“...Are you
Wi
my
of
tha
ROSCLAY
THE ABSOLUTE
Second General among
Aureatia’s Twenty-Nine Officials.
In his younger days.

ANTEL THE ALIGNMENT
Twenty-Eighth Minister of Aureatia's Twenty-Nine Officials.
Provides Force Arts backup to Rosclay.
JELKY THE SWIFT INK
Third Minister of Aureatia's Twenty-Nine Officials.
Brilliant civil servant who Rosclay placed his confidence in.
SABFOM THE WHITE WEAVE
Twelfth General of Aureatia's Twenty-Nine Officials.
Military officer who once crossed swords with the self-proclaimed demon king Morio the Sentinel.

"*Fwah-hah-hah-hah!* Impressive! Makes me wonder if you're really missing that leg of yours!"
"*Pfft*, lemme ask you, then. Are you really trying here or what?"
SOJIROU THE WILLOW-SWORD
Unparalleled blade appearing from another world.
Possesses masterful sword technique and a supernatural instinct that can single out how to kill a foe with a single glance.

"Can you stop me, Yuno the Distant Talon?"
HIROTO THE PARADOX
Known by the alias the Gray-Haired Child. A shura using his eloquence and scheming to control the playing field.

ISHURA

VIII

Blades of the Heretics

Keiso

ILLUSTRATION BY

Kureta

YEN ON
New York

ISHURA

VIII

Keiso

ILLUSTRATION BY

Kureta

Translation by David Musto

Yen On
150 West 30th Street, 19th Floor
New York, NY 10001

Visit us at yenpress.com
facebook.com/yenpress
twitter.com/yenpress
yenpress.tumblr.com
instagram.com/yenpress

First Yen On Edition: November 2024
Edited by Yen On Editorial: Payton Campbell
Designed by Yen Press Design: Andy Swist

Yen On is an imprint of Yen Press, LLC.
The Yen On name and logo are trademarks of Yen Press, LLC.

The publisher is not responsible for websites (or their content) that are not owned by the publisher.

Library of Congress Cataloging-in-Publication Data
Names: Keiso (Manga author), author. | Kureta, illustrator. | Musto, David, translator.
Title: Ishura / Keiso ; illustration by Kureta ; translation by David Musto.
Other titles: Ishura. English
Description: First Yen On edition. | New York : Yen On, 2022.
Identifiers: LCCN 2021062849 | ISBN 9781975337865 (v. 1 ; trade paperback) | ISBN 9781975337889 (v. 2 ; trade paperback) | ISBN 9781975337902 (v. 3 ; trade paperback) | ISBN 9781975337926 (v. 4 ; trade paperback)
Subjects: LCGFT: Fantasy fiction. | Light novels.
Classification: LCC PL872.5.E57 I7413 2022 | DDC 895.63/6—dc23/eng/20220121
LC record available at https://lccn.loc.gov/2021062849

ISBNs: 979-8-8554-0831-7 (trade paperback)
979-8-8554-0832-4 (ebook)

10 9 8 7 6 5 4 3 2 1

LSC-C

Printed in the United States of America

STORY SO FAR

The identity of the one who defeated the True Demon King—the ultimate threat who gripped the world in terror—is shrouded in mystery.
Little is known about this hero.
The terror of the True Demon King abruptly came to an end.

Nevertheless, the champions born from the era of the Demon King still remain in this world.

Now, with the enemy of all life brought low,
these champions, wielding enough power to transform the world,
have begun to do as they please,
their untamed wills threatening a new era of war and strife.

To Aureatia, now the sole kingdom unifying the minian races,
the existence of these champions has become a threat.
No longer champions, they are now demons bringing ruin to all—the shura.

To ensure peace in the new era,
it is necessary to eliminate any threat to the world's future,
and designate the True Hero to guide and protect the hopes of the people.

Thus, the Twenty-Nine Officials, the governing administrators of Aureatia, have gathered these shura and their miraculous abilities from across the land, regardless of race, and organized an imperial competition to crown the True Hero once and for all.

POWER RELATIONSHIPS

Country that seceded from Aureatia, ruled by the self-proclaimed Demon King, Taren. Defeated in its war against Aureatia and annihilated.
New Principality of Lithia
defeated
victorious
Aureatia
Nation of unified minian races, formed from merging all three kingdoms together during the age of the True Demon King.
???
wary
defeat
victory
Free City of Okafu
A country formed by the largest mercenary guild in the land. A group of elite soldiers that deploys a military force on par with any nation-state. Completely independent of any outside authority.
Toghie City
Trying to restore the kingdoms of old. The Old Kingdoms' loyalists gathered here. And taking advantage of the Particle Storm's attack, declared war on Aureatia and were defeated.

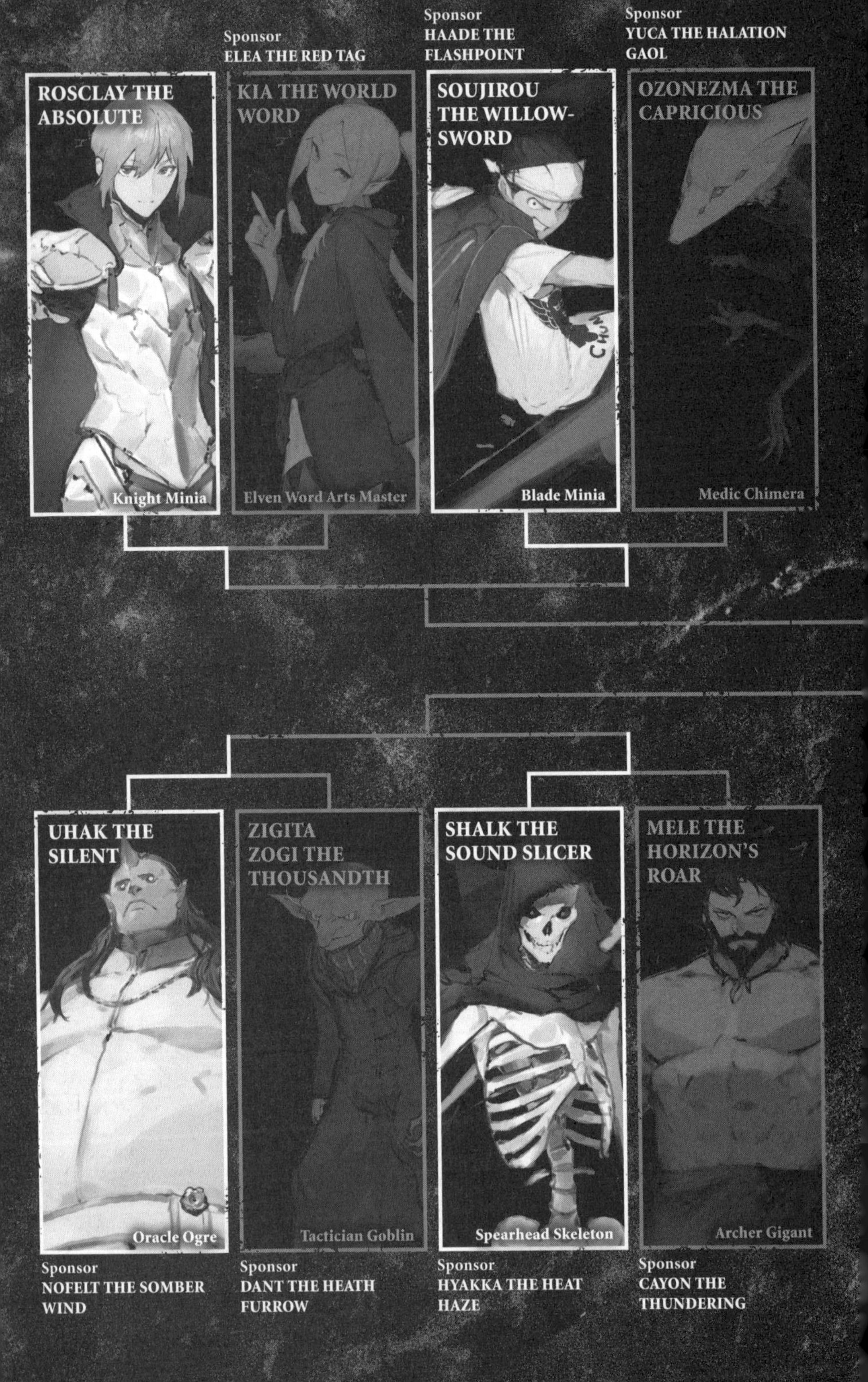
Sponsor
ELEA THE RED TAG
Sponsor
HAADE THE FLASHPOINT
Sponsor
YUCA THE HALATION GAOL
ROSCLAY THE ABSOLUTE
Knight Minia
KIA THE WORLD WORD
Elven Word Arts Master
SOUJIROU THE WILLOW-SWORD
Blade Minia
OZONEZMA THE CAPRICIOUS
Medic Chimera
UHAK THE SILENT
Oracle Ogre
ZIGITA ZOGI THE THOUSANDTH
Tactician Goblin
SHALK THE SOUND SLICER
Spearhead Skeleton
MELE THE HORIZON'S ROAR
Archer Gigant
Sponsor
NOFELT THE SOMBER WIND
Sponsor
DANT THE HEATH FURROW
Sponsor
HYAKKA THE HEAT HAZE
Sponsor
CAYON THE THUNDERING

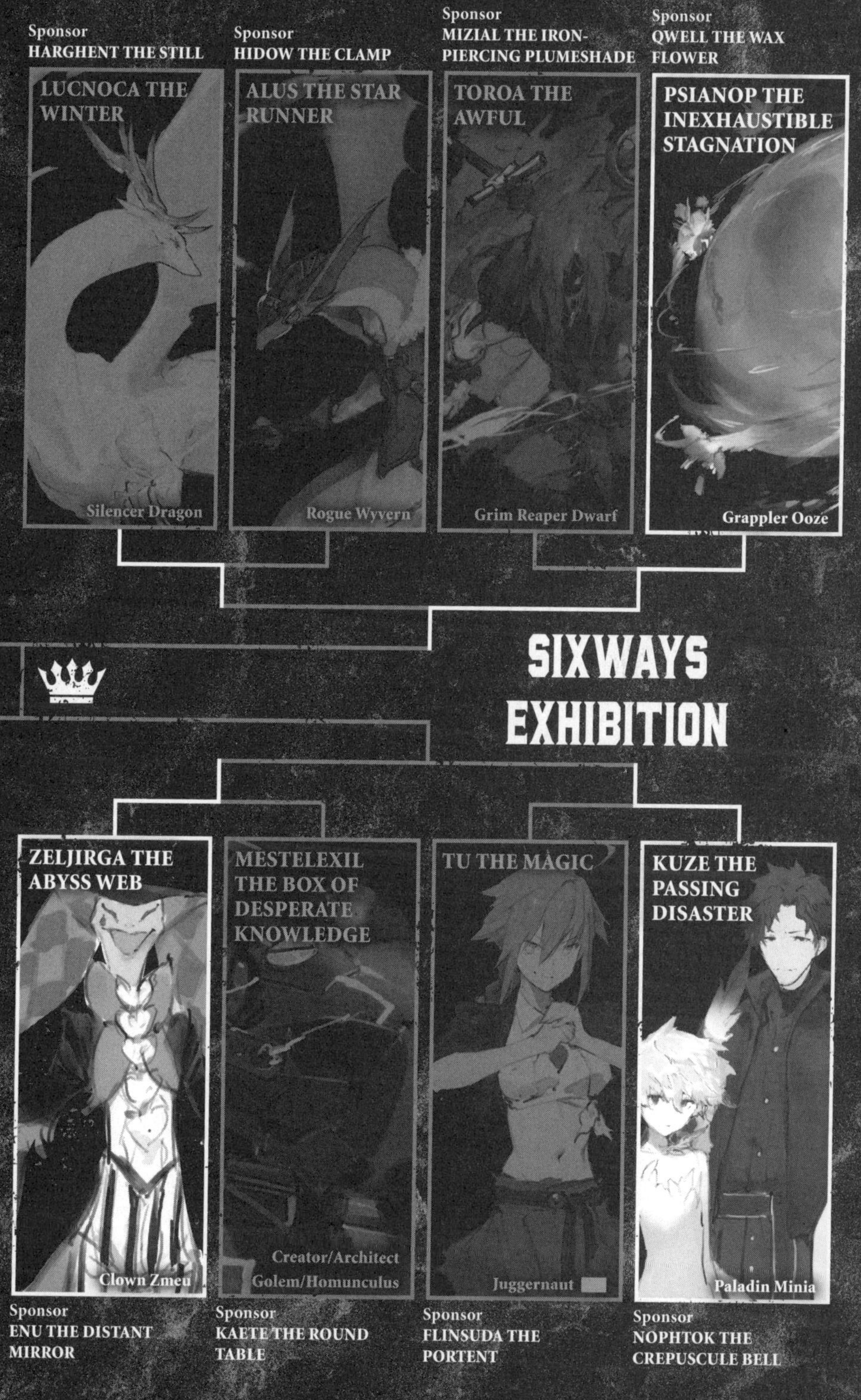
Sponsor
HARGHENT THE STILL
LUCNOCA THE WINTER
Silencer Dragon
Sponsor
HIDOW THE CLAMP
ALUS THE STAR RUNNER
Rogue Wyvern
Sponsor
MIZIAL THE IRON-PIERCING PLUMESHADE
TOROA THE AWFUL
Grim Reaper Dwarf
Sponsor
QWELL THE WAX FLOWER
PSIANOP THE INEXHAUSTIBLE STAGNATION
Grappler Ooze
SIXWAYS EXHIBITION
ZELJIRGA THE ABYSS WEB
Clown Zmeu
Sponsor
ENU THE DISTANT MIRROR
MESTELEXIL THE BOX OF DESPERATE KNOWLEDGE
Creator/Architect
Golem/Homunculus
Sponsor
KAETE THE ROUND TABLE
TU THE MAGIC
Juggernaut
Sponsor
FLINSUDA THE PORTENT
KUZE THE PASSING DISASTER
Paladin Minia
Sponsor
NOPHTOK THE CREPUSCULE BELL

GLOSSARY

Word Arts

① Laws of the world that permit and establish phenomena and living creatures that physically shouldn't be able to exist, such as the construction of a gigant's body.
② Phenomenon that conveys the intentions of a speaker's words to the listener, regardless of the speaker's race or language.
③ Or the generic term for arts that utilize this phenomenon to distort natural phenomena via "requests" to a certain target.

Something much like what would be called magic. Force, Thermal, Craft, and Life Arts compose the four core groups, but there are some who can use arts outside of these four groups. While necessary to be familiarized with the target in order to utilize these arts, powerful Word Arts users are able to offset this requirement.

Force Arts

Arts that inflict directed power and speed, what is known as momentum, on a target.

Thermal Arts

Arts that inflict undirected energy, such as heat, electrical current, and light, on a target.

Craft Arts

Arts that change a target's shape.

Life Arts

Arts that change a target's nature.

Visitors

Those who possess abilities that deviate greatly from all common knowledge, and thus were transported to this world from another one known as the Beyond. Visitors are unable to use Word Arts.

Enchanted Sword • Magic Items

Swords and tools that possess potent abilities. Similar to visitors, due to their mighty power, there are some objects that were transported here from another world.

Aureatia Twenty-Nine Officials

The highest functionaries who govern Aureatia. Ministers are civil servants, while Generals are military officers.
There is no hierarchy-based seniority or rank among the Twenty-Nine Officials.

Self-Proclaimed Demon King

A generic term for "demonic monarch" not related to the One True King among the three kingdoms. There are some cases where even those who do not proclaim themselves as a monarch, but who wield great power to threaten Aureatia, are acknowledged as self-proclaimed demon kings by Aureatia and targeted for subjugation.

Sixways Exhibition

A tournament to determine the True Hero. The person who wins each one-on-one match and advances all the way through to the end will be named the True Hero. Backing from a member of the Twenty-Nine Officials is required to enter the competition.

CONTENTS

ELEVENTH VERSE: **ATYPICAL COUP**

AUREATIA TWENTY-NINE OFFICIALS

First Minister
GRASSE THE FOUNDATION MAP
A man nearing old age.
Tasked with being the chairperson who presides over Twenty-Nine Officials' meetings.
Not belonging to any of the factions in the Sixways Exhibition and maintaining neutrality.

Second General
ROSCLAY THE ABSOLUTE
A man who garners absolute trust as a champion.
Participates in the Sixways Exhibition, supporting himself. The leader of the largest faction within the Twenty-Nine Officials.

Third Minister
JELKY THE SWIFT INK
A bespectacled man with the air of a shrewd bureaucrat.
Planned the Sixways Exhibition.
Belongs to Rosclay's faction.

Fourth Minister
KAETE THE ROUND TABLE
Sponsoring Mestelexil the Box of Desperate Knowledge. Kiyazuna the Axle's former pupil. Now a wanted man in Aureatia, he is on the lam.

Fifth Official
IRIOLDE THE ATYPICAL TOME
Old man, resembling a withered tree. Mastermind who controls Haade's military faction and a secret organization, the National Defense Research Institute, from the shadows. Attempted a coup d'état against Aureatia but was killed by Haade.

Sixth General
HARGHENT THE STILL
A man who yearns for authority despite being ridiculed for being incompetent. Not part of any faction. Killed his old friend-turned-self-proclaimed demon king, Alus. Former sponsor of Lucnoca the Winter.

Seventh Minister
FLINSUDA THE PORTENT
Corpulent woman adorned in gold and silver accessories.
Leads the medical division.
A pragmatist who only believes in the power of money.
Sponsoring Tu the Magic.

Eighth Minister
SHEANEK THE WORD INTERMEDIARY
A man who can decipher and give accounts in a variety of different scripts.
Acts in practice as First Minister Grasse the Foundation Map's Secretary.
Maintains neutrality just like Grasse.

Ninth General
YANIEGIZ THE CHISEL
A sinewy man with a snaggletooth.
Belongs to Rosclay's Faction.

Tenth General
QWELL THE WAX FLOWER
A woman with long bangs who hide her eyes. Sponsor for Psianop the Inexhaustible Stagnation. A dhampir who possessed powerful physical abilities, but was killed by Romzo the Star Map.

Eleventh Minister
NOPHTOK THE CREPUSCULE BELL
An elderly man with a gentle demeanor. Sponsor for Kuze the Passing Disaster. Head of the Order Division. Currently wanted by the Free City of Okafu.

Twelfth General
SABFOM THE WHITE WEAVE
A man who covers his face with an iron mask.
Previously crossed swords with self-proclaimed demon king Morio and is currently recuperating.

Thirteenth Minister
ENU THE DISTANT MIRROR
An aristocratic man with slicked-back hair. Sponsor for Zeljirga the Abyss Web. Linaris the Obsidian's pawn, but he is betraying Aureatia not as a corpse, but of his own volition.

Fourteenth General
YUCA THE HALATION GAOL
A simple and honest man, round and plump. Doesn't have a shred of ambition. Head of Aureatia's Public Safety branch.
Sponsoring Ozonezma the Capricious.

Fifteenth General
HAIZESTA THE GATHERING SPOT
A man in the prime of his life with a cynical smile. Possessed monstrous muscular strength. Secretly part of Kaete's faction, but was manipulated by Obsidian Eyes and killed.

Sixteenth General
NOFELT THE SOMBER WIND
An abnormally tall man. Sponsor for Uhak the Silent. Originated from the same Order almshouse as Kuze. Killed by Kuze and Nastique.

Seventeenth Minister
ELEA THE RED TAG
A beautiful young woman who walks a different path from her ancestral trade of sex work. Supervised Aureatia's intelligence apparatus.
Put to the sword for her acts of foul play during the Sixways Exhibition.

Eighteenth Minister
QUEWAI THE MOON FRAGMENT
A young, gloomy man with outstanding computational abilities. Collaborator with Iriolde's coup d'état, but was killed by Haade.

Nineteenth Minister
HYAKKA THE HEAT HAZE
A small-statured man who supervises the agricultural division. Straining himself to become worthy of his position in the Twenty-Nine Officials. Sponsoring Shalk the Sound Slicer.

Twentieth Minister
HIDOW THE CLAMP
A haughty son of a noble family and at the same time a popular, quick-witted man.
Sponsor for Alus the Star Runner.
Sponsoring Alus to ensure he doesn't win.

Twenty-First General
TUTURI THE BLUE VIOLET FOAM
A woman with grizzled hair tied behind her head. Collaborator with Iriolde's coup d'état, and headed the operation to slay Lucnoca the Winter.

Twenty-Second General
MIZIAL THE IRON-PIERCING PLUMESHADE
A boy who became a member of the Twenty-Nine Officials at just sixteen years old.
Possesses a self-assured temperament.
Sponsoring Toroa the Awful.

Twenty-Third Official
VACANT SEAT
Previously the seat of Taren the Punished, a battle-hardened and fierce woman who led the New Principality of Lithia in seceding from Aureatia. However, it is currently empty following her secession and defection.

Twenty-Fourth General
DANT THE HEATH FURROW
An exceedingly serious man. Commands the northern front army, containing Old Kingdoms' loyalists' forces. Part of the Queen's faction—and harbors ill feelings toward Rosclay's faction.
Sponsoring Zigita Zogi the Thousandth.

Twenty-Fifth General
CAYON THE THUNDERING
A one-armed man with a feminine speaking manner.
Sponsor for Mele the Horizon's Roar.

Twenty-Sixth Minister
MEEKA THE WHISPERED
A stern woman who gives a rigid and rectangular impression.
Acting as the adjudicator of the Sixways Exhibition.

Twenty-Seventh General
HAADE THE FLASHPOINT
A man who sincerely loves war. Sponsor for Soujirou the Willow-Sword. He was seen as the largest rival to Rosclay's faction, but secretly conspired with him and took advantage of the coup d'état to destroy Iriolde's faction from within.

Twenty-Eighth Minister
ANTEL THE ALIGNMENT
A tan man wearing dark glasses. Belongs to Rosclay's faction.

Twenty-Ninth Official
VACANT SEAT

ISHURA

Keiso

ILLUSTRATION BY Kureta

Eleventh Verse:

ATYPICAL COUP

CHAPTER 1 Sword of Faint Silver

"Vile dragon! O vile dragon! Wings of treachery defiling the heavens!" The grown man faced the garden tree and shouted. He was a tall man, just over the age of twenty.

His name was Narta the Mindful. Rosclay had only just turned ten, so Narta was twice his age.

Narta lifted the long tree branch hanging from his hip in an exaggerated arc and held it out in front of him.

"You ask me my name, do you?! Very well!"

The piece of wood Rosclay carried was simply the wooden plank his household used to shovel dirt, but when swung, it moved as gracefully as a beautiful silver sword.

"Know this! You have asked the name of your prey this day! The prestige of killing a single man, a royal knight and a minia! Thus, vile dragon, this battle is not a challenge from I, Altoy the Authority. No, you, Jigradeel, Blade of the Throne, are challenging *me* this day."

The clear and resounding voice seemed to shake the air.

The tip of the wooden plank, still gripped like a sword, was motionless in the air—it didn't tremble so much as an inch, even as he spoke.

A bead of sweat flowed from the man's temple and dripped from his chin. Then he whispered, "...How was that?"

"Can I point something out?"

Rosclay was sitting in the eaves by the back door and had watched the whole scene. He had also looked at the slightly overgrown weeds and felt that they would need to be cut soon.

"Whether you announce yourself or not, I don't think you're supposed to drone on like that. I think it'd be much better to strike at your foe *while* you're talking."

"Really…? *That's* the issue? You watched me for so long, and you're only saying this *now*?!"

"It bugs me. I mean, it's so weird. You're trying too hard to look cool."

"Rosclay…! You gotta dream bigger, c'mon! Listen. We're talking about announcing yourself in a show of heroism! It's the most important part of all!"

Narta the Mindful was a young man looking to join a theater troupe. Since Rosclay didn't have a father, his family had entrusted the man with some of their heavy labor, and on top of his pay, they would allow him to use their garden as his rehearsal space.

"That's seriously all you have to say after witnessing such a moving performance? I'm hurt."

"Oh, no, um… I think you're getting better, overall. That was really something, Narta."

"Your compliments always sound so half-hearted."

Narta sat down beside Rosclay and drank a water flask dry. While Narta hadn't actually been showing off in a real fight, Rosclay knew that true-to-nature acting was almost as exhausting.

"Can you really beat a dragon, though?"

"Huh? I mean, yeah. Don't you know the plot of Altoy the Authority? Afterward, there's this battle nearly to the death with Jigradeel. 'Jigradeel! If you boast that my skills cannot pierce you, then I dare you to defend against *this*!' Then he uses the arrow he stole from the Life Arts user Hittolip—"

"...That's not what I meant. I already know all of that. Even *I've* memorized the lines by now. I mean, is it really possible for a minia to defeat a dragon?"

"Hell if I know, but Altoy does it. He has to. Otherwise, he can't turn into some legendary hero."

"I learned about this in class. The minian from the past and the knight don't really seem to have this big difference in their physical abilities or anything."

This world had legends of its own. Passed down through people's memories across generations, there were some who made a living off them, like those in a theater troupe and poets. Though occasionally someone would find an old record written in the nobles' script, too.

Among his classmates at military school, there were those who looked up to these legends and sought to become mighty champions themselves. Rosclay understood the adoration, and he was aware that there was part of him that felt the same way.

"I feel like these sorts of legends are actually all made up."

"What did I just say, kid—you're crushing dreams with remarks like that! That's not gonna make you popular with the ladies. The quintessential trait of a guy who'll never get a girl, believe me."

"No, I'm really popular. Actually, just the other day someone asked me if I would take their daughter as my wife in the future. The girl was barely more than a month old..."

"D-dammit...cheeky brat..."

"*Pfft.*"

"All 'cause of that nice face of yours! Dammit! I wanted the girls to fawn all over me back in the day, too, y'know! I swear, it's all in the looks! No one cares about anything else!"

Rosclay regularly bantered with Narta like this.

He often heard he had inherited his handsome features from his dad, but without knowing what his father's face looked like, he had no way to confirm this for himself. He believed he looked more like his mother, if anything.

He was raised in the middle of a dark age. Shortly after Rosclay was born, his father was sent to the front lines with the initial force sent to subjugate the True Demon King, and he later passed away. His mother didn't want to talk to him about what sort of battle his father had fought against the terrible demon king before dying, and Rosclay tried not to ask her. He assumed it hadn't been a heroic death.

"I wonder if my good looks would help me become an actor."

"Wait, an actor? Didn't you want to be a royal knight?"

"Yeah, I guess. My mom told me to and all. But I don't really like knights or anything, either."

"...I don't think I've heard that before. You were so focused on your sword training, too. You hated it this whole time?"

"It's not that I hated it. I do like sword fighting, but...a knight is always putting his life on the line, right?"

Narta then made a complicated expression, sort of surprised and unsure how to respond.

"Yeah, that's true... Hell, the same goes for me. The truth is, I sort of chose the path of an artist in part because I didn't want to do that stuff. I get it. The demon king... That's one hell of an adversary."

"...I wonder if someone will kill them for us."

The students at military school all looked up to the legends and believed that someday they'd become the sort of grand champion that got immortalized in stories themselves. Rosclay didn't have the talent to dream like all of them did.

He imagined standing up against the Demon King's Army as a royal knight. The Rosclay of his imagination died all too easily. Rosclay couldn't believe—neither that he would leave something behind, nor that a minia could slay a dragon.

"All right, Rosclay, might as well try to become an actor then, huh? You could be my apprentice! I bet you could do it if you tried. You'll just have to practice every day. Society's all about appearances."

"No… I already know that becoming an actor isn't in the cards for me. I have my sword training and my classes, so… I don't have time to practice acting every day on top of all that. It can't happen, it's just too unrealistic."

"Sure it can."

"Okay, Narta. How, then? How could I make it happen?"

"You can practice together with your sword. "

Narta took the wooden plank and stood up. Thrusting out his *sword* in one hand, he stood at the ready. Rosclay felt like it was very rare to see him wear a serious look outside of his acting.

"What sort of stances are they teaching you at the military school? Standing with your legs in an L-shape, with your back leg set sideways against the front leg…placing your center of gravity on your tiptoes, and then stepping in to stab—would that just about cover it?"

"…Yeah, you got it."

"But, you see, there's no need to do that all the time when you're not in class or sparring. Look, Rosclay. Straighten your torso, from your heel to your neck. Pull your chin in tight and keep your eyes forward. What do you think would happen if you took a stance like this?"

"Well… It's a really weak stance. Your muscles are too tense, and your joint movements have gotten visibly stiffer."

"No, no! The answer's simple."

Narta flashed a dauntless smile.

"*You'll* seem *stronger.*"

"……"

The man had always been acting. He definitely wasn't strong, nor did he have some natural gift, either. Nevertheless, Narta had been an actor ever since he was Rosclay's age.

"Even in an actual fight, it isn't all bad. Steel your nerves and stiffen your muscles tight. Try moving while being aware of how others are seeing you. What happens when you do…? You get shockingly tired, that's for sure."

"I think that would be pretty obvious."

"Exhaustion signals just how much pressure was put on your body. So then, that'd mean you could hone your body just by standing, right? Just as a rule of thumb, though."

"*Pfft*. I really don't think it would be that easy."

"Wait, there are other ways to practice looking tough."

Narta bent down and placed a hand on the lower section of Rosclay's ribs.

"One way is how you breathe. I'm sure they teach abdominal breathing at military school, but when it comes to projecting your voice, the world of theater has honed the skill for a thousand years. Strictly speaking, you don't breathe out with your stomach muscles. You use the part behind that, the diaphragm, to exhale. You can do that, right?"

"…Yeah."

"Okay then, time to practice. Take a deep breath and project, and you'll be able to move better than anyone else, *and* appear way stronger. You just gotta do both acting and swordplay at the same time. Though, actually… I regret not doing that, so you do it instead. Then you'll be able to choose either path in the future."

"That's just more self-consolation. Narta, you're just making this up as you go, aren't you…?"

"I mean… Well… Sure, I might be, but still!"

"…*Ha-ha.*"

Although he returned Narta's lukewarm reaction with a sarcastic laugh, and despite saying nasty things about his technique, Rosclay figured he would give it a try. Though he didn't know if it would have any effect—or even before that, whether it was even possible or not—but he sensed there was a dream to have with it.

He felt that way a lot more than compared to what he had imagined—putting his life on the line, fighting, and dying without becoming a champion.

"You're really funny, Narta."

"Right? After all, you're looking at the guy who's gonna win the leading man's role."

"With a face like that?"

"Whaaat?! Listen, kid! My face— Okay, let me tell you something!"

It was the age when the True Demon King's terror had begun to spread, much like a dark mantle covers the world with the arrival of the setting sun.

Narta, setting off on a trip to the Kingdom as a member of theater troupe, had also been swallowed up in the mad butchery of the Demon King's Army, and died. It was said to be a miserable death, with his extremities torn asunder.

Rosclay later heard that Narta the Mindful's final role was as neither Altoy the Authority, nor any other champion, but a stagehand who engaged in the trivial chores of cleaning and maintenance.

◆

Months passed. At fifteen years old, Rosclay had become a royal knight of the Central Kingdom.

In the age of the True Demon King, strong and healthy adults were the first to die. As long as they were highly competent, it wasn't rare for a young man like Rosclay to be appointed to the kingdom's elite units.

Royal knights who were employed as periphery defense troops were assigned mock battle training twice every big month. During these mock battles, they trained while clad in heavy armor from head to toe.

Just as in a one-on-one duel, the training sword would actually make contact with the opponent's body. These combat drills were especially harsh on new recruits. After a drill ended, they would take off their helmets and a river of sweat would pour out.

However, when that time came, Rosclay would always be sure to wipe himself down while no one could see him. He did his utmost to make sure he didn't show any exhaustion or weakness to others.

The soldiers he would battle used the same dressing room as him, but none of them showed any hints of picking up on this charade. Rosclay felt confident when it came to this point, and this point alone.

"Rosclay, you must come from a family of knights, right?"

"No. My father was a knight, but he was simply conscripted from the peasantry."

"So then, it's more about talent than lineage, eh? Must've been a gap in effort, too… I felt like I couldn't get a blow in at all."

He had to make his strong points look even stronger. He took pains to either skillfully avoid revealing his weaknesses or hide them.

Rosclay was already a first-class knight when it came to his skills, but his opponent also fought as far as he had all while maintaining this somewhat childish posturing.

"Just between you and me, there's rumors you're gonna be named the next captain."

"No, that can't be. I'm too young, aren't I?"

"But even Commander Oslow has acknowledged your skills."

Oslow the Indomitable. Among the courageous generals like Haade the Flashpoint and Gilnes the Ruined Castle who made up the Central Kingdom's Twenty-Nine Staff Officers, he was renowned as being the strongest among them all, holding the position of Second General.

Rosclay's periphery defense troops served as the first shield against any potential invasion of the Central Kingdom by the Demon King's Army. It was also an elite troop helmed by Oslow the Indomitable. It was a post that Rosclay had wanted and achieved as a result of all his hard work—however, he had no interest in continuing up the path to further promotions.

If he was able to hold himself here as part of the Kingdom's defense corps, then just like he and Narta had previously hoped, he could live out the rest of his life without having to fight the True Demon King… Until the Kingdom was annihilated, at least.

Fortunately, ever since he had arrived at his post, the Demon King's Army hadn't launched a single attack. Rosclay had trained himself constantly to have the power to fight, but this power wasn't actually saving anyone. If there was any path to avenge Narta, dying with his ambitions unfulfilled, it must have been to use the skills Rosclay learned from the man to keep himself alive as another who didn't wish to fight. That's what Rosclay had believed.

"Besides, you've been training your Word Arts real hard lately, and that's gotta be to take the promotion exam, right?"

"Where did you hear that?"

"I overheard it in the cafeteria. Someone's spreading the rumor."

"...I see."

He'd had no knowledge of the rumor whatsoever. His reputation as a knight prodigy meant that, occasionally, he'd be hounded by baseless exaggerations.

Even when faced with these claims, Rosclay maneuvered to avoid denying them as much as possible. It was perhaps best for him to prepare a suitable excuse should someone seek him out for a Word Arts display.

...Though, if I just insisted that I couldn't, I could get by without having to go to such efforts.

Yet at the same time, Rosclay wouldn't have been able to grow as strong as he had if he hadn't been goaded on by such lofty expectations. Rosclay's lineage was average at best. His father had died as a perfectly mundane foot soldier.

By staying abreast of rumors and watchful eyes, he could infer others' thoughts. By pretending to be strong and using any methods at his disposal to achieve his desired results, he was forcing his real skills to catch up with his deceit.

He couldn't bear the thought that if he got rid of his affectations, exposed his weakness, and cut his performance short, the only end awaiting him was his own death as a trivial foot soldier.

"What's the truth, though?"

"Yes, I'm constantly practicing offensive Word Arts and the like. I... I swore to myself that I would only exhibit the skills that were worth showing. The same goes for the promotion exam—I don't plan on taking it whatsoever."

"*Ha-ha*. Too bad."

As if to interrupt the laughter, the alarm bell rang out. The blood drained from his fellow soldier's face. Rosclay first wondered if he was revealing the same degree of unrest of his own face at that moment.

"The south gate."

"......"

The pair immediately donned their practical combat gear and headed for the assembly point. In an alley along the way, they joined several others who flew out from the training grounds and gathered underneath the blue flag in the plaza.

Assembled there were not only knights, but even a squad of Word Arts soldiers led by Ownopellal the Bone Watcher. This wasn't a simple alert concerning the approach of the Demon King's Army. Rosclay could tell that the situation was out of the ordinary.

There, in front of the elite troops lined up in the plaza, was a tenacious long-haired man standing on the wooden platform. His name was known to all in the Kingdom. He was the unparalleled Second General, Oslow the Indominable.

"...This everyone then? I have a critical mission for you all."

Oslow was around forty years old, but both his expression and complexion were youthful and full of vigor. He seemed to have muscles that were denser than his already brawny appearance suggested. The broad double-edged sword he held was said to be an enchanted weapon that would send the bioelectric currents of anyone it touched into disarray.

"Currently, the Demon King's Army is approaching from the south! All members of the periphery defense troop will intercept them!"

"Commander!" someone from the squad shouted out. Oslow's commanding policy actually encouraged these sorts of questions and proposals from the squad members. "What are our enemy's numbers, sir?!"

"Tell me why you ask!"

"Yessir! Having an idea of the enemy troops' strength will greatly influence our plan of action on the ground! Depending on the situation, we will need to work with the town guards as well..."

"Your answer is correct. However, this time, you need not consider anything beyond intercepting the enemy!" Oslow declared. "Let me explain! In this fight, simply coordinating with the city shall spell our defeat! I will also inform of you our enemy's numbers! They number a single individual! It will be a battle with the fate of the Kingdom on the line!"

A sense of unrest spread among the soldiers.

Though this world was vast, there was only one race whose individuals could shoulder the fate of an entire nation.

"Our enemy is a dragon! Tiael the Crusher! Let me say once more! The fate of the Kingdom rests on this battle! There will be no exceptions! Every single one of you shall lay down your lives this day!"

Oslow's speech held an enthusiastic and absolute trust for the soldiers under his command. They were allowed to give their opinions regarding their maneuvers. Even if they didn't face the True Demon King, all of the soldiers deployed to the periphery guard troop, without exception, were the country's final shield, embodying the pride of Oslow the Indominable.

"It has all been for this day! This is the day you have all been tirelessly training for! Rise and become champions!"

In response to his voice, the stir among the soldiers changed from quandary to elation, then from elation to fighting spirit.

The terror of the True Demon King continued to spew dishonorable death to every corner of the world.

Much like Rosclay and Narta of the past, the young soldiers feared a purposeless death more than anything else.

Deep in their hearts, they still had the surging passion of their youthful days. They idolized legends and wished to someday become the same sort of grand champion themselves.

...Impossible.

Like the others, Rosclay's youthful passion had not wavered. Yet he had no faith.

Everyone will die.

A minia could never hope to slay a dragon.

◆

Before he learned how to put on an act from Narta—a memory came to mind from when he was ten years old.

Rosclay was in the garden of the house next door, fully absorbed in practicing his sword swing.

That day he had been invited to a small lunch party the neighbor's wife had hosted. There were no signs of any children his age, and the guests were mostly the wife's relatives.

It was awkward to talk with the adults, so he decided to work on the training that he had kept up every day without fail. While he knew it would leave a slightly unfriendly impression, Rosclay understood that his attitude would be well-received, and he would be praised as a fine and diligent child.

"Rosclay. Come here," the wife called to Rosclay from the house. "Quietly, now. Try not to make any noise."

"I'll be right there."

Brushing off the dirt from his indoor shoes, he entered through the garden door that had been left wide open. The wife was sitting down on the armchair in the living room, and held something small in her arms wrapped in a brand-new white cloth.

It was the wife's newborn daughter.

"...All the other guests have left, have they?"

"That's right. I only just realized that I still hadn't sent you home yet. Sorry, dear. You must have been bored."

"My house is right next door, so it wasn't any trouble at all. But are you sure it was all right? For someone like me...to be here."

Rosclay gazed at the now-silent room. There was another reason why Rosclay didn't join in with the adults' conversations: The gathering today was meant to be the funeral for her husband, who died in battle somewhere far away.

"...I ended up giving you the good news and the bad news all at once, didn't I? The truth is...I wanted to show my girl to you and your mother first, since you've always been so kind to me."

The wife passed him the newborn child and made Rosclay hold her. She looked cheerful and quiet. However, even when she smiled at Rosclay with innocent eyes, it didn't make him happy at all.

...What is going to happen to these two from here on out?

Would the support provided by the Kingdom to the bereaved family be enough to help the wife raise her daughter? Did one of the relatives he saw earlier have the power to provide for this widowed family?

With his father deceased, Rosclay's own family was similar, and he would eventually need to allocate the salary he received from military school, in addition to the income from his mother's work in the market, to provide for them both.

"...I'm sure she'll grow up happy."

Rosclay recalled saying something like that as he felt the tiny baby's warm body in his arms.

"Hmmm. Well, Rosclay is going to become a royal knight, so I'm sure you'll make this world a better place for us, too."

"I don't know about that..."

"In fact, why don't you take this girl as your wife someday? How does that sound?" she said, looking at her daughter and smiling.

Rosclay was at a loss for words. She and other adults like her would often make these types of irresponsible jokes. Perhaps in moments like these, it would have been better to respond with some flattery, too.

However, this was almost impossible for Rosclay. The margins in his life going forward had long been filled up with his own survival, and with supporting his life with his mother.

To go beyond his own orbit to extend a hand to another, to say nothing of saving the world from the despair of the True Demon King, was impossible.

Furthermore, Rosclay didn't wish to tell a lie.

"I-I...think you should save that stuff for...someone else...instead of asking me."

"Okay, then why don't I ask for something different? Could you give this girl her name—"

◆

Hearing a scream, Rosclay's consciousness returned to him.

He realized the scream was his own. A cloud of dust and blood mist assailed him from the right like floodwater, and he nearly collapsed just from the weight of it. He barely managed to hold his ground. His military boots dug into the dirt. He used his broken spear as a crutch.

"*Haah, haah...*"

If he got caught in the aftermath of the attack, he would die. Now that his feet had stopped moving, he needed to quickly hit the ground, but cumulative fatigue suggested if he chose to do that, he would never stand again.

He acted on the next priority instead. He steadied his breathing.

Taking in oxygen, he regained his judgment-making abilities.

Rosclay double-checked the wounds he had received. His upper right arm was dreadfully battered and bloodied. A deep gash left his fat exposed. There was no damage to any major arteries. He could continue to fight. He had maybe one more slash left in him.

The correct decision-making process, exactly as he had been taught.

He retraced his memories. His consciousness was muddled, and he viewed a scene from the past. He wasn't back in the living room of his neighbor on that day. This was Nanaga Hamlet. The entire surrounding tract was annihilated, with no remnants of the hamlet left behind.

Simply trying to halt Tiael the Crushing's advance had incurred this level of destruction.

Right now, Rosclay was right in the middle of the valley of death.

Tiael. What happened to Tiael? Did we take him down? What about Commander Oslow...?

Rosclay had come out with lighter injuries because he hadn't been directly caught in Tiael's claws.

Rosclay had been one of the men tasked with suppressing Tiael the Crushing with long spears. He had been slightly outside of the range of the dragon's strike.

The wound on his right arm was the result of the explosion of supersonic air, sending the flesh on his arm flying off.

Is this what a dragon's like? A true, absolute monster...

There was a rumble. A wave of dust hit Rosclay from a different direction.

He could tell it was the aftermath of Oslow's battle against Tiael. As they hectically attacked each other's blindspots, the area of their battle continued to shift. Oslow the Indominable had been fighting since before Rosclay lost consciousness. Was he even managing to evade the shockwaves from the dragon's claws?

"*Hiiiiiiiiiiiiss!* Do you know, Oslow?! Do you know terror?! D-did you know?!"

"......! Everyone, keep going! Regroup, three or more of you! Stop his movements with your spears, and I can finish him off!"

Suppressing the dragon's movements from behind was all the more dangerous with long spears. It put them right in the range of his tail attacks.

Rosclay's decision-making abilities were returning.

He could also understand the significance of the orders his commander gave in the extremes of combat.

That's right. If I don't help him, the commander will die. That famed champion.

Rosclay was at last able to see how Tiael and Oslow's fight was going.

The long spears the soldiers stabbed into the dragon one after another, naturally, were destroyed in the face of the dragon's physical strength, but each one of them hampered the speed of the dragon's initial action, and by weaving through the razor-thin opening this created, Oslow the Indominable dodged the dragon's claws.

Oslow was the only one not wielding a spear. Swinging his enchanted sword that halted bioelectric currents, Temilulk the Blade of Slumber, he kept forcing Tiael to focus solely on the sword's attacks.

At the start of the encounter, Tiael had been knocked down to the surface with wind-aspect Force Arts after the deaths of a tremendous number of Word Arts troops. Making use of the golden opportunity, the enchanted sword had stripped one wing and Tiael's left foreleg of all movement. The sections slashed by the Blade of Slumber were paralyzed, causing the adjacent limbs to lose all functionality.

The Kingdom's Second General. An unparalleled champion. There were few who had actually witnessed Oslow the Indominable fight with all his might.

Rosclay, much like many of the Kingdom's people, had only imagined what his strength must have been based on the many legends surrounding him.

He outdid all his legends.

Maybe... Just maybe, we could manage...

...to actually kill a dragon.

Oslow the Indominable was indeed a powerful fighter beyond anything Rosclay had imagined.

"*Jojingepf.*" (To Sanga Winds.)

A deathly chill ran through Rosclay.

"His breath! Get to shelter!"

Rosclay, retrieving his spear before returning to the fray, prioritized shelter above everything else.

The clustered soldiers, as well as Oslow himself, fled from the dragon's line of fire at full speed.

There was a single breath's pause...and nothing happened.

"*Haah, haah...*"

Rosclay couldn't tell if the terrified breaths belonged to him, or someone else.

It...misfired?!

Tiael hadn't stopped the incantation. Here in the Nanaga region, far from Tiael's domain, the dragon's Word Arts, with the ground at their focal point, had grown extremely unstable. Accordingly, dragons were a race who generally didn't stray far from the domain where they established their den.

Tiael the Crusher had been driven off by a threat that surpassed dragons.

Before, there hadn't been *anything* like that in this world, nor should it have ever existed, even now.

The True Demon King was the terror that should not have been.

"Off we go, Commander Oslow!"

"Be well!"

"...Advance!"

With a short back-and-forth, five soldiers challenged Tiael all at once. The light of the dragon's claws flashed, mowing down the earth, and all of them died in spurts of blood. Rosclay recalled that, amid the cloud of dust that just covered him, there was a lukewarm fluid mixed in it all.

Narrowly avoiding the horrific display of death, the second wave of soldiers put their lives on the line once more to pin down the dragon. Oslow didn't waste this second, and boldly flew inside the reach of the dragon's claws.

"......!"

It was right after Rosclay had picked up his fallen spear.

He was supposed to fight just like those soldiers. Their squad carried the weight of responsibility for the lives of the populace, and throwing one's life away to protect the people was, amid a hopeless world, the only path to becoming a champion.

He felt that the fallen had been magnificent people. Rosclay, too, wanted to be a courageous man, worthy to be counted among them. He wanted to prove himself useful to a genuine superman like Oslow the Indominable. That was what was righteous and proper.

As a soldier, there wasn't anything more valuable. That was how it was supposed to be.

"It's okay!"

Even when he should not have had any mind to spare in the midst of such extreme combat, Oslow called out.

Minia died the moment they entered a dragon's range. Oslow, with his supernatural combat intuition, had clearly discerned the limit of Tiael's mobility.

Taking in several shockwaves, just as Rosclay had, even as his whole body ruptured and his bones crumpled, Oslow the Indominable hadn't lost his fighting spirit.

The brandished claws demolished abandoned houses, foundation and all. From the gouged-out terrain, turbid waters from some irrigation channel flowed in. A single soldier, fluttering like scrap paper, fell into the water with less than half his flesh still clinging to his bones.

More than the destroyed terrain, the mountains of dirt and sand that piled up during the attacks' aftermath, and the corpses of shredded soldiers, showed in detail how ghastly the battle was.

"I...will fight! Nothing has changed! The same goes for you all, too! I'm following you all on your journey into death, got it?! Protect...*koff*... the Kingdom! Protect the people!"

"*Graaaah*... Minia...minia...! Eyes, those black eyes, the eyes...! Don't look at me! None of you, none of you...! *Hraaaaugh*!"

"Commander Oslow!"

"Commander!"

"Commander!!"

Standing in for those with broken spears, a new group surrounded

Tiael. Rosclay joined up with them. He thrust out the butt of his spear and formed a bastion around the dragon. Blades couldn't pierce dragon scales.

"*Ngh! Grraah…!*"

Rosclay was making a desperate effort that pushed him far past his limits, and yet he didn't feel like he could stop Tiael's movements. It was as if he was trying to push back the planet's crust.

"*Hrrrraaah!*"

"…! Commander! The neck! Tiael's neck!"

The whole time, Oslow had been searching for his one-hit kill—a single enchanted-sword slash at the dragon's neck.

However, Tiael didn't allow it, simply through his supernatural strength and speed.

As Tiael hallucinated out of immense terror and lost his judgment entirely, the virtue of being a dragon had put the ultimate minia-born champion out of reach.

"Die! Th-that's salvation. I'll provide it to you all…! *J-jojingebf!*" (to Sanga Winds!)

"Take shelter!"

Covered in wounds, Oslow still gave everything he had to flee from the line of fire.

The long spear soldiers didn't. In the middle of the battle of life or death, this time they gambled on the possibility the breath wouldn't come. They knew if they let go of Tiael, they would have to sacrifice as many people as before, and that they no long had the numbers to waste doing so.

"……!"

Rosclay alone jumped away.

"*Jekremjedorho!*" (Baleful black, boil and burst!)

Bwoom.

The armor worn by the soldiers standing in front of Tiael burst open from the inside.

It was caused by instantly swelling *internal pressure.* A second later, they all exploded together in the flash of tremendous heat and blinding light. Next, the trees. Then the stone well swelled up and exploded. Houses, boulders—every object in a straight line, one after the next, was brought to ruin.

Word Arts weren't as reliable when used in a region one wasn't native to. Even Tiael the Crusher, if he possessed his normal judgment and ability to reason, may not have exposed such a weakness. However, a misfire wasn't absolutely guaranteed to happen…

"*Aaah…ah, AAAAH…!*"

A terribly pathetic and inarticulate cry escaped Rosclay's mouth.

He had fled.

He watched those who hadn't fled die.

"Anyone…! Can anyone still move?! We must keep going! Don't give up the fight…!"

Oslow, showered in bullet-like fragments of the savaged soldier's armor, had been reduced to a bright red mass of viscera.

Even in his current state, Rosclay managed, just once, to read the trajectory of the dragon's claws and evade death. It was nothing short of a miracle.

"Me… I'm here, Commander! I can move!"

Rosclay was standing. Almost none of the Kingdom's elite troops remained. He was surely the only one who could still fight. He had to think so, or else he wouldn't have been able to keep himself upright. The mixed blood and dust harrowed the open wounds all over his body.

Why?

Why had he fled from the breath just now?

"You."

Oslow turned around at Rosclay's reply.

Then, he said something terrifying.

"The rest is up to you."

Tiael's claws made a full swing. Oslow had discerned the attack from the dragon's shoulder muscles and stomped. He escaped to just out of the dragon's claws' trajectory. However, the supersonic blast wave had shaved away the flesh from his face.

Scattering an immense amount of blood, his large body was slammed against the ground. Even then, Oslow still moved. In the cloud of dust, he threw his enchanted sword aside and took out his short sword. He kept trying to resist with eyes that could no longer see.

A loud *crack* rang out, and his upper body was crushed.

Tiael's forelimb stamped down on the unparalleled champion, and killed him.

"...Wh-why?"

Rosclay despaired.

Why did Oslow look at him?

Anyone else would have worked just as fine. Just by being close by, he had been entrusted to fight against despair.

For a soldier meant to be the people's shield, it should have been the greatest honor of all.

"...*Hngh*, why... Why me...?"

He wanted to flee. In truth, he always had.

At that moment, Tiael stopped moving. He was catching his breath.

Oslow's gallant fight had taken one of the wicked dragon's wings, as well as his left forelimb. The many slashes he made on the dragon had also paralyzed a sizable portion of the dragon's skin.

If Rosclay let this dragon be, in Tiael's current hallucinatory and wounded state, there was no guarantee that he would actually reach the Central Kingdom. Wasn't there a chance that he would die off somewhere from its wounds?

Rosclay didn't have to fight the beast himself, did he?

...Ahhh. Is that why? It's my punishment for thinking like this, is it?

Even after watching Oslow heroically die while fighting for the Kingdom up to the end, Rosclay...

I was the only one who didn't want to die.

He wanted to be someone courageous, who wouldn't bring dishonor to the dead. He wanted to prove useful for a true superman, Oslow the Indominable. He had thought that was proper and correct.

...Yet, deep in his mind, Rosclay hadn't *believed*.

He didn't want to end up dying like his father, amounting to nothing more than an insignificant foot soldier.

Even if he had true courage, and even if it were the result of acting with justice and honor, he didn't want to become a nobody who put his life on the line in battle only to die without becoming a champion.

He didn't want to die. *He didn't want to die.*

In the drawn-out moment on the verge of life and death, Rosclay had desperately sought a path of survival. It wasn't honor—he wanted victory. The ability to think, and to observe. Right now, that was what was necessary.

"...Captain...Ownopellal."

Rosclay murmured the captain's name of the Word Arts troop that should have been totally eradicated. Ownopellal the Bone Watcher. The Word Arts troops had done the essential work of knocking Tiael out of the sky with their Force Arts, but still, when faced with the dragon's tyrannical violence, they were never going to survive for long.

Ownopellal the Bone Watcher had been defeated just like the other Word Arts soldiers and was amid the mountain of corpses.

"...You're pretending to be dead, aren't you?"

"......!"

"I know. I'm also...very good at putting on an act..."

Rosclay wasn't interested in criticizing him. He couldn't possibly spare any mental energy for something like that.

Sharing a similar mind, Rosclay understood why Ownopellal had done such a thing.

In the middle of Oslow's battle, it had been impossible for Ownopellal to provide any Word Arts support without getting caught in the melee himself. In which case, he must have thought that pretending to be dead would let him wait for his best chance.

"Please. Can you use your Word Arts...and pass that sword to me...?!"

"...Rosclay. Yeah. Got it..."

"Antel."

There was another lone soldier nearby who was still standing. He had joined the squad at the same time as Rosclay.

"...Antel. Please rush to grab the sword. Right at the same time I do."

"Rosclay... I-I'm begging you. I can't do it. I can't charge into a dragon's claw range."

"I feel the same way... But Commander Oslow fought all by himself. I can't win without all three of us. I'll do it, but I need the help. Leave it to me in the end."

Rosclay calculated the remaining strength he had. Rushing over to where Oslow threw his sword in the end, and going from there to Tiael's throat—it was definitely possible. Oslow had understood that, and tossed away the enchanted sword instead of using it to protect himself.

Rosclay heard Ownopellal weave his Word Arts.

"*Ownopellalionan. Serpenomer—*" (From Ownopellal to Nanaga soil. Notching shadow—)

"*Grraaaugh… Grrngh…* Sword… The sword."

It seemed Tiael had finally noticed that the enchanted sword responsible for wounding him was no longer in Oslow's hands. Struck and torn apart countless times, Oslow the Indominable's body was now a mass of unrecognizable strands of flesh coiled around bone.

This was death. It was hideous.

Tiael shouted. "Where… Where is it?! The sword!"

Rosclay immediately ran. As if goaded forward by him, Antel ran too.

Tiael saw the area where Temilulk the enchanted sleep sword laid.

The dragon kicked the firm soil with both legs, and his massive body turned into a monstrous cannonball. Far faster than Rosclay and Antel, he pulverized the enchanted sleep sword into dust along with the ground where it laid.

However, even amid his hallucinations, Tiael soon realized the mistake.

"…*Grn*, This thing! This isn't…!"

It wasn't only the sword he had crushed underfoot. Imitations taking the form of the enchanted sleep sword, several fake swords generated from Ownopellal's Craft Arts, were lying on the ground or stabbed into the terrain.

Rosclay and Antel were racing in the opposite direction from where Tiael had charged.

"H-how dare… How dare you deceive me! Those eyes! If it wasn't for those eyes! *Croooooooo*! True Demon King…!"

"*Ownopellal io tem! Epthortemken! Modkeporte! Haspe6kormi…*

Artes!" (From Ownopellal to sword Temilulk! Broken and flittering water surface! Heavenly bridge! Axis sixth leg…! Choose!)

Among the numerous swords scattered everywhere, one flew with Ownopellal's Word Arts incantation and settled into Rosclay's hand.

Rosclay, and Antel, who had Tiael fast on his heels, were both brandishing an enchanted sword. Due to the paralysis, Tiael could only move one forelimb. Now, fully exhausted from his intense battle with Oslow, the dragon would be forced to choose one of them as his target.

"*Roooooooooar*!"

The dragon felt the most danger coming from Rosclay, closing in from the blind spot on his left side. Just before Rosclay reached the dragon, Tiael's claws immediately passed right in front of Rosclay's eyes, and the shockwave blasted him. He felt his flesh and skin burst open.

Yet, in the split-second before he was seriously wounded, Rosclay stopped moving. It was a feint.

Antel was approaching from behind Tiael.

Then, an attack from the dragon's long, thick tail blocked Antel's advance. Antel, too, stopped moving just out of range of the tail's attack.

The final counteroffensive had stopped. There was an insurmountable racial disparity that had shaken the resolve to gamble their lives into nothing.

Crazed from fear, Tiael spoke as if he were the one pleading.

"P-please, let this be the end. That blade… I-I can't take it, it's too terrifying…!"

"……"

A dragon was saying such a thing.

Just how unfathomably terrifying was the True Demon King?

Was the extent of the True Demon King's terror unfathomable?

Rosclay was incapable of becoming a champion. He couldn't defeat the demon king and save the world, either. Not until the very end.

If Tiael took a single step forward, that would be the end of Rosclay's life.

He didn't want to die.

"...Are you scared, Tiael?"

Even then, he stood. Standing with his back straight, from his heels to his head, he pulled his chin in and pointed his eyes out in front of him. As if he didn't fear death itself staring him down.

He should have run away. If he had pretended not to see the others' sacrifices, that would have been enough.

Even then, he had chosen to fight.

He had been entrusted with being a champion.

Right now, Rosclay had to deceive his own heart.

"This enchanted sword...! Wicked dragon! Is it not my own skill, but the sword of Oslow the Indominable that you fear?!"

Rosclay ran, as if to sacrifice himself to the dragon's claws. A charge into death—however, at the same time, he tossed away the enchanted sword in his hands.

Tiael's eyes reflexively followed the sword, as this blade alone was the last means of eradicating him.

It was at that moment...

"Rosclay!"

With the cry of his name, a sword came flying in. It was from the opposite direction, on the other side of the dragon's colossal body.

It was an enchanted sword, thrown to him from Antel. Right then, when he grabbed the silver blade, Rosclay had slipped in close to the dragon's throat.

"Tiael the Crushing!"

"M-Minia...! Cursed minia!"

If the dragon was arrogant enough to believe that Rosclay's technique truly couldn't penetrate him...

"Try to block this attack!"

The enchanted sleep sword Rosclay swung was blocked by the dragon's scales and broke.

However, the single attack brought the spinal nerves of Tiael the Crushing to an eternal standstill.

◆

The vile dragon closing in on the Kingdom had fallen.

The feat amounted to little more than narrowly preventing disaster with a wall built from a mountain of corpses.

The sacrifices had been too great. Every single one of the deceased, without exception, had experienced the unsparing training necessary to become the Kingdom's strongest elite soldiers.

Rosclay's group searched for any survivors of the chaotic melee, but there were only eight in total—including himself, Antel, and Ownopellal—and two among them would soon perish from their fatal wounds. Even more so, there was no one besides Ownopellal and Antel who witnessed the decisive final moment.

"...We can't...let this happen," Rosclay said to Antel and Ownopellal as he leaned his exhausted body against a stone wall, having finished giving emergency first aid to the last of the wounded soldiers. "Everyone is in despair. We think that we're powerless..."

"...This might be the end for us. A single dragon...a single, deranged dragon cost this many lives. Commander Oslow is dead, too... Without that man—forget the True Demon King, we might not even be able to stave off a self-proclaimed demon king's invasion."

"Oslow was an outstanding man." Ownopellal agreed with Antel's pessimism.

As Commander of the Word Arts troops, Ownopellal was a much higher rank than Rosclay and Antel, yet he looked terribly crestfallen and feeble.

"I don't think there's anyone who could ever serve in his stead..."

"In that case... In that case, we just need to make one. That's the only solution."

The terror of the True Demon King was sinking the people into the darkness of despair.

The populace needed a champion.

A symbol to prop up their legs as they threatened to give out.

"Let's say that one among us defeated the dragon all by ourselves. That Oslow the Indominable died an untimely death in battle—however, a champion took on his dying wish and slayed Tiael the Crushing."

"...Ridiculous. That lie'll get found out immediately."

"Even still, it has to be done. I'd like to hear your opinion, Commander Ownopellal."

"Rosclay... You intend to take on that role?"

"...That was my plan."

In the moment, he had ordered Ownopellal to pass him a sword, Antel to grab the enchanted sword, and for them to leave everything up to him—all with the smallest amount of words possible to ensure Tirael didn't sense their strategy. Rosclay's talent for commanding had bloomed.

His talent for commanding had bloomed. In a single moment, where a single wrong move spelled absolute death, he unflinchingly believed it had been enough to convey everything to his comrades.

"Bear witness for me. The two of you didn't offer me any help—I successfully carried out the task our fallen Commander Oslow entrusted to me, to slay Tiael, all by myself."

"Of course. Sorry for laying this on you."

"A difficult role, but we're counting on you."

He would play the champion.

A dragon-slaying champion didn't exist. That was the current reality. In which case, in order to make such a champion the new reality, the only possible option was for someone to lie and play the part.

This was the one thing Rosclay and his mentor, Narta the Mindful, had never stopped doing.

Just as he promised, Rosclay protected the people as an absolute shield guarding the Kingdom.

At the very start, there were those who doubted the unrealistic feat of dragon-slaying, but Rosclay continued to remain unrivaled, without ever falling to his knees in any of his battles.

The few survivors among the Kingdom's elite squad who headed out to slay Tiael—whose swordsmanship was on par with Rosclay's—no longer existed anywhere in the Kingdom.

The fact that he had begun to utilize Word Arts in his fights since the incident validated the rumors about him. More than anything, the popularity and authority that came along with his power of ingenuity suppressed any and all doubts and criticism.

Even as the Kingdom fell and gained the name Aureatia, he still continued to be the unequaled Second General.

Just like Oslow the Indominable had once been.

"You need a name." Antel suddenly brought up the topic on that day they killed Tiael. "Now that you've slain a dragon, you'll need a suitable second name. You can't keep up the commonplace one you have now, Rosclay."

"……"

Rosclay thought of the legendary champions.

Altoy the Authority. Oslow the Indominable.

What had they thought when they gave themselves those second names?

A champion who fought justly and proper, who perfectly wielded all kinds of techniques, overcame all their enemies, and slayed dragons.

Even these champions memorialized in stories must have known that such a thing never actually existed.

It was a wish.

They were wishing for such a champion to exist.

A light rain began to fall from the cloudy sky.

Rosclay quietly murmured. "Absolute."

The word that Rosclay believed in the least of all felt as if it was the most suitable answer.

"Rosclay the Absolute."

CHAPTER 2 Centripetal

The battles in the Sixways Exhibition began before the actual matches themselves.

To Hiroto the Paradox and Zigita Zogi the Thousandth—one pair among the shura who used their machinations as weapons—it went without saying that four small months before the start of the first match was nothing but a single moment in a massive plan that had begun even earlier.

Once Hiroto became active inside Aureatia, the first thing he required was a reception room. An office built in an upscale residential district in Aureatia, not very big, but not too small either. Special attention was given to the quality of the sofa and furniture his guests would come in direct contact with, and a reserve of tea and snacks was provided to ensure they never ran out—that was the extent of the accommodations.

As Zigita Zogi assembled the tactics he would apply to the Sixways Exhibition, Hiroto, with greedy enthusiasm, intermingled with various social classes, from high-level government officials to the owners of small shops, and poured his energy into establishing cooperative relationships in this role, regardless of how much fruit they bore.

"Master Hiroto the Paradox. Thank you very much for your invitation."

"I am honored to make your acquaintance as well, Katara the Crimson Water, Director-General of Elpcoza Peddler's Union."

Compared to the bald-headed elderly gentleman, Hiroto, welcoming him in, was young. His appearance would have been described, even at the highest estimates, as that of a thirteen- or fourteen-year-old boy. However, with his attire, tailored to resemble the suits from the Beyond, he strangely didn't compare all that unfavorably to the elderly gentleman, even when side-by-side.

"The name of the Gray-Haired Child was a great legend among us merchants. We wondered if he actually existed, what sort of technology he must possess… I can't help feeling a bit strange that someone like me would have the chance to actually meet you."

"If we're mentioning legends, you deserve that moniker yourself, Katara. Pioneering a trade route to the Arboreal Sky Spire the way you did must have been no ordinary feat. Personally speaking, I've been cheering on your efforts for a while."

"Goodness. You are familiar with me?"

"If anything, I'm absolutely shocked! I never thought a newcomer like myself would have a chance to talk to with you like this! It seems that Elpcoza Peddler's Union has great expectations for our business negotiations, then. In which case, I do hope our bargaining will be productive."

Using very natural and sometimes exaggerated emotional expressions, Hiroto opened up the heart of those he confronted.

He had investigated the reputation and career of Katara the Crimson Water beforehand, but this was a wholly common matter to him as automatic as breathing. As long as Hiroto was able to predict their inevitable meeting, then giving his everything for such an encounter was a purely matter of course.

"You would be General Dant, of Aureatia's Twenty-Nine Officials, yes? I look forward to speaking today."

In response to the elderly man's greeting, the shaven-headed man, sitting slightly removed from where they were, responded. "Yes, I am Aureatia's Twenty-Fourth General, Dant the Heath Furrow… I may be in the way here, but I'll be sitting in on these negotiations."

"Of course, I don't mind at all."

"Hiroto the Paradox is a crucial party to my hero candidate. Supposing there is any foul play regarding the match, it would be a detriment to them both. Hope you'll see me here as trying to nip that in the bud."

"Yes. I ask you to be a fair judge, then." The elderly man calmly answered, but inwardly, he couldn't have been too happy.

For such a big negotiation, it was possible that its success or failure would ultimately be influenced by legislative acts or changes in standards on the Assembly's side of things. There weren't any merchants who wanted the Aureatia Assembly to know about an important decision on the spot.

However, Hiroto didn't feel any weight to Dant's surveillance. More than that, he was even using it in negotiation to his advantage.

By having Aureatia's Twenty-Fourth General present for, Dant could give the impression that Hiroto's existence had been acknowledged by the Assembly.

"…in short, we are able to provide a workforce that is far more flexible than before. There is certain to be a sudden increase in manpower requirements with the advent of the Sixways Exhibition. However, as I am sure you are aware, this period of prosperity will not necessarily continue after the conclusion of the tournament… Should you contract with us, it will allow you to make plans that necessitate an increase in manpower."

"Quite. Being able to mobilize a labor force on a scale that the normal labor guilds can't match is an advantage. It would essentially be a labor guild the size of a small city—that said, what of their proficiency? Such skills cannot be taught overnight."

"That, too, is no cause of concern. I can guarantee the skills of our proud goblins, and I believe it will also be possible to dispatch laborers from the Free City of Okafu with an adequate foundational skillset. They administered a whole city themselves, after all. There will be experienced workers from any industry in their ranks."

"I see—you're absolutely right. If we can form a contract for the price you have presented me with, I believe it would be an amicable deal for us. That said, I will take this matter back to the Union for the time being… If you could kindly set up another meeting at a later date, then."

"Yes, of course. These negotiations were productive. I truly wish for your success in your Union's business."

From idle chitchat to business deals—Hiroto had spoken with a wide range of people, without any rest, even before the start of the Sixways Exhibition. Of course, the person on the other side of the negotiations wasn't always this civil. There were some who tried to take advantage of Hiroto's weak position to force disadvantageous conditions on him, and others who tried to manipulate the Gray-Haired Child with false trickery. Hiroto patiently kept his relations even with these people, too.

As he continued such taxing work, day in and day out, he didn't tire. It could be said that Hiroto had almost zero aptitude for combat or physical exercise, but when it came to negotiations, he could keep them going for a full day. Hiroto had the vitality of a teenage boy.

The bodies of visitors never deteriorated.

It was when one went to battle a mighty power that they truly needed to accumulate bonds and trust.

"Hello, Mr. Hiroto! You'll offer me another juicy story today, right?"

"Of course! It's my privilege to meet your expectations. There are several things we have discovered on our end regarding the hero candidates. I believe this will serve as an extremely profitable item for the Melmark Detective Agency."

For Hiroto's camp, the connection with the visitor journalist Yukiharu the Twilight Diver was a powerful advantage. As long as the person he dealt with needed the information—anything from the contents of the Aureatia Assembly's plans, investigating the movements of major players, or breaking news on disputes, accidents, and incidents—Hiroto would share it with them without seeking much payment in return.

When there wasn't any particular need to keep a meeting confidential, Hiroto would act like himself, without using his reception room.

—For example, when meeting with the hero candidate, Kuze the Passing Disaster.

"So, that's the whole reason why you gave me this information for free, eh?"

"With our strength, it's possible to trace the whereabouts of every single child in the Order across every region in the land. We are already fully aware of several pieces of information regarding your organization."

—For example, when meeting with Cayon the Sky Thunder, Aureatia's Twenty-Fifth General.

"I have no intention of changing the arena for the seventh match, thank you. I'll make it happen at the Mali Wastes… Though, to make sure things end up that way, I want to get rumors out there that *suggest it'll be held at the Dogae Basin*."

"Fair enough. If it's held in the Dogae Basin, the merchants will suffer big losses and sense an incoming crisis. You see, everyone has started preparing under the assumption it would be held at the Mali Wastes."

"I'll offer up as much collateral as I can. I might also be able to bring some flexibility to the decision on whether to get Mele involved or not.

"If you would allow me to ask that much of you, Lord Cayon, then I gladly accept. However, I will need to let this rumor spread in a way that ensures it won't disadvantage anyone else…"

Hiroto's way of fighting was different from the styles of both Linaris the Obsidian and Rosclay the Absolute.

His fight wasn't behind the scenes. It was among the people, a battle to openly build trust.

The construction of the widest possible network of interpersonal relationships that could prove beneficial in some way, somewhere down the line. Hiroto the Paradox believed that was truly the greatest trump card to have up his sleeve.

CHAPTER 3 Absence

There was no one who could prove the results of the ninth match of the Sixways Exhibition.

The battle between Psianop the Inexhaustible Stagnation and Lucnoca the Winter occurred without any audience present, and with the citizens of Aureatia ignorant to what happened, they were simply *told* the result that Psianop had won.

In part because the match ending in victory for Psianop was itself hard to believe, there were many complaints from the citizens of Aureatia, and from those involved with gambling and commerce in particular.

They questioned that maybe Aureatia, fearful that Lucnoca would progress onward to win out as the hero, might have made her withdraw by brokering some sort of deal. Or maybe Lucnoca abandoned the match of her own free will, seeing as it was against a lowly ooze.

Whatever the case, it was valid to believe there was no way that Psianop the Inexhaustible Stagnation had managed to kill Lucnoca the Winter, and the ninth match never actually happened.

However, even these voices of doubt were beginning to die down as the days passed. It was said that a small group of citizens, chosen to serve as representatives, had actually been shown Lucnoca the Winter's corpse.

Instead, another rumor began to circulate—during the ninth match, it was actually the Aureatia military led by Haade the Flashpoint who killed Lucnoca the Winter, and that his military faction possessed the might capable of rivaling the hero candidate judged to be strongest of the strong.

Did Rosclay's faction even have the strength to stop such a force? Would the Sixways Exhibition actually continue? Would Aureatia's political administration be maintained in its current state? Anxieties and speculation around the political situation begun to be whispered together with the suspicions concerning the ninth match.

Regardless, Psianop the Inexhaustible Stagnation was not bestowed the honor of victory.

Despite achieving the truly grand feat of slaying Lucnoca the Winter, there were still none who entirely believed it.

Having fought, won, and survived all for the sake of pride, he was ultimately left without a win.

◆

Rain continued to fall.

This was now Psianop's fifth visit to the Romog Joint Military Hospital.

There was still no trace of Qwell the Wax Flower after she had slipped out from her hospital room the day before the ninth match.

Though he tried to gather information from staff and witnesses, it was difficult given he was beastfolk.

...Where did you go?

A horrible premonition was boiling inside him.

Why had there been any need to slip out the day before the match? Even supposing she did so herself, what sort of fate had she met afterward?

If this had happened to anyone but Qwell, Psianop likely would have made the correct assumption.

Even he was aware that his daily, idle investigation was done in an effort to disprove his fears.

Qwell's survival was hopeless.

"Are you searching for Qwell the Wax Flower? Oh, no need to get ready to fight."

Psianop had merely turned his attentio toward the voice, and the speaker, a plump man with a camera hanging from his neck, was already raising both hands in surrender. He wore a plain wooden box on his back.

"Umm, I'm not hostile or anything, okay?"

"I wasn't even on guard to begin with. Yukiharu the Twilight Diver, then?"

"I'm surprised you know me. Suppose we can skip the belabored introductions. I'm a visitor journalist. In other words, I'm in the business of selling information."

"......"

Psianop didn't feel like pushing back to point out the man only sold information that would stand to benefit Okafu's camp.

They were in an alley that normally didn't have much foot traffic, but the scene around them was especially quiet. Perhaps it was simply that time of day, or nothing more than coincidence. It vaguely seemed like Yukiharu had carefully waited for a chance to appear when no other eyes would witness the exchange.

"In this story I'm pursuing, see, this National Defense Research Institute name keeps popping up. Idle gossip makes it out to be a research facility that uses self-proclaimed demon kings to make constructs and weapons in secret, but are you familiar?"

"......Rings some bells."

The unorthodox living organism that Psianop had no knowledge of, Acromdo the Variety. Sindikar the Ark, manipulating enigmatic flying machines. It had been a complete mystery where exactly Tuturi the Blue Violet Foam had found such combat assets. However, if such an organization did exist, that would explain it.

"Don't tell me you came asking me to confirm it for you?"

"That's part of it. Why don't we both confirm what the other knows? Assuming something resembling this National Defense Research Institute was mobilized...where would you have seen them, Psianop?"

"The Mali Wastes."

"Just came right out and admitted it, huh?"

"There's nothing to hide."

Psianop's victory merely stemmed from the interference of Tuturi's force. He recognized that it was reasonable not to be treated as the winner.

He wasn't meant to conceal the facts of the ninth match, for Lucnoca the Winter's own honor more than anyone else's.

"There were several mysterious weapons deployed in the ninth match—a monstrous race that originated from plants, a flying machine, something resembling a dragon revenant. Supposing this National Defense Research Institute or what have you does exist, then it has to be connected to Haade the Flashpoint or Tuturi the Blue Violet Foam."

"The so-called military faction, then. That lines up with the results of my own investigation." Yukiharu was recording something on a bundle of scrap paper. "In the middle of the ninth match, all entry and exit from the Mali Wastes was sealed off. The security really was quite tight, so I couldn't view the actual state of the match myself. I was only able to slip in late at night."

"...You're saying you waited the whole time? There had to be soldiers stationed at night, too."

"Oh, yes, there were. But it was definitely worth my while."

Yukiharu took out a photograph. On the ground of the Mali Wastes, the night illuminated by a standing fire, there were crushed metallic fragments scattered over the ground. Metal fittings to keep a cloak shut tight.

"...Any idea what this might be?"

"......"

Psianop immediately knew they belonged to Qwell.

It meant that something occurred there that was enough to smash metal.

"There's one more thing. I've identified a facility that I believe to be the National Defense Research Institute's base of operations. Only just recently, they took great pains to bring in this corpse, you see, and—"

"Enough," Psianop whispered quietly. "...Why?"

The words weren't meant for Yukiharu.

He felt neither anger nor sadness, only frustrated regret.

Why hadn't she listened to his instructions? Why had she slipped out of the hospital on her own? Why had she come all the way to the arena?

He wasn't confused by what Qwell had felt—he understood all too well.

Though they were of a different race, and though their connection had been temporary, only existing during the Sixways Exhibition... Qwell the Wax Flower had been the lone and sole disciple who had shared his sense of values.

"Why..."

When it came to Qwell's heart, he understood it all.

"...Why was she killed? If she only got in the way of their trap during the ninth match, there shouldn't have been any reason to kill her."

"Aureatia's side, at the very least, must have done so for the medicine."

Yukiharu tossed a small vial over to Psianop.

A long, thin vial, the size of a minia's fingertip. A transparent drug was inside.

"That's an antiserum. The invisible army—the vampires lurking behind the scenes of the Sixways Exhibition—wasn't just an expedient white lie to explain Alus the Star Runner's rampage. The Aureatia Assembly is actually busy preventing infection. Right now, in particular, the price for the silver bullet antiserum has climbed extremely high."

"So this... That's what this is."

Psianop held the vial up to the light.

The drug inside glittered in the light from the gas lamps.

Qwell.

He had to use his strength of will to curb this thing that threatened to explode within him.

Psianop could take it all out on Yukiharu, but ultimately the man was unrelated to this issue.

He had to remain levelheaded. He was supposed to have spent twenty-one years training to do just that.

"My original world had a medicine like this, too. Here in this world, though, I don't think you can make stuff like this without the Kingdom's technological prowess. Qwell the Wax Flower was a dhampir, wasn't she?"

Qwell the Wax Flower was a vampire without the ability to infect others. They were called dhampir.

From birth, she had possessed a vampire's body, which had surpassed other minia. It was a fact that had tormented her.

"One of the results from their history of fighting against vampires must be that they established a process to refine an antiserum from dhampir bones and the vampire virus antibodies they hold. The reason they always had a limit to how many they could produce was because the *materials* for them were so rare."

Even now, hearing the explanation, Psianop wondered why.

Was it to kick him back down now that he had advanced, for lacking a sponsor?

To use the produced antiserum to bargain with the government?

Is any of that...

Somewhere far in the distance, there was the sound of a bird flock taking off.

...a reason to kill her?

Having fought, won, and survived all for the sake of pride, he had nothing but loss.

◆

There was no prison that could contain Tu the Magic.

During Alus the Star Runner's invasion, not only had she headed out to fight, ignoring her sponsor's political coordinating and defeating her warden Krafnir in the process—she had also decided to go into battle against Alus and rescue the victims. Her actions, from Aureatia's perspective, could only be seen as chaotic and rebellious.

Tu the Magic had already sprung free from her sponsor's control.

However, she was voluntarily staying in Flinsuda's manor. Most likely, it was out of guilt toward Flinsuda and her acting guardian, Krafnir.

Now, Tu wasn't even under surveillance by Krafnir. The course of events that accompanied Alus the Star Runner's assault had merely proved that even a Word Arts caster of Krafnir the Hatch of Truth's caliber was unable to restrain Tu.

Tu herself wasn't moping around as much as she had after the fifth match, but instead, she had begun to lose herself in thought and move about as if she couldn't settle down.

Much like a child that knows someone is going to scold them, *that* day, Tu might have been waiting for Flinsuda to call out to her.

"Tu, darling. Come over here."

When Flinsuda summoned her, Tu timidly approached. She was awkwardly hugging a sphere that resembled a ball of mud. She walked around without ever letting go of Rotting Soil Sun, left behind by Alus the Star Runner.

"Flinsuda..." Tu's green pupils looked anxiously at her.

Flinsuda the Portent's hair was unkempt.

There were less accessories decorating her corpulent body, and her nails weren't polished.

In her current situation, she was forced to put aside the elegance that she usually put so much care and effort into.

Flinsuda was the head of the medical division. In addition to treating the heavily wounded victims of Alus the Star Runner's assault, along with her work identifying and coping with the considerable number of confirmed infected corpses, now her assistant in the field, Qwell the Wax Flower, was missing.

"I'm sorry I haven't been able to keep you company much lately."

"...Nah. That's okay." Tu feebly shook her head. "Um, Flinsuda... Sorry. About when I fought Alus and stuff..."

"Right, right. Why don't we start there, shall we? Tu, dear, you couldn't wait until I finished arranging things with the Aureatia Assembly?"

Tu shut her eyes tight with a terribly remorseful look on her face.

She was always honest in how she expressed her emotions. She was more minia-like than the actual minian races were. She behaved in an extremely impressionable way.

"Krafnir, too... I hope I didn't cause him too much trouble... But, but listen! Krafnir did his job like he was supposed to!"

"Tu, dear. I reduced Krafnir's compensation."

"B-but...! That was all my fault!"

"That's not true. Krafnir made a contract with me, and it included reining you in. While he may have given his all to stop you, Krafnir needs to bear responsibility for his failures."

"Responsibility..."

"That's right... Responsibility. In this world...everyone is carrying out their responsibilities, regardless of how strong they are, or how they may feel. This serves to protect people's confidence in each other, and ultimately ensuring Krafnir bears the responsibility proportionate to his work is for his own sake, too."

Flinsuda was thoroughly and wholly devoted to wealth.

Using the power of medical treatment to convert lives into money, she acted under contracts bounded by money, regardless of right or wrong.

If she could benefit someone, then it was fine to collect an equal benefit for herself.

Flinsuda raised herself up to her position on the Twenty-Nine Officials through this simple bargaining principle.

However, she shouldn't have applied such a simple principle to Tu the Magic. No matter how much kindness she showed Tu, Flinsuda understood that she couldn't genuinely bind this young girl's will.

"Tu, dear. Aureatia now regards you as a hero candidate who is impossible to control."

Flinsuda squeezed her rotund form into a chair and let out a long sigh.

"We've been instructed that, should we have a chance, hero candidates seen this way are to be disposed of by their sponsors."

"*Urk…!*"

Tu drew back in fear.

Flinsuda knew that Tu wasn't fearful of actually being killed. It was the fear of being resented and condemned by someone she trusted. In every aspect, save for her complete invincibility, she was a child.

"*Ho-ho-ho-ho-ho-ho-ho*! Now of course, this is something that I'm not supposed to tell the hero candidates. But I have to wonder, if there's no possible way to hurt you, how exactly then am I supposed to *kill* you?"

If that was possible, then Tu wouldn't have ever been chosen as a hero candidate to begin with.

Nevertheless, one of the sponsors' duties was to prepare, to the best of their ability, a means to control or expunge their hero candidate in case it ever became necessary.

Even Nophtok the Crepuscle Bell and Hidow the Clamp must have done everything they could to try and eradicate their own hero candidates who were far too much for them to handle. Perhaps Flinsuda was supposed to have done the same.

"…Flinsuda." As if she had made up her mind, Tu began to speak. "Why do you want money so much? Back then, if you didn't want money so much… if you had chosen instead to help everyone… I would've happily gone to help. You must have wanted to save everyone's lives, right, Flinsuda?"

"That's true. I do love money."

As she gazed out the window, Flinsuda leaned her weight deep on the chairback. It felt like her organs were being squeezed by her fat flesh.

Unable to see the stars up in the night sky, instead orange gas lamp bulbs flickered on the glass instead.

"Tu, dear. Take the sort of elderly people who can afford to live in this central city section—they will offer up an incredible amount of money just to live a single year longer. After all, no matter how much it may cost, there's nothing more precious than one's own life, is there?"

Flinsuda was also the very person who introduced technical medical treatments to Aureatia.

This was in part to make doctors learn surgical techniques and also to heal patients who couldn't be treated solely through Life Arts—however, the true goal was to increase the income of doctors by presenting patients who had reached an impasse with Life Arts treatment with expensive, state-of-the-art treatments instead.

"You see... I believe that doctors need to earn more money than any other profession. They bear a heavy responsibility and need to master difficult techniques and theory...yet, they aren't allowed to behave haughty and arrogant like aristocracy, either. They have to think of their patient above themselves. They need to be rich, or else no one would want to try to become one, don't you think?"

"Erm, Flinsuda... It's just, well... I thought about it...and there are people without any money, and people who doctors won't help, too..."

"You want to help everyone, don't you dear?"

Flinsuda was already coldhearted. With Tu's wish to help anyone and everyone, Flinsuda must have looked even more apathetic in her eyes.

She was also aware that Tu had frequented one of the Order's almshouses. As well as the fact that Tu wanted to prevent even one more person from falling through the cracks in society, this was what spurred her to enter the fray on the day of Alus's attack.

"The thing about saving the poor and destitute, dear? It's much, much simpler than trying to prolong the life of some rich person about to die from old age. Make sure they're well-nourished, use Life Arts on them, prescribe them medicine...and if there is some part of them that still can't be healed no matter what, you can simply excise it and sew them back up... But, see, even all of that treatment still costs *money.*"

The most common cause of death among the poor was merely a common cold or encephalitis.

Back when technical medicine still wasn't widespread enough, patients' only option was Life Arts treatment from a family doctor who knew them very well. It was an era where contracts weren't necessary, and treatment was established only through sympathy and obligation.

The lonely died alone. While doctors prioritized the needs of the nobility, the poor were left to fend for themselves and often died in obscurity.

"That's why I want to make it possible to rake in a lot of money, the kind used to give an extra year of life to the rich. Once I have that money, I can then buy forty years of life for twenty poorer citizens."

"......"

"The life of the weak is worth just a single gold coin, both for the people trying to save them and those who abandon them."

In which case, if she could possess countless numbers of gold coins, then she would be able to save countless numbers of lives.

Even if it meant deceiving someone whose time was coming to an end, even if meant giving up on the lives of several people in front of her, she could exchange one life for many more. That was Flinsuda's money-obsessed medical treatment.

"So it's true that, back then, I gave up on the people affected by the fire. I thought that by using the money I earned in that time, I would be able to save even more lives. Do you understand that?"

Tu's gaze wandered before looking down to the right.

She opened up her lips to try to say something, but then closed them.

She was holding Rotting Soil Sun tight against her chest.

"...Yeah."

Finally, she obediently nodded.

"I'm glad... That you were thinking about everybody like that. It was really hard for me...when I thought that maybe you weren't actually a good person at all..."

If Flinsuda had actually managed to convince Tu, and she followed the course Flinsuda indicated to her, then there wouldn't be any need to get rid of her. Flinsuda also understood that likely wouldn't happen, either.

"But, that day... I saved someone."

"You did, didn't you?"

"They were buried under the rubble... A man was calling out for help...and I saved him."

There were lives that Flinsuda had forsaken in order to negotiate the amount she would be compensated.

Flinsuda knew that it wasn't merely this one example Tu saved. There had been many more lives she saved just by heading straight to the scene and stopping Alus the Star Runner's advance.

"To that person, it was everything. He might've lost everything in the world... That's why, I don't... I don't want to think that what I did was wrong..."

"*Ho-ho-ho-ho-ho-ho*! You're absolutely right, dear. You did..."

Flinsuda's conviction was a false kind of justice, framed all around renumeration and contracts.

A true doctor was supposed to save all lives, without any compensation or contract.

It was already too late for Flinsuda to become such a doctor.

"...a magnificent job. You really gave it your all, Tu."

Tu looked on the verge of tears.

The Demon King's Bastard, true identity unknown. To Flinsuda the Portent, Tu was nothing but a lab rat to make her money by taking advantage of the Sixways Exhibition opportunity.

Even as she imposed cruel experiments on Tu, it didn't pain Flinsuda at all. Since, from the very start, Tu wasn't one of the minian races that doctors were meant to save, and wouldn't be harmed by anything done to her.

While she was openly lenient and soft on Tu, Flinsuda had been irritated many times at her for completely ruining a contract she had worked hard to secure, or for not acting exactly as Flinsuda wanted.

Nevertheless, after interacting with her for so long, had Krafnir's sickness been passed on to Flinsuda as well?

Despite being different in every regard, Flinsuda understood the way Tu thought.

Since her thoughts couldn't have been anything else but artless innate goodness, the sort that everyone naturally hopes for, Tu the Magic wasn't any kind of mysterious unknown organism at all.

"Get going now, Tu. If you remain here, you're going to cause me more trouble. After all, even if I wanted to kill you, it's not like I ever could, right? *Ho-ho-ho-ho-ho*!"

Tu the Magic was surely a singular gold coin.

A special gold coin that, regardless of its amount or value, could save the lives of many others simply from being left to run free.

Right now, the wealthy Flinsuda needed to let this coin go.

"Flinsuda. I'll think about it. I promised Rique."

Putting a leg up on the window, with the night air blowing in, Tu spoke with a serious look in her eye.

"What can I do…to save everyone? What's the best way to go about it?"

Flinsuda replied with a small nod.

She was letting a monster roam free.

However, this monster could figure something out, within this world cloaked in the shadow of terror.

The next time the wind blew in, the monster in the shape of a young girl was nowhere to be seen.

The fluttering white curtain looked like the remnants of a magic spell.

CHAPTER 4 Orde Old Town

Yuno the Distant Talon was long removed from the center stage of the Sixways Exhibition.

With her feat of bringing Soujirou all the way to Aureatia earning her employment under Haade the Flashpoint, Yuno had, out of sheer coincidence, laid eyes on the secret within Haade's camp right after the third match. Escaping with her partner in crime, Linaris the Obsidian, she had spent a fair bit of time in hiding.

Then, on the day of the eighth match, Linaris had returned to the mansion looking horribly exhausted, both physically and mentally. She still had yet to recover. As a mere child, there was surely not much Yuno could do.

Even still, there was something she had gained for herself from being wrapped up in the death of Nagan, the ruin of Lithia, and the fierce upheaval of the Sixways Exhibition—she learned about the types of powerful individuals who were far out of her reach.

There were eight days until the beginning of the tenth match.

Yuno, once again, met with the Gray-Haired Child.

"I'm honored to have another chance to meet with you, Yuno the Distant Talon."

"Th-thank you… It's nice to see you again, Hiroto the Paradox."

She nervously bowed. This office, located in a remote corner of Aureatia, was the dignitary parlor that he owned.

Next to Yuno sat a hollow-cheeked man. He barely showed any vitality, like a large doll. He was the very man who had accompanied Yuno, but she knew almost nothing about his identity.

"I'm Lendelt the Immaculate. I don't believe we've met before, Master Hiroto the Paradox."

Lendelt politely bowed.

He was an agent of Obsidian Eyes, sent to keep watch over Yuno's moves and behavior while she met with Hiroto. Nevertheless, while she was sojourning in the black mansion, Yuno had never once seen him around, nor had she ever heard the name Lendelt brought up.

He may have been an agent dedicated to attending meetings like this with other organizations, to ensure that there wasn't the slightest chance of any information around Obsidian Eyes' main force being exposed. Though this, too, was nothing but Yuno's own conjecture.

While Yuno was turning everything over in her mind, Hiroto and Lendelt's conversation had continued.

"...In any event, I am glad to see you are safe, Yuno."

Hearing her own name, Yuno reflexively looked at Hiroto's face.

Hiroto continued with a gentle smile. "I heard rumors that you had disappeared right after the end of the third match, you see. Right after that sniper attack as well. I was worried that you might have gotten caught up in some other...incident."

"Erm, well..."

She *had* actually been caught up in something. Yuno didn't know how to answer.

Despite wishing to feed her soul to the fires of her revenge, so many constraints wouldn't let her.

However, there was something she needed to prioritize over explaining her own situation.

"I can say the same thing to you, Hiroto. Thank you for taking time during your difficult circumstances to meet with me. Um…I hope my information can provide some help…"

This was all secondhand information from Lendelt, too—

Hiroto's camp, a coalition of Okafu mercenaries and goblins, was now left in an unfavorable political situation following Zigita Zogi's defeat in the eighth match. They had lost the protection of Hiroto's hero candidacy, while Rosclay's camp, having eliminated most of their rival powers, was extending their influence even further. The goblins, as foreigners in minian society, would end up being cleared out from Aureatia in the future.

If Linaris and Yuno's information was accurate, that future had become even more certain.

"First, can you take a look at this text?"

"…I see. It looks like a letter written in the welkin language. While I can read it…I'm afraid I'm not very proficient. Can you explain what it says for me, Yuno?"

"I can. This is a copy of information that one of General Haade's subordinates delivered in secret to the castle garden theater. I…and a certain individual, decoded it and realized what they were intending to do."

As Yuno explained the letter to Hiroto, she recalled that day when she and Linaris decoded the letter together.

Linaris, seen amid the soft sunlight, had been intelligent and beautiful.

Sitting beside her, Yuno herself had been the one to make use of Linaris's knowledge. She realized that though Nagan had been destroyed, the things she learned living there hadn't all been in vain.

The letter began with these words—

From the "cerebrum" to the "brain stem": Depending on results, may be necessary to adjust "terminus excision" period.

"...This part here is the content that we were able to understand from the reconstructed letter. Given what I just mentioned, the 'cerebrum' mentioned here would be Haade. The 'brain stem' could then be interpreted as Rosclay. This 'terminus' is, then, Iriolde. General Haade is pretending to work together with Minister Iriolde, but he is looking to cut him down at the appropriate moment and merge with Rosclay's camp."

"Thank you kindly. Just working from what you've laid out to me, it seems that interpretation is correct."

"This... This merging of their games must pose an immense threat that will greatly influence your course forward, given you're fighting to change Aureatia yourself! I would think it should be dealt with as soon as possible..."

"Where is the proof that this document *actually existed*?"

"Huh... What?"

"You didn't take the letter itself, but took down a copy to leave behind no trace that you read it. I can believe that. However, as long as we are unable to confirm the original article, this sort of document could have been forged to say whatever you want. That then means that the reliability of this information is lacking. You need trust to get people to act, after all."

"Er, that's... Th-that's fair..."

Yuno felt terribly embarrassed and dropped her eyes to the table.

The information she got a hold of was certain to shake the entire Sixways Exhibition itself. Nevertheless, Yuno's capabilities to handle such information weren't up to the task.

"Still, Hiroto. I... I don't have anything beyond my own word. If Haade's camp found any leftover evidence, I figured I'd probably be executed on the spot, so...won't you believe me?"

"I believe you." Hiroto laughed cheerfully. "*Ah-hah-hah-hah*! Of course I believe you. The information you laid out details one of the possibilities that Zigita Zogi the Thousandth was also worried about. So now I have someone giving concrete corroboration to something even he couldn't definitively prove. This is a windfall. Thank you very much."

"Um... Okay...?"

"Did I make you nervous? I do apologize for that. I'm sure that ever since you entered this room, you've been taking into account your word choice, your accuracy, and even my own interests, but as long as you're able to express your sincerity properly, whoever you're dealing with won't press you about all the little details. Instead of searching for a reason to refuse your proposal, they'll look for a reason to help. You're in your own dangerous situation already, Yuno, and I was the first person you came to for help. That alone is plenty of reason enough for me to aid you."

Hiroto the Paradox. This man, just like her acquaintance Soujirou the Willow-Sword, was someone who had deviated from the logic of the Beyond. A visitor. However, when she actually met with him face-to-face, she understood that the nature of his strength was something entirely different from Soujirou's.

If Soujirou's deviance was strength that terrified people, then Hiroto's strength was one that charmed them.

"You've made your sincerity more than clear to me. As for the advantages and drawbacks around this... Lendelt, I'd like to hear from you."

"Of course." Lendelt replied in kind. In contrast to Yuno, he appeared to be perfectly calm and composed. Had he anticipated that the negotiations with Hiroto would progress like this from the start?

"Regarding our identity, I don't believe I need to explain in detail, do I? I am Lendelt the Immaculate, seventh formation vanguard of Obsidian Eyes, and a minia."

Yuno had no way of knowing Lendelt's intent behind emphasizing his race while introducing himself.

Obsidian Eyes was a band of corpses under the control of a vampire. While it was possible for Linaris and her group to expand their control by infecting others through corpses, that danger therefore made it necessary when sitting at the negotiating table like this to guarantee the other party's safety.

Lendelt the Immaculate was an agent for that explicit purpose. Without ever once meeting Linaris, who was able to transmit her virus through the air, he maintained his allegiance to the organization while remaining uninfected.

"For you, Master Hiroto... I acknowledge that Obsidian Eyes are a hated and unforgivable foe. If my head will satisfy you, then I will gladly offer it to you at any time. Aureatia has turned into a singular behemoth. If someone doesn't stand against them, no one else has any hope of victory."

"......" Hiroto's smile itself didn't falter at all, yet Yuno couldn't surmise the emotions that lay underneath.

Or perhaps it was more accurate to say, Yuno could *no longer* surmise them. When Hiroto had laughed at Yuno just now, she had a clear sense that he was giving her a glimpse of how he truly felt.

"There won't be much time until Rosclay's camp wins and solidifies the overall power balance. If your own camp is in a disadvantaged position, then we could change the present state of the playing field as shadow actors with no connection to you whatsoever. To face the massive strife that is set to occur here in Aureatia, we ask you to *employ* Obsidian Eyes… That is our master's wish."

"Wait!" Yuno stood up without thinking. "I didn't hear anything about that! My request here… There is a patient in critical condition that needs treatment as soon as possible! I heard the results from Haade's investigation when I was with him! That Ozonezma the Capricious is a brilliant physician, and that he's a hero candidate with connections to you! I came here to ask you to save my friend!"

"I received these orders from my master after you, Yuno." Lendelt spoke in a clear voice that carried over and interrupted Yuno's shout. "If you intended to gain assistance from the Gray-Haired Child in exchange for information, then my master asked me to choose the survival of the organization over their life. It should be easier for Master Hiroto to accept Obsidian Eyes' request following my master's death."

"…If the parent unit is dead, then none of you will be under outside control. Is that what you're trying to say?" Hiroto replied, as if he was convinced of something Yuno didn't understand.

It was intolerable.

"Hiroto the Paradox!"

Yuno wanted to throw her anger at him. If she let the madness and hatred deep inside her take over and slammed her words at him, she could get through this without dwelling on the fear of facing off against the strong.

If she threw the unvarnished emotions inside her at him, then maybe, just maybe, everything would go smoothly.

"...! Hiroto, you just..." Yuno took a deep breath. "You said this just a moment ago. That it's not accuracy or talks about advantages or disadvantages that are needed when negotiating...but sincerity. In that case, I... If it looks to you like I am sitting here in this chair right now in good faith, th-that's because I've been talking about saving my friend."

Think. Think.

If she remained spurred on by her impulses, then nothing about her had changed.

She wished to feed her soul to the fires of her revenge. Why hadn't she been able to do that?

Because her desire to escape the oppression from the powerful was so great that she entrusted all her choices to her impulses in the moment.

The result was where she was now. Drifting farther and farther away from the person she wished vengeance on without achieving anything Yuno herself wished for, everything about her being swept away by the situation at hand.

She needed to decide with her own thoughts where she was heading.

Even if this was a request from Linaris herself, she couldn't back down here.

"I feel that Lendelt's proposal also outlines a very urgent problem. But the ones who gained this information and deciphered it...are myself and said friend. Since I've come here to sit and converse with you directly...I ask that you do me this favor. P-please... It's all I ask."

With a deep breath, Yuno bowed her head low.

She was able prevent her explosion of emotion from emerging.

To Yuno herself, it was an unbelievable feat.

"Master Hiroto. There is nothing more foreign to our organization than trust and confidence. Thus, we can only come to the negotiating table with talks around benefits and drawbacks."

In almost total contrast to the nerves and tension Yuno was feeling, Lendelt was cool-headed.

"As you have guessed, the patient Yuno wishes to save is our master. If you can spare her life, that would be more than we could ever hope for. Obsidian Eyes will swear in good faith to do everything we can for you. However, her life, or Obsidian Eyes—I also understand that the right to make that choice rests in your hands. If you are to choose between either, then choose Obsidian Eyes. Naturally, the other agents are unaware of the details around this deal, and I will not disclose it to them."

There was the option of waiting until Linaris's death to then take Obsidian Eyes in.

Just from the flow of conversation, Yuno could tell that this was bound to become an extremely important factor.

Hiroto replied, "Obsidian Eyes murdered my sworn friend."

The reception room went perfectly still, as if filled up with water.

Both Yuno and Lendelt both felt the weight of the enmity in Hiroto's words.

However, this atmosphere disappeared as if it had all been an hallucination.

"However, my friend created this situation himself. There's no need to overthink things here. When it's all said and done, I have guests coming to me seeking my help...and it's about whether I become friendly with them or not."

As he said this, Hiroto put down his cup.

Standing up, he stretched out a hand to Yuno and Lendelt.

A handshake held out to his mortal enemy, Obsidian Eyes.

"I shall grant both your requests."

◆

The coincidental course of events on the day that Zigita Zogi died seemed as if they had almost saved Hiroto the Paradox.

That was wrong.

Obsidian Eyes was comprised of broken failures who could only live in the midst of war and conflict.

Therefore, their goal had been to create a war-torn world that would allow them to survive.

Their strategy to do this was to eliminate Zigita Zogi the Thousandth, and with that, control Hiroto's camp with mass infection. By first manipulating their leaders, starting with Morio the Sentinel and Hiroto the Paradox, they could artificially orchestrate a longstanding cold war between Aureatia and the New Continent, truly achieving a victory for Obsidian Eyes.

However, this strategy was defeated. As Linaris the Obsidian secured her victory over her opponent, Zigita Zogi the Thousandth, his final stratagem made a change in their strategy unavoidable.

What exactly had been Zigita Zogi's final stratagem, then?

Making them question, for just a brief moment, if perhaps he was actually still alive—but that wasn't the true essence of it.

The actual aim was, by implanting the shadow of doubt that Zigita

Zogi was alive and everything was all a part of his plan, it would make continuing their controlling strategy more dangerous.

Once they understood that the path they needed to follow was dangerous, their only choice was then to retreat to the safer path—for someone sharp-witted enough to realize the existence of such an escape route, this was the only option.

Their escape route was forming a *united front* with Hiroto's camp.

If Haade's scheme was going to bear fruit, then it would inevitably cause a huge upheaval in the military of Aureatia. No matter how it all turned out, it would lead to increased tensions between Aureatia and Hiroto's camp.

It might not have become a long, drawn-out period of war. It may have only resulted in an employment relationship destined to someday be discarded. However, that was precisely the battlefield Obsidian Eyes kept wishing for, that they were meant to live through.

The real trap was the second-best strategy—the one they couldn't shake from the back of their minds even as they carried out the most viable plan.

Linaris the Obsidian understood Zigita Zogi the Thousandth's strategy, and as a result, chose surrender.

The gambit of her death could potentially change the whole balance of power.

Having lost their strategic linchpin of Zigita Zogi, Hiroto's camp would assuredly need an actually operating force like Obsidian Eyes. Furthermore, as long as Hiroto the Paradox survived, it was possible to win over a formerly hostile opponent to their side—that was what Zigita Zogi believed.

Hiroto, too, believed that it hadn't been the end. Thus, he made Morio the Sentinel enter Aureatia, forced Yukiharu the Twilight Diver to continue his investigations, and prepared himself for the favorable chance that was bound to visit him.

All he had to do was believe the time would come, and wait.

I haven't lost yet. It starts here, Zigita Zogi.

He could still continue to fight.

Trust is what's stronger than anything else.

CHAPTER 5 Yatmaees Garrion's Indoor Training Grounds

There were five days left until the start of the tenth match.

On this day, there was a single indoor training ground that wasn't scheduled to be utilized by any other squad or unit.

It wasn't unusual. A simply accidental coincidence. However, two people were in the facility taking advantage of such a coincidence. Aureatia's Third Minister, Jelky the Swift Ink—along with Aureatia's Second General, Rosclay the Absolute.

"I had just been hoping to borrow someone else's eyes."

Rosclay was lightly dressed in base colors of white and yellow.

He had summoned Jelky merely to confirm a smaller matter as they readied to carry out their operation, but Rosclay had also called him in part to look at his training form.

"I may be trying to move as fluidly as possible, if something looks a bit strange to others, then I can't say I've perfected it yet."

Jelky was sitting in a chair on the edge of the training ground. He slightly furrowed his eyebrows.

"...If you're aiming to be in perfect fighting form, then you should've spent more time on your treatment. Didn't the doctors tell you that?"

"They did."

They had needed to exhaust every method at their disposal to reconstruct both of Rosclay's legs, which had been broken during the fourth match. Rapidly regenerating extremities ended up consuming a considerable amount of one's cellular lifespan. There were also side effects brought on in exchange for the reduced treatment time. It was necessary to surgically remove the sections that regenerated crooked and warped. The wounds from the surgery were then treated with Life Arts once more.

The Life Arts specialists weren't the ones to recommend such a treatment method. Rosclay himself had asked for it.

"Still, I'm going to be the best I can be. There can't be even the slightest chance that Rosclay the Absolute is unable to fight on the day of the match."

"...And it's my job to ensure there isn't the slightest chance that match even occurs."

Hearing Jelky's reply, Rosclay smiled slightly.

"Either way, Aureatia is going to make big moves. I can't rely on my compatriots for everything and should prepare for any and all possibilities. Please watch."

Rosclay reached a hand out in front of him and released a tiny piece of cloth from his fingers.

It felt straight down.

He held his longsword straight up, right next to his face.

The transition from casual, everyday motions into his fighting stance happened naturally and in the blink of an eye.

"*Hup.*"

He stepped forward with a short exhale and slashed downward at an angle.

Though called a *strong attack*, it was one of the fundamental longsword techniques.

The piece of cloth, only as big as his fingertip and without the surface area to flutter through the air, split into two before it could reach the ground.

"How did that look to you?"

Rosclay picked up the cloth from the ground. The square scrap of cloth had been separated perfectly through the center.

"I do not have the combat experience of military officers such as yourself," Jelky commented with as stern an expression as always. "...Nevertheless, I thought it was fantastic. No different from how you've been up until now."

"Your lack of combat experience is exactly why I asked... With this, everything is perfect."

Mere strength wasn't enough for Rosclay's swordsmanship. It needed to be beautiful even in the eyes of a total amateur.

For instance, Soujirou the Willow-Sword's techniques would likely be seen as almighty by any person who was a fairly strong fighter in their own right. However, to the common eye they were uncanny and nothing more—liable to be come off as base and ugly.

"I'll say this again, Rosclay. You should *not* be facing this with the intention to fight. The tenth match will not happen. The plan is to announce that Soujirou the Willow-Sword has requested to withdraw and disqualify him. Once he is alienated by his sponsor, Haade, a visitor like him should have no means to protest."

"...I know."

It had been planned that way from the start. Anticipating that he would force his hero candidate to drop out the moment that they were matched up against Rosclay, Haade had chosen the freshly arrived visitor as his candidate.

Soujirou the Willow-Sword had no others to rely on in this world.

Additionally, having lost one leg during his match against Ozonezma, he wouldn't become a threat later on, even if he were left alive.

"However, even if Soujirou himself can no longer fight in the Sixways Exhibition, there is the possibility one of the other powers are planning to use him themselves. What are the chances that others in the Twenty-Nine, the Gray-Haired Child...or potentially the Old Kingdoms' loyalists, have contacted him?"

"Sabfom the White Weave is keeping watch over him at Romog Joint Military Hospital. Our information control measures work at that hospital. If anyone makes contact with Soujirou, we are certain to learn of it. If you have any worries on how we're handling things, then tell me."

"...Fair enough. Forgive me, while I was only asking to make doubly sure, I may have come off as a bit rude."

He flashed the same perfect smile as moments prior—however, this one was mostly self-deprecating.

It's not absolute.

Rosclay the Absolute proceeded forward with thorough discretion that occasionally bordered on cowardice.

That was how it seemed.

However, Rosclay was aware of it himself—this only extended to matters that concerned his own self-defense.

If it was truly in his nature to carefully think through everything, Iriolde's large-scale plan to slay Lucnoca the Winter and incite a rebellion would have never had the chance to go into action.

Rosclay's true thoroughness had always been reserved for schemes that kept fear at a distance: Psychologically attacking Gilnes the Ruined Castle, scattering water over the ground to block Kia's Word Arts, and manipulating the tournament structure for the Sixways Exhibition to make sure he fought against safe opponents.

He didn't expose his true self, even to his compatriots who knew the truth behind his candidacy and shared his goal.

Something is missing. I'm still scared.

On the day of the tenth match, Iriolde was going to enact his rebellion. Haade had made sure it would happen.

The massive coup d'état, including an attack on the palace, would become an event that left its mark on history. More than enough to paint over the grand entertainment and excitement of Rosclay the Absolute's match. More than that, his faction, manipulating the Sixways Exhibition as its administrators, wouldn't start the match. Per the rules, with Soujirou having lost his backer, he wouldn't participate in any more rounds. The tenth match would end with a default win for Rosclay.

"If there was anyone to be wary of, it would be the Free City of Okafu, but..." Jelky used his free hand to adjust his glasses. "There is no chance that they have been in contact with Iriolde's camp. We know this is certain not only from the information Haade sent to us, but also from the reports of our undercover agents. However, Iriolde's camp is also a power that's been taking in anti-Aureatian elements from the very start. It is possible that after seeing Iriolde make his big move, Okafu will independently decide to ally with them."

"That's true. The one factor that still has me worried is the Gray-Haired Child."

Should Okafu, led by Hiroto the Paradox, align themselves with Iriolde, subjugating would be *slightly* more involved than anticipated. Nevertheless, a majority of Okafu's mercenaries had been sent home to the Free City of Okafu following the string of deaths in the early stages of the Sixways Exhibition, which Obsidian Eyes was thought to have a hand in. No matter how skillfully Hiroto used his personal goblin army, they weren't enough to alter the big picture of something like a war.

If anything, for Rosclay, he was hoping that they would join with Iriolde's camp. If they pointed their blades at the monarchy, then he would be able to *legitimately and lawfully* put down the rest of Iriolde's group.

Which is why Hiroto the Paradox shouldn't make any moves... He has no reason to do so.

In which case, was there another enemy that could prove a threat?

The Old Kingdoms' loyalists were already without any real fighting force. The details surrounding Obsidian Eyes were mostly unknown, but Rosclay's group still had insurance from their exhaustive corpse testing and additional production of antiserum. He assumed Obsidian Eyes couldn't make any immediate moves.

"...I was thinking about the day of the tenth match."

He thought that it might be meaningless to think about it, anyway.

"Should any unexpected situations crop up on the day of, you likely won't be able to take any immediate action. Even if you subtract all the preliminary preparations, canceling the match is bound to bring you a huge amount of official work to handle. The situation on the day itself... our golden opportunity...was likely the only reason we were able to lure Iriolde out to begin with."

"I intend to give all my efforts to cope with any and all incidents, while keeping pace with my clerical work. When compared against the success of the Sixways Exhibition and the safety of the Queen, no matter how much work it may result in, it won't be more than a day's labor down the line."

The countermeasures against Iriolde's aims to overthrow Aureatia had a direct impact on the Queen's personal safety.

There was no doubt Jelky would give the mission everything he had.

"Thank you. I trusted you'd say something like that."

After replying, Rosclay returned to his sword training once more.

Footwork. Hand manipulation. Breathing.

Rosclay skillfully managed it all during his duels while simultaneously keeping his thoughts in motion.

In this Sixways Exhibition, where I should be suspicious of everything, Jelky is one of the select few companions I can trust.

Trust was very much the most powerful strength of all. Rosclay managed to come this far entirely because of Jelky's cooperation, and that was likely to hold true for what happened moving forward as well.

...Which is why I've preserved my trump card. The ability to send that man *into action.*

◆

The period Soujirou the Willow-Sword spent admitted to Romog Joint Military Hospital might have actually been longer than the time he had spent in Aureatia beforehand. Mathematically speaking, the number of days couldn't have been very long. At least, that was what Soujirou's internal clock told him.

His duel to the death with Ozonezma the Capricious had been a wholly new experience for him. In exchange for that, he had lost his right leg and was forced to endure a new flavor of boredom now that he couldn't move as freely.

While Soujirou didn't regret it, he did feel like he hadn't had enough.

"*Fwah-hah-hah-hah*! Every day, staring out the window! What are you looking at, Soujirou the Willow-Sword?!" A man's shout echoed from the sickbed next to him.

This was a patient by the name of Sabfom the White Weave, Aureatia's

Twelfth General. The smooth steel plate covered his face after having the skin over it sliced off, nose and all.

"Longing for the Aureatia city streets, are you?! I'm glad to hear it!"

"Yer way too damn loud all the time. You can totally get discharged at this point..."

Sabfom was supposed to be here to recover from his wounds, just like Soujirou, but perhaps due to all his wounds being on his face, he was brimming full of vigor, almost more than the average healthy person.

Allegedly, when Alus the Star Runner attacked, Sabfom had taken the lead to rescue the citizens, charging into the configuration himself—clearly not something anyone injured or infirmed should've been doing.

"Well, then. Isn't it the same scene out there, no matter how many times you look?"

"Nah...a shop's sending up advertising balloons. Just thought that they have a lotta different patterns to 'em. You guys in this world can't read or anything, right?"

"Oh, right, you visitors often make use of written characters, don't you!" Sabfom shouted, as if surprised.

Though, whether he was surprised or not, this man's voice was so loud it always sounded overexaggerated.

"The particularly big shops will put out ads and signboards with a unique color selection. The benefit to using them is that they can be discerned from farther away, and by putting them on balloons, they're visible from all directions! If I remember right, they have to apply to the Assembly to use a unique color combination. That said, save for the color combination, anyone's free to put whatever pattern they want on balloons. A lot of patterns are distinctive and elaborate."

"Words'd make it easy to tell a glance, but instead ya got this pain-in-the-ass setup."

"There are colors that all shops can use, too. For example, the color red by itself symbolizes that thirty percent of more of a shop's goods are on sale for twenty percent off and up! Useful info, isn't it?! *Fwah-hah-hah-hah*!"

"Oh, yah... Thanks. Might end up doing some shopping when I get discharged, who knows."

Sabfom was a stouthearted man who liked looking out for others, but one flaw of his was that his behavior was always so sweltering and overbearing.

For Soujirou, it wasn't more than he could take, but if any of the other hospital patients were sharing a room with them, the anxiety would have rapidly made their condition deteriorate. As a matter of fact, Harghent the Still, who once fought together with the man, had looked very exhausted mentally just from learning that Sabfom was staying in the same hospital ward as him.

...Actually, what even happened to Old Man Harghent anyway?

Ever since that day, Harghent hadn't returned to Romog Joint Military Hospital.

He challenged his old enemy Alus the Star Runner to combat, defeated him, and earned renown and glory.

The end result should've been everything Harghent had wanted.

However, what had happened after that?

Sitting in here ain't for me.

Soujirou felt like something was narrowing his own circumstances, slowly and torturously strangling him—something he couldn't defeat in a fight.

It wasn't the fear he was going to be assassinated. If anything, it was the opposite. According to what Yuno told him before, a doctor with the knowledge and ability to use Life Arts on a patient could easily cause fatal wounds by directly using them, but he hadn't felt the slightest hints of any such attack.

He was so bored, he had actually hoped such an assault would come for him, but even if it had, it probably wouldn't have been any challenge at all. The distance required for those Word Arts to reach him was also well within the range of Soujirou's blade.

Nevertheless, while he had an extremely strong intuition against attacks, it didn't have any effect against *not being attacked at all.*

Even as the situation outside the hospital was moving furiously on, the harm never reached them.

A majority of the rumors around incidents occurring in Aureatia didn't even touch this place, perhaps to avoid fanning the patients' anxieties.

"Hey, Sabfom. When's the next match? When do I get to fight?"

"There should be an announcement as the day approaches. After all, Rosclay is heavily wounded himself! Waiting until you're both fully healed to fight is fair for you, too, isn't it?!"

"...Nah. It's in five days."

"Well now, surprised to hear you know that!"

"It's that Rosclay or whatever's match, right? All sorts of guys gossiping about it."

There was an invisible power trying to remove Soujirou the Willow-Sword from the Sixways Exhibition.

However, even if he vaguely understood this, he couldn't challenge it to a fight, either.

In the second round, not a single match was conducted in a normal manner.

The tenth match wasn't going to commence.

There were five days remaining before the day of the tenth match.

◆

Aureatia was once the royal capital of the Central Kingdom, which transformed with the merging of the three kingdoms.

In some areas of the city, with its long history, it wasn't unusual to see structures from an age too old to be recorded in the annals of the Aureatia Assembly, and in fact, the city's urban development resulted in several instances where such underground structures and remnants of ancient buildings were rediscovered.

There was one organization who excelled the most in using these old structures from the age of the Central Kingdom, more than Iriolde or Hiroto's camp or even Obsidian Eyes—the Old Kingdoms' loyalists.

Aureatia's former Fourth Minister, Kaete the Round Table, had his hero candidate, Mestelexil, wrested from him in the fourth match As he was escaping from Obsidian Eyes' pursuit, together with Kiyazuna the Axle, he was taken, practically browbeaten, into the custody of the Old Kingdoms' loyalists.

Currently, he was in the ruins of an underground waterway together with an Old Kingdoms' loyalists' force.

He didn't know what age the ruins dated back to. They had been out of use for a long time, but the wall surface was paved in processed stone, and the space could support the lives of a large host of soldiers.

Of course, for Kaete though, this environment was far from meeting his standards for "living."

"What the hell's with this bread…?! It's practically a lump of wood! The dough's totally dense and hasn't risen at all!"

"No bellyachin' about the food, you dumbass pupil."

Cussing out and glancing sidelong at Kaete beside her, Kiyazuna devoured the piece of bread.

The bread was hard enough to chip a tooth or two with the way she was eating it, yet this old woman, easily over eighty years old, still had all of her teeth perfectly intact.

"You've always been way too picky! Living the life of a spoiled rotten brat."

"You're just way too uncivilized, Grams! You're a Craft Arts expert, why the hell're are you even used to living like this?!"

"'Cause I've been a demon king for a helluva long time!"

The terrible situation the Old Kingdoms' loyalists found themselves in wasn't limited to the conditions of their base and their food supply.

Formerly, the Old Kingdoms' loyalists had a powerful leader in Gilnes the Ruined Castle standing at their helm, and had powerful supports behind them like Iriolde the Atypical Tome and Hiroto the Paradox.

However, Hiroto used the Toghie City uprising by the Old Kingdoms' loyalists as a means to secure participation in the Sixways Exhibition, and Iriolde had accepted the outcome as well, cutting off his support and essentially abandoning the Old Kingdoms' loyalists after they were radically weakened as an organization. Not stopping there, Iriolde had been assimilating many of those who were actively working against Aureatia into his own group, too.

In short, at this stage, those who remained behind in this armed force were thoughtless rebels clinging to a fight they had no hopes of winning, purely out of pride and conviction.

"Dammit… You think we can win, Grams?"

Kaete looked out over the grubby group, sitting along the underground waterway and taking their meal just like they were.

"Win what?"

“Anything. Whatever the plan is, doesn’t feel like we’ll be able to pull it off. Say we invade Aureatia with the golems you’ve made—what do we need to capture to win? These guys may claim otherwise, but I doubt they’ll be able to change the tides in Aureatia since Rosclay’s got such a tight control over the whole place.”

Looking at it another way, the fact that the Old Kingdoms’ loyalists had been weakened as much as they had was itself an indication of how fierce Rosclay the Absolute was.

They had been given the name “Old Kingdoms’ loyalists” by Aureatia as part of a strategy to manipulate the public image of them, but their original identity was exactly as they claimed: the *Royal Army*. The very same Royal Army who, during the era of the Central Army, purported to be the mightiest in the land.

When the three kingdoms merged, they crowned their queen Sephite from the United Western Kingdom. This decision caused a backlash, and the hardliners of the new military division, splitting the Royal Army in two, became the prototype of the Old Kingdoms’ loyalists.

From the era of the True Demon King, they had tried several times to undermine Aureatia in order to regain the original state of the Kingdom. However, every time they did, the Old Kingdoms’ loyalists were the ones who were actually undermined.

Their assertions that, when considering the process in which Aureatia was first established, should have held a certain amount of legitimacy, also failed to shake Aureatia. During the age of terror, the people leaned not on legitimacy, but on a champion—Rosclay the Absolute.

While Kaete may have held no qualms about crushing anything to do with humanity and morality underfoot, he could still comprehend how significant this fact was. Even if these Old Kingdoms’ loyalists took on Rosclay the Absolute, their chances of victory were close to zero.

In other words, the reason Kaete and Kiyazuna were sheltering with the Old Kingdoms' loyalists wasn't so they could overthrow Aureatia.

"It's 'cause they're so hopeless that we gotta buddy up with 'em like this."

Kiyazuna bit down on the dried provisions she had been supplied.

"Eat the same stuff they do, and wear the same clothes. That's enough for 'em to start believing we're on their side, see. Everyone else just treats 'em like losers and all. A way to build up a bunch of underlings from nothing. So you gotta suck it up, too."

Kaete had never once heard of Kiyazuna the Axle leading minian followers before.

"Buddying up to them like that'll just mean that losers are gonna think you're another loser like them... What're you going to do if one of them starts to talk down to you, Grams?"

"Kill 'em!"

"...Right, right."

Kaete actually had a gentle look in his eyes as he stared at Kiyazuna.

Kiyazuna the Axle was someone with an intrinsic hostility toward the minian races.

"'Cept if my baby's life is involved, then things're different."

She had already finished eating her dried provisions. Kiyazuna had always been a fast eater, but Kaete thought he caught glimpses of another emotion in her mannerisms ever since they joined up with the Old Kingdoms' loyalists. Impatience.

"Gonna use these chumps...and get Mestelexil back. They ain't gonna be useful come wartime anyway. Gotta get some practical use outta 'em. Right?"

Neither Kaete nor Kiyazuna had any interest at all in restoring the Central Kingdom.

Without any hopes of victory, any plot to overthrow Aureatia and regain Kaete's power and authority was similarly unrealistic.

Nevertheless, when it came to the single goal of reclaiming Mestelexil, there was still a way to twist the situation to their benefit.

If the Old Kingdoms' loyalists could manage that, then it could serve as a breakthrough to solve not only many of Kiyazuna's problems, but Kaete's as well.

"I know, Grams. We'll *throw these guys* at Obsidian Eyes, use the fray of battle to destroy the homunculus core of Mestelexil, and regain control from the vampire..."

When he voiced their plan one more time, he couldn't stop himself from thinking.

"...Is it all really gonna go that smoothly?"

"*Heh*, we got any other options? If the two of us try to pin down Mestelexil just by ourselves, we'll definitely end up dead! Also, those Obsidian Eyes bastards gotta have other corpses wandering around beyond those guys chasing us."

Mestelexil is absolutely necessary... I still haven't given up on reforming Aureatia with science and technology.

Mestelexil the Box of Desperate Knowledge was not a hero candidate who was simply all-powerful and strong. He was a strategic weapon that could easily bring ruin to a whole continent. Under Obsidian Eyes' control, without the proper knowledge surrounding the weapons of the Beyond, Kaete and Kiyazuna likely weren't able to utilize even twenty percent of Mestelexil's full power—still, that *small degree* of additional fighting strength might have been enough to make it to the end of the Sixways Exhibition.

If Kaete and Kiyazuna were once again able to regain control of Mestelexil, this time there would be no need to proceed with caution or hide his true value. Kaete was confident that even a single one of the trump cards Mestelexil contained would be able to draw out major concessions from Aureatia.

"The real problem's about what's actually happening in Aureatia right now… We lack info! Even if there was that assault from the self-proclaimed demon king Alus the other day, should we accept that Alus the Star Runner is actually back in action? Rosclay might just be announcing combat damages sustained against other factions, like Haade's, as if Alus did them all. Even if we're going to steer the Old Kingdoms' loyalists, without a fairly precise information source, then—"

At that moment, Kaete stopped speaking.

There was someone heading over to them. Though, this person still wouldn't have been close enough to hear what they were talking about.

"Caneeya the Fruit Trimming."

"I know."

Caneeya was the de facto commander leading the current Old Kingdoms' loyalists.

Her muscular built and tall frame, burlier and stouter than any man around, stood out even from afar.

"Kaete the Round Table. Are our preserved foods not to your liking?" Caneeya smiled, looking at the piece of bread in Kaete's hands, barely halfway finished.

Of course, this woman always looked as if she was smiling. Her heart and expressions weren't in conjunction with each other.

"Yeah, not at all," Kaete replied, almost entirely on reflex. "We're lending your half-dead group a hand, out of the goodness of our hearts, and this is how you think to treat us? This dried food here makes better ant food than people food."

"You've been supplied with the exact same thing as everybody else. Unlike Aureatia, we hold equality as one of our guiding principles."

"Ohh, is that so? Then you won't have any problem with us doing the same exact work as any other soldier, then. Obviously, we can easily match whatever one of the ants in your loyalist army has to offer. "

"Well, I am sorry. If our aid has offended you, then you wouldn't mind if we sent you out of our ant nest to somewhere up on the sunny surface then, would you?"

"I haven't liked you Old Kingdoms' loyalists from the start. After I hack you up here, I'll—"

"Give that stupid mouth of yours a rest already, Kaete." Kiyazuna bluntly smacked Kaete's head. "Can't you maintain some damn self-control for once?"

"Ow! Why my head?!"

"*Keh*. That head o' yours can't get any stupider."

Kaete couldn't curry favor with someone he didn't like. While they may not have actually shared any blood, this aspect was something that Kaete had strongly inherited from Kiyazuna's own temperament.

Kaete and Kiyazuna were still considered wanted fugitives in Aureatia. If they hadn't had the Old Kingdoms' loyalists' familiarity with the city on their side, they likely would have been captured by Rosclay's camp and disposed of by this point. Either that, or Obsidian Eyes would have gotten to them first and silenced them, or even turned them into corpses.

"Screw it… Just get to your point, Caneeya the Fruit Trimming. If you're showing me that offensive mug of yours for no good reason, I really will cut your head off."

"I wanted to let you know which day we're making our move."

"*Hmph*… Except you must've been planning to do it on the day of the tenth match from the very start. A totally unsophisticated operation."

"Yes, very insightful of you."

"Do you even need insight to figure that out?" Kaete murmured with his cane propping up one of his cheeks.

Although few in number, it was hard to believe that so many Old Kingdoms' loyalists were hiding underground in preparation without any plans to make their move. The situation should have made the conclusion clear that they were enacting some sort of operation in the near future. The fact they were conveying this to Kaete and Kiyazuna now, with the tenth match starting in four days, must have been because they were worried about outsiders like them leaking information.

"During Rosclay's match, a huge number of citizens are going to move as a group to a set location at a set time. Not only will it be easy for you to take advantage of this course of events to send troops in, but if you target the arena, you can involve a great number of civilians in the attack… Artless twits. There's no way Aureatia hasn't assumed something like that would happen."

"Saying we'll attack civilians is quite a hurtful way of putting it. We are merely acting to free the citizenry from the control of the Aureatia Assembly."

"Oh? How admirable."

Needless to say, Kaete's backhanded compliment was dripping with spite.

This wasn't only true of the Old Kingdoms' loyalists, as it was the same for most of the other Twenty-Nine Officials, but they spoke as if they were taking violent action in the name of justice, or for someone else's sake.

What a pointless deception.

Kaete didn't have an issue with lying itself. He hated lies that were easily exposed.

There wasn't a single iota of him that wanted to serve justice or desired the welfare of the people, but he had always acted up-front about it. Even his plan of overthrowing Aureatia was for nothing more than to build what he himself thought was a more logical land.

These people's way of doing things, continuing to dance around a meaningless lie, could go on for a thousand years and still not change anything about the world.

"In any case, even I thought that attacking the castle garden theater mid-match was reckless. There were many among my men who voiced their desire to claim vengeance on Rosclay for killing General Gilnes, but… For once it seems you and I are on the same page."

"Certainly not happy about it."

"The end result being that the plan to attack the castle garden theater was rejected, since the match isn't going to happen."

"…What?"

Kaete agreed that, when thinking about the nature of the Sixways Exhibition, there was always the possibility that a match would be canceled for unforeseen circumstances.

Especially in the case of Rosclay, with his heavy wounds from the fourth match. The extent of his injury hadn't been officially announced, and even when Kaete was still part of the Twenty-Nine Officials, he hadn't been able to properly get all the details.

Therefore, it was bizarre for a mere Old Kingdoms' loyalist like Caneeya to assert that the match was canceled, unbeknownst to Kaete.

"If the tenth match is going to be canceled, why wouldn't I or Kiyazuna know about it? That sort of thing would be pointless unless average citizens are notified, too."

"It means they expect something to happen," Kiyazuna spat out next to him.

"Or they'll *cause* something to happen."

"You're absolutely right. The tenth match is *scheduled* to be canceled for *an emergency*. A massive coup d'état against the Aureatia Assembly is being planned, led by Haade the Flashpoint. The day of the tenth match is the day it is supposed to happen."

"...Haade is?" Kaete placed his hand on his chin in thought.

The tenth match was scheduled to be canceled due to Haade's intentions to overthrow the government being leaked to Rosclay.

Everything couldn't have been that simple. If that was the case, they could have announced the match cancellation beforehand. It would mean that Rosclay's camp knew about this plan, and were feigning to hold the tenth match in order to lure Haade out. Rosclay was intending to counterattack and kill the rebelling army.

Moreover, where exactly was Caneeya the Fruit Trimming able to get this inside knowledge from?

"This information... Who told you, Caneeya the Fruit Trimming?"

"I figured that I would fill you in about this at some point."

Caneeya sat down next to Kaete. Even when sitting, she was a whole head taller than him.

Just one of her brawny arms, thick as logs, would have been enough to strangle Kaete.

"I and several others in our leadership have a relationship with the Gray-Haired Child. The fact we were able to rescue you both from Obsidian Eyes' pursuit was due to information shared with us by Yukiharu the Twilight Diver."

"...Do you realize what you're doing here?"

"Yes. The Gray-Haired Child used us and our business together in

Toghie City to get himself into the Sixways Exhibition. He is an indirect cause of many of our comrades' deaths...including General Gilnes. He is an object of vengeance."

"*Hmph.* So you're saying, despite that, your organization can't survive without his help."

"The Gray-Haired Child…is a terrifying opponent. He wants to, one day, call everyone in the world his ally.

Caneeya's voice sounded as if it was trembling slightly.

Surviving by accepting support from someone who should be a hated and bitter enemy.

In the past, Kaete might have felt that this was a pathetic story.

However, Kaete and Kiyazuna were in the exact same position, unable to survive without accepting begrudged support.

"My men haven't been informed of this connection. The goods and information the Gray-Haired Child gives us are always precise and accurate. He acquired information that the one actually behind the massive coup scheduled to commence with the start of the tenth match wasn't Haade, but Minister Iriolde. In addition, Haade has been conspiring with Rosclay in secret, and is planning to cut Iriolde down on the day the plan goes into action.

"Wait, wait, hold on. There was way too much to parse out there! Iriolde?! Haade and Rosclay…?!"

From Kaete's perspective, none of it was anything he could have ever imagined.

"What does that mean, then? Haade's coup that kicks off with the start of the tenth match is a rigged affair of a united military force, and once it's finished, the political contest in Aureatia will end with Rosclay's reformation faction as the sole winners…"

How had the Gray-Haired Child come across this extremely important information?

Even if Kaete tossed this question at Caneeya, it would be altogether meaningless.

However, Kaete knew just how precise the Gray-Haired Child's intel was from the fact that he dispatched Old Kingdoms' loyalists to rescue Kaete and Kiyazuna, as though he had perfectly predicted how the sixth match would end up.

Kiyazuna spoke with a yawn. "I don't know a thing about this politics crap. So what's this all got to do with us, then?"

"Are you daft, Grams?! This changes our presuppositions… On the day of the tenth match, it's very true that Aureatia's ability to manage things will be stretched near its limit. The sole opportunity for these Old Kingdoms' loyalists to make any meaningful action. But, it's not the tenth match of the Sixways Exhibition that's going to keep them busy. The Aureatia army will lure out Iriolde's army and move to annihilate them. We need to outsmart this movement of theirs."

"Exactly. I knew I was correct to consult with Aureatia's former Fifth Minister. Based on your esteemed tactical genius and experience, what would then be the most effective move to make?"

"…Damn ragtag louts," Kaete bitterly muttered.

Needing to hammer out a decisive strategy in order to best utilize a presented opportunity, instead of having a decisive operation ready and waiting for the perfect chance to enact it, was, for an army, putting the cart before the horse.

While Kaete didn't want to believe Caneeya was too stupid to understand that, he didn't particularly expect much from her.

But this is fortunate. As long as we continue to survive, these golden opportunities are bound to eventually come around.

Kaete looked up at the underground waterway's low ceiling. He was piecing the logic together in his head.

The information the Old Kingdoms' loyalists had obtained, at the moment, must have been greatly biased in one direction.

He just needed to use that bias for himself.

"Okay, then. Given that the Aureatia army will be out in town suppressing Iriolde's forces, we can say it's basically impossible to attack Aureatia's key facilities. Whether it's the castle garden theater, the palace, or some random provision storage, the most we could hope for is to get driven off *along with* Iriolde's army."

As he spoke, Kaete soaked the tip of a stick that had been laying on the ground in a puddle on the edge of the canal.

He used the water to draw a simplified city map of Aureatia.

"Conversely, the protection around the secret facilities will be weaker... This is where you should target."

The forested section of Aureatia's Outer Ward.

It was a sparsely populated district that wasn't particularly worth any attention, but Kaete and Kiyazuna knew the importance of this area. Obsidian Eyes' base of operations had to be somewhere within this forest.

The signal that the plundered Mestelexil emitted through technology from the Beyond continued to transmit its location to Kiyazuna's receiver.

"They said that the vampire disease is what drove Alus the Star Runner mad, but...can you actually believe the nonsense explanation that a vampire, supposedly eradicated a generation ago, reappeared and was able to transmit the virus through their blood to someone powerful enough to be a hero candidate? Go ahead and imagine the reason why the Aureatia Assembly used the Sixways Exhibition to gather all these powerful fighters in one place. I see it as them moving forward with a scheme to artificially turn them all into corpses and render them powerless."

It was nothing but a made-up story he strung together on the spot using some of the information he had at his disposal.

Nevertheless, the Old Kingdoms' loyalists sought the sort of gambit they could pull off to turn the tables.

There were many who *wanted to believe* in this conspiracy Kaete laid out.

"Do you have some proof?"

"Proof. Proof, huh. Was there any of that in the information the Gray-Haired Child gave you? I had already estimated where their base might be. See, there were suspicious stories that reached my industrial ministry, too. Mestelexil and Alus seem to have failed, but…there was definitely a successful example."

"…You don't mean what I think you do, do you?"

"*There is no possible way* that Lucnoca the Winter was defeated through reasonable means. There's almost guaranteed to be some vampire that's been weaponized. With your manpower, we should be able to search for it—while Iriolde's army is drawing Aureatia's attention in the city."

"*Kweh-heh*. Not too bad, Kaete." Kiyazuna twisted her mouth into a smile.

He couldn't stand it. This deceptive eloquence wasn't how Kaete did things.

"Caneeya the Fruit Trimming. You… You understand your army has no hope of winning?"

Even then, something on this scale was possible.

He could see through the collective's lies and truths, since, to Kaete, all the people were ignorant sheep.

"Once an army that's degenerated into a reckless resistance finds a target, it's impossible to stop themselves from charging straight ahead.

Don't you think it's better to go with the option with less of a chance you'll die a hero's death?"

"Even if we fail, there won't be many wounded... That's what you're trying to say, isn't it? Should we succeed then, we would gain unwavering evidence of the Aureatia Assembly's foul play."

If there was ever a time when Kaete truly smiled from the heart, it was when he was ridiculing fools like this.

"I'll upset the outcome to it all. Even you lot must be thinking the same."

CHAPTER 6 Northern District of the Old Town

There was a young man named Surug the Double Shield. He shared the eight-person carriage with several other soldiers and was heading out with them to save the people of Aureatia.

Though not technically regular Aureatian soldiers, they felt that they had been preparing for this very day.

The people of Aureatia don't know. There are those who sacrificed a great number of lives to slay Lucnoca the Winter.

Surug held this sort of pride in him.

They, under the commander of Tuturi the Blue Violet Foam, had killed the strongest of all living creatures, more threatening than the one-and-only Alus the Star Runner, the dragon capable of annihilating Aureatia in a single breath.

Of course, Surug himself hadn't actually been present for the hellish battle at the Mali Wastes.

Nevertheless, it didn't change the fact that he belonged to the heroic camp that slayed Lucnoca the Winter. Powerful and prominent figures within Aureatia—Haade the Flashpoint, Iriolde the Atypical Tome—had guaranteed righteousness for them.

Aureatia's Twenty-Nine Officials, currently holding complete governmental control with Rosclay the Absolute and Jelky the Swift Ink the first and foremost among them, were traitors who schemed to use the

Sixways Exhibition's chosen aberrant freak hero to depose the Queen, and those in Surug's camp were the only ones who possessed the oppositional power to rectify this plan.

This Sixways Exhibition farce is unnecessary. We'll be the ones to truly free Aureatia from tyranny and fear.

The series of stories devised by Iriolde the Atypical Tome had manifested the exact results he had wanted.

The madness of this age, left behind by the True Demon King, could occasionally possess directional qualities with its effect.

It was the sudden spate of mass violence. As long as one was within this current flow, they could behave as if this chronic terror had been completely forgotten.

It was the day of the tenth match.

The fungi soldiers that appeared in several places around town signaled thus.

Around one-point-three meters from top to bottom, they didn't possess arms or any sensory organs, and with their stalks, ramified into three leg-like branches, they creeped along the ground at a walking speed. It was in their nature to perceive all animals with body heat as nutritional sources and ingest them into the structure of their mesh-like cap. A relatively simply construct that even a regular Aureatian soldier could take down.

Still, they were more than enough to induce fear. Fungi were an unknown construct never before seen by any of the residents of Aureatia, and the victims unfortunate enough to be absorbed into the fungi's bodies, met with a gruesome drowning demise due to its half-liquid internal tissue.

Above all, they had numbers. The constructs Yukis the Ground Colony had made fit for practical usage could be transported in a dormant state, dried out with only one seventh of their normal volume, and would immediately get to work after receiving some water.

Though a self-proclaimed demon king, who tended to seek out individual capability, the fungi soldiers were a mass-produced construct, developed with practicality as the main objective.

"That's them, huh..."

Arriving *as scheduled* to the points where fungi soldiers were deployed and witnessing them in the flesh for the first time, even Surug couldn't help being taken aback by the massive mycological monsters, filling up the whole boulevard as they creeped along.

An incomprehensible and terrifyingly grotesque construct. Surug had trained over and over to kill other minian races, but could his strength do anything to enemies like this?

They hadn't been informed that it was Iriolde's own National Defense Research Institute that had deployed these fungi soldiers. In fact, the cause of the fungi outbreak had been spun to say it was an Aureatian conspiracy, to further strengthen the troops' hostility toward the Aureatia army.

As his anxiety and soaring morale swirled inside him, Surug caught something that wasn't a fungi moving in the corner of his eye.

"Help! Someone! *Eeek*...!"

"*Ngh*!"

The instant he recognized a girl who had failed to evacuate, he flew out of the carriage.

Moving ahead of any of the other soldiers, he plunged straight into the sea of fungi soldiers.

"*Hrrrraaaaaaaaaaagh*!"

The stance of his opening step and the way he placed his body weight all seemed to line in up perfect harmony.

He severed the head of the fungi soldier chasing the girl and then, without stopping, cut down one more advancing in from the left with the rest of his sideways sweep.

The fungi soldier let out a gurgling noise. He couldn't tell if this was the fungi's cry, or simple a noise ringing out from having its body tissue slashed through.

"Behind me!"

He stood to shield the young girl.

The other soldiers, following Surug, rushed out from the carriage and had begun to battle. The grotesque monsters stopped moving one after another, whether vividly severed with a blade or shot through with a rifle bullet.

There was another specification required of the fungi soldiers Yukis had created.

Weakness.

The windups to their attacks were easily read, and the ability to see through their movements and evade, even for the youngest soldiers freshly finished with their training, was natural. Their bodies, constructed from unidirectional hyphae, were easily cleaved through, and gave a great tactile response when cut. With their nature to sense heat and swarm together, they had no ability to avoid danger, making it easy for soldiers to take down as many as they wanted.

This was because these constructs weren't made to invade Aureatia, but instead made for the soldiers of Iriolde's camp to defeat. The young, private army Iriolde had taught himself weren't scared of pointing their blades at Aureatia's regime. Nevertheless, there was no denying that their lack of actual combat experience was an obstacle against Aureatia's regular army.

Assuming that the elites of the anti-Aureatian forces, starting with

Haade's camp, were the main force preparing for what came afterward, then these soldiers were nothing more than sacrificial pawns to bring chaos to Aureatia—normally speaking, anyway.

The fungi soldiers were there to send these makeshift soldiers running wild and convert them into a fighting force.

"You lot! Which unit do you belong to?! Don't stick your neck where it doesn't belong!"

"Damn Aureatia army! What're you here to do now?!"

"We're just protecting the people of the city from *Aureatia's* attack on its own citizens!"

"What the hell're you—*hngl*?!"

"*Hah*, I got him! Got him right through the throat! With my very first shot!"

"Nice job!"

"That was impressive! Y'know, these guys ain't all that, are they?"

The goal of the fungi soldier's form, inspiring physiological repulsion, was to elevate the confidence the soldiers felt from defeating them.

In addition to this psychological effect, by making them brilliantly slay the fungi soldiers in large numbers, it was possible to collectively instill in them a baseless confidence and exultation.

A single group, moving like raging billows that had forgotten all hesitation and fear, would then become monsters who were capable of upsetting the gap in pure strength and technical prowess.

◆

This grand coup d'état, when broadly divided into political powers, was simply a battle between two factions within the Aureatia Assembly.

Rosclay's camp, the mainstream reformation faction in Aureatia, versus Haade's camp, the second, military faction, which possessed a huge influence over the Aureatia army.

However, the actual composition was more complex.

The mastermind who had been supporting Haade's camp in their opposition to the main faction from the shadows was former Fifth Minister, Iriolde the Atypical Tome. Longing for his political resurgence, Iriolde, with not only Haade's camp but also the National Defense Research Institute—a construct research facility helmed by self-proclaimed demon kings—under his banner, was for all intents and purposes the greatest political enemy of Aureatia's main faction.

The fungi soldiers deployed by the National Defense Research Institute across the land were the pretext for Iriolde to invade Aureatia with his rebel army.

Fungi soldiers filling up the city. Iriolde's private army, arriving on the scene as if the timing had been perfectly planned. As they mowed down the fungi soldiers, they even began to challenge the Aureatia army, arriving late to the scene, to fight.

Amid the chaotic maelstrom of countless intentions entangling together, there were very few who could command a bird's-eye view over the situation they found themselves in.

Conversely, there was one person who always commanded an overarching outlook of any and all information.

"They're being set up," a man whispered quietly from a rooftop.

A leprechaun. Wrapped up in a light brown coat, he had bandages wrapped pell-mell around his face.

I knew it already, but this wasn't a fight I should've had any business with...

Kuuro the Cautious. He too was part of Iriolde's camp.

Kuuro was originally supposed to deployed on this battlefield as a trump card in their attempt to overthrow Aureatia. He had only defected moments prior, right after the series of operations went into effect.

It had been easy. For the owner of eyes that reigned supreme over any and all perceptional organs in the land, an ability known as Clairvoyance, there were no eyes he couldn't deceive.

What he had needed was the right timing. Even if Iriolde's camp realized Kuuro's desertion, they couldn't interfere with Mizial or Cuneigh, whom they had taken hostage. He had needed to move when they weren't able to react immediately. In short, right now, as they put their operation into motion to overthrow Aureatia, activating the whole faction's forces at once.

The deployment of the anti-fungi soldier units looks random at first glance, but it's been done intentionally. It's all purposefully set up so every single squad can surround Iriolde's private soldiers simply by blockading two or three routes.

A spot that showed a road on the map but was blocked off because of repair work. There were places that seemed to be open with good sight lines, but actually only had a few ways that went in and out of the area. Even a unit that looked to be moving freely, when expanding the view to see the whole picture, was being driven back into a dead-end alley along with another two squads.

Not only that, it's being done to stop the fighters on the ground, or their frontline commanders from having any chance to realize they're being driven into a corner... Someone who possesses a strategic eye, who knows the configuration of Aureatia perfectly and is capable of deceiving their own allies... They're the only ones who could set this up.

The deployment of the fungi soldiers and employing Iriolde's private forces were all part of the operation planned by Iriolde's camp themselves. Was there any reason to purposefully move their men *in a way that made it easier to become surrounded*?

"...Gotta be Haade the Flashpoint."

After he let out his intuitive answer, Kuuro thought through why he had murmured the name.

Including the National Defense Research Institute first and foremost, Iriolde had brought several illegal organizations under his control and expanded his network. However, if there was this traitorous mastermind concealing themselves, but with complete command of the network itself...the only one capable was the head of the military faction, Haade the Flashpoint.

With the start of this operation, Haade has centralized the chain of command, including the National Defense Research Institute, and gained complete control. If he had been connected with Rosclay's camp from the start and planning to catch the entirety of Iriolde's camp at once, it would explain several of my Clairvoyance's premonitions.

In order to eradicate Iriolde the Atypical Tome's camp, one that had already been infiltrated but who never made the grand picture clear, Rosclay conspired with Haade and *brought about* this grand coup. Iriolde thought he had a grip on Haade's reins, and was using him in his planning, but in reality, it was the complete opposite.

That would then mean that Rosclay and Haade had been in a cooperative relationship from the start of the Sixways Exhibition, too. In the second round, Rosclay fights Soujirou in the tenth match... So that means Rosclay can force *Haade's hero candidate to lose at will, doesn't it?*

Kuuro the Cautious, with just a quick glance at the trend of battle in the city, was able to penetrate through Rosclay the Absolute's unearthly conspiracy with almost perfect clarity. Not only that, but even before he had abandoned his camp and began to make his move.

Clairvoyance, capable of gathering any and all information under the heavens, beyond the mere five senses, and minutely processing it all, was a supernatural gift of near omnipotence. In much the same way he had figured out his own camps' movements, if the matter was something Kuuro could theoretically predict using the information he perceived for himself, there were times when it would connect things beyond his own conscience and inform him in the form of nondescript premonitions. It could have been considered a type of pseudo precognition.

This observation is really just verifying what my Clairvoyance's already pieced together. In any event, if I can just use this confusion to save Mizial and Cuneigh, then I can settle things with Obsidian Eyes worry-free...

Obsidian Eyes, which Kuuro once used to belong to, had not only left him seriously wounded by using Mestelexil to bomb the clinic, they had also indirectly created the reason for Toroa's death.

The state of affairs had been brought on by Kuuro's own naïveté.

He had retreated too long from all the killing. Even back when he was wrapped up in the battle against the Particle Storm, he went and chose not to kill anyone. Even as he knew that he and those around him were being embroiled in the conspiracies of the Sixways Exhibition and Obsidian Eyes, he had only thought about how to live a peaceful life.

...I should have killed.

Right now, he had prepared himself to do so.

He planned to finish everything that he needed to do before the day was done. What he needed was the perfect opportunity, and the environment.

In order to deceive countless eyes, he needed to take advantage of the chaos between the two camps to act.

Observing the riot stemming from the fungi assault, he would wait until the time was ripe.

"Awfully disturbing, isn't it—Kuuro the Cautious?"

There came a voice.

From the very start, his Clairvoyance had perceived the man approaching from inside the building.

If he went away without talking to me, then I would've killed him before he had the chance, though.

He knew who the voice belonged to as well, without even needing to turn around to check. Aureatia's Twelfth Minister, Enu the Distant Mirror.

A man with ever-open eyes like an owl, wearing a bowler hat.

"The battle down below yes, of course, but the same goes for you as well... What exactly are you trying to do?"

"I could ask you the same thing, Enu the Distant Mirror."

He didn't have any kind of radzio or communication device. Of course, if Enu's objective from the start was making contact with Kuuro, he should have already known that cheap tricks like that were entirely meaningless.

"You should be back at the National Defense Research Institute during this operation... But this is the only good opportunity to make a move without the camp finding out. You're acting with motives that are different from Iriolde's. Isn't that right?"

"Your Clairvoyance is supposed to see through to my true intentions no matter how I answer your questions, yes? In which case, it's better to give you the truth. As you say, I am also planning on leaving this camp."

"What happened to Obsidian Eyes' surveillance? That's what Miluzi the Coffin Edict is for, right?"

"It seems his research is much more interesting than keeping tabs on me. There is little reason at this point for Obsidian Eyes to waste the effort in the first place. That's why I was fortunate enough to escape their surveillance network, and able to contact you like this."

Clairvoyance had come up with the answer without Kuuro spending time to doubt if this was the truth or not.

Nothing in Enu's answer had been a lie. This man was another member of the Twenty-Nine Officials known for his ingenuity. He did indeed possess brilliant abilities that could easily trick Obsidian Eyes' surveillance.

But it's unnatural. The fact that Enu is even still alive, if they don't have any reason to keep him alive anymore. Obsidian Eyes, for some reason, isn't in perfect form. That's what produced this delay in the chain of command. There was either a major, unavoidable change in their strategy, or something is ailing the young lady.

"Kuuro the Cautious. You're almighty, but right now you're just one person. Don't you need an ally? I believe we can form a relationship that benefits us both. I don't wish to let this good fortune go to waste."

"...Looks like you truly feel that way. What do you want?"

"Linaris the Obsidian."

Kuuro narrowed his eyes and turned around toward Enu for the first time.

He was met with round, completely unblinking eyes.

"...I want her living cells. Just her skin or finger will be difficult. I'd need at least a limb, or an organ...and I'd like you to share that with me long before their organization's necrosis. There is no need to kill her."

"It's basically the same as killing her. If you're familiar with the young lady, you should know about her physical constitution, too... Even just cutting off one arm is certain to kill her. That girl's constitution doesn't allow her to put any stress on her heart. It's a real serious request to make as one end of the deal for our collaboration."

"If you don't wish to kill, I don't mind if you take her alive. You are probably the only person who could capture Linaris the Obsidian. Of course, I understand that you have no obligation to accept this, but... that won't be too much of a burden for you, now will it?" Enu pointed his cane straight out and definitively declared, "You're trying to get revenge on Obsidian Eyes. That's why you slipped away from the camp."

"......"

There wasn't any reason for anyone else besides Kuuro to know the truth—that he had been attacked by Obsidian Eyes.

However, it was different for this man alone.

"In the sixth match when Zeljirga fought Mestelexil, I was still her sponsor. Once I knew the true objective of Obsidian Eyes in that match... I was able to deduce who could've carried out the bombing on the clinic that almost killed you, and who stood to benefit. Will all that in mind, I'll ask—what do you think?"

Obsidian Eyes weren't in perfect form.

Kuuro knew that even then, but it didn't mean he had a perfect chance to succeed.

"You need an ally, don't you?"

Enu had given Kuuro enough information to elicit an answer, even without using his Clairvoyance, in an orderly sequence.

There was one hurdle that loomed gigantic over any other when it came to defeating Obsidian Eyes.

"In order to defeat Mestelexil the Box of Desperate Knowledge. Is that it?"

CHAPTER 7 Rear Guard

Iriolde's army's battle had been progressing with them in a dominant position.

The Aureatia army, lured out by the fungi soldiers and arriving on the scene, were being defeated one soldier after another. Their individually superior abilities and experience were not enough to overcome the difference in numbers with Iriolde's Army, who were the first ones on the battlefield and with their morale soaring.

Iriolde's Army truly felt like they could win.

At the very least, it had been that way at the beginning.

Surug the Double Shield hadn't thought about losing at all, either.

Which was why his current situation had to be some mistake, a series of some sort of misfortunes.

"It hurts..."

Blood flowed from Surug's left shoulder.

The wound hadn't come from fighting Aureatian soldiers. In the melee, he had smashed hard into an ally, and either their armor or something else had cut open his skin. A painful gash.

Surug was probably the only one who had been able to flee from that place.

Before anyone knew it, Surug's squad, fighting in the streets, had been surrounded.

Several soldiers were cut down in a one-sided slaughter, unsure when exactly the tide had turned.

They had fallen into a trap.

Surug was sure of this, but the vital questions of who had set them up, and what sort of trap it was, were beyond the comprehension of a young soldier like him.

"A-Aureatia's…in danger."

He believed he had to fight.

However, in reality, all he could do was hide in the shadow of a fruit box and tremble.

There was the sound of something crawling and tearing about.

The fungi were trampling over the street out front. Surug cowered.

The courage that had temporarily sent shivers through his body had dispersed, and like an adverse side effect, the only thing left in his gut was terror.

I don't want to die…

◆

There was a man in the almost entirely deserted streets.

Iriolde's Army had been routed in this district, but as a result, a swarm of fungi were striding about like they owned the place.

"…What an awful sight."

This man, with tanned skin and a bald head, wore round sunglasses.

Aureatia's Twenty-Seventh Minister, Antel the Alignment, when compared to the lineup of monsters who had a home among the Twenty-Nine Officials, might not have left much of an impression.

He certainly wasn't incompetent. He had a calm and level disposition and had no difficulty mingling with the other bureaucrats. During the Sixways Exhibition, not unlike a period of wartime, he had been skillfully carrying out the work asked of him. However, Antel's abilities were never beyond the level of excellence seen among the common man. He possessed neither outstanding strength nor supernatural abilities.

Although he had experience serving as a periphery guard soldier, who were known for their elite skills, the reasoning behind his appointment to the Twenty-Nine Officials were his administrative skills and research into the national tax system. His appointment was relatively recent, as it happened right before the end of the demon king's era.

Normally, his position would mean he shouldn't have been here on the front lines.

"It's an ugly situation, but..."

First, Antel's group took notice of three fungi.

There was a single squad's worth of Aureatian soldiers in the wings behind Antel. They had already cut their way through two battles after arriving in the city, and every single soldier was elite, still without suffering a single loss.

"Before we head to aid the other squads, we should make it so we can use this street first. It runs north to south with the Jeanes Iron Bridge in the middle, and it will speed up the squads' movements."

"Definitely," the squad leader replied.

"Then let's mop up this area quick."

"No, I don't need you guys. If Iriolde's Army stragglers are pursuing us, they should be here soon. Watch my back."

"Understood. All troops, determine where the blind spots from the street are and stand by! Keep an eye on the rear!"

With the squad leader's voice behind him, Antel casually walked alone toward the fungi swarm.

Though these fungi were a new race that the Aureatia army was encountering for the first time, several of their standard tactics became clear while the soldiers fought them.

When taking on these fungi, naturally inclined to attack any heat source semiautomatically, what one needed to avoid the most was being a central target. They didn't possess any sense of pain, nor fear. Even if a superb soldier defeated one among the swarm, they would end up crushed by the rest of the swarm that came around them at the same time. These constructs needed to always be confronted with an equal number of soldiers or more, breaking up their targets.

Right now, Antel was being encircled by twenty-four fungi.

Antel the Alignment was a civil official. Even in this moment, he hadn't taken any fighting stance.

And yet, what was bizarre was that he carried several longswords on a wooden rack, worn on his back.

"Antel io jadwedo." (From Antel to Jawedo steel.)

His full lips spun his Word Art very quietly.

"Laeus 2 telbode. Temoyamvista. Iusemnohain. Xaonyaji." (Axis is second right finger. Pierce sound. Below the clouds. Rotate.)

Behind Antel, the numerous longswords spread out like a fan opening up.

Separately, a sliver flash raced through the air.

Shining objects rained down on several far-off home windows.

"Gwau—"

The muffled screams reached him, but only for a brief second.

These beams of light were longswords as well.

Launched at ultra-high speeds through Force Arts, they turned the people inside the residences into a splatter of blood.

The Iriolde army snipers that had been deployed in this region had all been experienced soldiers equipped with firearms from the Beyond, requisitioned from Kaete's camp. Nevertheless—

"They're using the new recruit's disturbance to lure Aureatia's squads into the open, then at important crossroads they have their elite troops lying in wait. As a kicker, this is all while the Aureatia army's attention is on the fungi swarm on the ground. Not a bad strategy... Although," Antel coldly murmured, his hands never leaving his pockets. "They made a grave miscalculation the moment they determined they could beat me in a sniper battle."

Even before Antel ostentatiously spread out his longswords to protect himself from the fungi, he had secretly used Force Arts on the longswords meant for his true target, and made them accelerate. Determining all the positions of the enemy snipers in the single moment he used himself as bait, he drove the longswords at them with precision, accelerating to top speed in midair and faster than any of them could shoot.

Antel's side had done just as his enemy had—narrowing their focus and luring them out. The moment a lone, defenseless Twenty-Nine Official activated his Word Arts, after stepping out on the front lines, it certainly must have looked like the perfect opportunity.

Antel the Alignment wasn't an exceptionally outstanding individual among the Twenty-Nine Officials.

However, he was in charge of providing Force Arts backup to Aureatia's strongest knight, Rosclay the Absolute. He was a master of long-range Force Arts, on par with all the others providing Word Arts support, one of them a self-proclaimed demon king.

While still within the realm of minia, each member was a monster of talent—*that* was what it meant to be one of the Twenty-Nine Officials.

"Enemy long-range fire support annihilated. All squads, advance."

The numerous fungi closing in on the ground were trying to ingest Antel.

In Antel's vicinity, a silver flash ran in a ring.

Six of the fungi were cleaved all at once in a straight line.

The fanned-out longswords revolved lengthwise and at an angle, mowing down the perimeter in a tempest of steel.

"Antel io jadwedo. Elcartomp. Xotehimelc. Risper." (From Antel to Jawedo steel. Bind sinew. Dark green drill. Strike.)

One of the longswords flew out from its formation like a bullet, skewered a fungi, and then, doubling back along its flight path, it tidily returned to its place in the line of swords.

Force Arts activation that maintained the inertia of his Force Arts, and sent it in a completely different direction.

Antel had called the squad back to him not for his own protection, but to have them look through the areas hidden from the main boulevard—outside of Antel's range—and clean up the remainders.

That said...

He turned his eyes to the alley on his right-hand side. There was one of Iriolde's fallen soldiers, mangled from the previous attack.

The weapon from the Beyond lying next to them would likely be impossible for almost all the residents of this world to identity.

Not a simple sniper rifle... It was likely some kind of artillery with enough destructive power to sweep away a whole squad.

By no means an enemy to take lightly. Even if you know you'll win the fight from the start, you still can't avoid casualties.

The amount of said casualties depended on how well Antel's group operated.

Rosclay the Absolute had done everything in his power to bring about the greatest opportunity possible.

Everyone else needed to give it their all in return.

◆

He thought that it wasn't worth risking his life to fight.

Ownopellal the Bone Watcher was a calm and gentle old man. Normally he pretended to be a genial old graybeard, far removed from combat, educating the children at Iznock Royal High School in scholarship and Word Arts as a first-class lecturer, while in his spare moments enjoying study and a stiff drink.

Both his position and personality suggested he wasn't the type of man to rise up to suppress a rebelling army.

However, by the time his train car arrived in Noen Station, it was occupied by Iriolde's private soldiers. Dragged out by himself from the train car, Ownopellal's life was now in their grip.

"Professor Ownopellal. We want to talk."

The woman sticking the pistol out at him was one of the rebel army's squad leaders.

It appeared that all the citizens who had been in the station were now locked out. They had brought the single station under their control so rapidly, no one must have had any time to resist.

"Hrmmm, for just a talk...this is quite a frightening way to ask. I'm a rather timid man, so I can't help seeing people with weapons in their hands as the bad guy..."

"Don't worry. We, too, hold what's best for Aureatia in our hearts. In fact, we are hoping that you'll be willing to take part in our actions today, Professor."

"...Do you plan to spark the flames of war...here in Aureatia?"

"It's necessary to drive out the evil infecting our nation."

Iriolde the Atypical Tome and Haade the Flashpoint had conspired together to use the slaying of Lucnoca the Winter as pretext to raise the flag of revolt against Aureatia. In all likelihood, things had happened exactly as Rosclay had projected.

Careful to avoid information leaks, Rosclay hadn't laid out any more of the plan to Ownopellal the Bone Watcher. He may have been in charge of Rosclay's Craft Arts backup, but he had already retired from the front lines.

It seems this enemy is strong. Not only does their discipline rival the regular army... those weapons must be the weapons of the Beyond I've heard about. I don't know to what degree the Aureatia army has a hold on the situation, but...retaking this station's going to be difficult.

Their intention was likely, by taking over the station, to pin down the railroad that ran north to south through Aureatia.

"Of course we won't harm you, Professor. Please, come with us."

"Hrm. I agree that it would be meaningless to resist at this point."

While it may have been different were he a mighty fighter with some monstrous skills, right now, Ownopellal was surrounded by several dozen soldiers.

Each one among them held weapons of instant death in their hands, and they were very well trained. The smart option was to act obediently for the time being and wait for the perfect opportunity.

After all, Rosclay hadn't filled Ownopellal in on the plan. It then meant that he believed *that even if he didn't, he could still come out victorious.* Ownopellal's actions didn't figure into his strategy at all.

This fight isn't something worth risking my life for...

Ownopellal believed Rosclay must have always had this sort of thought somewhere in the depths of his heart.

Memories of defeat, stained with bitterness, were carved into him like a wedge.

In the battle against Tiael the Crushing, he had lost all of the Word Arts soldiers under his command.

As he watched Oslow the Indominable, fighting to the bitter end to protect the Kingdom, Ownopellal chose of all things, to *play dead* and think only of preserving his own life.

They never had any hope of victory from the start. Perhaps his hesitation may have been born from confronting the terror of death right before his eyes.

Even then, at that moment, Ownopellal had forsaken the Kingdom.

"In that case, I suppose I will cooperate with you."

"I'm honored that you understand our position."

The leader smiled with relief.

She may have actually spoken the truth when she said she didn't want to harm Ownopellal.

"By the way, do you like to study?"

"...Do you mean, study in a class at school?"

"No, no. There are so many opportunities to learn outside of the classroom as well. For example, I've been riding this train every day to commute to the school, but...the truth is, it's faster to go by carriage."

"Forgive me, Professor, but we don't have time to stand here and chat. We'll be escorting you from the station."

"Ah! Could you wait just a moment?" Ownopellal said in a loud clear voice. "I'm talking to you all over there. I wouldn't step inside that train car...if I were you."

This wasn't said to the female squad leader in front of him. It was for the soldiers trying to get inside the train car.

While all passengers were blocked from boarding or getting off, since they had captured the station and secured Ownopellal, the most important person on the scene, the obvious next step was to check on the remaining passengers.

"Professor Ownopellal. This is our operation. I ask you not to interfere."

"Isn't that rather high-handed? Since I agreed to cooperate, I would've gladly included myself as part of that '*our*.' You should have heeded the warning of a teacher more carefully. *Ownopellal io kouto*." (From Ownopellal to Aureatia soil.)

A concussive boom echoed from inside the train.

The soldiers attempting to step inside stopped moving out of precaution, and their leader reflexively turned to look in that direction. That one brief second was more than enough.

"*Yurowastera. Vapmarisiawanwao. Sarpmorebonda.*" (Reflect in the substitute. Crack in the jewel. Halted water flow.)

"Professor Ownopellal—"

The squad leader turned back and tried to pull the trigger.

"*Ozno.*" (Fire.)

However, from this distance, a *sword was faster.*

"*Urg, hrnk*!"

The blade, sprouting up diagonally from the stone corridor floor, had pierced the squad leader's chest.

Expert Craft Arts, transforming a material's structure and attacking at high speed.

The process Ownopellal used to generate the longsword was all too smooth and quiet. The other soldiers, attentions drawn to the explosion, were slightly delayed in recognizing what happened.

"*Ownopellal io vollest. Lealten bogberbug.*" (From Ownopellal to vollest box. Turn over and open the stomach.)

"Commander!"

"Damn you, Ownopellal the Bone Watcher!"

They couldn't fire. At that moment, these soldiers could only verify that something strange had happened to their commander, that Ownopellal was chanting Word Arts, *and nothing more.*

They couldn't see over their commander's back to see the sword Ownopellal created. He had made the blade short enough to stop it from running the woman through. While Ownopellal's Word Arts were strange and suspect as well, no one could understand what their implications were.

They weren't positive that the commander had been attacked. She may still have been alive. If they fired right away, there was a chance they would hit the commander. For the rebel army, Ownopellal was an important figure they were supposed to capture, and if they mistakenly killed him, the soldier who fired the shot would have to bear responsibility.

"Nistarki. Sain min hel. Yestoloy. Qai samto..." (Light the point. Opening ocean. Angry river. When coming to the end...)

"Ownopellal, stop your Word Ar—"

Everything about the time it took to judge the situation proved fatal.

Ownopellal the Bone Watcher was a first-class instructor for the Craft Arts specialty at Iznock Royal High School.

"Histgrazia." (Howl.)

There came a roaring sound from the train's engine compartment, like metal being torn apart.

Behind the soldiers focusing on Ownopellal, the engine car *came flying at them.*

The large wurm-like mass pulverized the station platform and crushed seven of the soldiers first.

At this point, it was no longer an engine car. With its linkage to the other cars torn away and running out of control, it was now a grotesque monster, sprouting several metal legs like a centipede and driven by the flames in its internal combustion engine.

"Y-you!"

A soldier on the opposite side moved his firearm's sights off of Ownopellal and toward the massive, monstrous threat.

In Ownopellal's opinion, this too was a misstep. If they had shot through the commander to kill Ownopellal, they wouldn't have died—but their instincts made them do otherwise. Ownopellal was perfectly versed in how those driven by fear would act. Including himself.

"Ownopellal io vollest. Nex hort. Thirn." (Ownopellal to vollest box. Trickling, bubbling sand. Close.)

Even as the monstrosity struck the platform and continued to change shape, it swiftly bypassed Ownopellal on its path to mow down the remaining soldiers. Several gunshots, screams, and the wet sound of flesh being run over and crushed continued at Ownopellal's back.

The weapons of Iriolde's forces were indeed deadly against other people. However, it was impossible to shoot down a mass of iron closing in at high speeds, even with the assault rifles from the Beyond.

"Stop."

The instant Ownopellal murmured this, the monster halted without running into any of the passenger cars. With his last set of Word Arts, he had altered its structure to exhaust its remaining power on the spot.

He hadn't used the engine car to make himself a golem.

Just by using the already available internal combustion engine for power and remaking its structure with Craft Arts, he pulled off such a feat.

"Ever since the train began to run through Aureatia, I stopped commuting to work in a carriage."

He turned to the squad leader, who was growing hazy from having her lung punctured.

"By experiencing it for myself, I was able to get a deeper understanding of its construction, for one...and by touching it directly, I can also use Craft Arts on the trains, like I did here."

In the silence following the destructive chaos, the passengers began to fearfully exit the train.

Among the surging crowd, he spied students on their way to Iznock Royal High School.

Many among them were the children of nobility, useful as hostages for Iriolde's Army.

"Owno...pellal!"

"Over here!"

Ignoring the commander, Ownopellal loudly called out to the students.

"There's someone among you that used Craft Arts to make something explode, isn't there? That's the sound you get when you fail to shape-change properly. There's a low-frequency sound that comes beforehand, of the material creaking."

"Th-that was me." A meek, petite student stepped forward. This girl was the one who caused the explosive noise. "...I failed."

"You're brave. Good job."

She had attempted to fight the soldiers surrounding the train car with her sole, inexperienced weapon, all to protect her school friends.

The squad leader groaned as she collapsed against Ownopellal's body.

"Why...resist...?"

"You don't get it, do you?"

It wasn't worth risking his life to fight.

It was far too late for Ownopellal himself to have any pride worth holding on to.

While he had the intention to defend Aureatia, Rosclay would undoubtedly lead the way to victory. Even if Ownopellal didn't lift a finger.

Nevertheless, he did wish to negate the humiliation of the day he lost to the dragon.

Rosclay had managed to fight. He had continued to battle ever since.

Ownopellal wanted to prove it *hadn't actually* been that way. He wanted to rebel against the heart within that tried to flee.

That was the true nature of Ownopellal the Bone Watcher, hidden behind his gentle and mild, conflict-averse behavior.

Rosclay the Absolute possessed the power to encourage not only those who knew his strength, but those who knew his weakness as well, and make them his ally.

"Why wasn't I able to obey you, is that it? That's one thing that I'm afraid I can't answer… So shall tell you a different reason instead."

Ownopellal the Bone Watcher smiled as though he was a genial, mild-mannered old man.

"I won't let anyone get away with threatening my students."

◆

Tumult was a constant presence in the shopping district. This area in particular wasn't one of the nicer and safer ones in Aureatia, either. A bar couldn't make a living if it concerned itself with every disturbance.

This much uproar was basically a daily occurrence, and not worth acting on out of fear or a sense of impending danger—that was what Tika, working the morning shift at the Blue Beetle, was, at that moment, trying to tell himself.

Since this time of day brought in fewer customers, Tika was working alone. Given he knew that by noon there were bound to be more customers coming in, he couldn't entrust the place to someone else and flee.

Every now and then he thought he heard a gunshot mixed in with the screams.

"Tika. What do you think that sound was?" Nane quietly whispered, leaning forward from her seat at the counter.

"Knock it off, that's bad manners."

"What's the big deal? You and I are the only ones here anyway."

"Then there's no reason to get up close to my face, is there?"

"They might hear me outside if I'm too loud."

Four years younger than him, Nane was too young to drink, but he would come to the Blue Beetle just to have fun with her childhood friend, Tika, even though Tika was always warning her to stop coming since it wasn't the sort of refined establishment a young girl her age should be frequenting.

"Wonder what it is... Had to happen on the day of Rosclay's match, too."

"They're causing all sorts of mayhem because they know Rosclay's not going to come fight them. Don't you think so? Ever since Rosclay was set up in the fourth match and got really hurt...almshouses have gotten attacked, Alus the Star Runner came..."

"...It was nice and peaceful before all that, eh?"

Ever since the end of the age of the demon king, Aureatia *had never once gone to war.*

While he heard stories about tense relationships with the New Principality of Lithia and the Free City of Okafu, Lithia was said to have been destroyed in a huge blaze after its wyvern soldiers went out of control, and Aureatia ultimately made peace with Okafu, on good enough terms now to allow Okafu mercenaries come and go from the city.

To the citizens, the incidents occasionally caused by the Old Kingdoms' loyalists were a threat. However they, too, had been greatly weakened following a small-scale *battle* at Toghie City, and it didn't seem like the Aureatia army would lose to them.

However, all of that was before Rosclay the Absolute was injured.

Things had been fine for a short while after the start of the Sixways Exhibition. Even though Aureatia had cited potential danger as the reason to cancel any viewings for Lucnoca's match, *there had been spectators* during her first match.

It was said that during self-proclaimed demon king Alus's assault, which claimed so many lives, several hero candidates had fought valiantly to stop the damages, but Rosclay hadn't directly engaged Alus, either. Tika had heard that he devoted himself to leading the civilian evacuation, in spite of his serious injuries. A somewhat uncertain and precarious air hung around Aureatia as of late.

Wasn't it now necessary to show Rosclay's presence once more by having him in another match…?

"That's not right."

A young girl's voice came from farther back inside the restaurant.

The speaker was a young girl of sixteen. She had chestnut hair and was modestly dressed in a black a sweater?

She was a mysterious young girl with a fragile and otherworldly appearance about her.

"Rosclay isn't that strong."

"Iska… Miss—Miss Iska! Wait, if you're able to get up, you gotta tell me so…"

"Hold on, who's this chick?!" Nane slammed the counter and stood up.

"It's not me, it's—it's this restaurant, they're looking after her…! She's the daughter of Nikae, who died in the fire, so the boss, um…"

"You're talking way too fast! Liar!"

"Ummm... If I'm interrupting, I can go back inside, but...my water pitcher was empty."

Iska was an orphan who lost both her mother and her home in the assault by Alus the Star Runner.

Her mother was a factory worker in the second borough of the Eastern Outer Ward, but apparently she and the owner of the Blue Beetle had been trusted friends ever since their early days living in the gutter. The Blue Beetle had run an inn on the second floor up until recently, so the owner had decided to leave one of the rooms open to take in Iska now that she had been orphaned.

That said, there was no way that the owner, being who they were, would've done something as commendable as taking in an old friend's kid, so Tika thought that they had actually been after the disaster relief aid from Aureatia.

"Um... Miss Iska, are you one of the types who hates Rosclay?"

"Hm? I like him."

"What? My apologies. That comment just now made me think otherwise, is the thing..."

Tika wasn't great at dealing with Iska. He was supposed to be the older of the two, yet he couldn't help being extra polite with her.

Iska was a daughter of misfortune, sickly and now left orphaned, and yet she was neither subservient nor pessimistic at all.

"Who's this, then?!"

"I just told you, she's Miss Iska... Technically, she's one of our customers, so don't go being rude to her, okay? Sorry about her, Miss Iska. It's just that Nane doesn't really like it when Rosclay's bad-mouthed, either."

"Oh? Rosclay's not what's got her so upset, though." Iska giggled.

Tika could tell that Nane got slightly bent out of shape again.

"Th-that's not... That's not true! I'm mad 'cause you said bad stuff about Rosclay! We get to live safely thanks to him, right?! I'm really sorry that you lost your mom in the fire, but it's not good to resent his kindness and make it out like it's his fault!"

"Don't you think those two things are the same, though?"

Iska approached without any hesitation and sat down at the counter next to Nane.

Her hair gently fluttered, with the refreshing smell of disinfectant.

"Thinking something is *thanks* to someone else, and that something is someone's *fault*. If you think everything that ever happens is all thanks to the work of a single champion, then what if... What happens when something doesn't go perfectly well? You'll end up blaming them and saying it's their fault that they didn't save you, right?"

"Well *I'd* never do that..."

"Rosclay is always saying so. Have you heard it before, Nane?" Iska spoke gently, as if reasoning with a child. "'It is *thanks* to the support of Aureatia's citizens that I'm am able to act as a champion.' If he seems really strong and really dependable, that's all our *fault*—in reality, even without him here, our power is just as strong as Rosclay the Absolute."

Tika would often see her kind here in Aureatia.

Know-it-alls that wanted to talk like they understand Rosclay the most, what the "real" Rosclay thought, and how ignorant all the people of Aureatia were to the truth.

What was Rosclay the individual bearing such responsibility for, and what was he thinking as he conducted himself? Once someone began to consciously think about it all, they would eventually imagine whatever information they wanted in their head, regardless of the fact they knew

nothing about the man's life, and fall completely for the false image that their hopes created.

Was Iska another one of those fanatics, too?

However, her words, which seemed to disparage Rosclay's absoluteness at first blush, also seemed to hide an even stronger trust in him. Maybe that was possible—Tika merely felt that her words did.

"All right, all right, no need to get so worked up, okay?" Tika mediated the situation with an awkward smile.

"But—*eep!*"

What sounded like a gunshot rang out from afar, and Nane shrunk her body like a cat.

Tika didn't know what exactly was going on, but it was probably going to work out.

Rosclay the Absolute was a mighty knight, and always safeguarding Aureatia. They couldn't depend on him too much, and nothing good was going to come from letting their imagination run wild. Vaguely *believing in him*, like Tika, was the healthy way to look at it.

"Are the two of you going to watch today's match?"

"Hmmm, the arena's nearby, and I'd like to if possible, but… I'm stuck looking after the place, so probably not. How about you, Iska?"

"Oh, please. I can't afford to buy tickets." Iska giggled and lightly stood up from the counter. "…But I'm sure it'll be fine."

◆

Aureatia's Eastern Outer Ward, second borough.

Aureatia's Twenty-First General, Tuturi the Blue Violet Foam, forcefully ground her teeth.

"We were set up…!"

Through the binoculars, she saw black smoke billowing upward. A tiny shack along the canal had exploded. A lot of the soldiers who breached the hut were fatally wounded, but that was all that happened.

Rosclay the Absolute was supposedly deceiving both camps into coming and going from the area around this hut.

Something that could potentially be Rosclay's trump card, or weakness, was supposed to be here—this information itself had been a trap. Either that, or Rosclay had used the information they had gotten on him as a way to set them up.

"But…*koff, gahak*… Who benefits from this…?! Even if this lead was purposefully leaked to us, there's no way they could've anticipated… No way they'd think we'd mobilize, even bringing Romzo the Star Map, just to crush this unknown variable."

A dry cough slipped out from her throat. Her lung function was deteriorating, a lasting side effect from the battle with Lucnoca the Winter.

Rosclay was meeting with *someone* in the second borough of the Eastern Outer Ward. Tuturi and Romzo, along with a small part of their main force, were dispatched for preliminary reconnaissance in order to verify uncertain factors, true identities, and potential unknown dangers, then bring them to light and dispose of them before their operation began.

This meant that the dyed-in-the-wool warmonger Haade the Flashpoint had misread the situation.

If Rosclay the Absolute was able to predict and manipulate the future so effectively, then it would have signaled a supernatural ability that defied all logic, like those of a visitor. Given that Rosclay was just a regular minia, there was bound to be a logical explanation somewhere.

“This investigation, I believe—” Romzo murmured, standing next to her. In contrast to Tuturi’s own demeanor, he seemed perfectly cool and composed. “—was put together by General Haade himself, wasn’t it? As for what is supposed to be here, I haven’t heard any detailed evidence myself, but maybe you did, Tuturi.”

“Huh? Of course, I’ve heard…”

Her words cut off as she began to reply.

She hadn’t heard anything.

Haade was a brilliant commander. Ordinarily, he would have answered her if she asked for the basis behind the operation. Tuturi’s group had gone into action because it was right before Tuturi’s large-scale operation went into place, and because it was urgent. The preparations had already been arranged to mobilize Romzo out with a mixed squad of Haade’s subordinates, and this situation needed them to head into action right away. In fact, Tuturi had been given secret orders to dispose of Romzo the Star Map at some point during the chaos of the fighting. She was even thinking that this was the exact opportunity she had been waiting for.

Her trusting nature had been her undoing. Haade the Flashpoint would never have a lapse in judgment on the battlefield.

“No. It can’t be…*koff, gahak*, that’s not possible.”

“Tuturi.”

Romzo turned around and flashed a smile from deep behind his round glasses.

It was a dark smile.

“Romzo, you—”

Romzo’s flattened hand chop grazed Tuturi’s gut at the same moment she opened her mouth.

She staggered from the intense pain of her skin being cut open. She thought she had died.

Acute pain. It took another moment for her to then realize the sensation didn't come with her demise. If this man intended to kill Tuturi, then he could end her life without ever showing the movements of his attack.

"Hmph."

Tuturi tried to get a grasp on what was happening.

There was a miniature radzio in one of Romzo's hands. He had stolen it from her, cutting through the belt at her waist.

Romzo tossed it into the canal without looking particularly interested in the device.

"Hey! What're you trying to—"

An explosive blast echoed in the canal, as if to drown out Tuturi's voice, and a water pillar shot up into the air.

While it was nowhere close in scale to the explosion at the shack moments prior, the weapon had more than enough power to incapacitate and seriously wound a minia.

"So, it was an explosive. Hmph. Most likely one of the bombs on a timer from the Beyond... Our equipment was set to explode almost right as we breached the shack."

"Haade..."

The difficult-to-accept reality was thrust out in front of her.

Violence would be trampled over by even more powerful violence.

Minians needed ingenuity to fight against this cruel law of nature.

In that case, was that ingenuity then to be trampled by *even sharper ingenuity*?

"Romzo... Sir. Then, your radzio..."

"That's right. I never had it turned on to begin with."

"......"

Although he may have been an adept master of the First Party, he could have possibly been sure of this trap from the start. If it was a weapon from this world, he may have been able to detect it with his wealth of experience. However, there was no way he was thoroughly familiar with timed explosives from the Beyond.

"It truly is so very easy…Tuturi. No matter how much you may trust one another, no matter how much you may like someone, once you set your mind to it, it is far easier than one would think."

Even if there weren't any grounds to do so, he couldn't help but distrust and suspect others.

If there was ever a moment when this man, reduced to a beast, unable to believe in justice or conviction, felt joy, it was only when he learned that the heart of another, impossible to fathom from the outside, was that of a beast like himself.

In other words—betraying, and being betrayed.

"Ahh… *Hah-hah-hah*. I'm so glad the demon king didn't kill me."

Romzo the Star Map smiled with glee.

CHAPTER 8 Stone Stairway in front of the Joint Military Hospital

There were also those who didn't get wrapped up in the ravages of war breaking out all over Aureatia.

Romog Joint Military Hospital was not included as one of the Iriolde camp's targets, nor was it worked into Rosclay camp's operation, either. It wasn't for humane reasons. There was simply no benefit for either camp in getting the people admitted there involved in the struggle.

Within these walls was Soujirou the Willow-Sword.

"How many more times must I explain myself?" the nurse complained while jogging hot on Soujirou's heels as he walked down the hallway.

"The match today has been canceled! We've received an official notice from Third Minister Jelky!"

"What if it does happen, huh? You gonna take responsibility if I ain't there?!"

Soujirou had lost his left leg from the thigh down. He didn't have a lower leg prosthetic, but a transfemoral prothesis instead. By the standards of this world's technology, it was the same as supporting his entire right side with just a simple cane.

Nevertheless, the fact he could walk too fast for the average person to keep up could have been nothing less than the manifestation of his innate, supernatural physical ability and the natural sense to wield implements that extended from his own body.

"Gettin' real insufferable in here. I'm leaving. "

The recovery of the amputation wound and his walking rehab both should have long been over. The doctor asserted he needed to remain admitted for postoperative observation, but maybe the truth was that all these therapeutic processes were done to casually keep Soujirou away from the Sixways Exhibition and whittle away at his desire to fight.

Soujirou had suspected this for some time, but the fact they wouldn't allow him to be discharged on the very day of the tenth match had convinced him of it.

"I ain't gonna let anyone...make me lose by default."

It didn't sit right with him.

If Soujirou was such a nuisance, they should have just mixed poison into his food or medicine. They could've made the doctors in charge attack him with Life Arts. They could've surrounded him in his hospital room with a huge mass of soldiers and come at him all at once to kill him.

If his enemy had just done that, he would've been able freely fight back without any restraint.

Without ever sensing malice or hostility, he hadn't been able to bulldoze his way forward until the day of the match. A faceless somebody that he couldn't see from his position had chosen to use *that type* of attack against him.

Shaking off both doctors and nurses, he arrived at a window facing the street outside.

While it was a fixed window, when Soujirou's sword traced around it, lightly petting it almost, the inside fell down, window and all.

There wasn't any substance that Soujirou, having cleaved the Dungeon Golem with just a training sword, couldn't slice through with the indestructible sword he wielded, Alcuzari the enchanted hollow sword.

"That's dangerous! Stop it!"

"Oh yeah… 'fore I go, I should thank you. So, thanks."

Soujirou wondered where he was going to sleep later that night.

He had entrusted Yuno with almost all his daily necessities since coming to Aureatia, so he was being put in a bit of an inconvenient spot. It was better than camping out in the wilds, for the most part.

"Eh, I'm sure it'll work out!"

He jumped down a full three stories.

The instant he was going to smash his head against the stone pavement, he used the palm of his hand to land. Passing the impact through his whole body like a single bow, with a spin, he landed on his back and twisted sideways.

It was a strange technique, as if reversing the parachute landing fall.

"…Guess this is all I can hope for with only one leg."

He knew which direction to head in—toward the city. He could feel the presence of combat. This was a sensation he had felt numerous times in the Beyond, of numerous people, and numerous weapons clashing with each other.

In the past, Soujirou hadn't ever felt the allure of such a sensation.

The fighting had always broken out between some other comrades besides Soujirou, and there had never been any possibility that someone with the volition and strength to kill Soujirou would show up.

This world, however, was different.

There were threats that surpassed the realm of mankind, and power technique and weapons had been cultivated to fight against them.

"Yo."

Soujirou's feet stopped. He recognized the figure of the man blocking his path forward.

A sensation of violence, far richer and denser than the battle in the city.

He had a massive body, as if he had honed it day in and day out without any break.

The man brandished a long-shafted iron hammer used for firefighting.

"*Fwah-hah-hah-hah-hah-hah*! You should get back to the hospital ward right away, Soujirou the Willow-Sword! It's very *dangerous* for a patient to be walking around out here!"

With his face covered in a smooth steel mask, Soujirou had no way to tell what sort of expression this man wore.

"*Heh*... I should be the one tellin' you that. Stand around in a place like that, see."

This world tried to fight with the visitors whose own world rejected their existences.

They cultivated power, technique, and weapons to fight. That alone still wasn't enough for Soujirou.

"You never know! You may end up hacked to shreds 'n' all!"

"That'd make my day!"

Soujirou could fight because the people of this world still had the will to stand against him, even when they were fully cognizant of the threat.

The man was named Sabfom the White Weave, Aureatia's Twelfth General.

◆

Sabfom's iron hammer smashed the street's stone steps.

Soujirou had been standing right in that spot, however he sprightly fluttered through the air like a tree leaf and landed three steps higher on the stone stairs.

"*Fwah-hah-hah-hah*! Impressive! Makes me wonder if you're really missing that leg of yours!"

"*Pfft*. Lemme ask you, then: Are you really trying here or what?"

Soujirou the Willow-Sword wore a savage smile.

Sabfom the White Weave was taken with Soujirou.

That day when Sabfom had went into action, this man had also escaped from the hospital to go kill Alus the Star Runner.

Even after losing one of his legs, Soujirou's heart was unbroken. He wasn't a weakling who was driven only by the physical strength he had been gifted with from birth.

With his mighty ego, he continued to spur himself into intense battle.

"If you're not planning on taking me on, it's no skin off my back."

Furthermore, keeping Soujirou the Willow-Sword from going anywhere on the day of the tenth match was a role that Sabfom the White Weave had assigned himself to.

While he had no particular interest in Rosclay's political struggle, similar to many of the other Twenty-Nine Officials, he did owe him a debt.

Above all, the fight with Soujirou itself was more than enough of a reward for Sabfom. He wanted to battle this visitor even more aberrant than Morio the Sentinel and see who had the stronger force of will.

"Though, 'course, that's only if…you can shake me off and run away with just one leg."

"Not another one like this, dammit…"

Right now, Sabfom was putting space between himself and the stone steps where Soujirou stood.

The range of Soujirou's sword created a fatal zone. Against Soujirou, regardless of his limited mobility, Sabfom would take extra care to fight outside that range.

"Only ever coming at me with cheap tricks. You're pulling this crap, too?"

"If you underestimated me in thinking that I wouldn't use any tricks in a one-on-one duel, then you must've lost your eyes with that leg, Soujirou the Willow-Sword. If you're not going to come down here..."

Sabfom swung his hammer. He pulverized the rock wall.

While it would be a different matter if the vicinity was merely residential homes, the area around Romog Joint Military Hospital was land owned by Aureatia. Given that he was just destroying it all as part of Aureatia's operation, it didn't prick Sabfom's conscience whatsoever.

He smashed up the street even more. Cobblestones turned up into the air from the shock, flying higher than Sabfom was tall.

"...I'll just do this instead and *destroy* the path in front of you, to make sure you can't stand anywhere on it with that leg of yours."

Could a swordsman on a prosthetic leg put up a fight on thoroughly destroyed terrain without any proper footing?

Normally, Sabfom would have been able to answer that it wasn't possible. However, when his enemy was a visitor who had been driven out from his world due to his supernatural sword prowess, these conditions weren't likely to close the gap in their strength.

Sabfom knew that perfectly well himself. While he had also crossed swords with the visitor Morio the Sentinel in the past, even if Sabfom was able to exert the same near-death strength he had back then, the distance between himself and Soujirou was farther than the edge of the horizon.

"Just that'd be boring, wouldn't it, Soujirou?"

Sabfom the White Weave was fond of Soujirou the Willow-Sword.

That was precisely why he could sympathize with this man who could have continued winning throughout the tournament without a chance to taste a true fight to the death. He could sympathize with the strong ego and greed that made him cling to the Sixways Exhibition, his only opportunity to immerse himself in true combat, even if it was already impossible for him to participate.

Fight with your handicap, Soujirou the Willow-Sword. Under the worst possible conditions, unlike anything you've experienced in life before. Cheap tricks that manage to make someone like you fear death... are all that can truly grant your wish.

Soujirou the Willow-Sword claimed to have never tasted terror or death before.

This was why, even after defeating Ozonezma, he felt no relief, and continued to hear out the other patients' stories, to kill the enemy inside he had become aware of for the first time in the third match.

Someone who could stand up to fight, even after learning to fear. Sabfom wished to be the same way himself.

The extreme excitement that existed in near-death moments, and the pleasure of immersing oneself in truly feeling alive. He wanted to keep his truest heart, one that many others had lost in the era of the True Demon King.

"I mean, no skin off my back, but..."

Soujirou rested his sword on his shoulder atop the stone steps.

He was too far out of reach.

Sabfom the White Weave had rules of thumb as a seasoned fighter.

It was a result he could predict physically—using his body weight, speed, and parabolic path.

Soujirou was going to land right in front of Sabfom. Thus, his hammer would crush Soujirou's skull.

"You're gonna end up dead!"

"*Make my day*! Same as my first answer!"

"Heh."

The edges of Soujirou's mouth warped into a hearty smile.

His tracksuit fluttered. He jumped from the stone step. Sabfom had taken up his stance to counterattack before he sensed Soujirou's presence on his skin.

There was a loud rupturing *wham.*

Leaping with absurd speed, Soujirou had significantly lost his balance right beforehand. He was being thrown out into midair though the strength of his own legs.

"......!"

The prosthetic on Soujirou's right leg was crushed from the inside.

The prosthetic had been made by Romog Joint Military Hospital.

"Can't *sense death* through a fake leg, can you?""

It was an extremely simple artifice.

There would be a small explosion in response to a powerful impact, such as a leap made mid-combat.

It wasn't enough to be fatal, and it wouldn't activate through his daily life.

With the caution Soujirou paid to the meals and drugs he was given, the prosthetic leg he always wore on his body was then shifted beyond his consciousness. Such *diminutive* traps were the only method of attack that could slip past Soujirou's supernatural ability—a web of gut intuition, capable of sensing even long-range sniper fire, whose underlying principles remained a mystery.

"And this is would be the real—"

Impending sense of death.

Sabfom swung his hammer down toward Soujirou's skull as he free-fell, unable to move his body.

"Yup."

Sabfom felt like he had hit a metal spring of some kind.

Repelled by the mass of the great hammer, Soujirou was blown away onto the road, and shattered some of the debris and rubble.

The sensation that Sabfom felt in his hands wasn't that of bones being pulverized.

"......"

The blow that should have finished Soujirou off had been deflected. What had happened?

"Right before your head was crushed...you struck my hammer with your pommel, is that it?!"

In midair, where he should have been unable to make any moves, Souijrou had forcibly controlled his own trajectory.

Using the recoil of his strike against the hammer, Soujirou was blown away to open up space between himself and Sabfom.

Sabfom needed to compel his feet to stop heading toward Soujirou to press the attack. If he rushed in to pound Soujirou, stuck in the rubble, Sabfom was certain to be run through by the sword attack that followed.

If he got inside Soujirou's sword range, he would lose.

Right before he came at me with his slash, from atop the stone steps...

By thinking over their exchange just now, Sabfom reined in his combat instincts.

Soujirou was shouldering his sword.

If he assumed that wasn't a stance for slashing his sword, but instead to protect his head with its pommel...

I see now—that was my blunder. Even without knowing that I was aiming to destroy his prosthetic leg, he could tell that I was directing my killing instincts at his head. *Whether it was by some hidden projectile, or sniper ambush, he predicted that his head would be targeted in some fashion and readied himself to defend. Merely the act of confronting Soujirou the Willow-Sword indirectly gives him information.*

Soujirou wearily rose from amid the rubble.

They were squaring off against each other with the same amount of distance between them as before. However, now, they were both at the same elevation. Soujirou had lost his prosthetic leg, and was rendered physically unable to walk.

No matter how strong a visitor he may have been, he wouldn't be able to utilize his mobility that surpassed Sabfom. Furthermore, the area around Soujirou was the terrain Sabfom pulverized moments prior.

"Can't leap at me with that leg, can you?!"

"...Why would you say that? I'll never know until I give it a try!"

"Say what you will, but you aren't going to close this much distance."

Not yet. This still wasn't enough.

"*Fwah-hah-hah-hah*! As I just said, we can do this until nightfall, I don't mind. Though you'll probably get taken back to the hospital before then..."

"......"

"What will you do? Remain here, even if you it means killing the doctors that come for you?"

Sabfom's duty was to buy time to ensure Soujirou didn't leave Aureatia.

However, that of course didn't mean that he was fighting because he wished to settle things by running out the clock.

Soujirou had to be of the same mind himself.

To break through this deadlock, Soujirou, in the disadvantaged position, would eventually have to make a do-or-die attack. When he did, Sabfom could give Soujirou a taste of death's abyss for the first time.

All right then, do it. Any plan I could spend half a day scheming, I know you'd see through in a second. Now that you've lost your leg, what are you going to do about this distance? Try to use a steel beam from the rubble as a makeshift prosthetic? Or perhaps throw your sword, your only weapon, at me? Your only—

His thoughts had gotten then far when Sabfom's body instinctively moved.

Crossing his great hammer and gauntlet, then raising them above his head, he took a defensive stance.

The scalpel, descending at high speeds, was deflected with high-pitched sound.

The third match—

It happened at the same time.

A flash of light raced through the air and pierced through Sabfom's chest.

"*Hrngh, gaugh...*"

It was another thrown scalpel.

This man...stole Ozonezma's scalpels during the third match and used them to make a delayed attack!

"What, is that it, old man?"

Though he could hear Soujirou's voice, Sabfom merely flopped to the ground.

"Here I figured you'd have an answer to one more move at least. It's a trick I've used already, y'know. Ain't about my leg or my footing, I had you dead from the very start."

Soujirou's sword wasn't his only weapon.

When he had escaped, he could have stolen some number of scalpels from the hospital.

After Soujirou was sent flying in midair, he had been able to estimate where Sabfom would stand, where he would lie in wait, and everything up to Sabfom blocking the delayed blade falling from the sky, had been a part of the supernatural visitor's prediction of their fight.

But when did he throw those blades upwards?! I never took my eyes off him for a second! He showed a single sign of...

Sabfom's blood pressure was rapidly falling. His sight had begun to darken.

He had to fight. Even if he couldn't move a finger, even if it was only in his head, he had to fight.

...The explosion.

In the moment his prosthetic leg caused the small explosion, had Sabfom been looking at Soujirou directly?

Even assuming he managed to do so, in the moment directly preceding and following the explosion that threw Soujirou through the air, had Sabfom been able to perceive what the man's empty hand, dropped to his side, had done, while keeping his guard up against the sword slung on Soujirou's back?

In that second, Sabfom had concentrated his killer instincts on Soujirou's head to ensure he smashed his target.

Soujirou had been conscious of Sabfom's intentions.

"I get it... *Fwah-hah-hah-hah-hah...*"

So that was what it was after all.

Sabfom's targeting of Soujirou's head had been sensed by Soujirou. He was so absorbed in it that he didn't focus on anything else.

The all-too-strong fighting spirit Sabfom had possessed since birth had invited his own defeat.

But that was fine. It was the exact end of the fight he had wished for.

Just as it had been when he previously fought Morio the Sentinel, the fool. Haade's valor had allowed him to step beyond fear...

"This is...my truest...nature..."

His vanishing guffaw amounted to little more than a small groan.

◆

"*Tch*, making me waste...my damn time."

Using a bandage of torn-off cloth, he tied two iron bars together to his right thigh.

They were pieces of the hilt of Sabfom's great hammer, which he had cut off. Regardless of how sturdy they may have been, as a prosthetic leg, they were simply there to easily support his body.

Given that he doubted they were even affixed to his thigh, he obviously couldn't jump, as even walking took all his effort.

Even then, he was able to walk off.

"I'm here to fight."

Dragging his leg along the ground, Soujirou began to walk away.

"Like hell I'm letting this end...without a fight..."

On this day, the tenth match *was supposed to happen.*

If he made for where the arena was, Soujirou was sure he'd be able to fight.

Even as he was obstructed and suppressed by the very Aureatia that surrounded him, Soujirou the Willow-Sword could only gamble on a sliver of hope.

On this day, the castle garden theater was closed with the announcement of the cancellation of the tenth match.

The match wasn't scheduled.

CHAPTER 9

Central Assembly Hall First Communications Room (United Command Center)

Jelky the Swift Ink was esteemed as a brilliant civil servant.

With a precise, machine-like grasp of the economic activities carried out through Aureatia's vast borders, he was able to have a complete vision of his command to ensure continued economic growth at regulated speeds, all while ensuring no one noticed it was being closely managed.

This wasn't all thanks to his natural-born talents. These results were in part thanks to his own efforts, constantly learning from the many who came before him.

Jelky wasn't only blessed with his own talents, but also excelled at understanding the skills of others. Studying under bureaucrats he picked out as talented, regardless of their position or age, he had inherited their capability and personal connections.

This was not for his own promotion and social success. It was because he had always held regrets. The age of the demon king had produced countless monstrously powerful fighters, but conversely had killed too many noncombatants who possessed the strengths needed in peacetime. Those individuals, Jelky understanding their true worth, were pulled into the flames of war and revolt caused by True Demon King's terror and died like ragtag common soldiers.

He couldn't let the world regress back into a time of war and strife. He needed to protect Aureatia and the royal family that his predecessors had risked their lives to preserve. He thought that he had this duty, having survived and inherited their strength.

Jelky the Swift Ink believed that he was brilliant.

Therefore, this battle on the day of the tenth match needed to be possible too.

Iriolde's camp had revolted. Fights were breaking out in all corners of Aureatia.

Every single bit of information surged toward him in a deluge.

In response to it all, Jelky gave the same answer.

"We'll deal with it immediately."

Faced with the unrealistically large workload, Jelky established a mechanical priority order.

For problems that required immediate decisiveness, Jelky would take responsibility for making a decision, even if it went beyond his authority.

For problems that could be solved by others, he passed them on to other bureaucrats at the trade ministry, or immediately assigned them to other ministries.

Requests for his appearance from the various trade associations and other ministries would all be handled at a later date, and if necessary, he would send a representative in his stead.

Focusing as much as possible only on the problems that specifically required his abilities to solve, he continued processing the enormous, still overflowing, workload.

I still can't let this amount of work defeat me.

Exhaustion. Confusion. Resentment. Drowsiness. Intense pressure. Fear.

He needed to kill the normal reactions and functions of a living creature.

The problems cropping up everywhere were all emergencies, but as the greatest bureaucrat charged with Aureatia's internal affairs, there shouldn't have been any problem that was completely lacking any previously encountered precedent. He didn't need to spare considerable willpower or laborious decision-making on such things—and yet, following past examples alone would lead to failure.

Needing to respond to *everything* went for those on the scene as well. While they had fully prepared for this day to come, there was always a limit on how they could distribute their manpower and materials. To ensure the orders he gave himself didn't clash with those in the field, he planned to make them work together like cogs in a machine, always handling things even more appropriately than in past precedents.

He couldn't hope for anyone to help him.

"Urgent report! The battle in the sixth borough of the Western Outer Ward appears to be a civilian riot! I repeat, the battle in the Western Outer Ward, sixth borough is *not* the rebel army, but civilians! The protesting activities surrounding the cancellation of the tenth march are—"

"Notres Gina Craftsman Guild is declaring their support for the rebel army! Around ninety of said guild's private forces are joining in the battle in front of the guild headquarters, and with this—"

...If only Rosclay could act in this situation...

This was the greatest difference in all the precedents Jelky had overcome.

There was no need to mobilize a large force and overpower the enemy. If Rosclay the Absolute stood on the scene, the needless bloodshed and the citizens' hostility could be pacified like the closing of a poetic tale. From the eyes of those in charge of domestic administration, this superpower could be seen as far more unfair than any of the shura's masterful abilities of combat and destruction.

This day was the one time when they couldn't expect that power.

"The citizens' riot was projected to happen! We can mobilize a public safety squad instead of the military! Get in contact, and ask about how things are being handled on the ground! For the Craftsman Guild's revolt, I estimate that the military already had a handle on it from their own reconnaissance! However, continue monitoring the situation, and report immediately if another issue is about to crop up!"

"Urgent report! Lord Jelky. The royal palace has been attacked."

...It's reached there, has it?

He didn't believe that a man like Iriolde the Atypical Tome would aim to make such a short-sighted move as attacking the palace.

However, in the middle of the intensifying chaos and rage of the battle, both sides must have predicted that something like this was likely to happen.

"The defense structure around the royal palace is flawless. We don't need to take any steps from here. When we get a request for help from the Palace Guard Bureau, then—"

"Lord Jelky. It appears that Soujirou the Willow-Sword escaped from Romog Joint Military Hospital early this morning. We currently do not know his whereabouts."

"......"

Soujirou the Willow-Sword. They had planned to eventually dispose of Rosclay's opponent in the tenth match, but not *today*. At a later date, in the officially *delayed* tenth match, Rosclay was supposed to get all his preparations in order and engage Soujirou in front of the eyes of the public. However...

"How is Sabfom the White Weave?"

"He engaged with Soujirou and is in cardiopulmonary arrest. Currently he is trying to normalize his heart activity... That is something we are unable to handle ourselves, so I will postpone the report for later."

"...That's fine. Thank you."

This meant Soujirou had attacked Sabfom in his attempt to escape.

We can interpret Soujirou the Willow-Sword's actions as treason against Aureatia.

Soujirou must have understood this for himself. He must have had some clear and convincing reason. Right now, even the slightest bit of thinking time was a precious resource, however...

Aureatia's current situation...is somewhat similar to when Alus the Star Runner attacked, but very different. In the midst of this chaos, we can't mobilize the other hero candidates. Most of the hero candidates would end up interfering with our own maneuvers simply by fighting. Today is the one day when we can't designate Soujirou as a self-proclaimed demon king. If Soujirou is making his move now with that in mind, then—

"Lord Jelky... Th-this is urgent."

The new report came not with a shout but sounded almost like a moan.

"Kadan Third District was...*destroyed.* Not only the Aureatia army squads deployed there, but the civilians...and likely the rebel army as well..."

"What happened? What evidence is there to determine that?"

"I-it's...estimated to be from some sort of lethal weapon attack, engulfing both friend and foe alike as they engaged with each other. All schedule reports from field have stopped...and we asked for observations from the Tenth Fortress to report on the situation on the ground. They said that all life in the Kadan Third District died...*from having all their skin stripped off.* What appears to be a hitherto unseen type of glowing plant life has grown thick over the area."

It was one of the situations Jelky had feared. Before precise information or countermeasures, there was something else that needed to be done first.

"What's the state of the surrounding evacuation?!"

"In the final report, they said that since the area was expected to have fierce fighting, fifty percent of the residents in the directly adjacent sections were evacuated. Shall we send in personnel to guide the evacuation?!"

"No… We don't have time to send in personnel capable of managing the remaining fifty percent of the residents, persuading them, and leading them to safety! Depending on the nature of this enemy weapon, there's a chance it could cause secondary casualties among the personnel we send to lead the civilians! Have them consider isolating all of Kadan District and move to blockade the town!"

"But, if we do that…"

It will lead to far too many casualties.

They were absolutely right.

This level of responsibility was something he needed to shoulder.

Jelky and the others didn't possess some supernatural power that upset logic and reason. If they had anything close to such a thing, it was…

"I'll go."

There came a refreshing and cool voice from right in front of the door.

It was the voice of a champion who signaled relief and peace of mind, known to all in Aureatia.

However, Jelky questioned him, half astonished. He didn't turn around.

"…Rosclay. Why are you here?"

"I was the one who mapped out this operation. I can't push all of the burden onto you."

"However much we're able to minimize the scale of the damages will depend on our own efforts here. If you go out on the front lines, the entire goal of this operation itself will be turned on its head. I can't approve of any mobilization. You need to be kept unharmed."

"I'll approve it on my own authority. This is all to spare the citizens' lives."

Rosclay's tone was calm enough to send a shiver down one's spine.

"Right now, you've hit a *deadlock* for the first time. Isn't that right? For a little while now I've checked on the orders you've been giving through the radzio. In order to continue handling other problems, you've got into a situation where you will be forced to abandon many citizens to die. Let *me* solve that. Keep your mind working and make the next move."

He had known from Jelky's tone and the frequency of reports. There was a large amount of material beyond the content of Jelky's orders that made it possible to reach this judgment. Simply by hearing the uproar in the command center, and through a radzio at that, he had been able to understand the limits of Jelky's ability to process the situation.

"...I can't approve of it. We don't even know the truth behind this enemy attack."

"The report said that Kadan Third District was destroyed, right? If it was destroyed all at once, I believe that the enemy's attack is wide-reaching and instantly effective, like a dragon's breath. As long as we know that it will be prove lethal the moment one gets in range, any insights on the nature of the attack are unnecessary. In fact, the vital information here is the signs of an incoming attack. Please have the reports from the observation points in the vicinity come through to my radzio as well. The advancing direction and speed of this threat should be easier to grasp through long-distance observations away from danger."

"...Why?"

His mumbled question wasn't searching for an answer. He thought that Rosclay's thinking made logical sense.

Rosclay the Absolute's deduction was correct. Jelky could say it was almost too balanced, miraculously so.

He was able to take action to save the greatest number of people while maintaining a minimal level of safety for himself.

Why can he do that...? This is what makes him so dangerous.

Like it was with Iriolde the Atypical Tome, those gifted with ingenuity and a talent for self-preservation always put others in the line of fire and never exposed themselves to danger. However, Rosclay was capable of choosing to act heroically to save citizenry he didn't know, all while truly being terrified of his own death.

It was as if he loved each and every one of the citizens like his family. Or rather, as if he was terrified that his family was among the anonymous civilian masses.

This was what Jelky had apprehensions about.

When the people of Aureatia needed Rosclay the Absolute, he was bound to head out on his own volition to save them.

"I will agree on one condition. In a worst-case scenario, I want you to prioritize your safety over anyone else's."

Jelky's remark meant abandoning the citizens when necessary.

"I intend to."

Jelky knew that Rosclay was answering from the heart.

An artificial champion in and of itself was a balanced contradiction.

"Champions are those who save the people. Thus, they cannot be allowed to die."

◆

There was a bacterium by the name of *hemolytic streptococcus.*

In everyday life, this was nothing more than a harmless everyday germ. One that commonly inhabited the pharynx, digestive tract, and the epidermis. Very rarely it could cause an upper respiratory tract infection, or a skin infection.

However, the infectious diseases caused by *hemolytic streptococcus* could suddenly turn fulminant. The skin and muscles of the limbs underwent necrosis in a little over a day, leading to death from multiple organ failure. The symptoms would progress so rapidly that it could be already too late for a patient if the necrotic tissue wasn't swiftly amputated, and they didn't undergo antibacterial treatment.

The trigger to this advance in severity was unknown. There were times when someone who had been perfectly healthy one day would suddenly come down with an infection. The difference between fulminant *hemolytic streptococcus* and regular *hemolytic streptococcus* was said to be the fact that it would bypass the immune system by producing lipids to hinder the effects of immunoreceptors, but the specific cause that triggered this mutation was yet to be identified.

In short, with a very slight idiopathic mutation, an everyday commonplace bacterium could change into an unknown lethal pathogen.

The events that occurred in the Kadan Third District were close in nature to this example.

The corpses lying here and there in the road all had all their skin melted off from head to toe, exposing their fat and muscles. Several ribbons of blood were engraved alongside many of the corpses. They were the tracks left behind from their last gasps, writhing in agony and clawing hard enough to dig into the ground and buildings.

"B-beautiful. All too beautiful."

There was only one who was writhing about, still alive.

Of course, when it came to this man, it was more accurate to say he was squirming around on the ground because he was overwhelmed with excitement and intense emotion.

A white lab coat, worm-eaten patches all over it, and hair turned a garish color by chemicals.

He was a self-proclaimed demon king by the name of Yukis the Ground Colony.

"Nectegio, Nectegio, Necteeeeeeeegio! Tell me, how are you so flawless and so beautiful?! Actually, maybe it's hopeless…? I mean, whether I want to or not, I can't help but understand the gap in perfection between us as living organisms! I want even more people to witness how wonderful Nectegio is…! I want their feedback. I want everyone else to feel pushed to the limit like this, too!"

Yukis's incomprehensible motivations energized him, and he sprung his feet.

Then, he shook the melted corpse laying nearby him.

"W-wake up! Wake up, please! Strange. Anyone with a normal mind should be left screaming after witnessing the beautiful biological theory behind Nectegio… A clear scientific anomaly… Something else must have happened…"

After continuing this for some time, he released his grip on the corpse, as if suddenly remembering something. The corpse fell once more to the ground.

"Oh, right. Every other organism besides me had their resident bacteria mutated when Nectegio showed up, and died on the spot. Real selfish lot, aren't they…? They're getting the chance to witness Nectegio themselves, the least they could do is build up a minimal amount of resistance! Isn't there *someone* who's still conscious…?"

"*Br-brzzzzz*. Nectegio, is, awake."

Together with a flickering light, like a starry sky, there was a terribly quiet voice resembling the buzz of an insect.

Yukis fell on his back.

"*Uwaheeee*?! What a gorgeous voice!"

"*Brzzzzz*. Colonization, of city, environment, is satisfactory. Nectegio, is succeeding, at experiment."

The creature talking to Yukis was not an animal. It wasn't even a plant—it was the colony of strange fungi sporocarps that had overgrown the Third District. The stalks, growing taller than a minia, had broken through residential windows and towered overhead. Transparent gelatinous globes covered the fallen corpse. Pallid luminescent spores continued to flitter through the air.

The grotesque biota that was composed from it all was itself the fungi known as Nectegio the Ravenous Rot.

"Ahhhh, how wonderful...! Theoretically, of course, I knew it was possible for you to live in urban areas, too, but... Still, given these latest circumstances, I had no choice but to drastically change your environment! It seems that some number of people died, but what a lucky end result! We've proven that even in a metropolitan area with little exposed soil, you can maintain your stable form by using a large number of minians as your bedding! A chance turn of events and the experiment is a success! *Hee-hee-hee-hee-hee*! Ah, Nectegio, so beautiful, and so strong as to be nigh inevitable!"

Nectegio's attack had even engulfed its own allies in Iriolde's army and killed them. Yukis's presence here had nothing to do with Iriolde's camp's operation.

Just like Kuuro the Cautious, Yukis also disappeared into the confusion of the hostilities and severed the yoke of his camp's influence himself. He ran away to keep his own greatest work, Nectegio the Ravenous Rot, from being used in battle, and conducted a colonization experiment in a non-laboratory setting—in short, the mass slaughter of Kadan's Third District.

No one would have imagined from his behavior, but Yukis the Ground Colony may have been equipped with, in some senses, an above-average risk management ability. Even with his ferocious ego and heretical talents, he didn't fight against an enemy he had no hopes of beating, while conversely, he didn't hesitate whatsoever to separate himself from a force whose defeat seemed imminent.

Yukis wasn't a self-proclaimed demon king with a defined history of hostility toward Aureatia. While he repeatedly murdered others and performed reckless fungal experiments out on the frontier, the scale of the incidents themselves never went beyond the mold of a regular, run-of-the-mill criminal. Up until now.

Now he held in his hands the most fearsome biological weapon of all.

"*Brzzzzzz.* I, have identified, a weapon being, dropped."

"Whaaat?!"

Yukis looked up at the sky in surprise. He could see several lines of fiery rain, like meteors, through the buildings.

They were falling slow enough to see with the naked eye. The goal wasn't destruction based on their speed or quantity. Since the shells were ignited and then cast toward them, they were likely incendiary rounds that utilized fats and oils.

It was an attack from Aureatia's army. The observation towers in various places dropped the incendiary rounds with the intention to burn down Nectegio and the entire district the unknown fungus contaminated with it.

"I am, ana-lyzing the target. Analysis. Destruction. Disassemble."

The fungal colony that occupied half of the town's airspace exhibited steady bioluminescence, as if breathing.

Several mushroom caps slowly opened up, and the lichen covering the soil surface began to change its color.

"Understood. *Brzzzzzzzz.* Vege-table oil. Petroleum. Lead. Zinc. Phosphorous. Will incorporate into Nectegio's system, and perform, stabilization."

"N-not just beautiful, but clever, too…! So unbelievably precious!"

The incendiary bombs landed in a circle, surrounding the central part of the area where Yukis stood, and exploded.

The incendiary swiftly spread, kicking up a conflagration—before immediately being extinguished.

The incendiary weapon was designed to rapidly steal all of the oxygen in the area at the point of impact. It also could not be extinguished with water. It was triggered the moment it made contact with Nectegio's deployed colony, and combustion never happened.

"That didn't have any effect at aaaaalll! This would be the Suppression Species, *Triskus Nitanieh…*"

In the middle of a sea of fungus, Yukis the Ground Colony laughed along.

"*Brzzzz*—Six species, of compositional organisms, eradic-ated. Three, reborn."

The popping sound of bubbles bursting echoed.

A purple sporocarp, equipped with a rodlike basidium, had been developing out from the roof of a building. All of these sporocarp were turned toward the high-rise buildings that had a chance of being hit by the incendiary bombs.

"Dissemination Species, *Listanokazma.*"

Together small pop, the purple sporocarp burst open and scattered.

Likely due to the aftershock of the spores being released rapid-fire at supersonic speeds, the building where the sporocarp was embedded collapsed.

An observation tower collapsed far off in the distance.

One tower. Two. Three.

Nectegio the Ravenous Rot was a poisonous fortress that could kaleidoscopically attack and defend at once.

"Now do we move here or… Hmmmm, that's quite a stumper! While I don't really want to force any sudden environmental changes for Nectegio's sake, on the other hand, it's not my intention to get in the way of everyone in Aureatia, either… Well, for me, Nectegio is unequivocally an absolute priority…but part of me doesn't want to expose my oh-so-beautiful Nectegio to even the slightest hint of danger! Such a perplexing predicament! Alas, love-born apprehensions!"

◆

As he led the evacuation of the citizens from Kadan Fourth District, Rosclay received reports on the monster in the Third District.

Contamination that caused instant death on approach. Precision counterattacks against artillery attacks.

Currently accompanying Rosclay were only two squads who had been positionally able to reach the scene in time. They weren't Aureatia army troops. There were many young rank-and-file in their ranks.

"You're not going to move on yet, right, Rosclay?! Right now, my mom and uncle, they're calling all their customers and gathering people together!"

"Is Aureatia okay?! All morning there've been nonstop shelling sounds… There were some just now…!"

"All righty then, just sit tight in here in this plaza! We've sent out all the guild's youngest guys at once! We won't let a single person who hasn't evacuated yet get past us!"

"Ahhh, Master Rosclay… Thank you so very much for sparing the effort to save a senile old fool's life…"

"Rosclay! Please help, Rosclay!"

However, the ones Rosclay was motivating were the citizens. From the beginning, they all possessed more than enough power to motivate themselves. The catalyst that made them manifest this strength to its fullest potential was Rosclay's strength as a symbol.

"Thank you, everyone, for your cooperation. Against this rebellion, the Aureatia army maintains a dominating position… Nevertheless, our victory wouldn't be complete if we were to lose the lives of all you citizens. Work together with me and let us finish this evacuation without a moment's delay. Martel the Fortune-Viewer will be tasked with directing the situation from here on out. Please leave the rescue work in the Third District and the northern part of the Second District to us."

He had already transferred the work regarding the neighborhood's residential registry, and their action policies going forward. Entrusting the bureaucrat that accompanied him from the Construction Ministry to lead things, Rosclay was going to immediately move to the next area.

He couldn't stop for a moment. Although his wounds from the fourth match were healed, he needed to keep thinking over how to deal with the imminent threat without ever letting his guard down against any attack.

By going out into the field, he had gained several pieces of eyewitness information from the people.

Short of mobilizing the hero candidates, there was no method to deal with Nectegio the Ravenous Rot.

Rosclay connected to Jelky in command headquarters through his radzio.

"Jelky. I propose that we *don't deal with* the disaster in the Third District."

<*...What are you saying?*>

A slightly haggard voice came back to him.

Now that their arsonists' plan to torch the entire area ended in failure, the only option to preserve Rosclay's safety would be to shift to a strategy that would cost a certain number of lives. Jelky must have been thinking along these lines.

<*The offensive power of this enemy is* extremely *dangerous. I could say that it is as if you and the evacuated citizens are walking across a marshland inhabited by wurms right now. Even the slightest mistake could make everything end in failure.*>

"Yes. That's exactly why. This attack was made against both Aureatia's army and Iriolde's forces. Both camps recognize the danger that this enemy poses. The one who is too hasty in making their move will be the ones to suffer lethal consequences... This enemy has no intention of moving out from Kadan Third District."

<*The reason behind your conclusion?*>

"First of all, there are no signs that the range of the threat is spreading since we first got confirmation on this fungi. That means that sabotage is not its goal... Also, the fact that it appeared out of nowhere, and didn't go along with the enemy's movements. Wouldn't that mean that Yukis the Ground Colony chose the most advantageous area solely for the initial surprise attack and occupied it?"

<*Based on the surveillance reports, the multitude of fungi growing en masse in the Third District is the true form of the attack itself. It isn't a mobile construct like the fungi soldiers attacking the city, and is instead a*

construct that takes root, spawned by some manipulation on Yukis's side of things.>

Jelky thought through the situation on the other side of the radzio.

<*In other words, does that mean he needed a base of operations?! He captured himself a base in the Third District, and plans to turn it into a dungeon... The reason he made it wipe out both camp's armies all at once was to prevent any interference until the work was done...! Rosclay, we really do need to deal with it now, or it will be too late.*>

"That's why we'll abandon it. This area has become a no-man's-land for Iriolde's camp as well. Which then means that the only one left we're meant to deal with is Yukis the Ground Colony. If we make a move, we risk that he'll choose to move somewhere else or counterattack, but if we maintain the current position, we can finish the evacuation of the surrounding areas without issue."

The most important point wasn't to completely protect all of Aureatia. It was to end the day without any lives lost.

Yukis the Ground Colony could be taken down by mobilizing the hero candidates after this current battle, poised to be vital for everything Rosclay's camp had worked for, was over.

"Prepare for the possibility it might move, and closely observe Yukis's movements. One possible route the damage could spread is by using the water channels to contaminate other areas. I ask you make use of Liquified Rampart. We need the perspective of a Life Arts specialist. If we can deploy Ekirehjy the Blood Fountain, get in contact with me."

<*...Thank you. I was too hasty to solve the problem. I'll return to other matters. I'm fine letting you handle that.*>

Jelky's reply was brief, but there was a relieved tone to his voice.

Though Jelky may have been known for his rational, calm composure, it was still impossible for him to escape the guilt of abandoning something. With countless options piled up in front of him and an enormous amount of work imposed upon him, he had needed someone else to shoulder the great sense of guilt.

To fight. Or not to fight. This question has continued to trouble me day in and day out.

Rosclay was determined not to fight.

He knew that choice in it of itself was the strongest of all.

CHAPTER 10 Royal Palace Grounds

Yukis the Ground Colony wasn't the only one who acted outside the purposes of his camp in the midst of the melee.

There was a thin man named Kyaliga the Music Reed. He was a general in command of the fourth battalion of Iriolde's Army, united in the anti-Aureatia cause.

However, Kyaliga's own perception was slightly different. Kyaliga was now, just as he always had been, a general of the Central Kingdom, and he was only working with his benefactor Iriolde temporarily in order to reclaim the true Kingdom. As such, he was planning on taking advantage of the grand coup to carry out an attack on the royal palace.

Standing in front of his soldiers as they lined up around the moat encircling the royal palace grounds, Kyaliga wept.

"*Hic, mrr...sniff*—Everyone... Thank all of you...for serving under a man like me—*hic*—this far... From here, we will...recapture the palace."

He wasn't crying because he was overcome with emotion. Kyaliga was almost always crying no matter the occasion. It may have been some sort of illness, but there was a far more apparent ailment affecting Kyaliga.

Kyaliga the Music Reed professed to be a general who had had continued to defend the Kingdom from the age of the Central Kingdom. There were no actual records of this. A man of poor birth, ever since

Kyaliga received words of appreciation for his work from King Aur during an inspection visit to the slums, he had started to believe he was a vassal of the monarch himself.

In the age of the Central Kingdom, Kyaliga the Music Reed had been an odd sort. Even the Old Kingdoms' loyalists, aiming to reinstate the Central Kingdom, hadn't accepted his delusional claims. Ironically, it was by becoming part of a rebel army hostile to the Kingdom that Kyaliga's talents as a general shouldering the name of the Central Kingdom had blossomed.

Kyaliga's weapon was a large *naginata* nearly twice his height. At his feet there were several people's bodies cut up and scattered about, and the large bridge across the moat had been lowered.

Charging ahead alone before the bridge was down, he had wiped out all the Palace Guards protecting the moat.

As he swung his great *naginata,* deadly enough to kill a minia with the slightest grazing cut, he was able to fly right into the middle of the enemy force with his mad charge. Kyaliga was also a natural-born fighter.

"Th-there is nothing to fear. Sephite is *a demon king.* Claiming the title of Queen, *hic*, she brought crooks and scoundrels with her...a-and is nothing but a, *unnnnh*, self-proclaimed demon king who, *sniff*, captured the Kingdom temporarily with fear!"

The other rebel army who obeyed Haade's operational maneuvers had been encircled by traps artfully set up before the fighting began. However, the Aureatia army's superiority didn't work against Kyaliga, ignoring the operation and acting on his own. In fact, it had been possible to use the other battles as bait and invade far further than normal, reaching the doorstep of the royal palace.

Kyaliga's battalion, flying the flag of the Central Kingdom's restoration, was filled with regular soldiers from the era of the Central

Kingdom and with experienced combat veterans who had switched sides from the Old Kingdoms' loyalists. They were equipped with rifles from the Beyond, and to carry out a suicide bombing attempt, they were given Bomb Golems that would fly at high speeds.

They possessed more than enough fighting power. It was safe to say that there hadn't been any armed group in Aureatia's history that had managed to advance all the way to the royal palace with such quality and quantity of arms.

However, Kyaliga felt loathing as he shed his tears.

I knew I couldn't trust Iriolde after all. He was also nothing more than a politician. He isn't able to share my idea of righteousness...

This line of thinking didn't take into account the fact that he had mobilized the fourth battalion he was entrusted with on his own judgment, and disobeyed Iriolde's Army.

If we had the same weapons from the Beyond...if he gave us the heavy weaponry that could directly shell the royal palace, then we could have taken down the palace from right here... The truth is, he and his cronies never planned on taking back the Kingdom at all!

Obviously, the possibility of Kyaliga assaulting the royal palace was an extreme inconvenience to Iriolde's army. The pretext of their plan to overthrow Aureatia was to eliminate Rosclay's reformation faction for the sake of the people of Aureatia and Queen Sephite, and an assault on the royal palace would make them lose this moral cause.

The fourth battalion hadn't been supplied Iriolde's army's heavy machine guns and recoilless guns capable of destroying key positions because they were aiming to prevent the battalion from going out of control before it could happen, but this meant that Kyaliga the Music Reed had pushed ahead even beyond the expectations the leaders of the camp had for them.

It wasn't possible to predict with accuracy how the surging morale of battle would come into play. Much more, Iriolde's camp, which had swelled up from countless incorporated anti-Aureatian forces, possessed a structural weakness from being unable to unify all the ideologies within the camp. Some things actually grew weaker from growing fatter and increasing in number.

"Everyone, please fight with me! For justice!"

Instead of a banner, Kyaliga lifted his great *naginata* up high, and the roar from the soldiers followed after.

The powerful fortune to take advantage of the melee to then break through the Aureatia army's defensive battles one by one, and the excitement of having victory right before their eyes… The sound of hooves galloped like a thunderstorm, crossing over the great bridge and entering into the royal palace grounds.

On top of that were three Bomb Golems. The golems, with their massive round frames, were weapons meant to lead the way at speeds surpassing the calvary's mobility, to blow up the gate, and create an opening to storm the royal palace.

Since Aureatia needed to cope with the battles breaking out all across its borders, they only anticipated a counterattack from the Palace Guard Bureau. While the royal palace may have been the central seat of power, protected by the world's most powerful military force, as long as they aimed for the exact second when their defenses couldn't react, it was possible to cut off the head of power with a single short sword—

"Recapturing the Central Kingdom? Give me a break."

In the direction of the three golems' advance lingered a wiry man with a very sinister look on his face.

With both arms dangling downward, he stood against the golems.

"*Sniff*... It seems you've come here to die, Aureatia Ninth General, Yaniegiz the Chisel...!"

"*Hee-hee.* Kyaliga the Music Reed. Want me to fill you in? Tell you why idiots like you survived up until now?"

Before he finished talking, something flashed in Yaniegiz's hands.

The green light, tracing an incomprehensible square arc through the air, struck the feet of the Bomb Golems one after another.

The three golems, lined up together as they charged, all tumbled on the spot.

"...!"

Kyaliga forcefully changed his horse's direction.

Several of the cavalrymen on the front line had their advance obstructed by the golems and were thrown from their horses. Others were forced to stop altogether.

Yaniegiz laughed.

"We let you all live because you're a bunch of worthless fools."

The bomb golems exploded all at once.

The vanguards who had their advance stopped were blown apart with their horses and perished.

A moment later, the heat wave and aftershock hit Kyaliga. He gritted his teeth and withstood it. A Central Kingdom general couldn't let himself be defeated by something like this. Right now, Kyaliga cried out of sheer anger.

"Light arrows... Mote Nerve Arrow...! How dare you use the Central Kingdom's magic item...!"

"*Hee-hee.* What, you didn't know the full details on its abilities? The thoughts its wielder has the moment it fires are forcefully carried out on the life-form it shoots... I may not be able to 'self-destruct,' but it looks like as long as it's something the target can pull off, it'll happen without a hitch, huh."

Yaniegiz made an exaggerated show of his admiration.

Kyaliga wouldn't stand for it. Both that the man was selfishly using a magic item of the Kingdom, nor that it was likely done specifically to rob Kyaliga of his composure. However, Kyaliga was always crying. He could say that reining in uncontrollably strong emotions was something he did constantly.

Him choosing to talk from this distance means that he doesn't want to step inside spear range. Is he buying time for the Mote Nerve Arrow to reload...? By standing there unable to move—

Kyaliga's scowl at Yaniegiz was to keep the man's attention on him.

The rearguard calvary soldiers were equipped with guns from the Beyond.

You make for a good rifle target.

There were gunshots.

"Huh?"

Yaniegiz's thin body lurched and abruptly toppled over.

"You...lose, Yaniegiz."

There was another gunshot.

The bullets weren't flying in his direction. That was when he noticed.

Kyaliga turned to the rear guard. The group behind him were crossing swords with an Aureatian squad. Kyaliga's troops were the ones being hit with gunfire.

In the middle of the gunfire, a plump round man was fighting. Jumping through the gaps in the tight-knit formation with rabbit-like alacrity, he continuously struck with his sword, the tip mysteriously broken, using only minimal movements of his wrist.

"Y'know...I don't really want to do this."

Each time his blade connected, human and horse alike collapsed without a sound. They stopped moving as if their bodies were paralyzed.

The man murmured with artless simplicity as he single-handedly took down numerous soldiers.

"But you should stop trying to invade the royal palace. I'm gonna have to kill you otherwise."

"Aureatia's Tenth General...Yuca the Halation Gaol!"

Yaniegiz the Chisel was known as Rosclay the Absolute's right-hand man, but he also served as the head of the Police Agency. Kyaliga should have anticipated that he would cooperated with Yuca, tasked with preserving national peace.

Then, that first shot at Yaniegiz—

Following his hunch, Kyaliga jumped from where he stood.

The flashing shot of green light that came flying in from the side hit his horse, and the rest missed. The horse screamed in intense pain and flailed about.

Kyaliga looked up as he rolled across the ground.

"Whoops... Well, 'pose an ant-brained fool can at least figure that much out."

Yaniegiz lifted his body up. This man was never shot to begin with. He had simply pretended to collapse to the ground in sync with the gunshots. If Kyaliga had been a second late, he would've been hit by Mote Nerve Arrow's attack, and ordered to feel intense pain or pass out.

"Two from the Twenty-Nine Officials, and two magic items. Do you understand the meaning behind Aureatia deploying this much fighting power?"

Yet another scream erupted from behind Kyaliga.

Yaniegiz grunted with scorn. "It means the grace period we gave you fools is over!"

Kyaliga dashed forward.

With his great *naginata* in his hands, he ferociously closed the distance to Yaniegiz. Its slash, making full use of the great *naginata*'s mass and length, carried speed and force that was impossible to guard against, capable of sending an opponent's torso flying just by touching the tip up against the top of the shoulder.

I won't even let him realize he's dead.

In the middle of his charge, he bent his trunk, then shoulders, getting in position to mow Yaniegiz down.

A slash came rushing from two o'clock.

His fist, flexor severed and deprived of all grip strength, flung the great *naginata* in a different direction.

The pain signal arrived on a delay.

Forcing his way in was a man with a shaved head.

"Damn lunatic."

Aureatia's Twenty-Fourth General, Dant the Heath Furrow.

The leader of the Palace Guard Bureau. A loyal retainer of Queen Sephite since the era of the United Western Kingdoms.

"It's a disgrace that mongrels like you were even allowed to step foot within the royal palace grounds."

The course of the defensive battle for the royal palace, up against an unprecedentedly large fighting force, seemed to be completely decided...

However, not a single person had even imagined the reality.

Neither Dant, Yaniegiz, nor Yuca, not even Kyaliga, could have possibly known.

That an unimaginable, impossibly great fighting force was going to upset absolutely everything about the situation there.

CHAPTER 11 Friendship

There were those looking to slip under the cover of the chaos to achieve their goals underneath Aureatia as well.

One such group was the Old Kingdoms' loyalists. They had been reduced to a remnant force, led by Caneeya the Fruit Trimming.

However, the objective of their attack wasn't one of Aureatia's key positions—and put more accurately, this meant Kaete was technically guiding the Old Kingdoms' loyalists to invade.

"If Obsidian Eyes is truly the mastermind behind this vampire disturbance..."

Caneeya stood at the head of the army corps and advanced down the underground waterway, but even further out in front of her were tiny golems equipped with searchlights shuffling ahead. These were simple reconnaissance golems made by Kiyazuna the Axle.

"The organization should already be destroyed. Would they really employ one that they themselves weakened?"

"Are you kidding?" Kaete answered with deeply held disgust. "Think over your own situation, and then talk. Not only were you destroyed by the Gray-Haired Child yourselves, but now you're at his beck and call."

"......"

"Aureatia simply did the same thing. Since an ex-Obsidian Eyes member—Zeljirga—was chosen as a hero candidate, it's clear that there was a deal between Aureatia and Obsidian Eyes. Their organization was wiped out, so they can't support themselves without Aureatia's aid. Their only path of survival is to do as Aureatia orders, infecting the other hero candidates and then disposing of them. On top of that, as long as they follow their orders, it increases the chance of advancing their public-facing hero candidate."

Obviously, every word Kaete spoke was a lie.

Aureatia and Obsidian Eyes were in a constant hostile relationship, with Aureatia making efforts to test for infections and produce antiserums in order to pin down Obsidian Eyes as the spy guild trying to hide its true indentity and use the Sixways Exhibition for its own purposes.

However, Kaete never had any obligation to provide accurate information to the Old Kingdoms' loyalists.

What he and Kiyazuna needed to accomplish before anything else was to pit the Old Kingdoms' loyalists against Obsidian Eyes and regain control of Mestelexil.

"After Alus the Star Runner's attack, Aureatia revealed the proliferation of corpses themselves. Why would they purposefully present information to the public that would make the other hero candidates warier?"

For a dense Old Kingdoms' loyalist fool, she sure picks at the right threads.

Kaete couldn't get a read on Caneeya's emotions from her tone. Her expression never changed either, so for Kaete, she was the worst type of person to talk with.

"Figure it out yourself. I don't know about whatever purpose they may've had for announcements made after they kicked me off the assembly... But thinking over what Aureatia's aims were, given they're looking to eliminate hero candidates by using this vampire, they must have needed an excuse for Alus the Star Runner's rampage to ensure the Sixways Exhibition continued. If they made a false announcement while having the body in their possession, it'd cause them trouble...assuming they're thinking about continuing to dispose of the hero candidates in the later matches, too."

"Should an infection get discovered in one of hero corpses after that, then Aureatia could end up lookin' suspicious. That what yer getting at, Kaete?"

Kiyazuna the Axle picked up on Kaete's intentions and backed him up.

Kiyazuna's usual attitude was nonstop unpleasantness, but when it came to these types of sinister schemes, her malice became all too reliable.

"Aureatia managed to secure Alus's body, but there's no guarantee that the same'll be true for the other hero candidates going forward. Especially the ones like Lucnoca, where just cleaning up the corpse is a huge task on its own. Before her, there were other hero candidates that got outta control like Alus did, even if they were made into corpses. Some people'll start getting suspicious that *maybe Alus had been a corpse, too.*"

"And that's why they purposefully made that announcement. I see," Caneeya replied with a nod. Kaete had no idea if the explanation had truly convinced her or not.

Of course, for him, it didn't make a difference either way. Whether she believed him or not, he just needed Caneeya to use this logic to mobilize her troops and justify the attack on Obsidian Eyes.

...Regardless of whether I can make her believe me, I'll mobilize this dying organization.

Suddenly, a question floated into Kaete's mind. "Why did the Gray-Haired Child abandon you lot?"

"......"

"Of course, I doubt there's anyone in the world who would give any thought to saving a bunch of shabby anachronistic relics like you, but... Even still, it seems illogical for a man who allied himself not just with the Okafu mercenaries, but even goblins, to abandon your group and *your group alone*."

In the beginning, the Old Kingdoms' loyalists were a trading partner for the Gray-Haired Child.

However, Hiroto's camp had been thorough and painstaking in their treatment of the Old Kingdoms' loyalists after that.

Leading the Toghie City deadlock toward destruction, having Gilnes the Ruined Castle get captured by Aureatia, and disintegrating their armed forces all to ensure Hiroto's own participation in the Sixways Exhibition, even now he used the Old Kingdoms' loyalists as his pawns, all for the smallest amount of information and resources as bait.

"I said it before, didn't I? The Gray-Haired Child is a terrifying opponent."

Caneeya walked up ahead with slightly faster footsteps.

Kaete could tell she was trying to hide the expression on her face.

"You're aware that the Gray-Haired Child is acting to once again establish goblins on this continent, yes? However, in our ranks...as well as in Aureatia right now, anyone who holds the Kingdom's values possesses a firmly held prejudicial view against all non-minian races. No matter how intelligent they may be, no matter how beneficial it may be, no one would ever choose to live with goblins."

"Of course not. Who would want to coexist with a hideous monstrous race like them—"

"However, if you include the new continent, there are *more of them in number*. You understand what that means?"

"...What?"

The Gray-Haired Child made goblins his allies, rather than any minian race. Kaete could come up with a tentative explanation around this bizarre fact—perhaps that goblins had been the first ones to support him.

But, if that wasn't the case...

"It can't be. It's because the goblins...are the *majority*? That when you include the ones on this new continent or whatever...the largest population isn't the minian races...but goblins...?"

"That is likely it. We didn't understand that. Neither I...nor General Gilnes."

A cold sweat beaded on Kaete's forehead.

"W-wait... You said both in your ranks, and for Aureatia right now, didn't you? In other words, the part about the goblins not being accepted...was referring to you?! You're trying to tell me that the Gray-Haired Child...*chose the Old Kingdoms' loyalists before Aureatia*?!"

The Gray-Haired Child hadn't contacted the Old Kingdoms' loyalists pretending to be an ally before then destroying them.

The Old Kingdoms' loyalists had rejected the Gray-Haired Child themselves and met their fate.

"Hiroto the Paradox's financial power would have become a powerful trump card for us in our inevitable confrontation with Aureatia. We spent a great amount of time trying to convince him to give his effort for the sake of the Kingdom, and not the goblins...but he must have made up his mind at some point."

The Gray-Haired Child had first picked not Aureatia, but the Old Kingdoms' loyalists, to use as his foundation for making the world accept goblins. What would have happened instead, had they actually accepted his proposal?

In order to make his own allies win in the end, he used every possible means at his disposal. When in the process, as he was forced to snatch something away from someone, his targets became those he had determined *weren't his allies*.

If he continued that over and over, only his allies would remain.

"What...is he thinking?" Kaete murmured. He felt as though he was being watched...not by an enemy or an ally, but some nondescript massive, creepy thing.

The Gray-Haired Child had given shelter to Kaete, pursued by Obsidian Eyes, within the Old Kingdoms' loyalists.

On this, the day of the tenth match, it had been the Gray-Haired Child who had passed on the information about the grand coup that Haade and Iriolde were instigating.

The Gray-Haired Child knew that Obsidian Eyes had secured Mestelexil for themselves.

"What is trying to get us to do?"

Were Kaete's actions right now actually a true product of his own volition?

"Who's to say. In any case, it's probably a good thing you were chased out of the Twenty-Nine Officials. As far as I can see, from how they'll treat goblins going forward... Aureatia's already chosen the same path that we did."

Caneeya the Fruit Trimming purposefully turned back and wore deep, profound grin.

"In order words, they're *no longer* Hiroto the Paradox's allies."

◆

Slightly going back in time—two days before the tenth match was scheduled to start…

Yuno, visiting one of the old town's plazas on that day with Hiroto, was on guard.

This was partly due to the fathomless visitor Hiroto himself, but more than that, she couldn't stop herself from worrying about the eyes of the Aureatian citizens. Wearing a plain, burnt umber hood far past her face, she made sure not to meet anyone else's gaze.

"There's nothing for you to be so scared of, Yuno."

Returning to her, Hiroto wore a nonchalant smile. He looked to have been chatting about something or other with a shop owner just now, but was Aureatia really not cautious of the Gray-Haired Child doing such a thing?

"You don't need to worry. Neither you nor I have been labeled wanted criminals. At least, the Aureatia citizens won't try to capture you or anything of the sort."

"…But even then, you should be under surveillance by Aureatia, right?"

Hiroto the Paradox wasn't a hero candidate himself, but Aureatia's Twenty-Fourth General, Dant the Heath Furrow, was said to have been specially attached to him to keep him under surveillance. Though this, too, was information she had only heard through the grapevine while working under Haade.

"That's right. However, Aureatia's surveillance system has a large loophole. I understood that the one tasked with keeping an eye on me was Zigita Zogi's sponsor, Dant the Heath Furrow. He himself is an honest man, but he is with the Queen's faction, who stands opposed to both the mainstream reformation faction and the military's faction. There are very few who are going to unconditionally believe information from his faction. Even if he found something suspicious about my behavior and reported it, first he would need to prepare either enough proof or potentially benefits to get the other factions to act."

"In other words... You needed to pull the wool over General Dant's eyes whenever you did something?"

Hiroto smiled with amusement at Yuno's question.

"Oh no, of course not. This all happened before the beginning of the Sixways Exhibition. I've already built an amicable relationship with General Dant, and at this point, there's no need to pull the wool over his eyes at all. Besides, the person I am talking to is a fairly small-time entrepreneur. Even if there was a soldier keeping watch over me, there's nothing shady about our conversation. Aureatia's side doesn't need to constantly have a close eye on me anyway, since if they interviewed whoever I talked to that day for information, then everything that I mentioned would end up getting leaked to them later."

"But for these several days, General Dant isn't acting at all—isn't that right?"

"......"

Yuno was convinced, in some regards. While it may have seemed that he was simply moving forward with his business deals with private citizens, there was an inevitability to Hiroto's actions.

Including the fact that he had brought Yuno along with him to walk through the city.

"That's because the plan to overthrow Aureatia that General Haade—that Iriolde the Atypical Tome is advancing is *actually happening.* As long as there's the slightest possibility of an attack on the royal palace that day, as head of the Palace Guard Bureau, General Dant will prioritize that above everything, and needs to work out the plan to defend the palace…that's why he can't spare effort to keep an eye on you—Dant's in a situation where it's possible to make that sort of excuse, right?"

"Ohhh." Hiroto let out a sigh of admiration.

Ever since she had learned about one part of the conspiracy, right after the third match, Yuno had never stopped thinking about what might happen. She was accustomed to overthinking things. Her time spent worrying and wavering were the only long and plentiful moments she had.

"If General Dant is in an almost-ally relationship with you…then in few days until the tenth match, even if tried something that could be considered an act against Aureatia, it would mean that he could tacitly permit it. Since, victory for you…means that General Dant's Queen faction, not one of the main factions at play, would grow closer to victory…"

"*Hah-hah-hah-hah*, a fantastic read of things, Yuno. Such a young student, yet you have the power to really observe the state of affairs and parse them out. You didn't study this sort of stuff, did you?"

"N-no…it's not anything…to be complimented…on."

Faced with the unexpected praise, she couldn't stop her words from quietly petering out.

She didn't know anything specific about what Hiroto was setting up, for starters.

Over the past several days, desperately learning about the latest state of affairs in Aureatia, she believed she understood the situation Hiroto's camp was currently faced with. As a result of Zigita Zogi's defeat in the eighth match, they now found themselves at a severe political disadvantage. There existed almost no method at all to make Aureatia recognize citizenship rights of the goblins from this situation, with the economic activities of their mercenaries limited, and the loss of their hero candidate. Even if they formed an official collaborative relationship with Obsidian Eyes, it wasn't going to change anything about the situation, was it?

Should they aim to break into the deadlock situation with martial might and take advantage of the massive coup to mobilize their goblins and Okafu mercenaries, they had no means to conceal the flow of people and materials. If they showed even the slightest sign of doing so, even General Dant would be forced to report it to the assembly, despite leaning toward their side.

Just by conversing with the merchants he normally did business with, he fooled Aureatia's eyes and accomplished what he was after... Is something that sounds so magical even possible?

"I..."

Departing from the plaza, the two of them had boarded a carriage driven by a goblin.

There wasn't anyone around to criticize their conversation.

"...would like to have Soujirou the Willow-Sword fight in his match."

"...?! Wh-what...?" She thought maybe she had misheard him.

Even if he moved heaven and earth, it was totally impossible.

"There's no way we could do that! Soujirou had his leg amputated in the third match...! Besides, his sponsor Haade was working on the side of Soujirou's opponent from the very beginning...s-so there's no way the tenth match is even going to happen in the first place! With Aureatia having full control over the operation of the tournament, *they're going to make sure* not to hold it!"

"Yes. That's why you coming to us was such a profound boon. If the tenth match ends in victory for Rosclay, any possibility of victory on this continent for us will collapse with it. Now that Zigita Zogi has sacrificed himself, I absolutely cannot give up."

"But I don't have any means to contact Soujirou...and it'll probably be impossible to meet with him. The hospital is likely working for Aureatia, so most information is probably getting intercepted before it reaches him..."

"We understand Soujirou's true wish. As long as he has a match, he'll try to fight at any cost. It doesn't matter if he only has one leg or not—isn't that so, Yuno?"

"Well, yes, but..."

To Yuno, Soujirou was, without a doubt, one of the powerful individuals she detested, but in the Sixways Exhibition, her wish and Soujirou's had lined up with each other. For Soujirou, it was to enjoy an all-out battle against someone stronger than himself, which he had yet to encounter. For Yuno, it was to deliver the powerful to their dooms and carry out her revenge.

However, as long as they were battling within a tournament bracket that Rosclay had drawn up, this had been an impossible endeavor from the start.

When Yuno had learned that Soujirou was heavily wounded in the third match, she had been almost glad—that it would give her more comfort to know he lost after being depraved of his strength, instead of being treated as having been defeated while still possessing the strength and will to fight.

"It isn't only Soujirou, either—*you want Soujirou to still fight*, too, don't you, Yuno?"

"......"

"You want to force Soujirou to fight. You want to get vengeance for the ruin of Nagan. You want to make General Haade feel the same sense of inferiority you did toward him. You want to save Linaris... I can tell all this just form observing you. Each one of them is something you truly wish for. Your feelings have turned into a complicated jumble, but that is because every time you come into contact with someone, you wish for something more. A person's mental state isn't simple enough to allow one to live as a revenge-driven fiend, throwing everything in life toward a singular goal."

His gray eyes stared at Yuno.

A politician visitor. Yuno keenly felt that his strength was genuine. Though they had only interacted for a few days, he had completely seen through Yuno's nature, as if he were a decades-old friend.

"...Have I gone mad?"

Despite having thought it for so long, she hadn't been able to openly vocalize this suffering.

She hadn't even breathed a word of it to Linaris.

"All of the wishes you said...every single one, without exception, might all be a lie. I don't have the strength to go against the momentary rage urging me on. Even things I want myself I end up completely ruining."

"That's perfectly normal. Getting angry, struggling, resisting...all while simultaneously wanting peace of mind and bliss, it's not strange at all."

Hiroto closed his eyes. They were gentle words.

"It's because you're lonely."

"—"

"You've been in anguish this whole time, Yuno. Having lost your homeland, your friend, and yet without anyone understanding how you feel, it would be impossible to hold it all in without screaming. You so desired someone who would pick up on this scream and look toward you, you could no longer stand for anyone who wouldn't. On the other hand though, you know that no one necessarily hates you or dislikes you at all. That made it all the more unbearable...am I right?"

"...I'm...not so sure."

"I believe it is."

Yuno thought it was out of Hiroto's kindness that he purposefully made this sound like firm conclusion.

Was what Yuno considered to be madness truly just loneliness?

Had she wanted to surrender herself to something she knew was tormenting her because she hadn't wanted to forget the sadness from losing Nagan?

"...The reason I brought you along with me today, Yuno, was to ask about your wish. Since, right now, you don't have any Obsidian Eyes surveillance watching over you."

"Well..."

Lendelt the Immaculate, who had kept watch over Yuno, was holding a meeting with Morio the Sentinel regarding their actions following the tenth match at this moment.

There was no longer any need to worry that Yuno would leak information. Now that Hiroto's camp and Obsidian Eyes had formed a collaborative relationship, the sort of information Yuno carried was being shared by Lendelt himself. Obsidian Eyes needed to prepare for the chaos of the grand coup themselves, and their leader, Linaris, was unconscious. Even in a situation like that, did they have another person surveilling them besides Lendelt, to be ready in case Hiroto or Yuno made any unforeseen moves?

Hiroto the Paradox—was it also possible for this visitor, possessing the deviant nature to *meet* people as if it were fate, to pick out the perfect opportunity *to avoid any fateful first encounters*?

"Getting a doctor to look after Linaris the Obsidian. That was your demand, wasn't it?"

"...Yes. I believe in her current condition, she'll be in danger unless she's treated soon."

The leader of Obsidian Eyes was called "the Obsidian." Yuno had first learned that Linaris was said leader only after leaving the mansion. During this Sixways Exhibition, her guild was active in some kind of espionage activity away from the eyes of others, which was how they stole information from Haade's camp during the third match.

"However, right now, your own body is in need of immediate treatment, Yuno. Did you know that?"

"What...?!" Her voice cracked. The topic came like a bolt from the blue.

Yuno didn't feel physically out of sorts at all, and her understanding was that if there was anything wrong with her, it sure had to be some kind of mental disorder.

Hiroto continued. "There is one topic that Obsidian Eyes is purposefully keeping hidden. They are a collective of corpses headed by a vampire, and Yuno, you are already infected yourself. We performed a blood test on you as well, so we know this for certain. Right now, the parent unit, Linaris the Obsidian, holds the power of life and death over you."

"Linaris?"

A vampire.

A monstrous race that threatened the world in the past. A deviant strain of illness. With an infection passing from organism to organism, it changed people into corpses that loyally obeyed the orders of their parent units, eventually remaking any children they birthed as well.

Those infected by the vampire virus, even after being changed into corpses, didn't lose their free will. Thus, it was possible to never realize one was a corpse until it was pointed out to them by someone else.

Everyone was incredulous that they could possibly be infected right up until their infection was made clear.

But... That's...what it was. I'm sure of it.

Pale skin like moonglow. Deep golden eyes that seemed to suck Yuno in. A beautiful body that was thin and delicate while still possessing feminine curves. A face capable of charming anyone with a smile, or causing them to sympathize with a look of sadness.

Linaris's unearthly beauty existed *because* she was an unearthly vampire.

Linaris, a vampire...

That had been why Obsidian Eyes needed to flee and hide from Aureatia.

There must have been plenty of basis for Yuno to have noticed. Linaris was weak to sunlight. When they first met, she had made the Aureatia soldiers faint by some unknown means. The vampire that Aureatia announced to the nation, who had felled Alus the Star Runner, must have been referencing Obsidian Eyes, hadn't it?

Hiroto's tone sounded graver than it had just a moment prior.

"You were a Nagan scholar, Yuno, so you are likely familiar with how the vampire virus is transmitted. It's not one easily transmitted through simple touch or ingestion. They send in their own blood through a deep wound...or they infect others through even deeper physical contact. Does anyone in Obsidian Eyes, or Linaris the Obsidian herself, come to mind when I say that?"

"O-of—"

She couldn't hold back her shrill shriek. She nearly jumped out of her seat and to her feet in the carriage.

"Of c-course not, obviously! Th-that's a...really rude question!"

"Yes, it is rude. However, while I may have lacked delicacy, this is a truly important conversation."

Hiroto's eyes were not the eyes of someone telling a joke.

"Well then, Yuno, *what sort of process led to your infection*? Infecting someone with the vampire virus is normally not a feat that can be done completely unbeknownst to the infected. Going by the results of the sixth match, there's a chance that Obsidian Eyes took control of Mestelexil the Box of Desperate Knowledge… That happened when, and how? Furthermore, in the eighth match, my sworn friend Zigita Zogi was killed, also by an Obsidian Eyes attack."

Yuno could already understand what he was getting at.

Linaris was a vampire who had obtained a strange route of infection that was unknown to their world. And that if he granted Yuno's wish and healed her, Linaris may very well destroy Aureatia.

"Though the evidence is circumstantial, I believe it's fair to say chances are low that one of Obsidian Eyes' agents possesses this powerful infection ability. It is different for Linaris the Obsidian, however. More than a threat to myself or Aureatia, her existence is a threat to all miniankind."

"……"

"I wish to grant the wishes of those who will become my allies as much as possible. Furthermore, saving Linaris wasn't included in the conditions that Obsidian Eyes put forth. Now that you know the information she kept secret from you, would you like to change your request to me at all, Yuno?"

"…I…"

Yuno was at a loss for words.

Withdrawing her request to Hiroto here wouldn't count as a betrayal. It was only natural for the minian races to act on their own behalf. At the very least, there was far more righteousness to it than Yuno's choice to let a moment's fury lead her to separate from Haade and Soujirou.

Moreover, it wasn't that she was *killing* Linaris. If Linaris continued to die out as she was now, it would merely mean that her treatment was too late. Linaris had already chosen to sacrifice herself for the sake of her organization, and Obsidian Eyes had also accepted her choice.

"Even, still…I want to help her."

"Do you mind if I ask you here to explain why you think so…? I think you need to hear your thoughts out loud as much as I do, Yuno."

"…Sh-she's lonely."

She felt confused—several different emotions all flowed from her heart into her head.

"I think…she's lonely."

However, she felt this confusion was something different from the urge for revenge that had been spurring her forward.

She thought about the small month she had spent with Linaris. She was so very smart, and yet Yuno's innocent stories of her homeland and her travels made her so happy. If Linaris truly was the parent unit with a position of superiority over all of Obsidian Eyes, then why did she always have a vaguely troubled look in her eyes? She simply seemed to not have many friends, but she had the heart of a young girl just like Yuno.

"If I was naturally born to be an enemy to minians…and forced to always be suspicious of everyone…then I think, if I was ever betrayed, even if I thought they were someone I could bare my soul to, I'd be *forced to kill them*… Do you understand that sentiment, Hiroto?"

"Please don't worry. Right now, you aren't under surveillance by Obsidian Eyes. I've taken care to ensure that regardless of your choice, it won't be to your detriment."

"...That's not it. This isn't about whether I die or not... It's that, if she has to kill me, Linaris...I think it would be really sad and painful for her...not that I know that for certain or anything, I just *feel* it..."

Even sick in bed and vaguely conscious, there was no way the intelligent and bright Linaris who Yuno was familiar with wouldn't have realized the danger in dispatching Yuno. If she had intended on entrusting Obsidian Eyes to the Gray-Haired Child in exchange for her life from the very beginning, then Yuno's existence was nothing but a cause of worry that she might leak information.

Linaris must have wanted someone who would trust her, even after learning the truth behind Obsidian Eyes, right?

If they didn't still trust her, then wouldn't she be forced to kill them?

"There are perhaps few who can understand the reason why you view Soujirou with hostility after slaying the Nagan Dungeon Golem... It may seem bizarre at first blush, but it's a logical sentiment to have. What you loathe is the existence of such powerful people itself."

...That's right.

"You fear and wish to defeat those who can trample all else underfoot on a whim...who never consider the weak."

This man really is incredible. He probably understands these feelings I've never voiced out loud...better than even I do.

"You think Linaris the Obsidian is an exception?"

"Linaris is..."

Suddenly, she thought back to Dakai the Magpie, whom she fought in Lithia.

The visitor said he didn't have either friends or family. It had to be true for Soujirou, having come from the Beyond, annihilated in the ravages of war, as well.

Most of the hero candidates appearing in the Sixways Exhibition must have been powerful individuals who, even if they had experienced loss or fear before, were equipped with all-powerful might that allowed them to accept their fate to live a solitary life at the top.

"Linaris is probably...different. Though she is one of the strong, wielding organizational power, she's definitely different from you, Hiroto...and from the deceased Zigita Zogi. If you were to lose everything, and were left truly all alone, you'd be able to rise back up."

"......"

"I should ask you the same thing, Hiroto. Why?"

Yuno kept her eyes downturned. She probably didn't have the courage to look at Hiroto directly.

"...What do you mean?"

"...Hiroto, you understand me better than I understand myself, so...you should know for yourself that somewhere in my heart I sympathize with Linaris, and that I'm fond of her. Despite that...you revealed Linaris's true identity to me, risking the chance that Obsidian Eyes might hear you to do so... You wanted to *make me betray* Linaris of my own volition. Isn't that right?"

Hiroto the Paradox would take the side of his supporters no matter what.

He surely possessed a firm mental fortitude to be able to make his pledges to them a reality.

However, he had a heart, too. Behind the strength to survive on his own, there had to be a tiny bit of inconsistency and fragility, just the same as Yuno, left inside him somewhere.

"The truth is *you* want revenge, too. After they severed the goblins' ambitions that were staked on the Sixways Exhibition and drove your friend to their death...*you don't want to forgive* Obsidian Eyes, just for coming with heads bowed asking to work together. If I were in your position, I would wish for revenge. Like my hatred for the strong who destroyed Nagan."

"*Heh*... I am truly surprised."

Hiroto smiled like she had never seen him smile before.

The type of smile an elder who had lived through many decades wore, cynical and self-deprecating.

"Yuno the Distant Talon. It would appear that you've already become something far beyond than the mere powerless scholar you once were... You've grown far stronger than you think. This is based on my own experience, but...I believe that tasting emotions and doubts from many different perspectives, even for a short period of time, makes someone several times stronger than they would be spending a long time experiencing and learning in a single position."

"Hiroto...you planned to leave Linaris to die from the very start, didn't you?"

"Yes. However, seeing that you and I have made a commitment together, it would go against my own beliefs not to tell you this. Once someone has become a supporter of mine, I cannot lead them with lies. That's because, I know for myself that in truth, I'm not an unselfish politician at all. I shouldn't wield my power according to my own ego..."

Hiroto covered his face with both hands to conceal his expression.

Yuno could tell that the wide-open gray eyes peeking through the gaps in his fingers were looking at her.

"...Can you stop me?"

Yuno's hair stood on end.

It was because she felt a will.

For the first time, she learned that a will could be felt as though it possessed a distinct mass and weight.

Hiroto the Paradox was going to kill Linaris the Obsidian.

The Gray-Haired Child was unmistakably a devil. He would make all the wishes of his allies come true, but he would thoroughly use, exhaust, and crush those who wouldn't become his ally.

Knowing for himself that he possessed the power to transform absolutely everything in the world as he saw fit, he had used the firm limitation of being a politician to restrict his own rampage.

"I..."

Her words wouldn't continue.

Terrifying.

They were merely sitting across from each other inside a carriage, nor did he possess a single means to attack Yuno, and yet she felt a horror that this persona of his had a firm grip on her soul.

Hiroto understood everything about Yuno, but that didn't mean Yuno *understood Hiroto, too.*

Right before her eyes was unmistakably a shura who had transcended the limit of this land's understanding.

"...If I don't nod my head...then your only choice will be to do exactly as you promised, saving Linaris's life and letting a doctor see her! I-isn't that right...?!"

"Exactly. I will keep my promises to their completion. I will have a doctor examine Linaris the Obsidian while she still lives. Surely, Yuno, you understand that doesn't mean that she is guaranteed to be safe, yes?"

"No..."

It had been so long, she had forgotten.

Was standing face-to-face with a shura always so terrifying?

"If I may, Yuno. In order to maintain who I am, choosing not to get revenge was always inconceivable. That's why this isn't advance notice. It's *already in motion.* After the tenth match...if by some stroke of luck, Linaris and Obsidian Eyes are able to survive, I will promise you that I won't do anything more than what I've put in motion. I will save their lives, just as we promised."

Hiroto the Paradox was sure to keep his promise.

Which is what made this all the more terrifying.

He must have been capable of ignoring the will of a weakling like Yuno and still have his revenge, just as he wished for. Despite possessing such power, he was abiding by Yuno's own wishes instead of his own self-interest. He continued to regulate himself with his monstrous strength of will.

He wasn't someone like Soujirou, who acted according to his own desires and never considered weaklings like Yuno.

Nor was he like Linaris, who was strong, yet who would be unable to achieve what she wanted.

The Gray-Haired Child was…a monster that continuously realized the wishes of others, not himself.

"…I-in that case…Hiroto…"

The day of the tenth match was bound to be when everything would happen.

Iriolde would mobilize his army to overthrow Aureatia.

Soujirou and Rosclay would have their match.

Linaris would be killed.

"It's fine…i-if I make that stroke of luck happen then, right?"

It wasn't that Yuno had any prospects of victory whatsoever. This may have looked like the same desperate self-abandonment, spurred by uncontrolled emotion, that Yuno had exhibited up until now.

However, Hiroto the Paradox had to grasp that there was a similar, but different, motive driving Yuno now.

"Wonderful. I didn't expect any less."

The Gray-Haired Child, shadows still cast over his face, clapped without making a sound.

"I was correct to ensure you and I met each other, after all."

◆

"My reason for cooperating with Hiroto the Paradox? Weird to ask that now."

There was one other visitor who had come to the old town that day.

A plump man with an impressive camera hanging from his neck, and who shouldered a wooden box on his back.

Yukiharu the Twilight Diver walked through the alleyway alone. There wasn't any sign of someone to converse with.

"Because it's safe."

"Safe?"

A voice replied from the wooden box. It wasn't even big enough to carry a baby.

"'Never dies no matter what battlefield he ends up on'...some people talk about me like that, see, but even I'm making sure to calculate which power and what position I need to be in to remain safe and go around doing my thing, and that's how I've survived. If I'm going to expose Aureatia scandals, then I'm gonna get better protection if I'm doing that under the Gray-Haired Child, right?"

"Hmmm... You're a journalist, but you don't actually have any political principles, huh?"

"Whaaat? Listen, being a journalist with political principles sounds real nice and impressive, sure. But it means that those people are using their coverage to change society in a way that's convenient for them, right? There were a lot of guys in that position, actually. I don't want to be lumped in with them."

"You of all people are saying that…? You're using false coverage to manipulate people, aren't you?"

"But it's not false, I'm telling you."

Yukiharu's work for the day still wasn't over. He needed to propagate information.

From here he would go through several trade districts and finish laying the groundwork before the start of the tenth match.

Hiroto the Paradox's request was precisely for a news report that turned a lie into reality.

"If it becomes the real deal in the end, it's not actually a lie, don't you think? Even supposing it is a lie, I'm a doing the crime for fun, not any political reason, so I'm essentially innocent."

"Pretty sure it's more heinous than that…"

"Why? I'm not doing it maliciously at all, though."

Reporting on the truth that no one in the world had arrived at yet, and covering news in a way that made those who didn't know the truth panic, were, in Yukiharu's mind, two sides of the same coin.

As a result of working under Hiroto the Paradox, Yukiharu had a grip on what was, in some senses, the greatest secret this world had to offer. The identity of the True Demon King. The identity of the True Hero. He didn't want to announce all this, and fling the whole world into chaos.

On the other hand, there was a matter that Yukiharu himself was pursuing.

"Besides, if this report succeeds, we'll finally be able to get to the *real* reporting…"

Yukiharu licked his lips.

From his investigation up until now, he knew the target's location, who they were with, and the goal to their actions.

Nevertheless, Yukiharu the Twilight Diver always wanted even more information beyond all that

The target was under extremely strict protection, but the day of the tenth match, when the mass uprising would kick off, was guaranteed to create an opening.

"It'll make us able to get inside the National Defense Research Institute directly."

CHAPTER 12 Secret Detention Facility

The sporadic gunshots echoing outside the mansion had begun to subside.

The decisive battle to sway the power balance in Aureatia was on its way to its conclusion.

"It's ending already? Too bad."

Aureatia's Twenty-Second General Mizial the Iron-Piercing Plumeshade's current living circumstances weren't necessarily uncomfortable. It was definitely different from what he was used to when compared to the mansion he lived in, and he was worried about the servants he had left behind. Nevertheless, the food was quite high-class, and he could freely use the bath whenever he wanted.

More than that, though, living his life while some stranger stood guard over him was something he had experienced several times when he was younger.

Mizial had been abducted and was currently under confinement.

The perpetrator's identity was a complete mystery. At first, they said they were working on behalf of the hospital where Kuuro had been admitted, but they had been brought to this mansion instead after boarding their carriage.

"Here I thought that maybe if this house got attacked, we could slip out in the uproar and escape. You bummed, too, Cuneigh?"

"Yeah..."

"Are you okay?"

"Yup...I'm fine..."

What worried Mizial more than anything was that Cuneigh the Wanderer was growing weaker by the day.

Mizial wasn't the only one being confined to this mansion. She was a rare homunculus, small enough to fit in the palm of one's hand, with both her arms swapped out for wings. She was also Kuuro the Cautious's partner.

Kuuro the Cautious's location still remained a mystery, and she even heard that Toroa the Awful died, so it was reasonable for her to be so terribly depressed.

Mizial's apprehension lay in the possibility that this situation wasn't the cause of her lack of energy.

Homunculus are said to have pretty short lives, right? I don't know what happens when they die, but...it could be they just lose their energy like this and slowly peter out.

Assuming that was the case, what did he have to do to save her?

Mizial himself, while a member of the Twenty-Nine Officials, was a sixteen-year-old child. He couldn't do anything except worry and encourage her. Even if he could find a doctor somewhere that would go out of their way to treat a homunculus, it was more than he could ever hope for while imprisoned.

As such, Mizial had tried to escape several times by now. His thinking never went beyond wondering what would happen if he used force at the perfect moment, and all of his attempts had failed.

I don't care about the failures themselves at all. The fact my plans failed and I still have all my limbs means that these guys would be put out if I died or got injured, right? Then I've got nothing to lose *in just escaping...*

He had essentially unlimited time to think. Mizial the Iron-Piercing Plumeshade was dreadfully reckless, but when discounting this one factor, he still possessed the thinking abilities worthy of the Twenty-Nine Officials.

...I can assume they're either after money, or to use us as hostages. This has gotta be the third time...no wait, the fourth, I guess. The last time was back when I was ten, so I don't remember it too well... Since they haven't sent off my fingers or one of my eyes yet, it means that the kidnappers are threatening someone that that poses a danger to them, should they be offended. A powerful authority...or someone with military might on their side. There isn't anyone else in the Twenty-Nine Officials that would obediently listen to them over the safety of someone like me.

Mizial jolted up from the bed.

"Hey, Cuneigh. I bet Kuuro's alive, don't you?"

"Huh...?"

Cuneigh was laying almost perfectly flat in her birdcage bed.

"I think that since Kuuro's friendly with us, they figured if they captured us, he'd do what they asked of him. That and, just think about when they first contacted us."

He rattled on about his theory without waiting for any answer.

"If they had told us back then that Kuuro was dead, they couldn't have abducted us, right? Not knowing whether he was alive or dead means that they wouldn't be able to predict when his corpse might get found. So then, for them, the answer to that question *was never a mystery* to these guys. Yeah. Pretty likely chance that's what's going on."

"Really... If that's true then...that's great, huh..."

"...So c'mon, and cheer up!"

He flashed her a cheerful smile.

None of the problems before them had been resolved.

Mizial himself couldn't do anything but worry and encourage her.

While he was glad that Kuuro the Cautious was alive, if Mizial's theory was right, then him and Cuneigh were being used as hostages, and it meant that Kuuro was being forced to participate in something against his will.

It may have been the battle going on outside.

If only Toroa was around...

Strangely, when Mizial had been told Toroa the Awful had died, he hadn't felt an urge to cry. Apparently neither Toroa's body nor his enchanted swords had been found, but Mizial thought that he was probably truly dead.

He may have understood somewhere inside him that the conversation they shared that night was going to be their last.

There was a theory that Toroa the Awful, by plundering enchanted swords, had prevented several moments of conflict before they could happen.

Mizial hadn't admired Toroa the Awful because he believed in this theory, and it was dubious to think there was any meaning to his actions beyond pure slaughter.

Still though, if Toroa was here, he probably would've stopped this fight, too.

He may not have actually been Toroa the Awful. Still, he had been Mizial's friend.

Mizial thought so, even if Toroa had vanished somewhere on the edge of their world, and Mizial would never see him again.

"...Yup. We really gotta get outta this place."

After the two men had entrusted Cuneigh to him, Mizial wouldn't be able to face either Kuuro or Toroa the way he was now. If taking advantage of an attack on the mansion was going to be difficult, then what if he pretended it already had?

While it may have happened a while back, there had been gunshots on the main street right outside the window. He was going to make it seem like he had been hit with a stray bullet by breaking the window and cutting an artery with one of the glass fragments.

Abducting one of the Twenty-Nine Officials was an ambitious crime, so it was unlikely that the guard stationed to watch them could decide whether to let Mizial die or not. In that case, their only option, with Mizial's massive blood loss, would be to take him to a hospital, right?

The problem then, is how do I make the glass fragments from the window scatter inside… I could take the glass off the wall clock and try to use that. The gunshot was a while ago, so I can't immediately shout and call for help. If I pretend that I was severely wounded the moment I got shot, so much that I couldn't even call out for help…that might really make the rescue team panic. Next question is how long I can live after cutting a vein, I guess. And whether those guys will come by on their patrol within that timeframe…

Mizial knew that the abductors made their patrols on a purposefully irregular schedule. Even if he executed the escape plan, it would still be a gamble, with Mizial's very life on the line. Nevertheless, Mizial began removing the glass on the wall clock without any hesitation whatsoever.

"Cuneigh, this time it's gonna succeed for sure! I just had a great idea!"

"Mizial…"

There was a cracking sound.

Mizial hadn't broken the window glass. The noise came from the first floor, in a different room.

More out of curiosity than caution, Mizial's hand stopped moving forward with his plan.

"What was that?"

The sound of glass shattering didn't continue after that. In its place, *wham* and *thwap* sounds, like smacking something heavy and wet, rang out in quick succession.

This then made Mizial grow cautious. While strange, he felt these where the kinds of sounds one heard on the battlefield.

"...Cuneigh. Stay quiet."

Footsteps were approaching in the hallway.

Holding the glass from the wall clock in his hand, Mizial concealed his breathing and waited.

"Are you there, Mizial?" A man's voice called out, followed by two knocks on the door.

"I've come to rescue you. I won't harm you, so please come out here."

...This voice.

Mizial relaxed his guard and went out into the hallway on his own.

He had a feeling he knew who the voice belonged to.

"Uh, so tell me... What're you doing here, Enu?"

"Is it inconvenient for me to be here?"

A man in a bowler hat, both eyes open wide like an owl.

Aureatia's Thirteenth Minister, Enu the Distant Mirror. He and Mizial weren't especially close with one another, and his government post wasn't involved with handling these sorts of abduction incidents. It was baffling to Mizial on many levels.

"...Well, I mean..."

Mizial peered down the hallway. The scene was far beyond what he imagined.

The hallway guards were all dead, their heads smashed open. The ones downstairs all must have been wiped out, too.

"You don't do this sorta stuff, Enu."

"Perhaps I can. The facts to allow for such conjecture are there."

While it looked like there were bullet holes left in the walls, Mizial hadn't once heard the sound of a gun.

There was no way Enu could have slaughtered this many thugs all by himself. What exactly had happened while Mizial and Cuneigh weren't looking?

"It's just as impossible as ever to figure out whatever the heck you're thinking."

"I don't really intend to hide anything, though. In any case—"

With his emotionless, enigmatic eyes still open, Enu titled his head ever so slightly.

"You need to escape from here as soon as possible. That's why I'm here."

◆

One thousand, two hundred meters to the south of the mansion where Mizial the Iron-Piercing Plumeshade was imprisoned...

There was a tall, soaring clock tower that seemed to look down on the city.

Although there was a tiny silhouette sitting on the summit of the tower, almost none of the people crowding on the surface far below could see him.

The man was wrapped pell-mell in bandages meant solely to hide his burn wounds.

Kuuro the Cautious.

"Four from the building across the street. They sensed something strange happened and are coming to reinforce..."

Kuuro pulled back the bolt on his sniper rifle.

It wasn't one of this world's muskets—it was a Haenel RS9.

A sniper rifle from the Beyond supplied by Iriolde's camp.

The gunshot rang out from atop the clock tower.

"That leaves two."

It meant that he had finished off two of the targets simultaneously with one bullet.

Kuuro the Cautious's Clairvoyance possessed a downright absurd sensory range, as well as an omniscient precision, capable of parsing all the phenomena that occurred in this sensory range. This didn't just stop at foreseeing his enemy's placement and movements, with his aim and the trajectory of the bullets he shot being no exception.

"One tripped over a body. One, stopped in his tracks, is on guard. The front-facing third floor window. Next to it. He's going to look at the building diagonally out in front...now."

He pulled the trigger once more and shot his faraway target dead.

All of the guards in the mansion imprisoning Mizial and Cuneigh had all been shot dead, but Mizial hadn't heard a single gunshot. The reason was simple—*they were from a range too far for the gunshot to reach him.*

Kuuro had pierced through a window with his initial shot, killing the first guard, and then afterwards, continued to fire through the initially broken window, disposing of all the guards by making his bullets ricochet through the inside of the building.

At this point...there's nothing to think twice about. It's the same.

Now that he was killing, it wasn't any different from his old job.

He recalled that the fact he hadn't killed anyone since he regained his Clairvoyance during the Particle Storm battle was much more of an anomaly in Kuuro's life.

That naïveté had given Aureatia, Iriolde, and Obsidian Eyes an opening to leverage against him.

From now on, he wasn't going to be naïve. In accord with his murderous ire, he would pull the trigger on the foes that hindered him.

"Obsidian Eyes. The same goes for you."

Right now, Kuuro the Cautious was fighting united with Enu the Distant Mirror of his own accord.

The purpose was revenge upon Obsidian Eyes. As well as the capture of Linaris the Obsidian.

CHAPTER 13 Catastrophe

The course of the battle on the royal palace grounds had been completely decided.

Kyaliga the Music Reed, general of the rebel army, had been crushed, with close to half of the squad he commanded being killed and driven back in a rout.

Yaniegiz the Chisel, Yuca the Halation Gaol, Dant the Heath Furrow. Already Aureatia's greatest elite military officers were even utilizing enchanted swords and magic items to defend the palace. This wasn't because their enemy was Kyaliga the Music Reed's large battalion. Nor did it mean that if they could have defeated the enchanted swords or magic items, displaying their full power moments prior, Kyaliga's battalion would have been able to win.

It simply meant one thing—no matter how much fighting power Kyaliga could have attacked with, even if they shelled and bombed them with the technology of the Beyond, their enemy had more than enough means at their disposal to outdo it all.

Bent down upon the ground, tears poured down Kyaliga's cheeks.

"You should be ashamed…! Wicked traitors, turning your back on the Kingdom…!"

"Enough of your blithering," Dant spat out, still thrusting his blade at Kyaliga.

Dant's sword wasn't an enchanted one. It was a completely ordinary longsword. Even then, he was fast enough with it to instantly decapitate Kyaliga if he made any suspicious movements.

"Aureatia was established in accord with King Aur's dying wish. To ensure that without an heir of his own, the Central Kingdom wouldn't come to an end after his passing, he adopted Queen Sephite from the United Western Kingdoms, and the new metropolis that was built to take the people of both Kingdoms equally is the Aureatia before you."

"Wh-which one of us...is really blithering on here...*sniff*... The winner...always creates a convenient version of history..."

"You'll get more than enough time to talk later."

He felt it was inexcusable.

Dant the Heath Furrow was a palace guardian who had loyally served Queen Sephite, joining her in crossing from the United Western Kingdom to Aureatia.

Why couldn't this man even imagine what Sephite might be feeling, having tasted the tragedy of the True Demon King while still young, and shouldered with the heavy responsibility of governing an unknown land as the last surviving member of the royal family? All without anyone close to her to confide in and while enduring occasional slander saying she was a usurper of the crown?

The greatest crime of the attacks on the royal palace, starting with Kyaliga the Music Reed himself, wasn't the crime of rebelling against the royal family. Their crime was pointing their blades at a just barely eleven-year-old girl with no fighting strength of her own.

"I have to say, that was some real valorous work there, Lord Dant."

A man with a wiry physique grinned ear to ear from afar. Aureatia's Ninth General, Yaniegiz the Chisel.

"Though, I was planning on whittling them down here and there on my own you see, thinking that it wasn't worth disturbing you over. They put up such a feisty fight, I wasn't able to stop them."

"Don't talk like you mean that. You made sure to say 'two from the Twenty-Nine Officials' because you knew I was on my way to make it three."

A man from a poor background and known as Rosclay's right-hand man. Dant truly despised this man, but it certainly wasn't because of Yaniegiz's humble background.

Yaniegiz was part of the reformation faction helmed by Rosclay. A group who planned to hold the Sixways Exhibition and use the hero's name to depose Queen Sephite. As part of the Queen's faction, Dant had been burned by them many times.

One example was during the battle against the Old Kingdoms' loyalists who had captured Toghie City, when in contrast to Dant, who was deployed on the front lines, Yaniegiz had holed up in Imag City at the rear, and never sent out reinforcements despite Dant's repeated requests. Hiroto the Paradox analyzed it as an attempt to rout a part of the Queen's faction, reducing their military presence and voice in the government, and Dant's view on it had largely been the same.

Beyond just their politically poor relationship, the man personally irritated Dant, too, lacking character in his words and actions, and maliciously ridiculing his enemies. In any case, they didn't get along.

Even regarding this latest strengthening of the royal palace's defense structure, the proposal had come right before the day of the tenth match, by the reformation party. Yaniegiz must have done so in order to assert that it was the *reformation party* that protected the royal palace from attack.

In terms of their intent to rebel against the Queen, the reformation and this Kyaliga the Music Reed are essentially one in the same... Even worse, there's a chance that I'm the same, too.

While it may have simply been how the battle in Toghie City had ultimately played out, he had still allowed Hiroto the Paradox and the Free City of Okafu into Aureatia's borders and was giving them the opportunity to take over the kingdom.

Of course, if he hadn't gotten assistance from the Gray-Haired Child, the Queen's faction would have certainly lost and died out. It was likely that Dant, too, would have been removed from the playing field by some means before the second round. Be that as it may have been, warping his own convictions to win a political battle had brought him nothing but pain.

He also couldn't help but feel disgusted that he slowly began to see Hiroto the Paradox and Zigita Zogi the Thousandth as some kind of comrades-in-arms.

Dant, still with a look of iron, silently stopped the bleeding from Kyaliga the Music Reed's cut, and finished restraining him.

Kyaliga had moaned and groaned about royal lineage and the justice in this rebellion, but Dant ignored it all.

"Seems like the fighting has died down a bit, doesn't it?"

Yaniegiz squinted his eyes and gazed far off into the city.

The all-out war between two large factions competing for hegemony appeared to come to an unsatisfying end, like a flame withering out right as it began to burn.

It meant that the reformation faction had won.

Their power had grown stronger still. From here on out, the Sixways Exhibition would function entirely under the control of a single faction, too. Dant's small consolation was the fact that his battle to swing the pendulum had finished without spilling the blood of the people, and with the Queen safe.

"...Lord Dant. You must've realized it by now, right?"

"What're you talking about?"

"I'm talking about if Queen Sephite can govern Aureatia...and if she will be able to *stay safe* until she finally becomes able to. With this, all of her political opponents have completely vanished. That said... don't you think that someday, the terror of the True Demon King that's been carved into the people's hearts is bound to lead to the Queen's ruin, too?"

"..."

Those who knew of eras prior might have called the present age abnormal.

An age where perfectly normal citizens felt scared of something deep down in their hearts, avoiding conflict, oppressing the Order who preached morality, and going wild for these public slaughters done under the name of "true duels."

The fear toward those with power was out of control. The True Northern Kingdom had perished through an uprising of the people, deemed a revolution. Lithia, plunging into the depths of war and strife, as well as Mage City, retaliating against Lithia, and even Alimo Row, their oppression of the Order ending in a massacre, all displayed a fate guided by the terror of the masses.

"And you're saying *you* control this fear? Real conceited lot, aren't you?"

"Rosclay is doing that."

The city fire was dying down.

"Those who know how Rosclay fights may think that he's the only one among all the hero candidates without some special power of his own, but they're wrong. Rosclay *alone* has the power. To bring the people's hearts together and quell their fear. It's what's Rosclay's been doing this whole time."

"Influence over the people's hearts is a combination of things stemming from a balance of many factors. I think it is impossible to want the reason why to come solely from Rosclay's existence. Abolishing the monarch is bound to destroy the current equilibrium."

"We will be able to keep the Queen alive and make her step down from the throne. The forces likely to prop up the Queen and defy the government have been all cleaned up now... The throne's surely a heavy burden at Queen Sephite's age. You must agree, Lord Dant, that it would be better to go with her back to her Western Kingdom homeland and live a peaceful life."

This is just an excuse. I cannot go along with a pretext that's telling me to simply betray her. *No matter how one tries to explain it away, betrayal is* still *betrayal... I alone need to be the Queen's ally until the end.*

If he switched over to the reformation party, then everything might take a turn for the better. However, that choice would mean he was betraying Queen Sephite, Hiroto the Paradox, and himself, having supported them both up until now.

Dant opened his mouth to give his refusal.

"Is Sephite out somewhere?"

A young girl was next to him.

"—?!"

"...What...?!"

Green clothes and blond hair tied into pigtails high on her head. An elf.

This young girl had broken through to the interior of the royal palace, with its impenetrably strong defenses, and was questioning two of Aureatia's Twenty-Nine Officials like she was making idle small talk.

"You two work in the royal palace? What happened here?"

Dant noticed a strange phenomenon.

Yuca the Halation Gaol's forces, battling in the rear, had gone unnaturally quiet.

How had military officers like Dant and Yaniegiz failed to notice that?

Or perhaps, had it happened in a split second, without giving either of them the chance to?

"You..."

Yaniegiz's eyes opened wide.

He wasn't readying his deadly magic tool, Mote Nerve Arrow. Dant could tell that this wasn't because he had been late to react, but because his combat experience was stopping him.

It was telling him that if he showed this foe any intention to fight, it was highly likely *he would immediately have the tables turned against him.*

"Kia... The young girl from the fourth match..."

"World Word," the girl replied in annoyance. "Kia the World Word. I'm not some kid without a second name, so you'd better be sure to use it."

The unidentified Word Arts caster who had nearly disabled Rosclay the Absolute for life in the fourth match.

Able to produce any and all phenomena with a single word, and rendering any and all attacks against her, including surprise attacks she wasn't even conscious of, ineffective. Dant didn't understand how she possessed such a power, nor how Elea the Red Tag had managed to discover an exceptional creature like her.

"Why're you asking about the Queen's whereabouts?"

"Who cares why! I should ask *you* what's up with you guys. There's people *dead* in front of the bridge! All that blood…fingers and ears scattered about all over…"

"My name is Dant the Heath Furrow, Aureatia's Twenty-Fourth General. I'm part of the Palace Guard."

Dant walked two steps.

"…Give me a real answer."

"I do intend on answering your question."

After he walked, Dant stood with his sword in a low stance. In contrast to Yaniegiz who remained still, wary of instant death, Dant purposefully took an offensive stance.

Even assuming I fail to kill her, I can show Yaniegiz what Kia's method of attack is. If I can just give him an opening to get a hit in with the Mote Nerve Arrow…

"Dant." Yaniegiz murmured behind him. A restraining tone. "Yuca's entire squad has been defeated."

"Well, I put them all to sleep." Kia was plainly irritated.

Despite the sword held at the ready right in front of her—or perhaps because she hadn't registered it as being trained on her to begin with, Kia boldly took her eyes off Dant, and turned around.

"They were all fighting in front of the royal palace, so I put them to sleep. Making all those people fight for no good reason, it's so stupid… Does Aureatia really like war that much?"

An immature child. Dant couldn't pick up any behavior or air that was indictive of the strong and mighty.

His senses of danger weren't working. Dant couldn't help thinking that if he simply raised his sword up, without waiting for Kia to make her move, it would end everything.

However, the fact that she had made it this far…

"That can't be it."

Yaniegiz picked up on it one beat ahead of Dant.

In front of the royal palace… The battle in the central city had concluded silently, far faster than anticipated.

"D-did…did you do the same thing all the way here?"

"So what?"

Kia the World Word was in a bad mood.

It was because she continued to see scenes of fighting and slaughter while she headed for the royal palace.

The monster feared bloodshed and took precautions.

"I…I came all this way because I've got something I wanna ask Sephite! If she's the one who ordered you to do all this, then—"

"S-Sephite…is a demon king!"

Someone screamed at their feet. Kyaliga the Music Reed.

His continued vigorous struggling inside his restraints had made his gag slip off.

"H-huh…? What's with him?"

"*Hic*… The chaos of war continues even after the demon king's death! The Sixways Exhibition, and this rebellion…! That's because Sephite, *sniff*, a bloodthirsty self-proclaimed demon king, reigns, so—"

The rambling words spoken with a scream suddenly stopped.

Dant slashed Kyaliga's back as he crouched down without a moment's hesitation.

The blood throughout his body was startingly cold.

"Shut up."

"Dant! What're you…"

It all happened in a second. Dant heard Yaniegiz's reproachful reply. It wasn't a problem. Dant wanted to say it was the right thing to do.

He couldn't let Kyaliga say anything more in front of Kia.

Kia herself tried to rush over to Kyaliga, his spine deeply torn up.

Dant lined up his breathing, and slashed Kia's lower leg.

"Hey—"

Right as Kia said those words, the longsword should have passed right through her leg.

He missed his mark. Right before he made contact, a clearly unnatural force field turned it aside.

"*Heal*."

"......!"

When she put a hand on Kyaliga, his back and the wound on his arm regenerated instantly.

Unbelievably fast and precise, to the point it was questionable if it was actually Life Arts or not.

"*Sniff*...*hic*, *ahhhh*, King Aur..."

"*Stop*."

Far before he could make his next move, Kia halted Dant's movements with a single word.

From his neck down, his legs, and his arms, none of them budged, as if his body wasn't his own anymore.

"...*Repel*. You—you tried to slash me, didn't you?"

Then, once everything was over, Kia recited her Word Arts *from two moves earlier.*

I have no way to win.

She violated and transgressed any and all of the laws that built their world.

Yaniegiz was right. I shouldn't have tried to fight.

If Rosclay the Absolute wasn't able to win, then no one could. Yaniegiz had understood that, and thus, hadn't moved.

Dant's loyalty consequently made him react incorrectly. And now, he was going to die.

"So you were trying to kill me, were you? Why did those soldiers die?! If Sephite had a proper handle on things, that wouldn't have been necessary, right?!"

"King Aur... My life...just through your words..."

Kia interrogated Dant, and Kyaliga was groaning.

It may have been his instincts as a soldier that made him notice that something was off as Dant stood there, prepared for death.

Kyaliga the Music Reed still remained crouched on the ground. Why would he need to do that if his wounds were already healed?

"Yaniegiz! Kia the World Word!" Dant shouted, still prohibited from making any movement.

Iriolde's army possessed weapons of the Beyond.

"Get down!"

"Huh? What now..."

"...To your loyal retainers..."

—Kyaliga sent out a Bomb Golem ahead of him and charged toward the royal palace.

And if he had planned on joining in on this suicide attack from the very start...?

Dant's world was plastered white in explosive flames and a flash of light.

CHAPTER 14 Mad Passion

His consciousness was hazy.

He felt the inside of his body boiling hot.

He knew that he was approaching death.

Even then, Jelky still needed to keep on working.

While the fighting which had broken out all across Aureatia was settling down, it wasn't yet over. He needed to prioritize preventing any fires or building collapses generated from the fighting, as well as any secondary damages from the uprising while taking the appropriate measures against the damage that had already been caused.

Plenty of information came in to him at the command headquarters, set up in the Central Assembly Hall's First Communications room, but he prioritized matters involving people's lives and property above all else.

For this operation, Jelky wasn't only limited in the number of other Twenty-Nine Officials he could get to help, but also restricted to about half of the bureaucrats he normally tasked with assisting his work. Since this operation was all to ensure the reformation faction was the final victor, he couldn't expect any sort of help from the personnel in other factions. Even among their own faction, they needed to exclude those they suspected of getting any support from Iriolde.

Rosclay the Absolute, in accordance with his second name, executed thc plan with perfection.

He couldn't afford for any imperfections or mismanagement on the ground to ruin everything.

I've...been forcing pain on them.

Coughing into his handkerchief, it came away mixed with dark red blood.

The nausea had continued for a while, so he figured it was bleeding from his stomach.

On both the citizens of Aureatia, and others besides them as well. At this stage, I can't let this much pain stop me. Among those who I have sacrificed to get here, there were some who lost absolutely everything, and those who ultimately died—this is nothing. *I'm merely exhausting all that I have to keep moving, just for today. Compared to everything else, this is nothing.*

With the latest report, three new fights had broken out while six others had come to an end.

That may have been all the army was doing. All of the fighting was happening within Aureatia.

Buildings collapsed, bridges burned, factories had accidents, railroads cut off, roads jammed with traffic, an aristocrat's mansion with twelve people locked inside was attacked, gangs of robbers looted merchants, the Old Kingdoms' loyalists were spotted, the evacuation order was issued, then lifted, residences were destroyed to prevent the spread of fire, food stores were pillaged, deserted soldiers had become bandits, unknown weapons were being used, a belltower collapsed, poison flowed in the river, constructs had appeared, applications were submitted to utilize offensive magic items, an explanation was given for mistaken orders, the information from four reports prior was amended, people died, died, sustained injuries, and then died some more.

Even then, *this could all be dealt with.*

During a similar state of emergency, when Alus the Star Runner attacked, Hidow the Clamp had regretted making the incorrect choice among many different options, but Jelky always left himself the leeway to judge as he carried out his business.

He couldn't let there be any fatally erroneous responses with people's lives on the line. Though Jelky was set to bear all the responsibility in the end, Aureatia's blunders would be tied to Rosclay the Absolute's blunders.

"The Jeanes Iron Bridge fire is being contained. However, a specialist opinion says it's highly likely the bridge's integrity might be degraded, and continued traffic restrictions may prove necessary—"

"Master Jelky! Citizens are gathering in Orde Old Town! The soldiers on the scene are responding, but they appear to be protesting the cancellation of the tenth match—"

"The details behind the unknown weapon used in the Yatmaees Garrion attack have become clear! Going by the name of M120 mortar, the chances this has been deployed to the other squads in the rebel army is—"

"Emergency! Emergency! Please prioritize this!"

"—"

Jelky rushed to the operator's side without saying a word.

In this situation, the stamina needed simply to speak was too precious to waste.

"The palace...defenses...have..."

The operators were beginning to tire, too.

They needed time to steady their breathing to convey the information.

"Th-they've been wiped out. The Palace Guard squad is unconscious! Master Yaniegiz and Master Dant were caught in an unexplained explosion, their status unknown! They've already requested backup from the Aureatia army, sir..."

Jelky felt his consciousness fading, but he stood firm.

"U-understood."

The royal palace. Was the Queen safe?

Were Yaniegiz and Dant dead?

A self-proclaimed demon king. Or someone among the hero candidates. Although the Iriolde Army operation was led by Haade, clearly something that exceeded their estimations had happened— He cut off his thoughts there. It wasn't Jelky's job to think through things that far.

"Coordinate with the Aureatia army to take charge of the response. If there was an explosion, it's highly likely that civilians nearby heard it, too. I want us to spread our information before speculations run rampant. Say that an explosion was caused by the fighting in the Shinag Second Administrative District, directly bordering the royal palace grounds, and we're sending in more troops to strengthen the palace defenses. Tap the Information Bureau for help. I think the economic losses from royal palace grounds damages themself will be low, but on the civilian side, we're likely to get a number of inquiries from the nobility. Unlike when dealing with other citizens, there are large political ramifications with any loss in our image. Thus, no more than three personnel with at least three lineages or more should be sent out to deal with them. We can share some amount of the information to convince them as necessary, but for the truth of the attack on the palace and the state of the damage, the nobles should be given the false information mentioned earlier. Only share this incident with personnel of two lineages and above."

After passing on his judgment as administrative leader, Jelky shut his eyes tight.

He wouldn't think of anything unnecessary.

Jelky needed to throw all of his remaining energy into responding to this problem.

The royal palace might fall. Everything might end up being for naught.

A desperate torn seam.

◆

The army command room was red.

Even after Iriolde and the others' corpses were thrown out like garbage, the excessive crimson stains plastered to the walls and floor hadn't been cleaned, and Haade the Flashpoint commanded the entire operation from this blood-drenched command room.

Hidow the Clamp didn't really know if it truly should have been called an operation at all.

It was an abnormal war, as if one person was moving the pawns on both sides of the game board, and trying to see just how efficiently, and with as few casualties as possible, they could slaughter *just one side.*

"It's over."

Leaning his head deep against the backrest, Haade faced the ceiling.

It was the chair that Iriolde the Atypical Tome had been sitting in at the beginning of the operation.

At first, when this grand coup d'état had been planned, Iriolde's Army had been one.

However, consolidating the chain of command ahead of time, Haade had secretly divided this force in two. Those stubbornly wishing to resist Aureatia, starting with Iriolde's personal soldiers. And those who obeyed Haade and switched sides over to Aureatia, Aureatia army under Haade's command first and foremost among them. The former was eradicated, with only the latter left behind.

Regardless of whether they had been his own subordinates the day prior, he annihilated any who opposed Aureatia. Even as the city streets were turned into a battlefield, he restricted the harm to citizens to be as minimal as possible.

Despite being a senior citizen close to seventy years old, the actions and decisions Haade made when he took command were nimbler and shrewder than those of a young lad in his teens. It was as though this bloodstained room bestowed the old general with limitless vitality.

"...This was a good war. The kind no one's ever waged before, all to bring total bring total annihilation to their allies. There were a bunch of unavoidable choices, and unexpected turns, but...it was quite an interesting war, eh, Hidow?"

"I got no clue what you're going on about."

Hidow couldn't move. Until absolutely everything was over, he remained there unable to exit from this terrible room or turn his eyes away from it all.

"...You're insane. These soldiers, they idolized you so much... believed in you, and you just go and kill them? Hell, even Iriolde's men... look, I don't get it, but they had to be fighting with some amount of conviction or righteousness in 'em. How can you just stand there...? You don't feel guilty at all?!"

"Nope. It's a little late to talk about what someone believes in, or what's right, don't you think? This whole world's been smashed to hell and back by the True Demon King."

"......"

"Hidow. You're brilliant, but lack madness. Some part of your brain wants to believe that logic and interests mean anything. Isn't that why back in Lithia, Taren the Punished tripped you up? I showed you how I worked today because I figured you'd get something outta the experience. You'll need to keep Aureatia moving even after I'm gone."

"Come off it…! I may've been dragged into all this by force, but I was still treated like part of the camp's leaders here. Forget moving Aureatia, I'm a serious criminal."

"Right now the royal palace grounds've been attacked, and the defenses there are destroyed. I'll give you a new squad, so bring them along to the royal palace. Don't care whether the Queen lives or dies, but if we outline it all as a former Twenty-Nine Official investigating the rebel army from within and poaching their best of the best to *rush to the royal palace's defense*, that'll be plenty enough for a pardon. I've already filled the other side in, so you don't worry about any skirmish if you show up with troops."

"You think I believe you? You're the one who told me to watch you and learn."

"*Gwah-hah-hah-hah…* If I wanted to kill you, I would've done so from the start—but I doubt that excuse'll convince you. I was just talking about how interests and logic *absolutely aren't* at play, and all. Hell, doesn't make a difference to me… You're free to stay here and become a criminal, or leave and return to being a bureaucrat. Up to you."

"Putting it that way makes you sound just like that old fart Iriolde, you know that? He rub off on you while you were all buddy-buddy?"

Nevertheless, Hidow likely had no choice but to head to the royal palace.

Haade's proposal was probably so he could save his own subordinates with a pardon after they had penetrated into the core of Iriolde's army. In addition, the Aureatia Assembly were bound to need Hidow's help to process the aftermath of a coup d'état on this scale.

Everyone and his damn mother, using me however they want…

"…Oh right, this is all assuming you're going to return to Aureatia's side, but there's something else I want you to check for me."

Haade raised up his head, as though suddenly remembering something.

"Quit acting as if this is all a done deal."

"*Gwah-hah-hah*. Don't be like that. I want to know what Yuno the Distant Talon is up to."

"Yuno the Distant Talon... Oh, her?"

The Nagan scholar who claimed to have discovered Soujirou the Willow-Sword. Hidow himself had met her just once, during the plot to assassinate Taren. The young girl hadn't left any deeper impression with him than that, and he probably would have never remembered she existed if her name hadn't come up here.

"Weren't you supposed to be looking out for her? Can't you just get one of your other guys to tell you what she's doing?"

"As a matter of fact, Yuno is out of my reach right now. In the middle of the third match, a contact in charge of the correspondence about this operation was attacked. No one knows who did it, but the letter was probably read. From that day on, I haven't heard a word from Yuno. I made sure it wasn't easy to decode, but for a Nagan scholar, it's possible she deciphered it just from the words used in the message."

"Whaaat?! Why'd you keep that under wraps up until now?!"

Hidow couldn't believe his ears.

If this information was leaked by the time of the third match, didn't that mean there had been the chance that this whole operation, one that Aureatia poured all their strength into, might've gotten derailed?

Hidow didn't understand Haade's intentions. *Did Jelky and Rosclay know this?*

"*Gwah-hah-hah-hah*... She may be totally inexperienced young lass that one, but she really resembles me... Might just be a real illogical monster. I wanted to check for myself, so I decided to tell her to *do whatever she wants* during the Sixways Exhibition. Barely a few days afterward, she stole information from my soldiers and ran…"

It was beyond the pale. Not just Haade, but Yuno, too.

There were creatures in this world who acted in ways common sense couldn't even imagine, and these types never failed to knock Hidow down toward an outrageous fate.

"Yuno the Distant Talon didn't have a single person at her back. There wasn't any chance that when she was at my side, she was acting as an undercover agent for some other power. What do you think she could've accomplished on her own? Did she manage to use this secret of ours she coincidentally got her hands on as a trump card? You think she managed to wage a war against something all to stick to this will of hers I caught glimpses of? Even if her chances were next to nothing, I want to think Yuno managed to do something, and I want to know what."

"……"

Hidow would have loved to interrogate every point of Haade's, but it was more than likely that wasn't what Haade was getting at right now.

Haade was bringing up Yuno the Distant Talon to test Hidow.

This command room was dyed deep in the smell and color of fresh blood. Iriolde the Atypical Tome lost because he hadn't been able to imagine the thinking of those with a different sense of values.

"The war you talk about…it's just killing. You didn't want to have a war that was settled before the fighting started, where you're just going through the motions to victory. That said though, pulling your punches has gotta be against what you believe, right? First of all, you were resolved to throw away everything, all for this day, and intended on doing everything in your power to win. All the more reason, really, why you decided to overlook a small little bombshell… You were testing your and Rosclay's luck."

"*Gwah-hah-ha-hah-hah*... See, you can do it after all, eh, Hidow..."

Haade the Flashpoint simply laughed.

He didn't say whether Hidow's thinking was right or wrong.

"...There was a report just now that Soujirou the Willow-Sword escaped from the military hospital, right? You think...that it was Yuno's handiwork?"

"Soujirou's still trying to fight, it sounds like. If he still thinks he's got it in him, now wouldn't that be exciting."

Impossible.

The chances that Yuno had set something up without anyone knowing, as well as the chances that Soujirou would be able to do anything from here on out, were next to zero. It was close to sheer fantasy, Haade's hopes included.

Aureatia had no intent to hold the tenth match, and Rosclay wouldn't fight with Soujirou. Even when taking into account the fact that Haade overlooked what Yuno was doing, he wasn't going to give Soujirou any further help. Since he had lost his sponsor, Soujirou would lose by regulation, without the match ever happening.

Even assuming he was trying to join up with some power, Soujirou had been admitted into the Romog Joint Military Hospital up until now, with no means to communicate with the outside. Escaping on one leg today, when it was impossible to know where weapons from the Beyond or magic items were flying about, was close to suicide. Far beyond just losing according to the tournament rules, it was highly likely he'd lose his life.

The completion of the death match was absolutely inconceivable.

Or maybe, can they do it...? Soujirou, Yuno.

Their enemy's name was Rosclay the Absolute. An unrivaled champion who even bested the omnipotent Word Arts caster, Kia.

Something capable of upsetting the logic and reason of "the Absolute."

CHAPTER 15 Border of Old [redacted] Prefecture

Back when he met Tsukayoshi, Soujirou hadn't known anything of war.

It was like a living creature being unaware of the air. No one perceived something that naturally surrounded them from birth as a concept in and of itself.

All of the minia and weapons he encountered in his daily life generally greeted him with murder in their eyes, and he thought defeating them was what it meant to live. It may have been fair for Soujirou to refer to Tsukayoshi Yagyuu as his master, in the sense that he corrected this misconception.

"Okay, listen." This Tsukayoshi Yagyuu said in exasperation. "You really go way too far, Soujirou..."

The memory was from when Soujirou had first cut down an M1 Abrams, while he had still been living in the Beyond.

Debris was piled high on both sides of the road, and he knew that this road was for tanks to pass through, corpses and carcasses violently brushed aside willy-nilly by the heavy machinery.

There a tank was stopped with a deep slash carved into it.

Soujirou's katana had torn the main battle tank's armor apart and slain all the passengers inside.

"Cutting up a tank's just nuts. There's something off about you, for real."

"You're the one who's weird here. You and that damn wavy

outfit of yours. 'Cause of that stupid getup, the enemy's always picking us out."

"Huh? My clothes have nothing to do with it. I'm over here trying to stop us from being spotted and you're always jumping right out in the fight! Why're you so gung ho about killing people?!"

Even in times like this, Tsukayoshi was obsessed with always wearing the same ratty old casual kimono. He wore a sword despite being unable to fight, he always acted self-important despite being a complete coward, and he was completely, utterly useless.

He claimed to be the last legitimate heir of the Yagyuu Shinkage-ryuu sword style, but Soujirou didn't even know about any sword style called Yagyuu Shinkage-ryuu to begin with. He couldn't tell what the truth was, but he figured there was a pretty high chance Tsukayoshi was lying.

"If the other side's raring to go, what's wrong with going out to get 'em myself? What else are you wearing the damn sword for, then?"

"Let me tell you, okay? That's not what Yagyuu's about, all right?"

Tsukayoshi roughly scratched his head. He seemed to hold some annoying, illogical philosophy when it came to fighting that was necessary for their survival.

"Sekishuusai Yagyuu even says, 'Knowing one word makes you the master of those who know none. It is not other styles you must defeat. You must surpass the self you were yesterday,' okay? Basically, it's better to avoid the fight entirely before you end up crossing swords, and attacking someone yourself is something only the lowest of the low do. Just 'cause you're a strong martial artist, using that strength just to take down those weaker than you means that you aren't really all that impressive. I guess, in the end, it's the guys that can incorporate the areas where someone else excels who get stronger, not the ones that just get the upper hand in the areas where they're already stronger..."

"Enough already."

The people that thought over this pointless, boring theory stuff in the middle of a fight must've all died in the process.

In a sense, Soujirou could understand now why Tsukayoshi was as weak as he was.

"I'm getting at something here, okay? Even I've got my own really talented aspects that you don't, so I just wish you'd respect that a little bit instead of deciding everything based on whether you can cut it down or not..."

"What, then?"

"......"

"What specifically are you so great at?"

"......"

Tsukayoshi was at a loss for words, and his eyes wandered all over the mountain of debris.

Tsukayoshi Yagyuu was weak. If Soujirou didn't send their foes packing, there's no telling how many times the man would have already died by now.

He wasn't skilled enough with a sword to brag about it. Even setting aside that, when compared to Soujirou, the same could be said for everyone else in the world, Tsukayoshi's technique didn't look like anything more than a grown man swinging around a stick with brute force.

"...Oh! Right here!"

Tsukayoshi pulled out a book from the mountain of rubble.

"Okay then, can you read? Your generation never properly learned to read, did it?"

"Nope, I guess I can't."

"Well, in any case, one thing is for sure, that when it comes to education, I've got a huge leg up on you."

"Is it useful at all?"

"......"

"From here on out, is reading or writing gonna be useful for anything?"

"I mean...sure it might not, but still!" Tsukayoshi shouted in the uninhabited wasteland and slammed the book to the ground.

In all likelihood, the writing and books of this country were never ever going to be useful for anything again.

All of the nation states of the world were trying to erase the very existence of this country. The terror of the young girl named Shiki Aihara had changed absolutely everything forever.

"Why do you even go on and on 'bout Yagyuu this and Yagyuu that? I told you I don't care about any of that stuff. Saying the same crap over and over again when a guy doesn't care about any of it is just being annoying."

"Why do you care? Not like you'll listen to me anyway..."

"What're you sulking for...?"

Soujirou was truly appalled by the attitude of this man over ten years his senior.

He had to make him give up on it forever, or the same thing was likely to play out over and over again.

"Gimme a reason. C'mon. I asked a question, so answer it."

"I mean... You're strong, Soujirou."

"Yeah, I suppose so."

Soujirou was aware of it himself. While slashing up the fighters or missiles flying through the sky was still a bit of a stretch, if he didn't have to include losing by default to those things, Soujirou had yet to see anything stronger than he was.

"It's such a waste! Why then aren't *you some grand master swordsman*, then?! You've got all the strength of the sorta swordsman you hear about in legends and fiction and stuff...anyone would want to be just as strong as you...! Act the damn part at least! Yagyuu swordsmen are super badass, okay?!"

"That's a super stupid reason..."

Soujirou grew more and more disgusted. With it, he was also fed up with listening to the same meaningless preaching all just to appease some sentimental middle-aged man he wasn't even related to at all.

"Fine, how 'bout you make an effort to get strong, then? I'll start by teaching the easy stuff to ya first."

"N-no way! Your teaching methods are way too dangerous, and there's nothing easy about it!"

"Who's the one who was going on 'bout learning from what someone excels at?!"

"Ah-hah! Sekishuusai's words! If you're acknowledging what he's saying, then I'm gonna take that to mean you'll learn Yagyuu Shinkage-ryuu, thank you very much!"

"So then tell what you're so damn great at, then?!"

"......"

"Say something, dammit!"

◆

Soujirou the Willow-Sword was wandering through a war-torn city.

This was the same atmosphere as the Beyond. The world where he was born and raised, countless soldiers baring their bloodlust at each other.

While he hadn't cut down any tanks along the way, he had cut down constructs and carriages.

Some appeared to be part of Aureatia's army, while others looked to be with some other power.

He didn't particularly mind. He simply cut down all the foes that sent attacks his way.

"*Geh, heh*… The ones who avoid fighting are the stronger ones, huh?"

Remembering these words from sometime in the past, he couldn't suppress a laugh.

Even if using his far greater might to defeat his enemies didn't lead him to true strength, Soujirou would continue fighting for all eternity.

"No damn way that's right. You gotta fight… If you don't, no one'll know who's actually stronger…!"

Soujirou wasn't walking the streets aimlessly.

He hadn't been completely idle after arriving in Aureatia, nor while he was in the hospital with more free time than he knew what to do with.

Soujirou had some grasp of the city geography. As long as he knew which streets to go down, he could reach the arena.

In the process, he would have to pass through several battlefields, but that was a trivial issue.

Corpses piled up on the edges of the avenues, cars crushed people, gunshots flew this way and that, and explosions went off. This very scene was, to Soujirou, part of a nostalgic way of life.

"I'm gonna fight… Rosclay. You aren't getting away from me…!"

All these people who had "true strength" for themselves just had to come and face him, then.

◆

Two days before the scheduled day of the tenth match.

Yuno the Distant Talon didn't go back into the carriage she had shared with Hiroto, instead parting with him in the old town.

Given what she had heard from Hiroto, there was somewhere she needed to go immediately.

Hiroto the Paradox was trying to kill Linaris. This operation was likely to be carried out on the day of the tenth match, too. Something was bound to happen at the mansion where Linaris was on bed rest.

Will I be able to make it there on my own? Aureatia is so vast...but I only barely remember the path to the mansion, and I don't even know how far public transportation will even take me.

Should Yuno manage to reach the mansion somehow, during these past two days, Hiroto had surely set up something that far outstripped Yuno's abilities. In the case of both Aureatia, and the Gray-Haired Child, the situation beyond Yuno was beginning to drastically shift.

Expelled from everything that hemmed her in, if she simply waited around, everything would come to an end.

Yuno herself was in a situation almost like Soujirou the Willow-Sword's.

Will Soujirou...

Hiroto said that he would force the match between Soujirou and Rosclay.

...actually fight in the tenth match?

Even if the match did occur that day, Yuno once again wouldn't be able to see his fight.

There was some part of her that hoped the match would just get postponed according to Aureatia's scheming. Seeing the conclusion to the revenge she wanted for herself would have certainly been some salvation to the version of Yuno from that day long past.

However, Yuno now understood it all after seeing Soujirou up close.

Soujirou got heartfelt enjoyment from being able to fight in the Sixways Exhibition.

Nothing about that would change, even if he knew the truth—that she had led him here to kill him.

Yuno gazed at the sky.

He probably always wants to fight.

A peaceful sky, ignorant of everything and anticipating the Sixways Exhibition match.

However, as long as one had the power to remain true to their will, like Hiroto and Soujirou, they could even turn an impossibility like holding a match against Rosclay into a possibility—

"...Wait."

Then, she suddenly realized.

The schemes Hiroto laid out weren't from some power of will to never give up.

He was trying to make Rosclay participate in the match, in a more concrete way that gave him no room to escape.

That was why he said *a joke like that* during his negotiations with the shop owner.

Matters that sounded like jokes, even to someone with full knowledge of Hiroto's intentions, like Yuno, would actually happen.

Assuming...that is the case... Even so...!

That scheme wouldn't be made into a reality. There was a decisive hole in the plan.

Which was why, even someone who knew Soujirou like Yuno did, hadn't noticed up until that very moment.

It may have been nothing more than a spark of unpredictability.

Yet, Yuno the Distant Talon had, without a doubt, through her own strength, touched on part of a shura's line of thought.

"Soujirou... Soujirou is going to have his match!"

Of course. To Soujirou the Willow-Sword, Yuno's talk of revenge had nothing to do with him at all.

Having the shura who wished for battle more than anyone else end without any fight at all was something that could not come to pass.

Yuno had wanted to make Soujirou fight.

She needed to head out to save Linaris's life without a moment's delay.

As such, there wasn't very much she could do in order to make Soujirou battle.

Yuno had to have already possessed the information she needed to lead her to the answer. Could she give him that answer without letting anyone else catch on?

"...Soujirou! Until I see the end with my own eyes..."

First, Yuno scratched a mark into a nearby fence.

A mark etched by Yuno's sharpened arrowhead.

"...you can't lose and die yet, you hear me?!"

CHAPTER 16 Ideal

With noon on the day of the tenth match closing in, the Blue Beetle had a full house.

The bartender, Tika, who had way too much free time that morning, was now overwhelmed with serving the abruptly growing number of customers.

He even had his childhood friend Nane helping, hurriedly weaving around the tables and taking orders.

"Hey, Tika! The customer over here says their food still hasn't come out yet! Hurry up and bring over some fried potato and sausage!"

"Whaaat? Didn't I just bring that out?! The line order's a total mess!"

There was a change to the scheduled tenth match. As such, everyone stopped making their way to the castle garden theater and had come all the way out to the old town.

"Okay then, buddy, how d'ya think Rosclay's gonna beat Soujirou?!"

"Gotta be with Word Arts! Sure Soujirou's probably a bit better with a sword, but Rosclay doesn't even need to get within range, he can use Force Arts to make his sword..."

The customers' conversations could be heard even from behind the counter.

"I'm not going to stand for a repeat of the fourth match, you hear me...?! I've thought for a while now that there's gotta be some people on the Aureatia Assembly trying to set Lord Rosclay up!"

"*Hee-hee-hee*! On that point, Soujirou's real suspicious ain't he, hmmm? He's a visitor from the Beyond after all. Way I see it, he's gonna use some strange sleight of hand to interfere with Rosclay!"

Everyone was having these sorts of conversations.

If Rosclay the Absolute was going to fight Soujirou the Willow-Sword, what sort of method would Rosclay use to win? How was Soujirou going to struggle before he lost? Just what kind of brilliant martial spectacle would they be treated to?

...Everyone here believes in Rosclay, don't they?

Iska believed in Rosclay, too.

She treasured him from the bottom of her heart.

However, maybe what he truly needed was those who didn't believe him.

Anyone and everyone depended on Rosclay the Absolute, and wasn't that why he was then forced to doubt himself?

...Rosclay.

The sickly Iska hadn't been counted among the restaurant's helpers.

If the match in the castle garden theater had been canceled, then Iska thought she might get the chance to see Rosclay fight for herself.

Since she hadn't bought a ticket, Iska didn't believe she had any right to, but in either case, all talk about spectator seats had completely evaporated.

Quietly passing through the middle of the raucous tavern, Iska went up the stairs to the surface.

◆

Rosclay the Absolute had an ideal he needed to achieve.

He first became aware of it himself on the very first day he was asked about what would follow after the Sixways Exhibition, the royal games where hero candidates were pitted against each other.

"Any threat that exceeds the limits of mankind needs to be destroyed," Jelky the Swift Ink explained in a corridor within the Aureatia Central Assembly Hall.

"Due to the calamitous True Demon King, we the minian races have grown far weaker. If an uncontrolled war breaks out, the kingdom will be dealt a hard blow that it will be impossible to recover from."

"...I understand what you're trying to say here."

They continued to walk the corridor as if continuing on with some meaningless chit-chat.

The power that Jelky indicated wasn't pointing to a simple violent strength.

Aureatia, the amalgamation of the three kingdoms, had a historically unprecedented number of enchanted swords and magic items, strong personnel who had survived the age of terror, and resources gathered together during the chaos of wartime.

Rosclay understood, too. They couldn't label such power as the intrinsic strength of the nation.

The power of numbers. The people themselves were the cells that constituted the organism of a nation.

"You're thinking that the *people* won't be able to handle any further war and strife."

The True Demon King had etched a persisting fear in the hearts of all the people.

The terror that drove those who confronted it insane and turned them toward destruction had weakened, but still definitely remained behind. Even now after the death of the demon king, this world continued to face in the direction of destruction.

"War and strife that involves the citizenry will breed a sudden outburst of madness. If that ever should happen, no means of intervention will be able to rectify it… The persecution of the Order proves it."

"……"

The people continued to unconsciously search for a direction to point their hostility. The Order, a massive organization that was close at hand, was the first to fall victim to it.

The series of policies meant to cut down the Order, the largest social welfare organization, normally would have been nothing but detrimental, even to Aureatia. Though they understood this, the situation *forced their hand.*

Though they had formed a system to protect the Order and widely dispersed an accurate understanding of the situation to the people, they had been unable to quench the fires of animosity once spread.

As the next best option, they needed to position the Order to take the brunt of criticism so that no hostility was pointed at the Aureatia Assembly and to control the outbreak of madness. That was the reason why, despite severing ties with the Order and cutting off their funding, they established new institutions to take over the same functions the Order had previously performed.

"Just like the Order… Do you believe by pointing the people's spears at the hero candidates in the royal games, we can regulate their hostility?"

"…That's what I hope. This world was saved, but it wasn't saved in the correct way. We need to make it known to the people just how mighty a presence felled the True Demon King. Right now, the power and authority of the Aureatia Assembly is tremendous—tremendous, and as a result, fragile. The Aureatian citizens fear us as well. Believing that this tremendous power could turn us into rulers who harm the populace…"

While they were diverting the spearhead of the people's ire, the spearhead itself didn't disappear.

Even assuming that this royal games concept Jelky spoke of was made into a reality, after the Order was annihilated and the hero candidates eradicated, it was bound to be the Aureatia Assembly to fall next.

"We need to dissolve the Twenty-Nine Officials before the inevitable destruction. We'll create a symbol that properly gathers their awe and dread—the hero—and using that power, we'll transfer over the sovereignty of Aureatia. Keep the sacrifices to the bare minimum, and reform the national framework. That is goal of this scheme."

"...Are you including the monarchy in that reform?"

"Yes. I want to convert Aureatia into a republic. As long as there is someone who maintains enormous power and authority, the people's insanity will eventually kill them. Thus, I believe it necessary to turn the people who control the country into popularly elected representatives with a term of office. The symbol of the hero will be used as the banner for this systematic shift."

An altruistic plan.

If it became reality, Jelky would lose everything he had worked to accumulate.

Jelky the Swift Ink was trying to protect Aureatia, gambling all of his existence, even more than Rosclay.

"I intend to be completely unscrupulous about the means and deceive whomever necessary. In order to begin, I need a comrade to share my ideal. Someone who selflessly does the utmost for Aureatia, who earns admiration as a champion, with capabilities that outshine all others... Rosclay. I hope that you will work together with me."

"...I..."

Rosclay lifted up his head and looked at Jelky. Deep into the man's eyes, glinting sharply behind his glasses.

They contained none of the selfish calculations Rosclay had.

I should turn him down. There isn't any guarantee that Jelky's idea will work out smoothly.

The eyes believed in Rosclay, no matter what answer he gave to the proposal. At least Rosclay thought so.

Which is all the more reason why he couldn't join in.

Rosclay's hopeless self-preservation would hinder the virtue and nobility of it.

Should the plan hit a setback, he might sacrifice Jelky and escape all on his own.

He wouldn't necessarily be able to fulfill the role Jelky desired of him exactly as he wanted.

It's impossible for me... Impossible.

Thus, the thought was nothing more than a passing breeze, faintly caressing the back of his mind.

A vision suddenly came to his imagination.

A world of blood-soaked champions protecting people in the middle of surging threats.

A world where a single lone hero who had erased all such threats stood.

...There was a truth that everyone knew, but purposefully never spoke out loud.

This world was brutal.

The whims of a dragon or gigant could turn a built-up civilization into a vacant wasteland.

Goblins and wyverns attacked settlements, mocking, killing, and eating people, starting first with the weak.

The natural principles that allowed for non-minian beings to exist birthed creatures of slaughter, like constructs.

The Word Arts bestowed to all creatures with a heart and soul were used for violence because of that very heart and soul.

The Wordmaker summoned visitors. The visitors wielded their power to bring destruction to the world.

This creaking, warping world had, at last, broken down from the terror brought by the True Demon King.

However, everyone must have thought it before that, and simply never said it.

This world was insane and absurd.

Good fortune, wisdom, or even love, wasn't supposed to be trampled over by something incomprehensible.

Even children on the frontier, far away from the Kingdom, who had never seen a visitor with their own eyes before, believed that somewhere there was the Beyond, a world that was impossible to prove existed.

Poems and plays passed on the battles of champions who existed long ago. Because people *wanted* champions.

Someone who was *an actual person* even as they slew threats that far surpassed the limits of mankind.

No one like that exists.

Rosclay had known that ever since he was child. He assumed everyone accepted this fact, and coming to terms with the world's brutality was how one became an adult.

What about now, though?

Even supposing they didn't exist—

"The hero..."

The word popped out of his mouth before anything about the Kingdom's or the people's future.

"Deciding on the sole hero, strongest of all... *Hah-hah-hah-hah.* The weaker they actually are, all the more convenient. That's why you called me out, isn't it?"

"...I will admit that you were the first person I thought of when it came to establishing this hero idol. However, I don't intend on making you shoulder everything. We need to come up with an even better plan."

"No. That's the best option. I'll take up the hero mantle."

Nothing like it existed.

However, it was possible to present it that way.

Since the hearts of the people who wanted a hero were genuine.

Rosclay the Absolute smiled and answered.

"I've always aspired to be one."

◆

The minia who defeated Tiael the Crushing all on his own.

Rosclay the Absolute was set up to be the young champion taking over for Oslow the Indominable.

He understood that defending the Royal City, a job his ignorant young self had thought was a safe one, was a responsibility that required a great deal of labor and pain, with an even greater fear of death always assailing him.

The Demon King's Army would attack several times, much more often than the citizens were informed about, and every time he killed these former minian races, Rosclay feared, and hoped the True Demon King wouldn't arrive this time, either.

He had vomited countless times, unbeknownst to anyone else.

The more he understood the number of citizens he was protecting, the ghastlier his nightmares became.

Frequently, he would dedicate himself to training that would wreck his own body. If his comrade Antel, one of the select few who knew Rosclay's circumstances, hadn't stopped him, he may have ended up dead somewhere.

Did I really need to go this far?

The question came into his head, over and over, together with the taste of blood spreading inside his mouth.

...Why did I...

It was necessary. It was something he decided himself.

Even as he reasoned to himself each time the doubts would surface, the regular functions a person was equipped with would continue to shout at him.

Every time his body broke, he would undergo Life Arts treatment, accompanied by pain.

He always plastered a smile on his face, never showing the people his pain and exhaustion.

His mother had died from an infectious disease. He hadn't been able to be there in her final moments.

He didn't have anything to show for it.

He had to become a champion. It was something only Rosclay could do.

He continued to play the champion role, like the ones immortalized in the poems Narta had told.

In his bloodstained life, the moment he remembered with the most clarity was from when he was seventeen.

A slave-trader carriage was flipped on its side atop the stone pavement.

"*Haah...haah...*"

Rosclay's breathing was ragged.

Even he didn't understand how a seventeen-year-old youth had been able to make a carriage roll over.

He could only explain it as strength exhibited in a feverish delirium. All he understood was that he had brandished his sword in a way unbecoming of a champion.

Rosclay knew his right shoulder was dislocated. The slave-traders likely were far too terrified to move any further, but should they pick up on his wound, the chances they would move to counterattack were high.

He took a deep breath. To ensure they didn't even figure out he was hiding his pain, he managed to bring his right hand along his sword, supported in his left hand, as if it was the correct form his stance was supposed to have.

"...Stay where you are and wait for your arrest. The Royal City will levy their judgment upon on you."

He declared this with his champion's smile.

Inwardly, he even wished he could cut them all down right then and there. The fact he was panicked enough to think so had bewildered him.

The cargo bed had been cut off from the rolled-over carriage. When he opened it up, the paupers that were set to be traded as slaves all looked at Rosclay at once.

"Everyone. There's no need to worry anymore."

Rosclay forcefully reined in his emotions and showed them a smile.

Blond hair that drew eyes to it, even in darkness, and a pair of red eyes.

His features were the one thing he had always been confident in.

"I shall protect you from everyone."

"Th-thank you very much..."

"Rosclay the Absolute… You really go this far, even for poor people like us…"

"I-I'm…saved…?"

Everyone was all right.

Thank goodness.

The incident had been just a kidnapping of poor people. Rosclay was fighting against far more terrifying matters than something like this and saving a far greater number of people. Nevertheless, it was the first time he had felt this way from the heart.

He had been able to prevent an irrevocable sacrifice.

Among the paupers there was the figure of a young girl of only seven years old.

"You…you saved me?!"

He made out her face when the crowd cleared.

She was a young girl with chestnut hair. Her big, clever-looking eyes gazed at Rosclay.

"Yes, that's right."

Rosclay smiled, to stop himself from showing what he felt inside.

His fight, constantly saving faceless citizens, had threatened to crush his heart.

However, each and every one among them had someone else who held them dear.

Like this girl, who had been there among the inconsequential people he had saved that day.

"…Thank you very much. My name is Iska."

"Is that so? What a wonderful name."

Obviously, it had been a good name. Rosclay was the one who had given it to her.

He was certain that this name was the only proof remaining that the young boy had been there that day.

Like a child, he had wanted to take pride in being able to save her, in successfully becoming a champion.

Keeping that pride to himself, Rosclay smiled.

Rosclay the Absolute couldn't let himself be a champion to one person only.

As long as someone was watching him, that was how he had to be.

The boy is… The self is… The man is…

"My name is Rosclay the Absolute."

◆

He opened his eyes.

The tenth match was the pivotal day when absolutely everything would change. He had needed this time to focus his mind.

Finally…we've made it this far. Surmounting the jaws of death many times up until this moment.

Fighting was beginning to break out all over. The fungi soldiers and Iriolde's army flooding into the city might bring considerable damage to Aureatia. How capable they were to limit the sacrifices to the minimum would prove the justness of Rosclay and Jelky's plan.

Aureatia's power had slain Alus the Star Runner and Lucnoca the Winter. Both had been menaces capable of annihilating the Kingdom on their own.

Some number of the hero candidates died, while some others had been left seriously wounded. The true ringleader behind the anti-Aureatian opposition, Iriolde, was defeated, and Aureatia's divided strength would be consolidated into one.

They had produced plenty of results. He had thought many times he wished it could end here.

It wouldn't, though. Now that he started, the only choice was to keep fighting until the end.

He needed to use the vast superiority obtained from this operation to entice either Hiroto the Paradox or Morio the Sentinel to their side. He needed to eliminate the uncertain elements—the National Defense Research Institute, Kiyazuna the Axle, Obsidian Eyes. Then, deploying all that consolidated power together at once, he needed to neutralize Kia, Tu, and Mestelexil, the hero candidates that had been unexpectedly defeated out of the tournament.

Even then, it should be possible. Completely annihilating these threats that surpass the limits of mankind...with minian hands.

He wanted to accomplish what all the people wished for and what they had given up on.

A childish wish that he only became conscious of in adulthood.

Even then, in the depths of his heart, he had thought about it for a long time. If the dragon that killed Oslow hadn't been there. If the poverty that tormented Iska didn't exist. If the True Demon King had never been.

If an individual who could brandish power like the Kingdom's had been there, they should have been able to vanquish it all.

Rosclay the Absolute hadn't changed into a champion solely for the people, killing any and all traces of his self.

In truth, he hadn't been considering the image of the Kingdom's future, like Jelky.

By being used as a champion for the sake of the people, he was using the power of the Kingdom for his truest desire.

He suddenly imagined…

A world of blood-soaked champions protecting people in the middle of surging threats.

A world where a single lone hero who had erased all such threats stood.

Up until that day, Rosclay had been nothing but a normal young man. However, now at the end of a checkered destiny, if he was to hold in his hand the authority to choose which direction the world was going to head…

"Jelky. My ideal is—"

Which world was one he wished to leave behind for Iska?

CHAPTER 17 Match Cancellation

There was a young man named Surug the Double Shield.

He had been a soldier, roused to action as part of Iriolde's camp, but before that, he had had been a perfectly normal young man, a citizen living in Aureatia just like everyone else.

Surug had a young man's ideal to change Aureatia. Since some of his kinfolk were Old Kingdoms' loyalists, he hadn't been able to get the qualifications to enter the Aureatia army, but even then he wished to fight as a champion.

Then, he valiantly led the charge to save a young girl from the swarming fungi soldiers.

Unmistakably an act of a champion.

Surug's corpse was left stuffed underneath a carriage leaning over in the old town.

"...So ultimately, Aureatia planned on erasing all the nuisances in their way right from the start."

Morio the Sentinel looked at the fate of a nameless soldier involved in the coup d'état, Surug's carcass.

Morio was a visitor who led the Free City of Okafu and formerly a self-proclaimed demon king. As a result of Okafu officially coming under Aureatia's banner and having all sanctions against them lifted, he had become able to move freely in and out of Aureatia.

He didn't think that Aureatia was making a mistake. They were thoroughly annihilating all their enemies while trying to keep as many of their allies alive as possible. Then finally, after they had turned everyone into their allies, they believed they could guide everything to the best possible future.

Morio the Sentinel, along with Hiroto the Paradox, had been doing the same thing. They didn't have any qualms about getting use out of their foes before crushing them, and Morio didn't think he had any right to criticize that act itself.

Aureatia must be the same as us... But they keep making mistakes.

Morio was fond of war himself, but he felt that his way of going about it was fundamentally different from Aureatia's.

War was meant to happen as a last resort between camps incompatible with one another. There was an inevitably to the violence in this instance, and each individual soldier was able to risk their lives fighting to carry out something that they believed in.

However, this method of deceiving Iriolde's camp in order to destroy them wasn't a war waged as a means to solve a problem, but nothing more than a pretext to slaughter everyone in their way.

Aureatia is trying to become a different, inhuman monster. It seems like they can be negotiated with, but they can't. They've settled on their conclusions from the start and don't intend on compromising with their enemies at all. *That's why Aureatia is always able to make the first move before their enemies can. They're thinking that no matter who the opposing power may be...all they need to do is eradicate all their enemies.*

In their battle with Lithia, Taren the Punished ended up launching a preemptive and unjustified attack with the Cold Star. However, what had Aureatia been trying to do on their end?

They tried to assassinate Taren the Punished, whom they ostensibly maintained a cooperative relationship with, all just as a performance test for a recently discovered visitor—this was the story Hiroto had obtained from Yuno the Distant Talon.

Using Kazuki the Black Tone to attack the Free City of Okafu must have been a similar type of experiment. If Hiroto hadn't intervened, Morio the Sentinel would have been assassinated before the situation ever devolved into war, and Aureatia would have unilaterally imposed their desired conclusion.

There's no way they're gonna get their way.

Even assuming that they were convinced that they would never see eye to eye with their enemy, war wasn't *the first method to use.*

A large majority of the anti-Aureatiaists that composed Iriolde's army would have been former citizens of Aureatia themselves. The Aureatia Assembly must have had some amount of leeway to reflect on these former citizens' wishes. If they possessed this much power, then they should have put in the effort to find some compromise that both sides could accept.

The ones truly driven mad with blood and fear weren't the citizenry, but Aureatia itself.

By eradicating absolutely everything, they were trying to realize *absoluteness.*

"Rosclay the Absolute. You're strong, all right. But, if you win here… no one else will be able to win again. This continent will be ruled under minian supremacy, and no one different from yourselves—no goblins, no mercs—will be able to survive."

The cheers of the people echoed from the direction of the plaza across the main road.

The alley where Surug's corpse remained abandoned and discarded was, in comparison, quiet.

"There isn't anyone besides you lot that wants that. Gonna need some sort of big upset soon, before you end up turning into the true monster."

◆

"Rosclay! Don't head to the plaza!"

At the same time, in command headquarters...

Jelky the Swift Ink yelled into the radzio.

He was backed into such a corner, he couldn't even afford to go through an operator.

"I will deal with it all... The communication to the citizens was mismanaged on my part! If you go there now, you could potentially end up in danger!"

<I understand the danger. However, your own physical endurance must already be near its own limit. Instead of talking with me, please prioritize the safety of the royal palace...of the Queen. Unless I explain things directly, the situation will have repercussions on the people's trust in the Aureatia Assembly itself.>

"Even then...!"

Jelky began to protest, but he understood that it was a meaningless reaction driven by his emotions. Deploying Rosclay was indeed the optimal move to get the situation under control.

The one who set this all up understood that, too.

...This is a trap!

The citizens of Aureatia thronged the Orde Old Town plaza.

It wasn't only the residents who had always lived in the area. Countless people were gathering in this plaza from quite literally all the regions in Aureatia.

It stemmed from the people getting ahold of a piece of information. It wasn't the same as what Aureatia had announced, yet contained exactly the same scheduled time and place, a specific rumor that had been disseminated to ensure the citizens across all of Aureatia heard it uniformly.

The tenth match in the castle garden theater that had been canceled *would have its venue changed.*

There are too many citizens gathered together! At this point, having Rosclay declare the match canceled himself is now the only way to get things under control...! There's only one person who could accomplish a feat like this!

"Lord Jelky, there's a radzio call from Hapule Feather Guild headquarters. It's not the guild representative calling, they c-claim...to be the Gray-Haired Child..."

"...I'll take the call."

Jelky took the receiver, but his grip strength had grown significantly weaker, and threatened to drop it.

More than any mental unrest, the exhaustion from overworking his physical body to its absolute limits was manifesting on the surface.

<Thank you for all your trouble, Third Minister Jelky. I apologize for interrupting you while you're so busy, but I am calling today to negotiate with you as the Gray-Haired Child.>

"The Gray-Haired Child...!"

The rumor dissemination.

Spreading information with even more influence than Aureatia, all while slipping past the eyes of Jelky as he gathered information from all over Aureatia—this seemingly impossible contradictory combination had, for Hiroto the Paradox, been possible.

<Stamping out any wicked influence on Aureatia as much as possible,

while keeping all sacrifices to a minimum—your order of priorities, while commendable, neglected to account for the natural feelings of the people... No, actually, with just you and the reformation faction alone only processing things from the top of that priority order downwards, it was naturally out of the question for you get that far.>

"Given the scale, you're not the only culprit at work, are you? You've spanned several commercial districts, and Yukiharu the Twilight Diver must be involved, too... Small-scale guilds and independent merchants, the ones without a direct deal in place with the Aureatia Assembly... you wedged yourselves *downstream* of our own information, beyond our direct line of sight! All those frequent invites you sent to shopkeepers to come to your office within Aureatia, this is what they were all for...?!"

<*I was simply conversing with some of my business associates. Nothing unusual about that, is there?*>

Starting when the tenth match was several days out, Hiroto had slowly informed shop owners and small-scale guilds alike of the rumor that the tenth match would have a venue change on the day of. Even if he slipped in a joke about it with his negotiations, he was speaking with a regular citizen, not people he needed to be especially guarded with. On top of that, the ones put in charge of surveilling Hiroto were Dant the Heath Furrow's troops, who had to prioritize their duties as palace guards.

It was inconceivable that Rosclay the Absolute's match wouldn't be held in the castle garden theater, the largest arena of all. Given that moves had already been made to sell the spectator tickets, the chance of a venue change was close to zero.

Therefore, he couldn't have provided definitive information that presented a basis to make them believe as such. As Jelky's group was busy constructing countermeasures against the grand coup, Hiroto had planted the seed of doubt asking *what if it was true* to ensure the citizens who heard the rumor kept it fresh in the back of their mind...while also making sure not to incite a conspicuous amount of inquiries to be sent Aureatia's way on the subject...

In fact, a rumor about a venue change had been circulated once before in the Sixways Exhibition, during the seventh match. If Cayon the Thundering had received the Gray-Haired Child's cooperation when disseminating that rumor, then it would mean that he had already proven whether or not this scheme would work effectively.

What was even more ingenious was that they didn't instill people with different facts around the situation that negated Aureatia's own official announcement, but instead leaked out information the people could interpret as a type of supplement to the announcement.

The tenth match in the castle garden theater was canceled—"*but there has been a change to hold it in the old town plaza instead.*"

Then, on the day of, the first half of this rumor came true exactly as Hiroto the Paradox had communicated it would.

Since the information was from the Gray-Haired Child, who knew about the hugely important change ahead of time, many people who had learned of the rumor would be under the impression that the second half must have been true, too.

The Gray-Haired Child channeled their desire. Even if Aureatia officially declared the match canceled, he used the people's desire to watch Rosclay's fight today...*and created a rumor that made them believe it was true. The citizens' mindset here was obvious, and therefore, we were delayed in handling it...*

From Jelky's perspective, had there been any possibility of recognizing the rumor's spread and stopping it?

In order to tackle this day of turmoil, Jelky had assigned a priority order to all information, and was forced to focus his efforts on saving people's lives and preventing economic loss. The deluge of inquiries about the cancellation of the tenth match was something *they assumed would happen as a matter of course*, and even when it came to the whispers that the match would actually be held with a venue change, when compared to urgency of the constant battle reports and political responses, it had simply been a problem that could be put off for as long as necessary.

The problems that could be solved by others besides Jelky had been swiftly allocated to the other bureaucrats in the Trade and Industry Ministry, or other government agencies.

The requests for Jelky's presence from the different trade associations and government ministries were all treated as something that could be dealt with at a later date, and if necessary, he sent a representative in his place.

Jelky himself was the one who had decided on this policy. The Gray-Haired Child had then used this blind spot in the political responses Jelky was capable of during his limited time in the morning, all while being on the outside of the commander headquarters.

Simply by conversing with the merchants he normally did business with, he fooled the eyes of Aureatia and achieved his goal.

Such magic was possible. The Gray-Haired Child had used magic against them.

"...This then means that Rosclay will be dragged out to the exact place at the exact date and time you intended for him. In front of a countless throng that could contain any number of your pawns concealed within the crowd...is that it?"

<That facts of the matter would dictate that, yes.>

Jelky couldn't leave this radzio call. If anything, Jelky needed to continue these negotiations and prioritize them over all other business at hand. Hiroto had gotten in direct contact at this stage with Jelky because he was going to use Rosclay the Absolute's life as his camp's bargaining chip.

Ozonezma the Capricious. Zigita Zogi the Thousandth. The two hero candidates under Hiroto the Paradox's control had been defeated in the first round. Okafu had their movements as an army restricted, and even when including the goblins, their combined military force was nothing that could compare to Aureatia's army. The Gray-Haired Child had been left on the playing field as a presence to remain vigilant against, but they had believed they could see all of the cards he could use in any negotiations with Aureatia.

Nevertheless, even after this aberrant politician was defeated, he prepared a devilish wild card on the spot.

The blade of the very first person to be defeated was pointed straight at the throat of the one that was meant to always have been the final victor.

<Now, I believe the next order of business is to talk about our proposal to you.>

"...That won't be necessary."

However.

Just as it was in real life, the one pointing the blade wasn't always necessarily in a superior position.

<I thought you to be quite an understanding fellow, Jelky.>

"...You're the one who needs a better understanding, Hiroto the Paradox."

The lawless outlaw wouldn't gain anything in the end.

The one brandishing his sword would be judged by the law and end up descending toward their final destruction.

"You don't understand what it means for Rosclay the Absolute *to be there in that plaza*. Judging from what you've said here, I can tell that your move is to attack him with the men of yours you've slipped into the crowd. At present, it has now become impossible for you to attack Rosclay."

The entirety of his conversation with the Gray-Haired Child was being leaked to Rosclay.

<*...I'll need to hear some reasoning to believe that.*>

"Go ahead and try your attack. Rosclay has openly shown himself in front of the masses countless times before. Do you think that he was never prepared for a sniper attack or assassination attempt?"

At that moment, when Jelky understood the Gray-Haired Child's plan, he had truly resigned himself to defeat.

Since, if some sort of attack was made against Rosclay immediately after he was drawn into the old town plaza, they didn't have any means to prevent it.

Jelky had needed to continue these negotiations and prioritize them over all other business. Especially in order to draw information out of this enemy and buy Rosclay time to cope with their attack.

"...I will admit it. You brilliantly outfoxed me and showed you could outdo Aureatia's response capabilities with a minimum amount of power. However—you took Rosclay the Absolute too lightly."

◆

The old town plaza was like a raging sea of noise.

"Where is Rosclay?!"

"The match should've started by now!"

"Seat tickets! I've got a seat ticket, dammit!"

Lost among the senselessly dense throng was a man in a black overcoat.

His mouth was covered up by his black mask as well. A glimpse out of the corner of anyone's eye wouldn't be enough for anyone to make out his face, nor that he was wearing armor underneath his cloak.

"...I've got a read on the plaza surroundings."

The buzzing of an insect rang in the man's ears as though it was a person's voice.

"There aren't any snipers in the buildings overlooking the plaza. About twenty goblins hidden in the crowd, but they aren't armed. For the Okafu mercenaries, though, I can't get a clear read from an insect's sightline... Instead, I went ahead and ensured the ones carrying firearms won't be able to use them."

Creating a great number of heartless revenants out of birds and insects, and controlling them from far away as if he had transferred his own heart into them—as vast as Aureatia may have been, the only one capable of such a feat was Krafnir the Hatch of Truth.

The man in the black coat answered by hitting his palm with his finger a set number of times, to stop anyone from hearing him. "Agreed." "Now." "Going."

"...I don't plan on holding back. I'll gladly help as long as you ease the punishments on Flinsuda and Tu."

Krafnir's original status was very close to being a private soldier of Flinsuda the Portent. Flinsuda maintained a neutral position among the factional struggles within the Twenty-Nine Officials, and regardless of any vast reward or trade, she never mobilized Krafnir, tasked with protecting keeping Flinsuda herself safe.

One result of the upheaval was that this situation had changed.

During Alus the Star Runner's attack, Flinsuda had been unable to stop Tu the Magic from taking action. Afterward, prior to the tenth match, Tu had escaped from Flinsuda's supervision and was considered to be a hero candidate who had left the control of their sponsor—it meant that Tu could be recognized as a self-proclaimed demon king and targeted for subjugation.

If that should happen, Flinsuda would have to take some responsibility for letting a self-proclaimed demon king loose. While it may not have been as much of a shake-up as in Hidow's case, her personal position would take a large turn for the worse.

That's precisely why it was important to negotiate with Flinsuda first when Alus attacked. Even if Tu was an uncontrollable pawn, as long as we established the fact that we had negotiated on how to use her, we would be able to draw Krafnir over to our side... Jelky's judgment was correct.

He advanced unwaveringly through the people, all while never letting his guard down.

Despite the terrifyingly dense throng, the black-cloaked man wove through it with brilliant martial control over his whole body, and preventing himself from being swept up in the flow of people.

The black-cloaked man was Rosclay the Absolute.

Rosclay utilized Krafnir, able to deploy the perceptions of several thousand simultaneously, to guarantee the area's safety. The metallic insects were physically weak, but destroying a single section of a gun's structure was a very easy task for them.

Even as their foe schemed to suppress him with numbers, without using any such weapons, Rosclay always had *more moves* available to him.

"...However, is *that man* really not a problem? Just him being here will greatly increase the chances you'll end up dead. Not just that, he's likely hostile to all of Aureatia itself."

While Rosclay had filled him in beforehand, Krafnir still had misgivings about the man's presence. If by any chance he acted to dispose of Rosclay, it would be almost impossible for Krafnir to respond.

Rosclay tapped his fingers. "Negative." "No problem."

All of it was already accounted for in Rosclay's estimations.

However, he needed to contain this uproar quickly. The longer he stood by watching, the higher the chances grew that he would be hit with some unexpected attack, and Rosclay still needed to keep acting to keep the casualties that accompanied any battle to a minimum as well.

In this plaza, with every iota of space filled with people, it appeared as if there was almost no leftover spot where one person could stand out among the crowd and address the masses.

However, there was no wavering in Rosclay's footsteps.

He stepped toward the structure that stood in the middle of the plaza—it was a fountain, repaired like new, and taller, after it was destroyed in the first match.

This fountain had stopped spouting water from the moment Rosclay had started to head toward the plaza. As such, he could climb up to the top of the central structure.

When the black-cloaked man reached the top, as if stepping up on to the stage, the gazes of the throng all turned to the man and his peculiar movements.

"Everyone, quiet down, please."

Abdominal breathing like in a play, expelling breath solely using the diaphragm.

Even throughout the uproar, his unblemished voice rang clear.

"Rosclay…!"

"No way."

"Isn't that Rosclay?"

"But the rumors said he wouldn't come."

The crowd's voices calmed slightly with the confusion that accompanied their attention on him.

At that exact moment, the black-clad man placed a finger up to his mouth in an elegant motion.

"Quiet." His voice was almost a whisper. "I am truly sorry to you, the people of the Aureatia. There will be no match occurring today. Instead of telling you through the mouths of the soldiers, I have come myself to explain things as a small show of good faith to you all."

"—"

The plaza fell into a dead, stunned silence.

People's emotions flared higher and hotter the more they came together.

Once the fire had been sparked, no matter how powerful one was or how much authority they commanded, it was essentially impossible for a single person to quiet down a crowd of several thousand all at once.

However, Rosclay the Absolute had managed to do so.

The result of his life as a champion, he had polished his behavior and voice to produce the largest effect possible.

He was furnished with a natural charm that fascinated people, beyond merely his excellent facial features.

"I am Aureatia's Second General, Rosclay the Absolute."

He tossed aside the black coat from atop the fountain.

Blond hair and crimson eyes, reminiscent of sunlight, or a sparkling jewel.

Skin brimming with youthful vigor, as if it had never once been scarred before in his lifetime.

A figure that combined both sturdiness and beauty, more well-balanced than a sculpted statue.

Rosclay the Absolute stood, wrapped in sparkling silver armor.

"Woooooooooooooo!"

The silence shifted into eardrum-splitting zeal.

And thus, the sound of arms swinging upward. The sound of stamping feet. The sound of hands clapping, screaming, and bursting into emotional tears.

The disordered mob of moments prior had fallen under the order that was their passion for Rosclay.

"Rosclay! Rosclay! Rosclay! Rosclay!"

The citizens shouted in unison.

Rosclay didn't move to immediately stop them.

After he had used the excitement to focus the people's thoughts and attention on him, he did the exact opposite.

Atop the fountain, Rosclay stood motionless, not saying a word.

As if to make all the attention he gathered at once flow backwards, Rosclay's own silence began to propagate among the entire crowd. All of the citizens waited for Rosclay's next words and wanted to hear them.

"Once more, I ask for your understanding."

He had told them about the decision to cancel the match right at the beginning, but he didn't think that what that meant had been conveyed to the whole crowd. He simply laid psychological groundwork in order to make them accept his announcement.

"The tenth match will not be held. This is not my own decision, but one Soujirou the Willow-Sword has consented to as well. As you are all aware, he cut off his right leg during the third match. While everything has been put into his treatment up until now, the wound has yet to fully heal...and it was determined that should the match happen in his present condition, the wound would reopen and potentially threaten his life."

He was mixing in information that diverged from the facts at many points, but a majority of those gathered here didn't have the means to confirm the veracity for themselves. Not only was all communication to Soujirou cut off while he was in Romog Joint Military Hospital, they painstakingly made sure no information on Soujirou's present health leaked out, either.

"I also needed to cope with the frequent fires and riots, so once again, allow me to apologize for this announcement coming at the last minute. We have already announced the decision to compensate everyone for the full sum they have lost due to the postponement of this match."

Rosclay put his hand up to his chest and closed his eyes.

Then, opening his eyes, he raised his sword.

"However, I promise that this match will absolutely occur at a later date! Soujirou the Willow-Sword also strongly wishes for this match, and I wish to respond in kind as well! The day will soon come when Soujirou's wounds are healed. Please, I ask that you to see things through until such a time comes—"

"It's Soujirou."

"—and cheer him on."

For a single moment, imperceptible unless one closely paid attention, Rosclay had stopped mid-sentence.

He had heard someone amongst the throng murmur Soujirou's name.

"Rosclay! Rosclay! Rosclay!"

"Rosclaaaay!"

"Rosclay! Rosclay!"

"Rosclay! Rosclay! Rosclay!"

As the people screamed out the name, an eerie premonition began to creep up Rosclay's back.

...Soujirou the Willow-Sword.

Despite saying that very name himself just now, up until this moment, it seemed as if he had forgotten about the man's existence entirely.

Currently, he had escaped from Romog Joint Military Hospital. While his objective was unclear, there were reports of him getting caught up in the fighting in various places… However, the man himself was simply an irregular and unusual swordsman, an individual fighting force. He couldn't exterminate a battalion with massive destructive power, nor did he possess elusive and effective mobility, or abilities of instant death that were impossible to predict.

He didn't have any impact on the war situation itself—outside of these current circumstances.

"Master Krafnir. Are there any cars in the area?" he quietly murmured, mixed in among the excited cheers.

No matter how cowardly it may have seemed, he needed to squash all possibilities.

"No. More precisely put, there's a wrecked carriage in an alleyway one street over, but it had been abandoned on the street to begin with. The region around here has a lot of stairs and narrow alleys. Even the residents don't use carriages… Didn't you enforce traffic restrictions the moment the fighting broke out anyway?"

"…"

He understood. He had called out to Krafnir to confirm if there hadn't been any anomalies.

Rosclay focused on the crowd's voices.

"Rosclay! Rosclay! Rosclay!"

"Hey, isn't that…?

"Soujirou."

"Rosclay! Rosclay! Rosclay!"

"Rosclay! Rosclay! Rosclay!"

"Willow-Sword's..."

Rosclay caught his breath. He ensured his unrest didn't show on his face.

An insect communicated in his ear.

"ROSCLAY... THIS IS THE FIRST WARNING. HE JUST ENTERED INSIDE MY SENSORY RANGE. STEPPED INSIDE THE DISTRICT. CLOSING IN ON THIS PLAZA."

"...Who has?"

Even knowing the answer, he couldn't help but ask back.

Krafnir answered.

"SOUJIROU THE WILLOW-SWORD."

A section of the surging crowd began to part into two, forming a path.

It wasn't a champion-like nature or technique moving the throng, but danger and ferocity contained within a minian form. Much like a pack of herbivores moving all at once without anyone ordering them to, after sensing an incoming predator.

"It's Soujirou."

"Isn't that..."

"The red clothes—"

"He's missing a leg—"

"Soujirou's really—"

Rosclay could see even from his angle.

A red tracksuit from the Beyond. Hair messily bundled together. His features were asymmetrically distorted, more reminiscent of a dangerous reptile than a person.

The aberrant master blade master. A being that was never supposed to appear there.

"Soujirou the Willow-Sword..."

There hadn't been even the slightest chance of encountering him here.

Even if he had been cognizant of Soujirou's threat from the beginning, Rosclay still would have come out here to this old town plaza. The losses Aureatia could have incurred from this crowd going out of control were immeasurable.

There wasn't any possibility that a man on one leg wandering through the vast expanse of Aureatia would coincidentally arrive in the old town plaza.

"Soujirou."

"Soujirou's here."

"What about Rosclay?!"

"If Rosclay's here, then—"

This atmosphere...

"Will Rosclay fight, then...?"

"I mean, him coming signifies..."

"But the match in the castle garden theater was canceled, right?"

"Soujirou's here?! Scary!"

"Rosclay! Rosclay!"

"It's Rosclay and Soujirou."

"They said the venue changed to the plaza."

...It's too late. The Gray-Haired Child used their desires.

It hadn't been necessary to go out of their way to deal with an escaped Soujirou the Willow-Sword. In the off chance that an important figure, Rosclay, first and foremost, ran into him, it would have been easy to get through the encounter while avoiding any engagement with the one-legged man.

The risk of him revealing himself before the crowd in the old town

plaza hadn't even been enough to prompt misgivings from Jelky. Only a limited number of people, primarily Flinsuda, knew that Rosclay had enlisted the aid of Krafnir in preparation for this day. Even if an assassin slipped in among the crowd, they had eliminated most of the probability of that happening.

However, *these weren't supposed to both come at the exact same time.*

These factors *that, while not fatal on their own, are coming together... all in the worst way possible.*

"Rosclay! Rosclay! Rosclay!"

"Soujirou! Soujirou! Soujirou!"

Even from a distance just barely close enough for his voice to reach him, Rosclay could clearly see Soujirou's twisted smile.

"All right... Let's do this, huh?"

Match ten. Soujirou the Willow-Sword versus Rosclay the Absolute.

CHAPTER 17 Match Cancellation

CHAPTER 17 Match Ten

<I was never attempting to assassinate Master Rosclay to begin with.>

Jelky the Swift Ink listened to the Gray-Haired Child's voice with his consciousness hazy from exhaustion and shock.

Rosclay had been perfect. He even managed to defend himself from unavoidable traps laid out in his path.

That was how it was supposed to have been.

<*This isn't a threat. In order for our negotiated consensus to be effective,* we *couldn't attack Rosclay through any dishonest means, and had to use some method that left you no room for fabrication or lies, no matter how you tried to control information.*>

Rosclay the Absolute had truly responded perfectly to all the traps set in the old town plaza.

He should have ensured his safety, guided the citizens, and left.

However, Rosclay's whole reason for personally guiding the throng was because they had gathered together out of a desire to see his match against Soujirou. Right at that point, Soujirou himself went and showed up, too.

Now, the only option was to start the match.

<*There's no room for any foul play. The* exact thing Master Rosclay wished for himself *is happening* exactly as scheduled, *nothing more.*>

"What do you want?"

Jelky decided to bend without a second thought.

If he didn't admit defeat here, Rosclay would be beaten. Defending the symbol Rosclay stood for was far and away more important than saving his own worthless pride.

<*...The first part of my proposal is a revision to a part of the slave law. Due to the vagueness around the current law's definitions and punishments, in regard to the hotbed of illegal work—monstrous race slavery—I would like to clarify how they are handled, and legalize their trade among the citizenry. By opening up legal markets, along with curbing the slave trade of other races through labeling them as handled "as monstrous races," as well as monstrous race slave dealings done by criminal organizations, it will guarantee a laborer population throughout your territory. Also, we would like to offer reconstruction support for the damages*

caused by self-proclaimed demon king Alus's attack and this series of military coups. Our government shall loan resources to Aureatia including funds and labor, and donate some as well. I look forward to hearing a positive response regarding these two proposed policies—now, while I have answered your question, there is one important point to add.>

Before Jelky could think over his reply, the voice on the other end of the radzio smoothly continued.

<*Let me stress that* this is not a threat. *We will not save Master Rosclay in exchange for your acceptance of our demands, nor do we possess any means to stop Soujirou on our end. Please consider our proposals as simple negotiations aimed toward after the results of this match.*>

"Wh-what—"

Jelky's breath caught in his throat. Jelky's throat trembled not out of unrest, but purely from exhaustion.

"What are trying to do here?! You didn't set up this grand scheme to negotiate?! All to get a political victory for your nation in spite of your defeat in the Sixways Exhibition…?! If this isn't a threat, then what the hell is it supposed to be?!"

<*It's a* campaign pledge.>

Despite unmistakably being the voice of a young boy, there was a terrifying, weighty pressure to his tone.

From the moment that Aureatia refused to accept the Gray-Haired Child, Aureatia was no longer the man's ally. They were nothing more than an offering to ensure his allies' victory.

<*It wasn't me.* You *were the ones who publicly promised a match. You lied too much to your citizens. That the destruction of the New Principality of Lithia wasn't a result of war, that the Order is exploiting the underclass, that the Sixways Exhibition is a fair and aboveboard fight to decide*

on the hero—Master Jelky the Swift Ink. There's one other area where you have an error in your perception.>

All for something as trivial as that?

Jelky couldn't incredulously question if he truly was doing this out of a sincerity toward a citizenry of a completely different nation.

The Gray-Haired Child understood.

<*I certainly haven't been intermingling with the people of Aureatia all in preparation for today. I built up many day-to-day interactions and intercommunication, while you hide a large amount of information from the people. As a result… Each and every person among them believed the rumors we told more than what you publicly announced.*>

He was nothing but a monster, as far removed from the people as he possible could be.

So why then, why did he understand?

<*Trust is what's stronger than anything else.*>

◆

Rosclay muttered as he remained standing atop the shut-down fountain.

"Master Krafnir. I ask you to ensure the safety on the outside of the venue. There may be someone who tries to make a move while all the focus is gathered on Soujirou the Willow-Sword."

"…I'd much rather do that sort of work. Given my position, I don't want to antagonize a hero candidate."

Soujirou—death in minian form—was closing in.

All around him, the people pulled back like an ebbing tide, creating a strange blank space right in the middle of the old town plaza. While there wasn't any boundary line, no one else made any attempt to fill in the arena-like area. Everyone was anticipating it. A match between

Aureatia's strongest swordsman, and the almighty swordsman from the Beyond.

"You're Rosclay, yeah?"

"That's right. It's a pleasure to meet you... Why are you here?"

Herein lied the Rosclay's biggest question.

The Gray-Haired Child most likely had floated a rumor several days ahead of the tenth match and resolved to lure Rosclay here to the old town plaza.

However, *where were the means to convey* such a decision?

This definitely wasn't a coincidental encounter. There was a considerable distance between here and Romog Joint Military Hospital. Since he only had one leg and couldn't utilize any sort of carriage, it would have been physically impossible for him to get here in time unless he made straight for the plaza upon his escape.

"Not sure you'd really get it even if I explain, to be honest."

Soujirou idly looked up to Rosclay.

"I'll try my best to understand."

"Sure... I know this girl, Yuno, see. A while back, she did the same type of thing. Used her arrowheads to mark things, make signals for me, so... I was only able to get here 'cause whenever I was about to get lost, I'd see one of the marks she left behind."

A cipher that only a specific individual could understand. He had considered the possibility. While Soujirou's senses may have been able to distinguish simple marks scratched into a building, the soldiers patrolling about wouldn't have been able to recognize it as a type of cipher. However, that wasn't the problem.

"...It's not the place that I question, but the date and time. Why did you escape from the hospital and come here, believing that there would be a match?"

“’Cause this is where we’re having our match, right?”

“No. The tenth match is canceled. You should’ve been informed about this ahead of time.”

“Huh, ain’t we fighting, though? You say some really bizarro stuff, y’know that?”

They weren’t on the same page. Why had Soujirou…been convinced that a match that couldn’t possibly happen while he was still in the hospital was going to happen? Why, also, hadn’t anyone been able to get a grasp on his method of communication?

“After making such an impressive show of it to me, what the hell’re you on about?”

There existed some type of obvious reasoning in Soujirou’s mind.

Inside Rosclay’s brain, he thought at full speed in the pause of a single breath.

He “saw” it. What sort of visual method was used? On top of that, something he recognized as being shown specifically to him… In which case, was it something he could see from his hospital room? At least, if the information was conveyed to him through some secret writing, he wouldn’t phrase it like this. Soujirou is a visitor, for starts. There isn’t any script in our world he could read—

Then, he hit upon it.

There was only one. One method that could convey something to Soujirou in an impressive manner without hiding it from anyone.

Rosclay looked up at the sky.

Balloons.

The shopping district’s colorful advertising balloons could be seen from the window of his Romog Joint Military Hospital room.

Hiroto the Paradox had a powerful influence over the shops he bargained with. It couldn't have been hard to make them fly balloons in the exact pattern he specified.

Even throughout the course of the Sixways Exhibition, there hadn't been any point of contact between Hiroto the Paradox and Soujirou the Willow-Sword. Rosclay thought there couldn't possibly be any cipher that the two of them could mutually understand.

However, there was a single one.

If *this code* was boldly hoisted up into the air, no one, none of the Aureatia citizens, nor Rosclay, would be able to read it.

"I see, there is a method he could use…to tell you something…"

"No way you'd write that if you weren't tryin' to tell *me* something. You didn't want anyone else to know that you were holdin' the match in secret here in this plaza…"

A blind spot in their thinking due to living in this world, and not the Beyond.

A code that only Soujirou and Hiroto could understand.

"*So you wrote it in Japanese*, right?"

…Hiroto the Paradox.

Disguising it as a notice from Aureatia, he had gotten Soujirou to act on this day.

The patterns of notification balloons were complicated to emphasize individuality. If one of the patterns among the notices that numerous shops flew into the air happened to coincidentally align with the writing script of another world, was there anyone here in this one who could have differentiated it?

…It was impossible to ever predict. How could there be someone who could understand one specific language among the thousands that exist in the Beyond…?! Even worse, it happened all while we were pressed with

responding to the grand coup erupting all over Aureatia... With an inevitability as if fate itself was being manipulated, he forced me to come across him*!*

Hiroto the Paradox had lost. He had been defeated by the colossal nation of Aureatia, both politically and militarily.

Was there anyone else who *could manage to do all this* from a state of affairs that left them without the slightest possible chance to turn the tables?

Truly a paradox. Hiroto the Paradox was, without a doubt, a monster.

Now, right in front of his eyes, Rosclay was faced with yet another monster.

"Rosclay! Rosclay! Rosclay!"

"You got this, Rosclay! We're cheering you on!"

"Don't go easy on him just cause he's missing a leg!"

"I'm gonna brag about this to my mom! It's like a dream come true!"

"Soujirou's a helluva fighter, too, y'know!"

"Rosclay! Rosclay!"

"Rosclay! Rosclay!"

He had to fight. Rosclay couldn't ever run away.

Since no matter who he fought, Rosclay the Absolute was never supposed to lose.

"Run if you want, I don't mind."

Soujirou alone spat out his words amid the chorus of cheers.

"Ever since I showed up...seems to me like you've been scared stiff, eh? Lemme tell you, ain't any fun for me to cut down guys like that."

"*Heh*... Thank you kindly. However, that is one thing I cannot do."

Rosclay descended from the fountain and stood at the same height as Soujirou.

It was a necessary move to convince the crowd, but because he stepped over the fountain, the inside of his shoes were wet and now worked to his disadvantage in battle.

Of course, when it came to disadvantaged footing, Soujirou fighting on one leg had it far worse than Rosclay. Nevertheless, the discrepancy between Rosclay and Soujirou's fighting skills was on a whole different level.

"...How should we signal the start of the match?"

"Feel free to come at me whenever you want or whatever... I'll even give you a handicap and say I won't attack first. We're gonna end up in sword range anyway."

"That's fair. In that case, how about when our breathing's synchronized."

As he talked, he put plenty space between himself and Soujirou.

What he needed to do was verify his foe's range. The attack range including what Soujirou showed in the third match, reflecting blades and throwing them.

"Please, citizens of Aureatia, I ask you to remove yourselves from this plaza! As this is a true duel, your safety is not guaranteed. Your assistance is unnecessary!"

Openly turning his back to Soujirou, he put space between them as he called to the people.

He was aiming for a psychological effect by openly turning his back. Along with their conversation just now, he was making Soujirou and the audience recognize that they weren't at the fighting stage yet.

The tall buildings adjoining the plaza... No, I can't use any of them. The residents should all been completely evacuated by the start of the first match, but there are far too many people gathered on the roofs looking down over the plaza.

His gaze then arrived on the observation tower soaring on top of the hill. The tower was a massive stone construction of a bygone age, and the observation deck at the top was narrow. There was maybe ten or so citizens who had grabbed these "box seats."

"I beg those of you watching from the observation tower as well, please come down and leave this plaza… Even should I win my match against Soujirou, if any of you were caught in the battle and injured, then it shall not be a true victory."

"M-Master Rosclay!"

"Hey, hey! Rosclay talked to me! Yeah he spoke to *me*!"

"Oh, listen to you! We're causing him trouble, you dolt! Quit putzing around and get down!"

"Master Rosclay, I'm rooting for you…! I believe in you, I know you'll never lose!"

The citizens in the observation tower departed, each one commenting as they went.

Continuing after this, Rosclay did something similar several more times.

When Rosclay first arrived, he had needed to climb a fountain just to avoid people, but the droplet of terror that was Soujirou the Willow-Sword served to make them keep their distance.

As long as he was able, as much as possible, to create a space that they absolutely weren't supposed to approach, then crowd psychology would make it difficult for them to step into the area again. Rosclay extended out this area to construct an advantageous arena for himself.

The castle garden theater wasn't Rosclay the Absolute's only battlefield—also…

"C'mon, already! Quit dragging this out! How long're you gonna keep me waiting here?!" He heard Soujirou's enraged voice from behind.

Rosclay was just about to head over to double-check that there wasn't anyone near the observation tower a second time.

"You are the one who said I was free to set the start of the fight at my leisure. While it may be of no concern to you... For myself, the safety of the citizens is paramount."

"Okay, sure, but...ahh, what a pain! Time to cut you down! If you don't got any plans to fight, I'll just attack from behind, got it?!"

I'm sure you would. You'll blow your top and come at me yourself. Your current position...means you have to make sure that this fight actually happens.

Rosclay turned back around near the tower and faced him with a smile.

His feet had already dried after being soaked in the fountain water.

Soujirou's movements, wobbling forward and drawing his right stick leg along, resembled a clumsy clockwork doll.

It thus meant it was impossible for him to run, jump, or make any other sudden evasion movements. On top of that, if he was also in an excited mental state, his movements would naturally grow more linear and straightforward.

"This should be enough."

Rosclay wasn't in sword range. Soujirou was at the bottom of the hill.

Rosclay swept his left side with a sword slash. It wasn't an act of intimidation.

The very tip of the sword grazed the foundation of the observation tower, scratching as it went...

There was a loud stone *creak*.

"We can begin now if you'd like."

The observation tower was leaning precariously in Soujirou's direction.

The tower, severed diagonally at its base, began to reveal its rectangular cross section.

"Ohhhh!"

It crashed. A destructive sound of everything, stone, earth, and steel smashing together.

Shouts and cheers echoed from the audience, at last understanding the situation.

Rosclay's goal wasn't to kill Soujirou in one attack. The aim had been to prevent him from making any evasive moments with the descent of a mass far too large to meet with a sword slash. He concealed it among the noise...

"Antel io Jadwedo. Laeus 2 telbode. Temoyamvista. Iusemnohain. Xaonyaji." (From Antel to the steel of Jawedo. The axis is the first right finger. Pierce sound. Descend from clouds. Circulate.)

—the Force Arts coming out from the radzio.

The longswords *that had already been generated* within the collapsed tower transformed into a tempest of silvery white and pierced through the gaps in the debris. Six. Ten. Thirteen. Nineteen of them. They rushed out at speeds too fast for the onlookers to even perceive.

They passed through from above, left, right, and from front and behind.

These swords started to make a buzzing sound from their terrifying speed.

Rosclay took several steps back.

...Wasn't able to kill him, was it?

A person's arm peeked out from a gap in the rubble. This single arm alone managed to grab onto two of the longwords, but by the time he had gotten his shoulder out, the shape of the longsword was crumbling away to dust.

He couldn't allow Soujirou's hand to grab onto any sword whatsoever.

"Ownopellal io tem. Nactekcca. Siliyo axolis. Nika." (From Ownopellal to Temilulk sword. Winged night. Thorny snow cover. Exhaust.)

The Craft Arts that continued to flow from Rosclay's radzio had destroyed the observation tower and made the numerous longswords all collapse in on themselves. Needless to say, it wasn't Rosclay who had used the Force Arts moments prior, either.

Determining it was impossible to avoid the match, Rosclay had drawn out the start time as long as he could.

He knew that even with that slight bit of extra time, Jelky the Swift Ink could summon them all. Antel the Alignment, clearing out the rebel army in the vicinity of the old town, and Ownopellal the Bone Watcher, stopping around the station, had arrived exceptionally fast. His Craft Arts support and his Force Arts support had both arrived.

Light shot from among the mountain of debris.

With a crunch like a bug being crushed, the trajectory of the light changed in midair. Two of the longswords, brought together in a midair cross, were sliced through, and because Rosclay had reacted late, it stabbed most of the way through his sword blade.

It was a fruit knife, seemingly obtained from some residential home.

Rosclay's hair stood on end.

"...!"

"Awww... Shoulda figured throwing stuff at random wouldn't do it."

I can't react... Krafnir and Antel protected me with everything they had, and just barely made it in time. Even a plain knife...can reach me from this far away?!

Soujirou the Willow-Sword hadn't been injured whatsoever.

It merely seemed that he had been crushed underneath the mountain of rubble, but looking closer, within the mountain was an open space just big enough to fit one person. It wasn't a coincidence—the rubble that Soujirou had dismantled in the span of a second had accumulated in shapes that mutually supported one another, so if anything, it had protected Soujirou as he stood in the middle of the destruction.

On top of it all, that slight amount of space must have been plenty of room to defend himself from the longswords rushing in from the openings in the debris and leaving him nowhere to run.

A deviant blade master with complete control over a sword, even those not in his grasp, on a technical and theorical level.

Even after reflecting the scalpels precisely thrown by an almighty chimera and having a blade forced against him with a visitor's brute strength, his wounds hadn't been fatal. He understood absolutely everything as if the blade and him were of one body and mind.

"Is that all you got?"

...If I assume the projectile just now was a feint, then he can't have many hidden weapons on him. Collapsing the observation tower and confining Soujirou inside was to stop his line of sight with the rubble. It was worth it just to try. Attacks via Force Arts aren't effective, and if anything, there's a greater risk the swords will be used against me.

"You can run away if you want. 'Cept you'd better be running to try and win."

Rosclay put space between them. He couldn't himself get closed in on here.

Suddenly, it seemed like Soujirou's clumsy steps changed their pace completely.

"Krafnir!"

"Piss off already!"

Metal insects swarmed Soujirou, trying to bite and tear at him. Although the swarm should have been just barely dense enough to avoid the audience's eyes, there was a blade whirlwind with godlike speed, and the bug colony that should have been impossible for any swordsman to deal with dropped to the ground without a single one of them reaching their target.

Aberrant leg strength. If Rosclay had been fighting Soujirou at full strength, he wouldn't have even had the chance to breathe once the match had started.

"If you ain't got any chance of winning, then cut it out!"

"I CAN'T KEEP THIS UP, ROSCLAY!"

"Please, just a little bit longer!"

Krafnir's fighting force, each bug on par with a single minian soldier, was being worn down. This wasn't an opponent they could hold back against. If their army came to an end, it was death.

Rosclay was continuing to back off, but there were some in the audience who grew suspicious of Soujirou as he slashed the air.

"What's that move of Soujirou's there, ya think?"

"He's not hiding some invisible thrust up his sleeve or something, like Toroa, is he?"

"This can't be happening… Rosclay, unable to finish him off…?"

Soujirou advanced, and Rosclay withdrew.

"Antel io—" (From Antel—)

Assuming it could even get a square hit on Soujirou, throwing longswords was a completely ineffective method of attack. Antel must have understood this for himself, too.

Rosclay went down the hill while conversely Soujirou was on top of it, where the observation tower had originally stood. While there was plenty of space between them, Rosclay's experience was warning him that he was in danger.

Right now, Soujirou's taken the high ground.

He saw a long thin shadow, changing its shape atop the hill. Rosclay murmured.

"…Professor Ownopellal. Craft Arts on the post of the gas lamp."

Orders given through the radzio.

Since there had once been an observation tower constructed there, it meant there were gas lamps to illuminate the night view as well.

This post, far thinner than the tower, aimed at Rosclay and collapsed straight toward him.

It had been sliced on top of the hill.

"Ownopellal io orde. Ikutes dea—" (From Ownopellal to Orde pillar. Waterfall eyeball—)

Right. I'll do the same myself.

"Don't try to—"

A sound of metal scraping together.

"—screw with me!"

The sound of Soujirou sliding down the diagonally tilted post as it collapsed down the bottom of the hill.

The two-cylinder structure he had in place of his right leg was locked together with the pole.

"Arpistera. Gill." (Unpeeled glimmer. Open.)

"...!"

The post, fulling its role as a railway to slide down, warped in the middle and bent.

Soujirou grabbed on to the post with his left arm to stop his body from being sent flying.

Conversely, Rosclay closed in on Soujirou for the first time in the match.

Swordsmanship exactly as drilled, correct and just above all else. His step forward and stab happened all at once, as part of a single flowing body movement.

However, as long as the move came from a blade, this visitor's sword would catch the tip of Rosclay's own and—

"...What the hell?"

Immediately beforehand, Soujirou blocked the thrust with his fake leg.

There was a shrill bursting sound, and one of the two poles that made up his fake leg bent and went flying. The leg strength he felt through the fake leg's kick, like that of a savage beast, repelled Rosclay's right arm, throwing it out wide.

In that brief second, unable to defend his midline—

"..."

"..."

Stillness.

Soujirou rolled without attempting any follow-up attack and landed on one leg.

Rosclay the Absolute, too, remained still where he stood.

The opposite side from his right hand, thrusting out and deflected away wide. In his left hand, held at the ready behind him, was a strange navy blue sword, baring a thick blade like a *liyuedao* sword.

Making him grab the post with his left arm, he had blasted Soujirou's fake right leg. If Soujirou had attacked him, Rosclay would have been able to cleave his face down the middle with a slash that was guaranteed to strike first.

"Why," Soujirou spat, "are *you* using that thing?"

"*Hah*... Well, here I'm wondering why you didn't block that with your sword for me."

"Rosclay! Rosclay! Rosclay!"

"Rosclay! Rosclay! Rosclay!"

As if the condensed moment in time had returned to normal, suddenly the reverberating cheers reached his ears.

When Soujirou sliced through the gas lamp and came flying into Rosclay's melee range, the Force Arts activated. Launching longswords at Soujirou wouldn't get a proper hit in, regardless of how many hundreds they fired at him.

However, it could easily manage the task of *handing over a sword* to Rosclay.

In his thrust-out right hand, Charijisuya the Blasting Blade.

In his left hand behind his back, the Magicked Blade of Razhucort.

Jelky had pulled out all the stops in his arrangements. The plan to pass through certain death range and then counterattack should have been a guaranteed kill.

For the blade master from the Beyond, even that didn't touch him.

I'm different from Soujirou.

Right now, Soujirou and Rosclay needed to fight together, standing on the same ground.

Rosclay stood face-to-face with Soujirou slightly outside his sword range.

"...Close to letting down my guard for a moment there when I broke through your defenses. A real good performance, eh?"

"I'll gladly accept that as a compliment."

Both of the swordsmen were smiling.

A fiendish smile searching for blood, and a virtuous one praising his enemy.

Krafnir. Jelky. Antel. Professor Ownopellal.

Nevertheless, Rosclay the Absolute remained intent on victory.

Even if he deployed all the dastardly and heretical tricks and eroded himself completely—

"Rosclay! Rosclay! Rosclay!"

"Rosclay! Rosclay! Rosclay!"

He would still win *in a way befitting a just champion.*

...I'm not fighting this battle alone.

◆

The chestnut-haired young girl was nothing more than a single person among the jostling crowd of countless onlookers.

The fervor in the old town plaza felt like enough to crush Iska.

No spectator seats had been set up, so she couldn't really see Rosclay himself due to the heads of the people jostling to look.

However, she had caught several glimpses of him through the gaps in the crowd.

She saw Rosclay topple a tower with a single slash and press in on his enemy with a flurry of Force Arts.

She saw him as he reclaimed a superior position over Soujirou in a momentary clash, as he been moving backward, as if driven into a corner by an invisible blade.

"See, look, Rosclay did it! Soujirou's only got one part of his fake leg left!"

"You idiot, that's cause he blocked the attack with his leg! Even still, I've thought this for a while, but Rosclay's crazy strong, huh… Just barely left a scratch and look what he did."

"Hey, Dad, you went to watch the third match, right?! What sort of moves does Soujirou use?!"

"No clue, but if Rosclay's gotten him that close, then it's over!"

"Rosclay! Rosclaaaay! Over here!"

…He was doing this the whole time, wasn't he?

Iska's body wasn't able to frequently make trips outside. She had never actually witnessed Rosclay fight for herself.

Up until now, she had only been able to imagine how he fought based on Rosclay's confessions, or the stories her mom would catch while out and about.

Rosclay the Absolute was a scoundrel who tricked his enemies and deceived the people according to Rosclay, and a flawless, upright, and bold knight according to her mom.

Even though she knew the dream would never come true, she still thought to herself—if Iska ever did have the chance to witness how he fought, what did Rosclay truly look like?

He's putting on a front.

Watching Rosclay as a spectator, he did indeed look like the sort of strong and beautiful champion her mom had relayed to her.

Even the Force Arts she briefly glimpsed were performed in a way that made it seem like his own technique, even as she knew the truth of it all, and Rosclay could have revealed the truth to everyone present, and it still would have been hard for anyone to accept.

However, Iska could tell he was pushing himself far too hard, as well.

This normal young man, the type that could be found anywhere, was fighting in order to remain a strong and beautiful champion.

Frantic and desperate, without anyone knowing the wiser.

Rosclay. The fact I'm feeling this...may all be a misconception on my part.

She thought it was a misapprehension stemming from her knowledge of Rosclay the individual.

But this misconception should just remain mine and mine alone.

Iska loved Rosclay.

She wished for a future together, just the two of them.

However, as long as Rosclay the Absolute remained as Aureatia's wonderful champion, he would continue to fight battles just like the one Iska saw.

It's okay. At this point, I'm not going to stop you or anything... Rosclay.

If that was his wish, at the very least, she would watch over him here.

Should things be as Rosclay the Absolute's own words said, and the individual power of the people served as Rosclay's strength—then, at the very least, Iska must have possessed the power of one person inside her.

◆

Soujirou the Willow-Sword didn't particularly have much interest in Rosclay the Absolute.

He was fine with letting someone else who wasn't in the ring themselves offer him help.

However, even if he did win the fight with these cheap tricks, was that actually enjoyable for Rosclay?

Whatever happened, they were the ones who would die when they lost, so if they didn't have the most fun battle to the death possible, to account for their lives being on the line, then ultimately, weren't they just missing out?

When it came to the man's skills and abilities, while Soujirou agreed that Rosclay must have honed his body to the absolute limits of the minia form, that was basically all there was to him. He hadn't reached the standards needed to properly cross swords with Soujirou whatsoever.

That was how Soujirou thought of it.

"I should be able to make quick work of 'im..."

Soujirou scratched his head right in front of his foe.

It appeared that Rosclay the Absolute wasn't as weak of an enemy as Soujirou sensed he was.

Soujirou should have seen a clear route to Rosclay's life, but with Rosclay constantly enacting two or three schemes at once, he couldn't reach the correct path forward. Soujirou was being outwitted.

Rosclay was always ready with a card to play to bridge the gulf of their abilities. The clash with his enchanted swords just now had been exactly that.

Much like it was impossible to distinguish between a visitor and the minia of this world based on appearances alone, he couldn't judge whether something was an enchanted sword or not simply by looking at the blade itself. He been able to dodge the Blasting Blade because he had watched the intents of its wielder, Rosclay, instead.

On top of it, simply by seeing through the first Blasting Blade attack, he ended up with the tables turned back against him. Rosclay the Absolute had even foreseen that Soujirou would break through it and kept the Magicked Blade secret.

"All right...well, what're you gonna do from there?"

"Whatever it is, I'm sure the same move won't work on you again."

"I mean, 'course not."

Repelling the first part with precision via the tremendous recoil from the Blasting Blade, Rosclay would find his prey with the Magicked Blade guaranteed initiative when Soujirou came flying down at him. It was logical, but still ultimately confined within the realm of logic. It was a move that was entirely composed under the premise that the enchanted blasting sword would score a hit. For Soujirou, he could simply evade it from the start and be fine.

Soujirou lightly bent his left knee, and prepared to kick out left, right, up, down, front, back—in all directions at once.

Rosclay, meanwhile, remained in the same stance as before.

The Blasting Blade held out in front in his right hand, and the Magicked Blade in his left hand, held behind his back.

He maintained his decorous smile as he spoke.

"I'll came at you with the same move."

"...Oh yeah?"

"Ownopellal io arte." (From Ownopellal to Arte sword.)

Word Arts. Soujirou kicked the ground faster than his brain could think.

The Magicked Blade was already being swung down at him. As if Rosclay had perfectly predicted the moment Soujirou would move.

However, the truth was he hadn't read Soujirou's moves. The sword, merely swung down as fast as possible, exploded on the ground without hitting its mark.

Something's not right.

The blast was bereft of bloodlust. It guided him to opened-up low ground. A distraction. Aural camouflage.

Soujirou had instinctively stopped Alcuzari the enchanted hollow sword that he meant to follow through with.

He felt an intensely heavy resistance. A rifle bullet had made contact with the sword blade. A sniper.

Even before the shock could demolish his wrists, he deflected the bullet by *rolling it* with the flat of his sword in accordance with the bullet's rotational direction.

Rosclay's response...

Soujirou was paying attention to Rosclay's left hand.

"Yones hamsh. Rix te neshel." (Left side of the mount. Crime-knowing curtain.)

...is coming from here.

Soujirou didn't move.

The Magicked Blade of Razhucort did.

Soujirou knew that the blade of ultimate initiative had passed by right in front of his eyes. The enchanted sword, because of this guaranteed forestalling move, needed to be precisely aware of its opponent's form and speed and *placed* along their trajectory to hit its target, or it was rendered meaningless.

The blade flew, and right as the second attack, fastest of all, began, Soujirou responded with his own blade. The enchanted hollow sword entangled the tip of the Magicked Blade and wrested it from Rosclay's hands with the same terrifying acceleration. If the wielder wasn't a shura himself, then slaying an enchanted sword was simple.

The Blasting Blade was still stuck into the ground. The Magicked Blade repelled down.

Another half pace forward, and he was within lethal sword range.

"*Dis terda.*" (String of dark tone.)

"I saw it. That..."

"*Nim a.*" (Become hollow.)

"...life of yours."

A killing slash.

"—"

He felt his hands cut through air.

Soujirou's intuition had perceived a definite path of slaughter.

However, Soujirou hadn't reached his target.

The sword blade had crumpled like dirt.

Alcuzari the enchanted hollow sword, supposed to never break or chip.

"Break open my defenses and get careless."

The Blasting Blade, pulled out with one hand, grazed Soujirou's left elbow as he lifted it up.

The impact nearly sent Soujiro's tiny body sailing straight into the audience.

"*I said I'd come at with you the same move, didn't I?*"

"*Gwaugh, gahak!*"

The aberrant blade spit up blood as he laid on the ground.

The problem was less that his left elbow had been blown away almost down to the bone, and stemmed more from one lung being crushed from the point-blank blast wave. Regardless, he was robbed of most of his faculties in one arm.

...I got played!

Rosclay the Absolute was weak.

While he may not have been the absolutely weakest, when it came to pure fighting capabilities among the hero candidates, myriad freaks and demons all jumbled together, he was undoubtedly near the very bottom. Anyone would recognize him as such.

...This guy's strong.

Strong—as long as visitors were themselves people...

Then it was possible to deceive them, including by ensuring one's strength was never shown.

Alcuzari the enchanted hollow sword was, from the beginning, *something he had received from someone else.*

"Gifting me...an enchanted sword. Haade, that bastard. *Gwahk, hah hah, hyrk.*"

From the beginning, it had all been to make him use it here in this fight.

All in case he won out against his first opponent, Ozonezma...and fought Rosclay in this match.

"Y-you were...thinking up something awful after all!"

It was impossible to distinguish whether a sword was an enchanted one just from looking at it. Even if it wasn't an unbreakable enchanted sword, but instead from the very beginning one that was destined to break, destroyed with Craft Arts after waiting for a fatal opportunity—Soujirou's technical prowess meant that he wouldn't have broken the blade to begin with, even after parrying a rifle shot.

A lie that was impossible to see through, presupposing the visitor's supernatural gifts.

Rosclay couldn't allow Soujirou's hand to grab onto any sword whatsoever.

"Hey look, it's Soujirou."

"No way... He got thrown away that far just from a single blast?"

Behind him, the crowd stirred.

"Rosclay even had his sword repelled."

"Hey, Soujirou, you okay? Give up yet?"

"Stuff it, all of you..."

As a result of getting blown far away, he was out of range of any follow-up attacks.

In his current situation, with the crowd near, there was little chance of any Force Arts attacks or attacks from those tiny bugs.

In order to pick himself up, Soujirou thrust his untouched right hand into the ground and felt something gross and wet.

"...What the hell's this?"

A swarm, looking like metallic beetles melted together into a muddy mess, happened to lie dead exactly where Soujirou had fell. They were undoubtedly the bugs that the friend of Rosclay's was using. Why were they dead, though...?

"...*Gaugh, hngh!*"

An intense pain began to rapidly spread from his right fingertips.

Writhing, he scratched the ground with his right hand. His nails were easily peeled back, and there were several red lines drawn on the ground.

The crowd screamed and backed off, circling wide around Soujirou.

"Wh-what the…hell is this…?!"

"Nectegio, the Ravenous Rot."

In the middle of the shrieks, Rosclay coldly murmured a reply, in a low whisper to make sure no one else would hear.

What exactly had Rosclay done just now? What was going to happen to Soujirou? At the very least, Soujirou knew one thing for certain.

I was wrong. My estimation was totally wrong.

This man wasn't the type of naïve opponent to give up on a follow-up attack for any halfhearted reasons like *Soujirou being out of range*, or *the crowd standing nearby*.

Much more than that, he had driven Soujirou into the most effective follow-up attack of all.

After one learned the truth behind the champion of Aureatia, they started to lose sight of an extremely simple fact that even the nameless city children knew very well.

Rosclay the Absolute had slain all of Aureatia's enemies.

Including *the* Lucnoca the Winter.

"You're going to die. I'm not going to step in range of you any further."

Ever since Aureatia was first established, no one had been able to best him.

◆

Command headquarters. Jelky, in a state of complete exhaustion, listened to the sounds coming from the radzio with his head facedown on his desk.

He couldn't give in now.

...Ekirehjy the Blood Fountain examined Nectegio on Rosclay's orders and gathered its toxins... Did he manage to coordinate with Krafnir...?

It was one of the trump cards they had prepared for emergencies, but they had deployed several of said trump cards in this fight already. Rosclay had prepared and accumulated them all.

Antel the Alignment. Ownopellal the Bone Watcher. The enchanted swords for defending the palace. Dally the Coin Repeller. Ekirehjy the Blood Fountain. He had arranged to have as much fighting power present as possible.

Jelky's head was in terrible pain, and he had almost no sensation in his left arm.

In addition to the daily, chronic overwork, the mental pressure and enormous amount of work that surged in one fell swoop that day was shortening Jelky's lifespan.

Everything I was able to do...all so Rosclay may win...

He thought that, to be precise, this attachment he had wasn't toward Rosclay.

It was an attachment to the yet-unseen Aureatia.

The Aureatia that would become a unified nation upon overcoming all the dangers that threated the world without killing the monarch or the people.

Jelky may have lied this whole time, just as Hiroto the Paradox said.

Even then, he didn't believe that they had been mistaken in their methods. If they had progressed down a just path, free from any deception, it would have led to a great many more sacrifices than there were now.

The true value of a nation wasn't the approval rate of the people. It was guaranteeing the people's safety and having the faculties to perpetually maintain it.

“I should have…said that back to him…”

The radzio call with the Gray-Haired Child had already ended.

Jelky also hadn’t any energy to spare to counter back in the moment. First and foremost, he had needed to give all the effort he had to support Rosclay right away.

“How frustrating…”

◆

His body was beginning to die.

Defeat meant that there had been some part of Soujirou’s way of fighting that had been wrong.

It wasn’t that he had come into the battle missing his right leg, nor was it that he hadn’t been suspicious of Alcuzari the enchanted hollow sword. It was that, despite wanting his match against Rosclay, he hadn’t been able to slash at him at the start.

The guy who avoids fighting is the stronger one?

If he hadn’t given Rosclay time to prepare, he wouldn’t have been ground down by the sheer amount of reinforcement he was getting like this. In that regard, Rosclay the Absolute was terrifyingly brilliant.

Presuming he would fight in the castle garden theater, this match should have been under the worst possible conditions for Rosclay, egged on by the crowd and forced to fight on the spot.

However, when faced with the worst possible conditions, he had immediately found himself weapons—the vague start for the match, and the need to let the people escape the area.

Back then, Rosclay had observed the surrounding terrain as he moved about the plaza and bought time to give him the greatest possible advantage.

Even someone who seemed inferior in strength to Soujirou had areas in which they excelled compared to himself.

If Soujirou could obtain that strength for his own—

"That...ain't...right...!"

He wriggled and struggled as he got up.

It wasn't about next time. It was *now.*

Right now, he had to close the distance and kill Rosclay, or it would be over. He would die first.

His left leg amputated, and his prosthetic broken. Explosive trauma to his left elbow. His right hand was soaked in lethal poison.

"What the hell're you running away for! Champion, my ass...!"

"Soujirou the Willow-Sword! I do not wish to slay a swordsman of your caliber! The blood loss from your elbow must be quite severe. Should you move, it will only put you in even greater danger. You can be saved if we attend to your wounds immediately. I ask you to rest there and wait for a doctor to arrive!"

That wasn't it. The harsh pain in his right hand was beginning to reach his wrist.

Rosclay was saying that Soujirou had to move, or the poison would circulate through him and he would die.

Rosclay the Absolute wanted to kill Soujirou more than anything.

"I...can still...fight..."

Mustering up the last of his strength, Soujirou tried to kick off from the ground.

His shoulder was pulled back.

"Huh?"

It was an Aureatian citizen.

A well-built Aureatian citizen had stepped forward and grabbed Soujirou.

"Whoa now, buddy… You can't push yourself so hard in a state like that."

"You okay?! We'll take you to a clinic."

"That bastard…!"

Rosclay hadn't been calling out to Soujirou.

It had been to the Aureatian citizens. More precisely, he had purposefully called out to create a situation where *it would make sense* for the Aureatian citizens to act this way.

He had someone at the ready. Waited…for this worst possible second. Rosclay…you were this *thorough?!*

Unable to waste a single second in his situation, Soujirou's potential options were few.

Just gotta go for it.

With his destroyed left arm, he stole a knife from the citizen right next to him. Something he could manage.

Soujirou just needed to cut off the fingers of the large man grabbing his shoulder and peel him off.

The large man murmured, "Sorry, but…"

Slash them—

"You can't cut me down."

The slash that was supposed to fly as fast as his nerves fired, stopped before he could move a single finger.

It was none other but Soujirou himself who stopped it.

"…Wha…what the hell're you here for?"

He recognized the large man's voice. To blend in amongst the citizens, he wore a black hat and glasses to greatly alter his image, but Soujirou's intuition for slaughter was the one thing that couldn't be tricked.

If he attacked this man, he would end up dead.

"*Fweh-heh-heh*... Been a minute hasn't it, Soujirou?"

Kuze the Passing Disaster dug the fingers of both his hands even harder into Soujirou's shoulders.

"*Ngh*... Screw you...!"

"But today's going to be goodbye for good."

◆

Kuze the Passing Disaster was an assassin. He needed to assassinate Queen Sephite.

In order to save religious faith, he needed a crime heinous enough to pin all the Order's notoriety on him.

If he advanced to the second round, when the royal family would come to watch the matches, he could get his wish. To win and proceed on, he should have only needed to kill only one person, his opponent in the first round.

That didn't happen. Kuze killed Alus the Star Runner himself, as ordered by Aureatia.

"Well...who do I need to kill next?"

He was in the second borough of Aureatia's Eastern Outer Ward, after it was struck by a conflagration—in a small shack along the canal.

Kuze sat down on a wooden box in the room, looking fatigued.

"Rosclay the Absolute. That must be what this is about, if you've called me out to a place like this."

"No one else knows about this conversation, even within the Aureatia Assembly. That's why I needed to hide myself and meet you in person."

There was a man hidden under a robe inside the shack.

His facial features were more well-sculpted than a theater actor, but when he wasn't inside his glittering silver armor, Rosclay looked like a normal citizen, as if his usual impressive presence was a complete lie.

"I see. Well, what is it, then?"

"Let me make my thinking here clear. I can assist your organization in your goal."

"...!"

Killing.

The choice flickering in the back of his head brought him disgust, like his entrails were rotting, but he needed to steel himself. It wasn't guaranteed that things would get to that point.

"*Fweh-heh-heh*... Goal? Our goal, huh... If Rosclay himself is willing to help with restoring the Order, I'd accept the offer with open arms."

"Regrettably, restoring faith at this point will be impossible. Your organization thought that yourselves, yes? If those who lived a proper life are enterally left unrewarded, then you need to create someone to shoulder the blame for that—"

"It's the same thing that you lot are doing to us, isn't it?"

In the age of the True Demon King, there wasn't a single person who had been saved by the teachings of the Wordmaker.

The Order was rotten, exploiting the poor and destitute to eke out its survival.

In exchange for forgetting their faith in the Wordmaker, the people of the world started to believe these stories instead.

They didn't want to believe that the tragedy and atrocities that befell them had all happened without any reason whatsoever. At this point, the Order was seen as necessary in order to serve as that reason.

Kuze needed to detach the reason from the Order he needed to keep protected.

"...How much do you know?"

The plot to assassinate the Queen was something that not even the head of the Order Division in the government, Nophtok the Crepuscle Bell, knew about.

If the plot was discovered, all the sacrifices up until now would be rendered meaningless. If it meant protecting the secret, Kuze would even manipulate Nastique of his own will.

"I've already made my conclusion clear. *I* can assist you. You wish to take responsibility for assassinating the Queen and use it to prolong the life of the Order. Is that right?"

"..."

Kuze wasn't so much preserving the silence on purpose, but was unable to answer.

He simply thought that it showed Rosclay the Absolute's extraordinary tenacity, to identify the truth all by himself.

"Why do you think I've gone to these lengths?"

"Good question. Trying to use me for yourself?"

"The answer is similar, but a bit different. I don't want to die."

Rosclay gave a fatigued smile.

"The Order may teach that even when the body dies, Word Arts will be woven on eternally...but I don't want to die. Simply imagining that I may lose myself forever is terrifying... That's why I don't want us to remain enemies."

Everyone must have felt that way.

Since, even at that moment, Kuze could kill Rosclay with a thought.

"You sure about this? If it comes out that you overlooked the Queen's assassination, you're not going to get by with just an execution."

"...In order to achieve our faction's goals, it will mean abolishing the monarchy in the end anyway."

"...What?"

"I'm sure your Order never even dreamed of it, did they? That we would both share the same goal of dethroning the Queen. We intend to use the symbol of the hero to convert Aureatia into a republic. The Six-ways Exhibition event is for the sake of this reformation as well."

"*Hah-hah-hah.* Is that...really true? *Hah-hah, hah-hah-hah-hah-hah-hah.*"

Kuze laughed, but it wasn't the sort of laugh that came out on purpose.

What exactly was the point of all the killing he had done?

His emotions were horribly dry, and empty.

"Huh, I get it, sure, sure! Instead of dethroning her while she's alive, it'll make everything go along faster if she dies and the whole monarchy is broken instead...! Not only that, but the perpetrator is going to step up and admit it for himself. How ideal! You'd definitely be getting everything you wanted that way, wouldn't you?"

And with absolutely everything without hope.

If it had to happen either way, that wouldn't be too bad, either.

Even when it came to the Gray-Haired Child who he was currently working with, Kuze intended to assassinate the Queen in the end and betray him.

Even the Gray-Haired Child who he was currently working with intended to assassinate the Queen and betray him.

Assassinate the Queen and take on the Order's persecution. At this point, for Kuze the Passing Disaster, this was all he had left. Much as it was so for Nastique, he simply had to be the blade focused solely on achieving this singular goal.

"Sure. To say thanks for giving me a good laugh, I'll work with you. Who do I need to kill?"

"Lucnoca the Winter," Rosclay answered. "There are some who are making moves to use the beginning of the second round, the ninth match, to take down Lucnoca the Winter. I expect there will be a tremendous amount of military force deployed against her, but should even that be not enough, there is a chance she will attack Aureatia... I need you as a trump card."

A single one of Lucnoca the Winter's Ice Arts breath attacks could easily annihilate all the areas of Aureatia at once.

Which was exactly why Kuze the Passing Disaster could be called her natural enemy. As long as Kuze was included in the enormous radius of the attack, that alone would be enough for Nastique to *kill the strongest of all dragons.*

"...So you're not telling me to go out there directly and kill her?"

"Yes. *Making them exhaust themselves* is part of the operation."

Whatever Rosclay the Absolute was planning was none of Kuze's concern.

However, in all likelihood, Rosclay the Absolute was another schemer like Maqure the Sky's Lake Surface, able to think up ambitious, far-reaching plans.

I wonder who's stronger, you or the Gray-Haired Child.

"Kuze. I'm sorry that I am unable to save your Order."

"...No worries. When the time comes, just let me know. At this point in the game...a little betrayal's nothing at all."

The ninth match. Psianop the Inexhaustible Stagnation and Tuturi the Blue Violet Foam's hard-fought and brave battle resulted in the death of Lucnoca the Winter.

Rosclay the Absolute had preserved his trump card for later.

◆

Rosclay the Absolute was always fighting with stratagems meticulously laid out around him.

Among them were tricks that were ultimately never used.

When he stepped into the old town plaza, he had spread out a cautionary net of Krafnir the Hatch of Truth's constructs, but normally even this couldn't be called an entirely flawless defense.

For example, it wouldn't be guaranteed against arrows from Mele the Horizon's Roar, or bombs from Mestelexil the Box of Desperate Knowledge.

When facing attacks that would destroy the plaza in its entirety, keeping an eye out for onlookers would be meaningless.

Therefore, having Kuze the Passing Disaster *happen to be present there* was significant, as a precaution against such attacks.

He *just needed to be on the scene*—simply by having Kuze caught within the attack radius, he would serve as the ultimate shield of all, killing the attacker—before they attacked.

Save for Soujirou, the fact Kuze the Passing Disaster and Rosclay the Absolute were connected was known to no one else. Even to Rosclay's back-up support, looking in from the periphery, Kuze currently resembled any other Aureatian citizen.

Furthermore, at this point, Soujirou was going to die, simply by being stuck where he was.

"Damn…you…!"

"Just pack it in. There's no saving you at this point, even if I didn't do anything here."

In the confusion earlier, Soujirou had grabbed a knife for himself.

If Kuze was the only one to approach where he was standing, then he wouldn't even carry this one weapon, but in a situation like this, crowd psychology meant that completely unrelated people also came to stop Soujirou.

As long as Soujirou held it in his hand, the knife wasn't simply a tool for fighting off the crowd.

"Still…ain't enough…! This much is…nothing! *Ngh, gwauuugh!*"

"*Eeeek!*"

"*Eyaaaah!*"

His arm fell with a thud.

Everyone in the crowd except Kuze screamed and backed off in terror.

Soujirou had cut off his own right arm, which was infected with the lethal bacteria.

"…!"

Kuze, pinning Soujirou down, was forced to follow those around him and separate himself, too. He was a hero candidate, whose face was already well-known. Once all of the other citizens had put space between them, he couldn't make any conspicuous moves of his own.

"Wh-whoa now, what the heck're you doing, buddy…?! Your arm may've been a mushy mess, but cut it off and the blood loss is going to knock you out of this fight way faster…!"

"I don't…wanna hear, any crap from a damn…bystander!"

Turning to Rosclay, Soujirou began to walk, one step at a time.

Most of the cells in his four limbs were dead. His right arm and left leg were lost, and most of his left elbow was beginning to get torn off.

Since he wouldn't be able to reach that far on his own, his only option was to make his enemy approach him.

Soujirou needed to learn how Rosclay fought.

A way of fighting where the weak could kill the strong. A battle using psychology and the environment to draw his enemy toward the battlefield he wanted.

"Rosclay! You really cool with this, huh?!"

"..."

"Aureatia's strongest knight, huh?! Say that after you've lobbed my head off! A real knight? They cross swords back 'n' forth right up to the end! I'm not admitting defeat unless *you're* the one to kill me!"

He was closing in.

Rosclay the Absolute lingered where he stood.

...No. He was observing. He was watching and waiting like a cold-hearted beast for Soujirou to die off.

"I have a different set of values. I do not condone tormenting and killing an opponent who can barely stand... Please, I ask you to fall where you are and accept treatment."

Soujirou didn't budge. In a battle of words, not swords, his enemy naturally surpassed him.

Could Soujirou come up with the words capable of moving Rosclay from where he stood?

If he didn't, he would die. Fall and perish meaninglessly on the plaza ground, unable to do anything.

He needed to fight until the end.

"Rosclay! Finish him off!"

"C'mon, Rosclay, give him the fight he wants!"

"Just give it up! It's too cruel to watch!"

"Soujirou's not right in the head!"

"Rosclay! His head! Take his head!"

Rosclay couldn't keep running away forever. With an audience looking on, he was bound to move.

From his now largely fuzzy consciousness, Soujirou spat out his words.

"I'm Yagyuu…the Earth's last Yagyuu. The strongest…swordsman…"

That's right—Yagyuu Shinkage-ryuu. The last.

"Indeed. You fought brilliantly, worthy of your name. Soujirou the Willow-Sword, I will never forget you."

"…You could win now, y'know."

"…"

Soujirou could tell, mostly through intuition, that there was a small change in Rosclay's expression.

"I'm saying that…even you can win *in a fair…and honest* fight."

◆

Just how much further could the swordsman fight with a left hand that had its elbow blasted off?

At the very least, for Rosclay, it would have been impossible. If the extensor carpi radialis longus muscle on the outer side of the elbow was lacerated, it would become extremely difficult to bend the wrist. His grip strength would weaken, and naturally, it would grow difficult to maintain his grasp on anything. The motions to throw a projectile were physically impossible.

Even with all of that, Soujirou the Willow-Sword was the Beyond's strongest blade master.

If Rosclay waited for him to die, he would win. It was how Rosclay had fought to that point.

"Rosclay! Rosclay!"

"Rosclay! Soujirou's serious here!"

"This guy's got some real spunk, huh?!"

"Rosclay! Be careful!"

"Please…stop! Just put him out of his misery!"

...Looks like this is the limit.

Judging by the air of the citizenry, Rosclay couldn't drag out the conclusion to the fight any longer.

Rosclay the Absolute's matches couldn't come to a cruel conclusion.

Soujirou likely understood that and was thus advancing forward, challenging him.

Rosclay looked one more time at the crowd. At each and every one of their faces.

He took a deep breath.

I've weakened him enough at this point. I'll end it with a melee duel. After continuing this far, I need to carry it through to the end.

Soujirou advanced forward one step at a time.

Even as he was dying, each individual step was strong.

Rosclay too began to walk—and then murmured.

"...Krafnir."

Something was swarming toward Soujirou's feet, out of view from the spectators.

Rats, centipedes, spiders. Krafnir's revenants.

"Hrn, yaah!"

A white afterimage remained chaotically behind.

As if Soujirou could perceive each individual revenant in the swarm, they were all cut down before they could touch him.

It was monstrous. Even now, after losing most of his limbs.

We only gathered enough of Nectegio's poison to use in the attack a few moments ago. This is about the maximum number of rats and bugs we can have attack him while still ensuring they are out of the audience's sights.

Nevertheless, there was no wavering in Rosclay's eyes as he closed the distance. He was observing.

Soujirou the Willow-Sword has been weakened to the absolute limit.

Just what sort of response can he make in that state? How fast will he be? How much strength does he have? Is he truly weak enough *for me to win on my own?*

Soujirou's gait seemed not to have weakened at all.

Had it really been possible for Rosclay to watch and wait for Soujirou's blood loss, and the poison, to kill him?

It seemed like Soujirou possessed the same deviant vitality as Lucnoca the Winter, that he could drive himself forward infinitely as long as it was to keep on battling.

Rosclay readied his sword as if in response.

He was an in extreme state of focus. Rosclay murmured all the information he was processing in his mind.

"All right. Using Force Arts to send longswords flying isn't the right move. While it'd be possible to launch a heavier saturation attack than with the revenants, there's still the slim chance of giving him a sword to use..."

"...?"

"No sniper attacks. I would need to drown out the gunshot with the Blasting Blade at almost the same moment as the shot, and swinging it at this range would look unnatural, too. Then, if I use the last bit of strength to close the distance—"

"*Whoa!*"

Soujirou instinctively swept the air with his knife. There was a loud metallic *clang.*

"—that was what you were thinking, wasn't it?"

This latest sniper attack didn't come with any gunshot. It was a silenced sniper shot using a subsonic bullet.

"If fair and honest is what you wish..."

"...!"

The exact moment Soujirou slashed away the bullet, Rosclay swooped in to close the distance like a bird of prey.

"Then I shall battle you with my proper and just technique."

A sword stab. Soujirou swiped with the knife, diverting the blade. Even attacking his enemy in a completely unguarded moment, he still had aberrant reaction speed.

Rosclay didn't fight the momentum from the knife parry, and rotated his sword blade in a half-spin. Soujirou's knife, having stopped the blade, was wrapped up by the spin and thrown from Soujirou's hand.

It also served to shift Rosclay to his next sword attack. A slash toward Soujirou's amputated right-hand side.

I can kill him.

A kick of the prosthetic leg caught it.

The blade dug into the last remaining support in the prosthetic. An explosion.

Charijisuya the Blasting Blade.

I can kill him.

Soujirou held with this pivot foot through conditions that would have made a regular person crumble from the blast shockwave. However, Rosclay was stepping toward him with a kick to pin down his hip joint.

Soujirou couldn't physically maintain his balance. Rosclay kicked him to the ground.

Each and every motion beautiful, the very exemplar of orthodox swordsmanship.

Ah... I can do it. Even I can properly—

He had defeated the Beyond's strongest blade master with his orthodox and rightful blade.

Rosclay swung the Blasting Blade down at Soujirou and—

"...aw it. That life of yours."

"...?"

His shoulder never lowered. Instead, *a blood-drenched something* had pierced him from inside his ribs.

"*Kwaugh!*"

There was a physical, coughing reaction.

He spat out blood.

Rosclay understood that right before he lowered the Blasting Blade, he had been stabbed by something.

Yet, Soujirou should have lost all of his weapons at that point.

His own thoughts were all that circulated at high speed.

Soujirou...lifted his body up. What stabbed me?! We're too close. Even if he concealed a weapon, he certainly didn't have enough time to take it out. The third match...did he throw something up in the air, like during the third match, and hit me with it? No. There's no way I would overlook an attack he had already used before!

Rosclay was an ordinary man. Being wounded was enough for him to drop the Blasting Blade.

Letting out a viscous *splurt*, the blade piercing Rosclay was pulled back out.

A majority of the spectators couldn't understand what happened, but a section of them let out a terrified scream.

With the same dying breaths, Soujirou savagely laughed.

That's not it. He wasn't hiding any weapons. This man...

"*Ngah, ngah...* I didn't...cut off my arm, to stop the infection..."

The bloodstained blade was terrifyingly white.

It was growing straight out from Soujirou's arm itself.

...made *his own weapon.*

For a blade master of Soujirou's skill, such a feat was possible.

When he cut his right arm off as it was gnawed by disease, he had

made a sharp cross section...as if the bones of the cross section themselves were *blades*.

He created for himself a sword that, far more than his steel prosthetic leg, or his left arm with the elbow smashed up, was directly connected to his physical body.

1582, the tenth year of Tenshou.

Takeda Katsuyori and his retainers, driven into a corner by the Oda following the betrayal of Oyamada Nobushige, were about to meet their final battle at Mount Tenmokuzan's Seiunji Temple. However, the Oda army had already gone around their destination of Mt. Tenmokuzan, and Katsuyori was forced to double back.

Among the remaining retainers, numbering less than fifty at that point, was a general by the name of Tsuchiya Souzou Masatsune who was responsible for the rear guard during the retreat.

The rear guard laid in wait for the Oda army on a narrow cliff path along the Nikkawa River, barely wide enough for one person at a time.

Tsuchiya Souzou was said to have kept fighting with one hand. Grabbing the wisteria vines that covered the cliff in one hand, he mowed down the enemy army pressing in with the katana in his other and kicked them down to the Nikkawa River flowing below.

The legends said the enemy numbered over a thousand—he thus earned the name *One-Handed Slayer of a Thousand*.

Killing just one person with quite literally *only one hand*. How easy of a feat was it for a deviant visitor?

"What did...I tell you?! Crossing swords till the end is what it's all about!"

Soujirou slashed him. It was unmistakably a sword attack.

Using the longsword Antel's Force Arts wedged between them in midair, Rosclay barely defended himself.

"Why...why're you fighting?! Soujirou the Willow-Sword!"

He could wield any and every sword better than anyone. He was fighting with the cross section of his own arm, which should have been agonizing and painful with each slash, and yet if anything, it was faster and stronger than a fully healthy arm.

Slash. Block. Slash. Sword clash.

The strongest swordsmen across two different worlds finally contended against each other in a battle of their utmost limits.

"Is fighting really so fun?!"

"Sure is! Nothing but fun!"

If he could just pick up the Blasting Blade.

If he could just hold out until Krafnir's insects came to reinforce him.

If he could just demolish Soujirou with sniper fire and Word Arts.

Too fast, too close for Rosclay to think about anything extra—his absolute limits.

The bone blade ripped apart his silver armor, gouging his innards while his silver blade cut into flesh and severed Soujirou's ribs.

Rosclay continued to fight, swallowing back blood and gritting his teeth as he did.

He didn't want to die. He didn't want to die. He didn't want to die.

Rosclay the Absolute...

He continued to recite it to himself like a curse.

...needs to always remain a champion.

No matter how much pain he endured, he couldn't fall to his knees.

No matter how wounded he was, he couldn't die.

No matter how tough the battle, he needed to keep on winning.

With his powers of concentration facing down death, time seemed frozen.

...Why did something like this...

No matter how many sacrifices were necessary...even if it meant betraying the people and assassinating the Queen herself, all of the threats across the horizon needed to be defeated by a champion.

With that, a future where no one would see a need for champions was bound to come someday.

He had needed a gift for when that day came, that would leave something concrete behind.

With Iska, he—

"*—Ah.*"

Red.

"Don't go dwelling on useless crap—"

The bone blades had pierced through Rosclay's stomach.

His small intestine and some other internal organ were caught by the blade and spilled out from his back.

"—in the middle of a battle to the death!"

The longsword in his hand was still aimed straight ahead at his opponent's face.

In the final move, he had been slow to react. He hadn't been able to knock Soujirou down.

Rosclay wobbled and took three steps back.

He had lost. Even exhausting all of his strength couldn't bring victory within reach, and he had lost.

A defeat there was no excuse for. He had done everything he could.

"*...Hah-hah, ah-hah-hah-hah-hah...*"

Even though he had lost, he found himself laughing as all his tension came undone.

He had kept it up for so long that he had even believed it was in fact an intractable part of himself, yet it took but an instant for all the nerves to unwind.

He could tell his life was trickling down.

Just as it did for any ordinary minia.

Just as it had been for Oslow the Indominable, Rosclay the Absolute, too, would die.

My internal organs and arteries have been torn apart. Still, for me, none of that is important...

His diaphragm, lungs, throat, and face.

Those were all he needed. Rosclay used his sword to hold up his body as it threatened to give out.

"People of Aureatia."

It was a normal voice, with no technology assisting him, but it silenced the screams and cries in the venue.

With his ambition left unfulfilled, Rosclay the Absolute was going to die.

However, he had no intent on just simply dying there.

He would set up his final attack.

"There is nothing...to mourn. Since I...from the beginning... I was no hero. H-how...however, I have one final wish...! Please, I ask you to find them—do not let my fight here be in vain."

Rosclay the Absolute had used absolutely everything he could in order to achieve his goal.

Surely he was able to use his own death as well.

"A hero. A real hero, the title I fell short of. Please, find them...

Please continue with the Sixways Exhibition! Until the end! Until one, final person remains…!"

Even if the path would be accompanied by innumerable sacrifices.

When the champion died, all the monsters were going to be dragged along with him.

He was convinced that the winner, Soujirou, must have collapsed at that point.

However, Rosclay wouldn't do the same. He was an absolute champion.

He smiled with his blood-covered face.

With his sword supporting him, he stood straight up.

His vision, and his pain, began to dissipate.

Grief, shouting, applause.

The only thing in his sense until the end was the all-too-familiar sound of applause.

Match ten. Winner, Soujirou the Willow-Sword.

CHAPTER 18 Red Coral

Jelky continued to hear reports from the radzio.

Rosclay had lost.

Falling one step short in his battle against Soujirou, he had suffered fatal injuries.

It was uncertain whether the voices that reached Jelky's ears, where he lay collapsed on the ground, were real or not.

...Rosclay.

They should have been able to gain complete victory.

Rosclay was supposed to continue fighting their long fight.

Jelky had been forcing a terrible burden on him the whole time.

He couldn't ask Rosclay to forgive him.

It's...my responsibility. I need to...cover...Rosclay's portion, too. Right until the end...

He could tell his consciousness was fading. He needed to get himself up, but he couldn't.

Jelky needed to use his mental fortitude to prop up his physical body, but he couldn't.

The only ones capable of that had been champions like Rosclay the Absolute.

......

Something warm flowed down his cheek.

At this point, Jelky's reality was vague and unclear.

It may have been sadness. May have been anger. It may have been frustration.

Or perhaps, it was nothing more than a simple physical reaction to his exhaustion.

However—did even a man like Jelky cry at times?

"...Rosclay. Why did you lose...?"

Still with his face planted on his desk, Jelky forcefully clutched his fingers.

"Rosclay...!"

◆

At that same moment, Hiroto the Paradox had, too, learned the result of the match from a transmission of a goblin spectating in the plaza.

Soujirou the Willow-Sword had defeated Rosclay the Absolute.

When comparing their pure fighting strength, it might have been only the natural course of events.

However, Hiroto knew just how big this fact actually was.

The chances had been far greater that Soujirou wouldn't be able to win.

Still, Hiroto had thrown everything behind this final gamble after Zigita Zogi's death.

It was an awfully simple, and tremendous, gamble. If Soujirou won, Hiroto's camp's fight would continue. If Soujirou lost, Hiroto would lose everything he had built up.

Hiroto the Paradox's way of fighting meant that in the end, he needed to entrust the conclusion to someone other than himself.

Since that was what it meant to *believe in people.*

"...Mr. Soujirou Yagyuu. You fought valiantly."

In his reception room, without any other eyes on him, Hiroto silently clapped all by himself.

"You've won."

◆

From the very beginning, there hadn't been any preparations for Soujirou the Willow-Sword's victory.

Soujirou the Willow-Sword and Rosclay the Absolute, both in critical condition from their unofficial tenth match, were put into the medical squad carriages that got as close to the plaza as possible through the tangled and intricate old town streets, and immediately transported away.

However, the one who had arranged for this medical squad was the same one essentially in charge of the Sixways Exhibition, Jelky the Swift Ink.

Rosclay the Absolute had been an individual, and an entire faction. As long as it was beyond the eyes of the people, *they could do anything.*

Therefore, the two doctors that rode along in the carriage bearing the unconscious Soujirou were there to finish him off, and make it appear as if he died in transport.

Even if they had lost, they would never let their enemy win.

"I'm stunned. He's in this terrible state, yet he hasn't lost very much blood. From what I can see of the bones, his right arm was keenly severed...and yet, the tissue around his artery, and only that tissue, is crushed closed, as if on purpose. Just what sort of technique are you supposed to use to manage something like this?"

"Best not to try to understand anything about a visitor. I'm guessing he'll die if we leave him anyway, but things'll get hairy if we wait until he's conscious again. Dose him with a vasopressor agent, and open up the wounds."

It was right as the carriage was beginning to leave Orde Old Town. Their "treatment" had begun.

"Not very sportsmanlike, now is it?"

"Huh?"

Without them noticing, a third man was now sitting inside the carriage.

A man with a moustache and a muscular physique reminiscent of a savage beast.

There was no way he had been there from the start.

"Ah, wait, is it bad manners to board a moving carriage?"

"Wh-what the, how did you get in here?!"

"Oh, you know. I happened to hear you docs chatting about something I couldn't just ignore, see. Consulting with each other about how to kill a patient? I sure hope that was just a joke..."

"..."

"..."

"If you're saying it was a joke, then I'll ask you to get started on giving Soujirou emergency first aid right away. If you can fool me and fail on purpose, though, you're free to try."

The two doctors could do nothing but sit in silence.

The Gray-Haired Child understood that Rosclay's methods would be thorough. Thus, to prevent any assassinations, he had dispatched a different monster beforehand.

During these Sixways Exhibitions—as long as someone was involved with a deviant, they were guaranteed to encounter other deviant beings, as well.

"Now then—I know this weird for me to say, but..."

Morio the Sentinel cut himself a new cigar and lit it.

"Sure don't have any good memories when it comes to other visitors."

◆

Inside Rosclay the Absolute's coach, also transporting him from the old town plaza, the scene was the opposite from what happened with Soujirou the Willow-Sword.

The carriage carrying Rosclay had stopped in an old town alleyway, and the doctors riding along were being questioned about the details. Apparently, Rosclay had suddenly vanished mid-transport.

"...Yes. Master Rosclay himself requested that we stop here... Though they were his orders, since we were in the middle of an emergency transport, I did refuse him at first, but...he told me it was something that greatly related to the administration of the Sixways Exhibition."

"You're trying to tell me that he ran off?! That's absurd... Let's assume you're telling me the truth, how in the world did you fail to capture a critically wounded man on his deathbed?!"

"He used medicine to blind us. To be precise, it was a liquid contained in a medical bottle, so it was harmless, but...there are some powerful drugs among the medicine we use for emergencies."

"Dammit... That doesn't give me anything to work with! Argh, I need to find him and fast. There's no time to waste!"

The policeman scratched his head.

If their diagnosis was correct, Rosclay had lost his small intestine and kidneys. The massive hemorrhaging was too much for even emergency Life Arts treatment to completely stop. Even with treatment, there was almost no hope of saving him.

If it truly was impossible to treat such severe injuries, then that meant...

"Throwing medicine to blind someone... Rosclay the Absolute would never do something so cheap and despicable like that!"

◆

The plaza was quiet, as if the uproar from moments prior that had seeped into her bones had been a figment of her imagination.

A lone chestnut-haired girl in a jumper skirt was walking.

Once she had distanced herself from the plaza and entered this area near the Outer Ward, there were very few people walking around Orde Old Town.

Since most of them were all crammed into the plaza right now, Iska may have truly been the only person walking through the alleyway which had never been home to many residents to begin with.

She had decided that even if the day did come, she wouldn't shed any tears.

Rosclay the Absolute had fought until the very end. As the champion to the people of Aureatia, he had died a noble death in an honorable fight, so Iska understood there wasn't anything to be sad about.

Thus, the fact she was even walking along this street was nothing but sheer sentimentality.

The era of the Central Kingdom, when this old town still hadn't gotten old yet.

One time, her mom told her that Rosclay the Absolute had saved Iska on this road once before.

It happened when Iska was still young, so she only remembered fragmented memories of flashing silver.

However, it was a road that held memories for her. She wanted to bring back the past one last time.

The sound of her shoes clacked atop the cobblestones of the empty street...

"Sheesh… I swear, you're always…"

Then, she was unable to suppress a laugh.

Since Iska felt truly exasperated.

"…being so silly, putting on that cool front like that."

In the abandoned street, Rosclay was sitting down, leaning against a stone wall.

The blood flowing from his stomach traveled along the cobblestone lattice, spreading out in a terribly bright red pattern.

Rosclay was smart. He seemed to be childishly boasting that he easily predicted that Iska's feet would lead her back to this memorable road.

"…Iska."

Rosclay smiled.

It wasn't his normal, flawless one, but a weak smile of a man on his deathbed.

Oh. But, it was his true face.

Iska crouched down, not caring that her skirt would be soaked in blood, and brought her palm to his cheek.

"I've come home, Iska."

"Yes, you did, Rosclay. You did great."

Just like she had done some time before, she held Rosclay's head and stroked his hair.

Rosclay the Absolute had been a perfect champion.

The people never grew disheartened in the age of the True Demon King, no matter how much terror assailed Aureatia, because the champion Rosclay was there.

It had been that way always and forever, right up to the very end, even in places unbeknownst to Iska.

To the point where he made sure not to let anyone else see the moment his life ran out in defeat.

"Iska… I'm, sorry… I, in that moment…"

"…Yes. I know."

In that moment, when Rosclay accepted Soujirou's challenge.

Iska thought that if he hadn't fought, then he wouldn't have lost.

But at that moment.

"I wanted to win…with my righteous…my just sword…"

Iska had seen Rosclay's figure out in front of her.

She understood.

"Right… Rosclay. It must've been hard, and painful."

"I'm glad… Iska…this way…no one will know where I am…"

Rosclay's hand gripped down on Iska's.

Rosclay the Absolute had used several schemes and stratagems.

However, if there was one true final scheme up his sleeve…

"S-so…from here on…we can…together…"

"That's right. Always… There was nothing to worry about. We were always together, weren't we?"

She had decided that even if someday the day came, she wouldn't shed any tears.

After all, Rosclay had never stopped playing a role far more difficult than what Iska had to endure.

In return, she smiled like a mother would.

Good job. Thank you. You worked really hard.

She thought that no matter how many words she added on, it still wouldn't be enough.

Since she was sure that all of the people throughout Aureatia felt the same way.

"I love you."

These words were the ones Iska alone said.

"I love you so much, Rosclay."

No matter how many times she tried to resign herself, these feelings were one thing she was unable to throw away.

Iska slipped onto his finger what she had never been able to part with.

It was a ring of red coral.

"*Uhn, uuuuhn.*"

A feeble cry echoed through the empty cobblestone street.

She had decided she wouldn't shed any tears.

It was the crying voice of a young child.

"*Unwaaaaaaaaaaaah, waaaaaaaaaaaah*!"

Rosclay the Absolute was crying.

Upon Iska's chest, he shed tears and cried.

"Rosclay, I'll love you forever. Rosclay..."

Iska merely wore a gentle smile and rubbed his back to comfort him.

"*Waaaaaaaaaaah... waaaaaaaaaaaaaaaah...*"

She stayed that way until everything grew quiet.

A champion died.

Rosclay, the man Iska loved.

CHAPTER 19 Confluence

There was a young girl walking the city streets far away from the royal palace.

Her name was Kia the World Word. She hugged her shoulders, and quivered.

"Wh-why…why would you do something like that…"

The horror that happened in front of the royal palace had completely exceeded Kia's comprehension.

Had that man crouching down really blown himself up? At the very least, it didn't seem to be something the other two military officers there with him had set up themselves.

"H-he tried to die…of his own will…?"

Just as it had been for Rosclay in the fourth match, and with Lana from the New Principality of Lithia.

Kia's body was unscathed. Even when suffering an explosion at short range made by a weapon from the Beyond, her omnipotent Word Arts could avoid any and all danger at all times.

However, the Word Arts that automatically protected Kia, naturally, only had an effect on her. But a mere child herself, Kia hadn't *even imagined* until that very instant that Kyaliga the Music Reed would blow himself up.

The other two military officers had been barely breathing, her Word Arts perhaps shielding them to some degree.

For Kyaliga, in the epicenter, however...

I can do anything...*and yet. Bringing someone dead back to life is the one thing I can't.*

She should have been able to fully heal the bodies of all three of the people caught in the explosion.

Yet one among them would never open their eyes again.

...Is it my fault?

This area was far from the royal palace grounds. With Kia's power, it was easy to instantly move across this much distance.

Still, she had run away. She hadn't wanted to remain in that place.

Kia didn't want to witness terrifying death.

Someone...

The citizens didn't know anything. Of how many tragedies had occurred in the underside of Aureatia, or how many people had died on that day alone.

She could hear applause from somewhere.

The roadside stores, with their illustrated posters and balloons, were going crazy with excitement in anticipation for Rosclay the Absolute's match.

Someone, help me...

She didn't know how long she continued to run.

However, while she was running, simply to put distance between herself and a man's death, Kia the World Word had wandered into a district of Aureatia she wasn't familiar with.

Kia knew, logically, that Kyaliga the Music Reed's death was not her responsibility.

His cause of death was his suicide bombing attack, and he had planned on doing that regardless of how Kia acted.

However, if by any chance *that hadn't been the case*, what was she supposed to do?

Kia's power was far too strong. Elea had strictly told that Kia that she shouldn't overuse it however she saw fit. If Kia visiting the royal palace caused something to go wrong, and *end up the way it did...*

She could make anything at all happen, so perhaps, she had unconsciously changed everything for the worse on accident.

Will it happen again? If I go to the royal palace, is the same thing going to happen?

It was that moment when an echoing metallic sound of something overturning reached her ears.

A group of ne'er-do-well men fled from the alleyway in front of her.

"Hey, wait!"

A young girl's voice tried to get the men to stop from further down the alleyway.

"Sheesh... I was just asking in passing, you don't gotta run away like that!"

"Uhhh...?"

She had been cautioned at school about scoundrels that chased after young girls, but what about the reverse? Kia peered down the alleyway out of pure curiosity.

It was a young girl with green eyes and a single long braid in her hair. She didn't seem to be carrying any weapons.

The girl immediately noticed Kia's presence.

"Waaait. Have you and I met before?"

"Um, where'd that come from...?"

Kia wasn't very knowledgeable about this stuff, but if the girl was trying to invite Kia to some weird guild, then she wasn't going to have any of it.

She had been taught that they apparently had several tricks to do so, such as using a good-looking girl like this.

"Oh, actually, maybe you know! Seems like you two are pretty close in age! Oh, right, my name's Tu."

"Wait, was that you asking for my name? It's Kia..."

"Kia! Do you know any way to meet with Sephite?"

"With Sephite?"

If there was such a method, then Kia wanted to know, too.

Kia's Word Arts were capable of absolutely anything, but if it was possible, she wanted to meet Sephite properly, without using said *absolutely anything.*

Since it was possible that even Kyaliga the Music Reed's death was all because Kia had cheated her way there.

"Sephite and I used to go to the same school, but...now it's a bit different."

"It is?"

"Forget school... Right now I don't even have a house, and Aureatia's chasing me down..."

"Whoa, really?! What a weird coincidence! Me too!"

"You can't be serious..."

However, in a strange turn of events, Kia's suspicious feelings toward Tu began to dissolve. Despite looking far more like an adult than Kia physically, Tu's mannerisms and way of speaking were much more straightforward and honest than any of the adults Kia had ever met before. In that sense, her attitude vaguely resembled Acromdo the Variety's somehow.

"Hey... So, I actually wanted to meet Sephite, too."

"Wowee! We're three for three?! Okay, let's look for a way together, then!"

"Let's look… Right, that's what I was going to say."

She needed to search for the best possible method, even if it was something she could do by herself.

In order to do that, even the invincible Kia needed allies.

People encountered one another. This coincidence may have instead been something even more powerful than omnipotent Word Arts at work.

Their journeys that had crossed once before now converged together.

◆

Meanwhile, opposite the grand coup d'état by Iriolde's camp, in an area far removed from Aureatia's attention, there was another armed force on the move with a different goal in mind.

They were the remnant forces of the Old Kingdoms' loyalists. Among the group of armed men were also golems of various sizes.

Dense forest surrounded them on all sides. Flowing spring waters, with the light of the sun blocked by the tree leaves.

The mansion erected in the forest was Obsidian Eyes' base of operations within Aureatia's borders. Kiyazuna the Axle had been the one to expose the location that had been so thoroughly concealed from the eyes of others.

By following the homing device signal coming from the plundered Mestelexil, they had deduced the location.

One of the soldiers walked along the ground, covered in branches, without making a sound, and gave a report.

"General Caneeya. The west side search report indicated that they've gotten a visual on a residence."

"That's good. Prepare to storm the place immediately. Though hopefully there's no battle, of course."

Even when placed in this strange situation, Caneeya the Fruit Trimming wore her unchanging smile.

On the other hand, Kaete and Kiyazuna were discussing their strategy.

"A bit late to ask, but do you have any vampire antiserum, Grams? I was inoculated as one of the Twenty-Nine."

"Of course I don't, why would I?"

"So then, our only method to fix Mestelexil is to destroy him and make him regenerate?"

"Haven't I been saying that from the damn start?! Smash through Mestel's armor, and knock Exil outta there, along with his preservative amniotic fluid! Violence is best! What's hard to get?!"

"...I understand that's the only option, but is Mestelexil going to be okay with that?"

"It's fine! I've taught him as much already."

When she asserted herself like this, there wasn't anything Kaete could say back.

Kiyazuna the Axle's love for her golems was unquestionable, but it was just as true that her sense of ethics was far removed from that of a normal person's.

"...Fine. Let me just tell you my idea then. Even if using the antiserum is impossible, if this really is their base of operations, isn't there another method that won't require us to struggle with destroying Exil?"

"Huh? Well, ain't like you ever think up anything good. What is it, then?"

"...Anyone could come up with this. If anything, it seems like the one with a far better chance to work."

Kaete looked west. Up ahead, past these trees blocking the way, was the mansion they were after.

"Assassination. We can wrap this whole thing up just by *killing the parent unit*, right?"

◆

Linaris might get killed.

Yuno the Distant Talon was tired.

She had returned to Obsidian Eyes' mansion almost entirely on her own. While she had made it back for the tenth match, she didn't know if she had truly returned in time.

The Gray-Haired Child was already enacting his plans for revenge. She didn't know what they were, or what she needed to do to stop them, but she needed to let Linaris escape before anyone else.

Can I do it? What can I even do right now...?

She didn't have a single person on her side. She tried to at least get in touch with Lendelt, but was unable.

Yuno wasn't even sure about the number of arrowheads she still had hidden in her sleeves. Ever since coming to Aureatia, she had continued to make her arrowheads day in and day out, but her plan to make Soujirou head to his match had used up a lot of them.

"...Don't tremble. Not here, not now...!"

She cursed at her own feet with irritation.

Yuno didn't know what was waiting for her up ahead, or what sort of dangers there were.

At the very least, she thought, she didn't want feel scared when she still didn't know for sure.

Above all, if she was going to save her friend, Yuno needed to advance forward, even if she was gambling her life to do so.

...I've never stopped thinking it, after all.

Nagan Labyrinth City burned, and Yuno's dear friend died.

She felt like she needed to redeem that regret someday.

"At that time, I could've saved her."

That time was now.

The absolute weakest piece in play was advancing forward alone.

◆

"I see, so Obsidian had their base of operations hidden in a place like this."

Enu the Distant Mirror walked along the forest path, murmuring with admiration.

"A true private villa, not even contained in the Central Kingdom's records... I'm surprised they even found this base of theirs. They never filled me in on where they were staying, you see."

"I haven't been told, either."

Lined up with Enu's footsteps was a leprechaun in a dark brown coat, walking silently.

Kuuro the Cautious's face was messily wrapped in bandages.

"Then how did you know they were here?"

"I have my Clairvoyance. No matter where they had their base of operations in Aureatia, *if I tried searching for it*, it wouldn't even take a full day. The reason I found them is because they made me want to search them out."

"What wonderful confidence."

On one hand was Obsidian Eyes' strongest killer, a man who had so much stolen from him by the spy guild.

On the other was a sponsor with his life firmly in Obsidian Eyes' grasp, who was now scheming to use them for himself.

"I've made sure not to pry, but..."

Kuuro the Cautious asked with the same sullen look.

"...What's your objective, Enu the Distant Mirror? It appears that you all were the ones who supplied the National Defense Research Institute with its base of operations. You also have connections with Viga the Clamor. And, for some reason...you've been gathering living vampire specimens and made contact with Obsidian Eyes. Your activities began long before the start of the Sixways Exhibition, and you've been moving secretly among several of the different powers in play for this sole goal of yours."

"I don't intend to do anything ominous or disruptive. The opposite, if anything."

"A peaceful use for whatever it is, huh?"

"Does it appear that I'm lying?"

"...It doesn't. I've just never seen someone say that and mean it before, so it felt a bit unsettling is all."

"What about yourself? Any doubts about your revenge against Obsidian Eyes?"

Kuuro bore a strong grudge against Obsidian Eyes.

However, the fact of the matter was they were his former comrades as well.

"I'll do that *my way*. Deal the proper reprisals to the proper people, and that'll be the end of it. I'm not seeking to harm them any more than necessary."

"Hm. You're worried about Linaris the Obsidian, aren't you?"

"When I was still there, she was a good-natured and bright child. She never had any involvement in our work. If I had to give my opinion...I can't say I'd be fine with you handling her however you see fit."

"Nevertheless, she *is* killing people." Enu thrust out his cane. "That is a fact. You don't need your Clairvoyance to see that. While I admit she ended up being treated somewhat inhumanely, I don't believe it's uncalled for in the girl's case, either... Can I convince you with the explanation that, even in the worst case, *there's no need to deprive her of her body parts*?"

"...A valid line to draw, I suppose," Kuuro the Cautious answered with obvious displeasure.

The leprechaun likely knew that there were several effective means of torture that didn't involve any bodily harm.

"In that case, if anyone besides Mestelexil or Obsidian Eyes were to interfere, what was your plan then? I don't want any meaningless killing if possible..."

"Others? There can't be anyone else who would come to a place like this on purpose."

"They're already here."

Kuuro pulled the breechblock on the submachine gun from the Beyond.

In his eyes, he could see everything, always.

"Better hurry. If your goal is to capture Linaris alive."

◆

The warehouses connected to the Tim Great Canal.

Though camouflaged on the outside to look nothing of the sort, a section of these warehouses was in fact a research facility for the grotesque and fantastic—known as the National Defense Research Institute.

Among the conspiracies swirling around the Sixways Exhibition, occasionally the name would pop up, but there wasn't anyone who actually knew its location or what they did. It was that type of organization.

There was also a man who had been tracking down its existence for a long time.

"Wonder if they've already got started on their end."

Yukiharu the Twilight Diver brought his hand up to shield the sun and looked in the direction of the city.

A plump man with a camera hanging from his neck. For some reason, he carried a wooden box on his back.

Thin smoke trails rose from the city. The Aureatia army was going to claim unilateral victory anyway, but the mere fact that any war broke out meant that a flawless victory was impossible. Victims and sacrifices would always follow.

The being inside of the small wooden box spoke up.

"I know you're thinking about how much you want to cover what's going on over there."

"*Ahah-hah-hah*, sorry, my bad. I mean, I was a war correspondent, so it's just sort of instinctual, really… But now's basically the only chance we'll have to directly go inside the National Defense Research Institute. Don't worry, I know what to prioritize."

Yukiharu was a journalist who had been tracking down the National Defense Research Institute since before the start of the Sixways Exhibition.

He had even gotten his hands on the broader information, like what sort of organization it was, and who was the person behind its operations.

However, as a journalist, he needed to directly learn the deeper truths for himself.

Several of the dark sides to Aureatia that Yukiharu was continuing to chase after had originated from the National Defense Research Institute.

"But this is weird, isn't it? You managed to pin down information on the True Demon King, and the hero, too, right? Heck, you even talked about the hero with Shalk the Sound Slicer the other day. Rude, really. You don't have any idea how I feel."

"C'mon, what's the big deal with that… He's not someone who's super involved with you anyway, right?"

"Okay, fine, putting that aside, why have you spent more time on this National Defense Research Institute instead of on the secrets everyone in the world's looking to know? I'm pretty sure at this point, any report you made on the National Defense Research Institute would be too late, anyway."

"Hmmm. Honestly, I don't think you'd sympathize with me, even if I did tell you… Either way, this is all about my way of thinking as a journalist, so I never thought it'd be something everyone would understand."

Yukiharu put a hand to his soft chin and, in a rare twist, looked serious.

"The True Demon King and the True Hero stuff, collecting the material on all that was fine—but it doesn't make for a really interesting news report."

"Why?"

"There's no story to it."

"It's all back to the entertainment factor, is it?"

"See, I knew you'd say that. But seriously, I want you to actually think about it. If I told this to everyone, what would they even do? This person's the hero, this person was the demon king, the end—what else is there? That's not what it's about, y'know… Ultimately, I think everyone wants the sort of truth you get from the people involved in a story having these complex hearts and minds, and the sort of result that comes out of it all."

"I really don't get that fixation of yours, Yukiharu."

"Everyone has a part of them in their heart somewhere, so I really think they should just be more honest about it..."

As he talked, he had already stepped inside the warehouse.

While most of the soldiers were all out participating in the grand coup, there were still a fair number on guard.

Nonetheless, Yukiharu had done plenty of prep work this time. There weren't so many that he couldn't break through them all.

"You! Stop right there."

Then, he was rightfully stopped. Yukiharu wasn't trying to conceal himself at all.

The guards were equipped with the normal, widely circulated muskets, but it was obvious these weren't plain warehouse staff.

"This land belongs to Lulaze Transport. Civilians aren't allowed here."

"Oh, sorry, today's my first time so you probably don't know, huh."

Yukiharu spoke very naturally and with confidence.

"I'm a Life Arts caster sent here by Yide the Bundle Garment. Oh, if I remember right, you're the head of security... Orija the Ear Tearing? Looks like Yide forgot to mention me to you when he talked with you during the new drug deal. Oh yeah, here's the referral stamp. So anyway, is Viga the Clamor in? I've some business I need to talk to her about ASAP."

"...This referral stamp does look legit. Viga the Clamor is in the biological experiment building, but..."

"Oh, do you need to search my belongings or anything? This is a camera. I'm here because they said they needed to leave a record for the latest experiment. You're going to check inside the box, too, right? Give me a sec to open it up."

With an attitude that made the guard never even dream he was an outsider trying to sneak inside, and the speaking skills to overwrite the guard's thoughts in rapid-fire succession, Yukiharu got out ahead of any wariness and dispelled it.

On top of it all, the information he casually mentioned offhand were all facts that no one besides those involved with the National Defense Research Institute should have known about. In Yukiharu's experience, the more an intruder was confident and bold, the less likely they were to be distrusted.

"All right. Put the wooden box down there and..."

The guard noticed something. Yukiharu's reaction was even faster. He fell down to the ground.

There was a *pow* from a gunshot, and the guard's head exploded.

"Yikes."

Yukiharu's eyes went wide as he was showered in blood.

"It's the Aureatia army!"

"What's going on?!"

"Tell me how many they've brought, and where they are! Head over to intercept!"

From listening to the guards' voices in the distance, Yukiharu could tell that the Aureatia army had launched a surprise attack.

Gunfire immediately rang out, and there were constant moans and shrieks, though it was impossible to tell which side they belonged to.

This was an unexpected development for Yukiharu, too.

"...That's weird."

"What, no it isn't. If the National Defense Research Institute is connected to Iriolde's Army, then obviously Aureatia's going to want to crush them, right?"

"On any other day, maybe. But right now, the city's under attack, right? Do they really have the luxury to take over the National Defense Research Institute today, given how much trouble's happening all over Aureatia? Who knows what sort of constructs could be waiting here, right? Could be a revenant like Vikeon in here, even."

"...So you want to say that this *is being done on the side*?"

"I wonder. Either way, this is our chance! All the patrolling guards are dead, so time to use this opening to slip in."

"You're really *too* positive, you know that?'

Ignoring the grumbles from the voice in the wooden box, Yukiharu entered into the warehouse.

Rubbing his hands together for no reason in particular, he glanced around the building.

"Whew boy, this stuff always gets me excited!"

"There are dead people here, aren't there?"

Though it was called a research facility, it was exactly as its outer appearance suggested for the most part: a warehouse that was partitioned into several rooms with thick walls. However, each individual room was progressing with their own research.

Right at the outset, Yukiharu went up the metallic stairs inside the warehouse and, passing through the second floor accessway, headed toward the location he had wormed out from the guard, the biological experiment building. It was the next structure over—

"Uh-oh."

Right after entering into the biological experiment building, Yukiharu's feet stopped.

"What's wrong?"

"Soldiers have come inside. Those aren't Iriolde's troops. Must be Aureatia's army..."

"You're skilled at running and hiding, aren't you?"

"That's true. Guess I'll handle it as usual."

Scratching his head, he made for the closest room in front of him along the wall.

There was a loud smacking sound.

Yukiharu thought it was the sound of a door closing forcefully and turned around.

He then collapsed where he stood.

"Yukiharu?!"

"Huh...? What? Hold on..."

The intense pain didn't hit him until afterward. Yukiharu's right ankle had been blown off.

The Aureatia army had entered into the downstairs floor of the biological experiment building. Yukiharu was on the second floor, which would have been a blind spot from where the soldiers stood. They couldn't have possibly shot him from their position.

However, this was a windowless interior, and there wasn't any logical way his leg could've been sniped from outside.

"What happened?"

"I-I was shot...from the accessway...! But, seriously?!"

He had known that someone was advancing from the accessway.

He dragged his body to conceal himself in the shadow of some machinery.

"C-crap...! Is it the Aureatia army?! Someone with the National Defense Research Institute?! It wasn't a stray bullet was—*gwaugh*!"

Yukiharu's body bounded upwards from his sitting position, and his left shoulder slammed into the wall.

It was the impact from being shot. His left shoulder had burst wide open.

"Didn't you find some shadows to hide in?!"

"I was hidden…! I'm *still* hidden! Th-the bullet…they *curved the bullet's path, after they fired*…! Th-the…the only one who can do that, though…!"

Yukiharu found himself at a loss for words because he in fact *had an idea about* who this champion was.

Except…she should have been dead.

There was someone approaching them.

There was a silhouette illuminated in the light. A lithe female arm holding a bayonet-affixed rifle—spinning it around as if beating out a rhythm.

A visitor gunner.

"K-Kazuki the Black Tone…!"

The shadow answered him. "THAT IS CORRECT."

It was a grotesque beast that didn't bear any resemblance to Kazuki at all.

An eight-legged beast with bluish-silver fur, who looked like a colossal, terrifying wolf. A red line ran horizontally across his streamlined body with one section of it open, and from it sprouted out a musket-wielding arm.

"THIS IS KAZUKI THE BLACK TONE'S ARM. I WAS A BIT UNDERSURE IF I COULD USE THIS TECHNIQUE JUST WITH HER PHYSICAL ABILITIES, BUT…"

Spinning the musket around as if these fingers were a single part of his own arm, it pointed the gun barrel at Yukiharu, left with nowhere else to run.

"IT SEEMS I CAN USE IT TO SOME EXTENT."

"Ozonezma…!"

Ozonezma the Capricious.

The strongest chimera in history, and formerly part of the Gray-Haired Child's camp, just like Yukiharu.

"PUTTING ASIDE THE FIRST SHOT… YUKIHARU THE TWILIGHT DIVER. YOU TOOK THAT SHOT IN THE SHOUDLER BECAUSE *YOU WERE SHIELDING THAT WOODEN BOX*. WHAT DO YOU HAVE IN THERE?"

"I-I don't really want to tell you…!"

"Hold on! Isn't Ozonezma on *your* side?! Why is he attacking us?!"

"He's not…! The fact he's using Kazuki the Black Tone's arm like this means…he's got a connection to the power that managed to collect her body…!"

Yukiharu's hunch had been spot-on.

It had clearly been strange for the Aureatia army to come attacking on that day.

They had their sights set not on the National Defense Research Institute, but on Yukiharu, and planned to dispose of him.

"Th-this guy's…*on Aureatia's side*!"

Yukiharu the Twilight Diver knew far too much information that was deadly to Aureatia.

Aureatia had been constantly waiting patiently for their chance to get rid of Yukiharu without anyone knowing about it.

"I HAVE MY OWN REASONS FOR DISPOSING OF YOU. THE TRUTH ABOUT THE TRUE DEMON KING…IS SOMETHING THAT SHOULD NEVER BE TOLD TO ANYONE IN THIS WORLD… THE TRUTH ABOUT THE TRUE HERO, EVEN MORE SO."

"*Hah-hah.*"

A laughter unbecoming of the situation slipped out from Yukiharu's throat.

A journalist who knew too many things that he wasn't supposed to, getting killed.

It was such a terribly cliché story, he found it hilarious that even in a world where tremendous power came and went, this was ultimately the plot that it settled on.

"I-it's not just, me...you're killing but Viga the Clamor, too, right? Now that she's finished spying on the National Defense Research Institute...there's no longer any reason to keep her alive..."

Which was why Aureatia had brought in someone who would definitely be able to dispose of them both.

Ozonezma the Capricious, unaffiliated with any power himself, possessing a deep connection with the demon king's terror...and who could act for the sake of this connection on his own, if necessary.

Yukiharu was driven into a gap between machinery, but the door to enter into one of the rooms of the biological experiment building was right next to him, past the machinery. Was Viga the Clamor in there? Was there some means to turn the tables in there?

For starters, was there any way he could escape from this situation, given Ozonezma was pointing a gun straight at him?

From Yukiharu's viewpoint, he could see that there was a single Aureatian soldier coming up the stairs from the first floor.

Psychological warfare was likely ineffective against Ozonezma, but even if the chances were close to zero, he had to make the gamble.

"Oh right, Ozonezma. There's this interesting story I want to tell, see..."

"UNNECESSARY. I HAVE GIVEN PLENTY OF EXPLANATION."

He wouldn't make it in time. That was what Yukiharu had expected.

However, reaching the second floor, the Aureatian soldier's right arm was then *torn off and sent flying* with terrifying speed.

It flew in at Ozonezma like a bullet.

"..."

Faster than any bullet, Ozonezma's back opened up.

Countless blades, gushing out from the gaping hole, mangled the arm faster than the eye could see.

The cross section of the arm had what looked like plant roots extending from it, but Ozonezma obliterated them in midair without touching a single fragment of the roots.

Right at that same moment, the building shook with a vortex-like rumbling portending destruction.

It was a wurm. Appearing from inside the earth, it leapt at Ozonezma while pulverizing everything in its path.

"...REINFORCEMENTS, HM?"

Confusion and destruction ran amok.

As it did, Yukiharu jumped over the machinery, opened the door, and rushed inside the room.

It was less like an experiment lab and looked more like an operating room. On the dissecting table laid the body of a headless young girl—

"*Blraugh!*"

There, his vision spun.

He spit up blood. He realized a bullet had pierced through his stomach from behind.

Yukiharu was, for Ozonezma, nothing more than a target he could dispose of offhandedly while dealing with a wurm. There was an even more serious problem.

"...Ah, d-damn..."

If he was shot in the back, was his wooden box still safe?

Lifting up his head in a haze, Viga the Clamor, wearing an apron, was looking down on him. If she had heard Yukiharu's conversation just now, she must have recognized that her life was in danger.

"I-I'm begging...you...*hah-hah*..."

He needed to tell her before he lost consciousness.

"She's...a really good...partner, see..."

◆

"...Yukiharu the Twilight Diver is in here?"

The Aureatia army soldiers who had stormed the National Defense Research Institute had suffered an unexpected attack.

First, one of them was infested by what looked like plant roots, and almost as if guided there by the same soldier, a wurm appeared, clearly targeting Ozonezma.

Ozonezma the Capricious dealt with both—or perhaps, the singular—biological weapon by himself, drawing it outside of the warehouse.

The wurm's arrival had destroyed half the building, but they couldn't let their high-priority target escape death.

Spreading ropes and boards over the collapsed sections, the squad crossed the destroyed scaffolding.

Yukiharu looked to have used an opening during the battle to tumble into an experiment room, but Ozonezma had still dealt him the fatal blow.

"Yukiharu the Twilight Diver might already be dead."

"Even if he is, we have to verify the body."

This wasn't a man who could be ignored.

He was a threat to the world that that eventually someone needed to kill.

All that was left was Viga the Clamor—presently there were no signs of any dangerous constructs, the wurm from earlier perhaps their last enemy to worry about.

"Viga the Clamor...a self-proclaimed demon king, huh."

"She's a Life Arts caster. Double check your anti-poison gear."

"Yeah. Don't let your guard down. Everyone rush in on my signal."

The elite squad stepped into Viga's lab all at once.

Yukiharu the Twilight Diver was collapsed on the floor.

Beside the operating table, there stood Viga the Clamor.

There was one other person there.

A soldier held up their musket.

"...Who're you?"

A naked young girl stood on top of the operating table with her back turned to them.

Her skin color wasn't merely porcelain, but pallid.

What was bizarre was the blood bleeding across the nape of her neck in a straight horizontal line.

The wooden box on Yukiharu's back had been grazed by a bullet and smashed apart, but...

There was nothing inside.

"*Tee-hee*... Hmm, isn't that a good question?"

The young girl appeared to be laughing for the first time in a long while.

There was once a man by the name of Dakai the Magpie.

He remained behind to fight in Lithia after their defeat was written on the wall He knew that Lithia had no hopes of winning, but thought that even if they were going to lose, there still remained a chance to *stop the enemy from claiming victory.*

He was a bandit visitor with errant powers of observation.

He could even steal away the proof that Aureatia used a construct weapon to attack Lithia.

Either way, to Dakai the Magpie, incapacitating a revenant without destroying their life core was an extremely easy feat. This *living proof* would pass through the hands of the remnants of the New Principality, like a ticking time bomb waiting to blow as it wandered through different powers at play and through different hands—as the biggest scandal possible.

Yukiharu the Twilight Diver had, at long last, detonated the bomb.

"*Hee, hee. Hee-hee-hee-hee-hee—*"

Extending out from the girl's naked back were nerve-like tentacles.

Then, holding both of her hands behind her, she turned around and smiled.

"I'm back."

Afterword

Thank you for your support. Keiso here. While this may be a bit boring to chronicle in the afterword eight volumes in, I would like to explain the origins behind this series, *Ishura*, up until it was published by Dengeki's Shin Bungei imprint. *Ishura* was originally serialized on the web novel site Kakuyomu, and the printed edition of *Ishura* is a significantly retouched and revised reconstruction of this web novel. The end.

You could get the general match results and story itself up to the seventh volume from reading the web novel (though with significantly less content). As such, the story in this eighth volume is a brand new part of the story that hasn't been fully released anywhere else. I was able to successfully deliver the story that laid beyond the web novel thanks to all you readers who have supported this work, to Kureta for always providing the most badass illustrations that perfectly match what I'm looking for, to my editor Satou who is always ready to give me his advice no matter what state I'm in, and to the all the other people in involved with publishing and advertising the series. I am truly grateful to you all.

Also, as a new policy starting from this volume, I've created a new Q&A corner concerning the worldbuilding of *Ishura*, as proposed by my managing editor. Some areas will spoil the story in the volume itself, so I hope you'll enjoy it as a nice extra after finishing the rest of the book, and to prep yourselves for the *Ishura* anime beginning in January.

There is another new experiment I wish to try. A spaghetti aglio e olio peperoncino recipe. Regarding this dish, while I don't really think there's much new in regard to the recipe itself, what I'd like to present to you this time is version that doesn't use actual peperoncino, but wasabi instead.

Spaghetti aglio e olio peperoncino is said to be challenging because of how simple it is, but if I'm just eating it at home and not showing it to anyone, as long as it tastes good, I don't particularly care about if I'm good at it or not. Spread a layer of olive oil enough to soak two cloves of garlic in a frying pan and cook them on low heat. During that time, boil the spaghetti in the microwave. I've been boiling pasta in a microwave cooker for a long time now in these *Ishura* afterwords, but a microwave cooker is especially important for this spaghetti aglio e olio peperoncino recipe. This time, please set the cooking time to be about two to three minutes less than what you normally use to boil the pasta. I'll explain why further on.

Once the garlic's turned a golden brown, take it out and place it in a dish, while in the same pan, fry chopped bacon in the garlic-infused oil. This is where you also add salt, but a scant teaspoon should be plenty. It might be better to adjust the amount to match the saltiness of your bacon and the amount of spaghetti. When the bacon has been browned nicely, turn the heat off.

Once the spaghetti is finished cooking, add it to the frying pan along with all the pasta water left over in the microwave cooker. Turn the heat on once more and mix everything together, emulsifying it until all of the pasta water has boiled down. We needed to shorten the initial cooking time earlier since this will heat up the spaghetti even further.

Once it's completely boiled, mix it up well with the garlic in the dish to spread the flavors, put in your preferred amount of wasabi, and it's finished. The wasabi version of the dish has a bite and freshness to it that's slightly different from the peperoncino's spiciness, and wasabi paste in a tube is much easier to use and prepare than peperoncini. I encourage you to try it out as it's a simple, yet novel, dish.

Even now that the story has gone past the scope of the web novel, I still have more and more intense plot developments planned. I hope you'll continue supporting the new *Ishura* going forward as well.

In-depth *Ishura* Analysis! Here's what Keiso-sensei told us!

All of a sudden, we find ourselves with only five matches left of the Six-ways Exhibition. While more and more of the shura are dropping out, this work still has a fathomless and enormous amount of worldbuilding concealed within.

Even the managing editor hasn't been given the full picture...and with that in mind, I conducted a Q&A with Keiso-sensei to find out more!

Q1: What sort laws and principles are behind the phenomenon called "Word Arts" within the world of *Ishura*?

Truth be told, even within the world of *Ishura*, Word Arts aren't actually strictly defined.

Currently, even just what's referred to as "Word Arts" in the story covers a wide range, from the more broadly defined Word Arts that point to the laws of nature that establish the existence of dragonkin, beastfolk, and constructs, to the narrower definition referring to the techniques of the five Word Art systems—Heat, Force, Craft, Life, and Soul—that interfere with the world, with all of them, as well any mechanics of the world that aren't included within the verifiable laws of physics, being collectively referred to as "Word Arts."

However, the perception of life is undoubtably concerned with many of these mechanics, and it's believed that, for example, the Word Arts that establish life continue as long as the perception of that lifeform does, and the Word Arts that work on the principles of the outside world must function through a language that expresses the lifeform's perception.

To go further, the currently widely known classification of the five Word Arts systems is nothing but a provisional one propagated for practicality by the people, and the types of beings who reach the realms of the shura or the self-proclaimed demon kings utilize Word Arts that are an advanced composition of several systems, or aren't contained within these systems whatsoever.

Q2. Conversely, are there any mysterious phenomena within the world of *Ishura* that *aren't* from Word Arts?

There are. The supernatural abilities that enchanted swords and magic items possess, and which are believed not to have any cognitive abilities themselves, are one example of a phenomenon that would be unsuitable to be called Word Arts, under the above definition.

When Uhak experimented during his journey with Olukt, Uhak's supernatural ability was depicted as nullifying other supernatural abilities besides just Word Arts, and it is likely that when they did, they also experimented with if he could erase the abilities of enchanted swords and magic items as well.

However, there are conflicting theories on this point, and there's the undeniable possibility that enchanted swords and magic items with special powers possess a perception that can utilize Word Arts in and of themselves. Toroa the Awful, being able to read the notions of his enchanted swords, may have been living proof to corroborate this theory.

Also, it can be said that the world-deviating powers that visitors possess, while impossible to verify, are very unlike to be Word Arts. This is because these supernatural abilities were powers that they've displayed without any change from when they lived in a world without Word Arts.

In which case, by that same principle, wouldn't it negate the Word

Arts theory around enchanted swords and magic items, that are also transported to the world of *Ishura* like the visitors? While this is something to consider, that is not necessarily the case.

This is because, for enchanted swords and magic items, no one is able to prove that their world-departure was due to their abnormal abilities. Essentially, one explanation could be that a vessel without any special abilities in its original world was capable of world-departure by possessing its own perception, and was then able to gain its special abilities, Word Arts, from said perception.

Also, the terror of the True Demon King can be considered an exception that isn't included in any of the established classifications. It's something that is completely without cause, and Word Arts, of course, are not a world-departing power, either.

Q3. If Rosclay had defeated Soujirou with a win by default, what strategy was he estimated to use to win the tournament afterward?

Rosclay's semifinal opponent if he had beaten Soujirou would have been Psianop, but having lost Qwell, Psianop is currently without a sponsor, and he would have to get a new one to back him if he wished to continue his participation in the Sixways Exhibition.

Since on top of claiming victory over Soujirou, the grand coup d'état would have eliminated the hostile forces against Rosclay within the Twenty-Nine Officials, almost no matter who became Psianop's sponsor, it would have been possible to make them act in line with Rosclay's intentions.

In terms of the final, he hadn't established a concrete strategy from the very beginning. The mental taxation that would come from controlling exactly who among the eight in the other bracket would advance was tremendous, and he thought it more logical to acquire information through the ongoing Sixways Exhibition itself while building a strategy.

However, at present, the hero candidates on the other side of the bracket who are left are Kuze, Zeljirga, Shalk, and Uhak. For Kuze, the hostage strategy employed by Nophtok would be effective. While Zeljirga had run away from the Sixways Exhibition, Shalk's weakness lay in his sponsor, and Uhak's sponsor was dead as well.

No matter who among them advanced to the final, Rosclay could attack the weak points of them all.

Q4. What are the Twenty-Nine Officials' jurisdictions over the governmental ministries and agencies?

They're all as laid out below. For those who have left their position, the government officials below the Twenty-Nine Officials act as heads in their stead.

First Minister	Grasse the Foundation Map Internal Affairs Ministry
Second General	Rosclay the Absolute Personnel Bureau (Underneath Internal Affairs Ministry)
Third Minister	Jelky the Swift Ink Trade Ministry
Fourth Minister	Kaete the Round Table Industrial Ministry
Fifth Official	Iriolde the Atypical Tome (Vacant) Foreign Affairs Ministry
Sixth General	Harghent the Still Air Defense Bureau (Underneath Defense Ministry)
Seventh Minister	Flinsuda the Portent Health Ministry
Eighth Minister	Sheanek the Word Intermediary Education Ministry
Ninth General	Yaniegiz the Chisel Police Agency (Underneath Internal Affairs Ministry)

Tenth General	Qwell the Wax Flower Fire Defense Agency (Underneath Health Ministry)
Eleventh Minister	Nophtok the Crepuscule Bell Order Bureau (Underneath Education Ministry)
Twelfth General	Sabfom the White Weave Disaster Prevention Bureau (Underneath Construction Ministry)
Thirteenth Minister	Enu the Distant Mirror Construction Ministry
Fourteenth General	Yuca the Halation Gaol Public Safety Bureau (Underneath Internal Affairs Ministry)
Fifteenth General	Haizesta the Gathering Spot Inspection Bureau (Special Organization)
Sixteenth General	Nofelt the Somber Wind Geographical Bureau (Underneath Construction Ministry)
Seventeenth Minister	Elea the Red Tag Information Bureau (Underneath Defense Ministry)
Eighteenth Minister	Quewai the Moon Fragment Technology Agency (Underneath Trade Ministry)
Nineteenth Minister	Hyakka the Heat Haze Agriculture and Forestry Bureau (Underneath Trade Ministry)
Twentieth Minister	Hidow the Clamp War Damage Reconstruction Agency (Underneath Internal Affairs Ministry)
Twenty-First General	Tuturi the Blue Violet Foam Communication Bureau (Underneath Defense Ministry)
Twenty-Second General	Mizial the Iron-Piercing Plumeshade Physical Education Bureau (Underneath Education Ministry)
Twenty-Third Official	Taren the Punished (Vacant) Frontier Development Bureau (Underneath Foreign Affairs Ministry)
Twenty-Fourth General	Dant the Heath Furrow Palace Guard Bureau (Special Organization)
Twenty-Fifth General	Cayon the Thundering Transport Agency (Underneath Trade Ministry)
Twenty-Sixth Minister	Meeka the Whispered Justice Ministry
Twenty-Seventh General	Haade the Flashpoint Defense Ministry
Twenty-Eighth Minister	Antel the Alignment Finance Agency (Underneath Trade Ministry)

THE SAGA OF TANYA THE EVIL, VOL. 1–12

Reborn as a destitute orphaned girl with nothing to her name but memories of a previous life, Tanya will do whatever it takes to survive, even if it means living life behind the barrel of a gun!

Manga adaptation available now!

SO I'M A SPIDER, SO WHAT?, VOL. 1–16

I used to be a normal high school girl, but in the blink of an eye, I woke up in a place I've never seen before and—and I was reborn as a spider?!

Manga adaptation available now!

OVERLORD, VOL. 1–16

When Momonga logs in one last time just to be there when the servers go dark, something happens—and suddenly, fantasy is reality. A rogues' gallery of fanatically devoted NPCs is ready to obey his every order, but the world Momonga now inhabits is not the one he remembers.

Manga adaptation available now!

VISIT YENPRESS.COM TO CHECK OUT ALL OUR TITLES AND. . .

GET YOUR YEN ON!

YEN ON Yen Press